PENGUIN CLASSICS

BANAAG AT SIKAT
(RADIANCE AND SUNRISE)

Lope K. Santos was a Filipino Tagalog-language writer and former senator of the Philippines. He is best known for his 1906 socialist novel, *Banaag at Sikat* and for his contributions to the development of Filipino grammar and Tagalog orthography.

Santos pursued law at the Academia de la Jurisprudencia, then at Escuela Derecho de Manila (now Manila Law College Foundation) where he received the Bachelor of Arts degree in 1912. In the late 1900s, Santos started writing in his own newspaper *Ang Kaliwanagan (The Light)*. This was also the time when socialism became an emerging idea in world ideology.

In 1903, Santos started publishing fragments of his first novel, *Banaag at Sikat*, in his weekly labour magazine *Muling Pagsilang (The Rebirth)* and was completed in 1906. When published in book form, Santos' *Banaag at Sikat* was then considered the first socialist-oriented book in the Philippines which expounded principles of socialism and sought labor reforms from the government. The book was later an inspiration for the assembly of the 1932 Socialist Party of the Philippines and then the 1946 group Hukbalahap.

In the early 1910s, he started his campaign on promoting a 'national language for the Philippines', where he organized various symposia, lectures and headed numerous departments for national language in leading Philippine universities. In 1910, he was elected as governor of the province of Rizal under the Nacionalista Party. In 1918, he was appointed as the first Filipino governor of the newly resurveyed Nueva Vizcaya until 1920. Consequently, he was elected to the 5th Philippine Legislature as senator of the twelfth senatorial district representing provinces having a majority of non-Christian population.

In 1940, Santos published the first grammar book of the 'national language', *Balarila ng Wikang Pambansa (Grammar of the National*

Language) which was commissioned by the Surian ng Wikang Pambansa (SWF). The next year, he was appointed by President Manuel L. Quezon as director of SWF until 1946. When the Philippines became a member of the United Nations he was selected to translate the 1935 Constitution for UNESCO. He was also appointed to assist in the translation of the inaugural addresses of presidents Jose P. Laurel and Manuel A. Roxas.

Danton Remoto was educated at Ateneo de Manila University, Rutgers University, University of Stirling and the University of the Philippines. He has worked as a publishing director at Ateneo, head of communications at United Nations Development Programme, TV and radio host at TV5 and Radyo 5, president of Manila Times College and, most recently, as head of school and professor of English at the University of Nottingham Malaysia. He has published a baker's dozen of books in English, including *Riverrun, A Novel*. His work is cited in the *Oxford Research Encyclopaedia of Literature*, *The Princeton Encyclopaedia of Poetry and Poetics*, and the *Routledge Encyclopaedia of Postcolonial Literature*.

PRAISE FOR *BANAAG AT SIKAT* AND DANTON REMOTO

'*Banaag at Sikat* first appeared as a series in the Tagalog newspaper *Muling Pagsilang (Renaissance)* in 1904 . . . It is now recognized as the most prominent work of the period known as the Golden Age of the Tagalog novel (1905–1921) and a milestone in the history of Tagalog fiction for its engagement with social issues...'

Dr Patricia May B Jurilla
Tagalog Bestsellers of the Twentieth Century:
A History of the Book in the Philippines

'Lope K Santos' *Banaag at Sikat* was the most important Tagalog novel of the early 20th century. Avidly read by the intellectuals and the masses, it influenced the workers to fight for economic, social, and political reforms. It became a Bible for the working men and women of the Philippines.'

Professor Teodoro Agoncillo
Author of *A History of the Filipino People*
National Scientist of the Philippines

'The hybrid plot of *Banaag at Sikat* makes it not just an important political tract but a love story as well. Its importance in the history of the Tagalog novel is assured.'

Dr Resil Mojares
The Origins and Rise of the Philippine Novel Until 1940:
A Generic Study
National Artist for Literature

'The vigour and charm of style of *Banaag at Sikat* never fails. Santos knows how to sustain interest: he lets his people move and speak in a manner the reader can easily identify with. He knows the folk—both of his novel and his audience. He knows perfectly their mores, their ways of thinking, their vices and especially their language. The novel is rich in folk wisdom and homilies, which give added charm and character to this Tagalog classic.'

Romeo P. Virtusio
Award-winning writer of *Bilibid: Beneath the Prison Walls*
and *Padre and Other Short Stories*

'In *Banaag at Sikat*, Lope K Santos succeeded in condensing the whole spiritual history of the Filipino *ilustrado* ('the enlightened or educated ones'). . . The novel is a true exemplar of revolutionary art.'

Dr Epifanio San Juan
Winner of the Association of Asian American Studies
Outstanding Book Award
Emeritus Professor, University of Connecticut

'In the novel, the two lead characters want to plant the seeds of socialism and anarchy. The narrative of their resistance is a struggle against the old order inherited from colonial Spain and the new order being imposed by the Americans. Danton Remoto is one of Asia's finest bilingual writers. In this book, he renders *Banaag at Sikat* in a fluent and contemporary English that introduces this Tagalog classic to a new generation of global readers.'

Dr Bienvenido Lumbera
National Artist of the Philippines
Winner of the Ramon Magsaysay Award for Literature,
Asia's Nobel Prize

'Lush, limpid and lean, Danton Remoto is a stylist of the English language. Read him.'

Bernice Reubens, winner of the Man Booker Prize
for the novel, *The Elected Member*

'I am a fan of the works of Danton Remoto.'

Junot Diaz
Winner of the Pulitzer Prize and the National
Book Critics' Circle Prize for the novel, *The Brief
Wondrous Life of Oscar Wao*

'Danton Remoto is an accomplished writer whose fiction is marked by elegant and intense language. I am also impressed by the social concern in his writing, wrought well in images so clear it is like seeing pebbles resting at the bottom of a pond.'

Sir Stephen Spender
Winner of the Golden PEN Award
Appointed as United States' Poet Laureate

'Danton Remoto's books are vivid, well-written and enthralling. He is an adroit writer: his works form part of the Philippines' new heart.'

James Hamilton-Paterson, winner of the
Whitbread Prize for the novel, *Gerontion*

'Danton Remoto can capture curves of feeling and shapes of thought in both English and Filipino. His language is chiseled and lapidary. His structure is musical in its control and tonality. His eye and ear are perfect.'

Professor Rolando S. Tinio
National Artist for Literature and Theatre

'Danton Remoto—who writes poetry, fiction, and creative nonfiction—is one of the Philippines' best writers.'

The Age, Melbourne

'Danton Remoto is a smart and sensitive writer whose works ask many questions about our complex and colourful country.'

Jessica Hagedorn
Shortlisted for the National Book Award
for the novel, *Dogeaters*

'Danton Remoto is an outrageously good writer. He writes with substance and style and he knows history—the context that shapes fiction—like the lines on the palm of his hand.'

Carmen Guerrero Nakpil
Author of *Heroes and Villains* and *Myself, Elsewhere*
Winner of the South East Asia Write Award

'Danton Remoto did something different. He has such sharp powers of observation. In his books in English and Filipino, he sees and gives importance to telling details that others ordinarily don't see. This is what separates him from the rest: he can capture feeling and image exactly, especially feeling which is difficult to show, since it is elusive and fleeting.'

Professor Rogelio Sicat
Dean, College of Arts and Letters
University of the Philippines

'Danton Remoto is such a wonderful writer. His books deal with the tropical Catholic magic that saves and destroys.'

Tiphanie Yanique
Winner of the American Academy of Arts
and Letters Award and the Flaherty Dunnan Prize
for the novel, *Love and Drowning*

'The Ateneo de Manila University has produced some of the best Filipino writers in the last three decades. One of them is Danton Remoto, who writes poetry and prose of the highest order—in both English and Filipino!'

The Manila Chronicle

'Danton Remoto is a poet, fiction writer, translator and journalist— one of the finest in Asia. He shows depth of feeling and great skill in his works. But I am also impressed by his compassion for the weak, the poor, the suffering in his books. He is a writer who cares.'

Father Miguel A. Bernad, S. J.
Editor-in-Chief, *Kinaadman: A Journal
of Southern Philippines*

Banaag at Sikat (Radiance and Sunrise)

by Lope K. Santos

Translated by Danton Remoto

PENGUIN BOOKS

An imprint of Penguin Random House

PENGUIN CLASSICS

USA | Canada | UK | Ireland | Australia
New Zealand | India | South Africa | China | Southeast Asia

Penguin Classics is part of the Penguin Random House group of companies
whose addresses can be found at global.penguinrandomhouse.com

Published by Penguin Random House SEA Pte Ltd
9, Changi South Street 3, Level 08-01,
Singapore 486361

Banaag at *Sikat* was published in 1906 by Lope K Santos

This translation is published in Penguin Classics by Penguin Random House SEA 2021

ISBN 9789814914055

www.penguin.sg

This translation is dedicated to the memories of the National Artist for Literature and Theatre, Rolando S. Tinio, who shared his thoughts on creative writing and the art of translation

and Director Marilou Diaz-Abaya, who, with Rolando, had long conversations with me on life, love and literature.

Contents

Introduction: The Novel as a Social Text

In 1902, Isabelo de los Reyes—a radical scholar, propagandist and founder of the Philippine Independent Church—started the Union Obrera Democratica, the first labour union against the Americans. The Americans had been in the country for only three years when they snuffed out the dreams of Asia's first independent country and turned it into just another colony. The Americans, always quick on the draw, promptly imprisoned de los Reyes to prevent the growth of the seed that he had recently planted.

The young writer Lope K. Santos was a member of this labour union. Remember that this was just a few years before the Spaniards had executed the novelist and poet Dr Jose Rizal at Bagumbayan field, for being 'the spirit of the Philippine Revolution', and just three years after the United States had colonized the Philippines. Nationalist feelings still ran high. American culture—its language, literature, music, film and basketball—had yet to take root. The soil in many parts of the country was still soaked in blood. Poems and novels in Tagalog were being published in the newspapers. These works that harked back to a glorious past and satirized the troubled present were being written, published and read widely. Love of country was the mantra of the day.

The eminent historian, Professor Teodoro Agoncillo, wrote: 'Most influential of these works, however, was Lope K. Santos' *Banaag at Sikat*. Avidly read by the masses and the intellectuals, the book in no

1

small measure influenced the workers fighting for economic, social and political reforms. As a result, more and more labour unions sprouted; strikes were resorted to by the labourers, particularly those engaged in cigar and cigarette manufacturing—to the discomfiture of the capitalists who had been accustomed to pushing the workers around.'

But who was this person who wrote not just the first proletariat novel in the Philippines, but also the first one in Asia?

Lope K. Santos was born in 1887 in Guipit, Sampaloc, Manila, the son of a worker in the printing press. Even at a young age, he was already familiar with the printer's ink. Unfortunately, his father died when he was still young and the boy had to work as a helper in another printing house. That printing house published the *Balarila ng Wikang Tagalog* (*Grammar of the Tagalog Language*) by Father Mariano Sevilla. The young boy showed an early interest in the arts: he read the poems his father had written, helped in theatre productions, and joined poetry jousts.

He took a course in Education, but was forced to work for the Spaniards, so he could draw his salary as a government employee. After the signing of the Pact of Biak-na-Bato Peace Treaty between the Philippine revolutionary forces and the Spanish colonial government, Lope K. Santos worked as a guard in Intramuros. Later, he helped distribute firearms and food under the command of General Pio del Pilar when the Philippine–American War erupted.

He moved houses, always on the run from the enemy, and then he met a group of journalists, the brightest and bravest in the country: Rafael Palma, Teodoro M. Kalaw, Rafael Corpuz, Jose Palma, Patricio Mariano, Honorio Lopez, Valeriano Hernandez Peña, Faustino Aguilar and Francisco Lacsamana. These gentlemen were not only journalists; many of them were also poets and novelists. Lope K. Santos had found his milieu.

After the Americans finally subjugated the Filipinos in a long, costly and bloody war, the second wave of colonization began. Along with the entry of the Thomasites, the American teachers who came aboard the cattle ship *U.S.S. Thomas*, arrived the long container vans with books in English: Longfellow and Shakespeare, Keats and Lord Byron; as well as the explosive books of Hegel, Marx, and Engels, among others.

Lope K. Santos became a militant journalist in *Ang Kaliwanagan* (*The Light*) and *Kapatid ng Bayan* (*Brother of the Country*) in 1902. He later edited *Muling Pagsilang* (*Rebirth*), the Tagalog supplement of the *El Renacimiento* (*The Renaissance*) newspaper. Both the Tagalog and Spanish newspapers were fearless until the Interior Secretary, Dean C. Worcester, brought a libel case against Fidel Reyes for his scathing editorial, '*Aves de Rapiña*' (Birds of Prey). The American won the case. All the printing machines of the newspaper were confiscated to pay for damages and in exchange for the freedom for the publisher and the staff.

Later, Lope K. Santos edited the satirical newspaper *Lipang Kalabaw* (*Carabao Nettle*), published by the then rising star in Philippine politics, Manuel Luis Quezon. Later, Santos was persuaded to run for governor of Rizal province, which he won. After serving as governor, he edited the newspaper of the Nacionalista Party, from which President Quezon plucked him to work as governor of Nueva Vizcaya province. He later ran for senator of Mindanao and again, he won. Santos was well-admired as a governor and a senator: someone who never lined his pockets with stolen money, and someone who tried his best to apply, in the real world, the words he wove in his fiction. He later served as a director of the Surian ng Wikang Pambansa (Institute of the National Language). He died on 1 May 1963, fittingly enough, on Labour Day.

Banaag at Sikat is considered as the fountainhead of social realism in the Tagalog novel tradition. It starkly mirrored the various forces clashing during the early days of American colonialism; in this guise, the novel could be seen as a social text.

Santos wrote the novel when he was only twenty-five years old. He was a voracious reader and his great learning was shown in the authors and books cited in the novel. He also knew that he was standing on the shoulders of a literary tradition. His novel sprang directly from *Ninay* by Pedro Paterno and the *Noli me Tangere* and *El Filibusterismo* by Dr Jose Rizal. The *costumbrismo* tradition of the novel as a document of mores and manners, customs and traditions, that was shown in *Ninay* can also be found in some chapters in *Banaag at Sikat*, especially in the description of the luxuriant flora in the countryside, as well as the wedding and funeral scenes. The embers of Rizal's novels can be seen in the subject matter of *Banaag at Sikat*: like philosophy, it was written 'to help change the world'.

Moreover, *Banaag at Sikat* was the child of the nineteenth-century didactic novel. This can be seen in the long passages where the characters debate on capital and labour, socialism and anarchy. Sometimes, Santos laid too heavy a hand and would veer a chapter toward another theoretical discussion on capitalism and its discontents, and why the Philippines should embrace socialism instead.

The poet and critic Roberto Añonuevo admired the novel's 'breadth of vision' and the way 'it catalogues the events, as well as its depiction of characters, conflicts and scenes'. However, like many previous critics, he noted the 'flaw' of the novel: its characters who were wont to deliver long speeches, which marred the 'aesthetics' of the novel.

National Artist Bienvenido Lumbera also wrote a musical version of *Banaag at Sikat* and noted that 'in the process of adaptation, he said his biggest hurdle was the polemics of the characters. For example, the two male leads spent a lot of time discussing socialism and anarchism'.

For his part, the Marxist critic Dr Epifanio San Juan noted that 'criticism of the novel from Adriatico to Agoncillo to Laya has invariably directed attention on the insistently didactic and therefore "anti-literary" or programmatic content and thrust of Santos' narrative method. I believe this view . . . is based on an erroneous premise and a short-sighted conception of art's function vis-à-vis objective social experience.'

Banaag at Sikat, then, should be seen from the lens of its own historical context: the nineteenth-century novel—a vessel of opinions and an instrument of enlightenment for the readers on the burning issues of the day.

Dr Soledad S. Reyes also said that this is the context in which *Banaag at Sikat* should be seen. While it also deals with love as well as family issues, it does not deal with personal issues alone. It shows the contending forces in a society divided between the few who are rich and the many who are poor. Many of the passages in the novel still have implications relevant to the present, like pebbles thrown on the surface of a lake, creating ripple upon ripple of meaning.

This is also illustrated in Dr Resil Mojares' reading in his book, *The Origins and Rise of the Philippine Novel Until 1940*, where he said: 'There are points in literary history when novels in the conventional mode begin to bear tenuous relations with the historical realities of the time during which they are written. The intrusion of these realities will necessarily result in a 'deformation' of the conventional plot. This distortion can take several forms: chiefly, it can be freakish and mechanical (as when the new is simply superimposed on the old) or it can be artistic and creative (as when the two elements are successfully integrated). This is the problem illustrated in an interesting group of early novels, the best-known representative of which is Lope K. Santos' *Banaag at Sikat*.' This led to what Mojares calls the 'hybrid plot' of the novel: it is a political tract and a love story as well.

Banaag at Sikat will continue to generate new meanings, or regenerate old ones, through the passage of the years. Translated here as *Radiance and Sunrise*, may it inspire new readers to take their individual and collective lives into their own hands, and shape them in order to 'help change the world'.

References

Abueg, Efren R. Marso 1970 'Sosyalismo sa Panitikang Tagalog'. *Panitikan* (Vol. V, Blg. 2). Maynila. Pangwika Publishing.

Agoncillo, Teodoro A. 1970. *A History of the Filipino People*. Quezon City: R.P. Garcia Publishing.

Añonuevo, Roberto. 2008. '*Muling Pagbasa sa Banaag at Sikat ni Lope K. Santos*. Posted on October 15, 2008. http://alimbukad.com/2008/10/15. Accessed 10 March 2021.

Mangahas, Rogelio. 1969. 'Ilang Silahis ng Banaag at Sikat'. *Philippine Studies*. Quezon City: Ateneo de Manila University.

Mojares, Resil. 1980. *The Origins and Rise of the Philippine Novel Until 1940. A Generic Study*. Quezon City. University of the Philippines Press.

Reyes, Soledad S. 1982. *Nobelang Tagalog 1905-1975: Tradisyon at Modernismo*. Quezon City: Ateneo de Manila University Press.

San Juan, Epifanio. 1971. *The Radical Tradition in Philippine Literature*. Manila. Manlapaz Publishing, Inc.

Santos, Bayani, 2019. 'Translating Banaag at Sikat'. *Unitas Journal*. Manila. University of Santo Tomas. October 2019.

Torres-Reyes, Maria Luisa. 2010. *Banaag at Sikat: Metakritisismo at Antolohiya*. Manila. National Commission on Culture and the Arts.

Villanueva, Antonia F. 1980. 'Si Lope K. Santos, Lider ng mga Manggagawa'. *Mga Sanaysay sa Alaala ni Lope K. Santos sa kanyang ika-100 na Kaarawan*. Maynila: Surian ng Wikang Pambansa.

'Lope K. Santos 1906 novel *Banaag at Sikat* gets the indie-rock treatment', *Philippine Daily Inquirer*, August 2, 2010. p. C5.

A Note on the Translation

This translation is based on the 1959 edition of *Banaag at Sikat*, the final edition that Lope K. Santos personally supervised. Anvil Publishing would later reprint this edition in 1988, 1993, 2008 and 2018, as possible required reading for classes in Filipino and Philippine Literature in colleges and universities.

When I first began translating this novel, it was clear in my mind that I will be translating it for a twenty-first-century reader. Therefore, I telescoped the long speeches and dialogues mentioned earlier, some of which are repetitive, into shorter paragraphs.

Lope K. Santos also wrote this novel in his early twenties. Thus, it showed the blessing and curse of writing a novel at such a young age. There was the passion and enthusiasm, as well as a deep well of sentiment from which the novel sprang. But there was also the tendency to show off his vast storehouse of learning—the flora and fauna of the Philippines, the many books on economics, sociology and political economy. These, along with the speeches, slowed down the pace of the novel. Thus, while I translated this novel, I kept in mind the mantra that I used when I was revising my own novel, *Riverrun*, for Penguin Random House South East Asia: keep it moving. A novel is a story, and the pages have to turn.

I also used the English equivalents of words ('Java plum' for '*duhat*') and translated directly into English the words, phrases and sentences that were originally written in Spanish. I retained the satirical spellings of English used by the young people learning English for the first time, and I maintained the florid language and tone in the letter written by one of men besotted with Meni. I think the intention of the author was to compare and contrast this with the clarity and sincerity of Delfin's letters to Meni, and I have preserved that in this translation.

In many cases, I have retained the names of places and proper names, as well as most honorifics (Don, Señora). I have also retained the original spellings used by Lope K. Santos.

I would like to thank Bayani Santos, the grandson of Lope K. Santos, who encouraged me to undertake this work; Dr Maria Luisa Torres Reyes, as well as Gilbert Francia and Niccolo Vitug for their help given to me while preparing this difficult work of translation.

Finally, I would like to thank Nora Nazerene Abu Bakar, the Associate Publisher of Penguin Random House Southeast Asia, for calling me up one morning and asking me to translate this book, which I did through the many days and nights of the Covid-19 pandemic.

The generosity of heart is all theirs but the faults of this translation, if not in the stars, are all mine.

And finally, my forever love goes to James, my partner, for reminding me that the world of words is where I should be.

Chapter 1

At the Antipolo Springs

'People have been coming here for years, but this year, even more visitors came,' an Antipolo resident was boasting to his guests from Manila. 'It could be that other than the fire that recently razed and devastated the town, our people's resistance against the Spaniards, and then against the more powerful Americans, could have further impoverished our people. But by the grace of Our Miraculous Lady of Peace and Good Voyage, this year's festivities were truly joyous! Only this time, the most popular attractions were the spring waters, where the visitors come to bathe . . .'

The Antipolo resident recalled the story accurately—recent visitors between early May and the last days of June 1904 would have described it in a similar fashion. Did people come because of their faith or the attractions that enticed almost the whole of Manila and those from the provinces to go up the hills of Antipolo? Undeniable was the town's magnetic power to pull people up to the ridge, even those who were cold-hearted and those who scrimped.

Without doubt, the sheer faith in Antipolo's healing powers drove sick people to bathe in the springs. But now, the people came to enjoy the endless attractions for pleasure, rather than for the waters 'that were made miraculous by the Virgin Mother.' Those were bygone days when the springs were sacred, a balm for souls guilty of sins. Most often, the springs became flowing witnesses to the secrets of a young woman's heart, the obscene glaze of a young man's eyes and the opportunities for admiring the embellishments of the body and lovers exchanging affection.

'To bathe in the springs' no longer meant healing someone of some sickness. Now, it meant 'to enjoy the stars in heaven'. Indeed, it would be like the use of the phrase 'to go to church', now meaning, 'to see people in their Sunday best'.

Pity the soul of him who had 'discovered' and 'made' those waters 'miraculous' for his failure to sense what would happen to his 'discovery'. Just as sure as the sun setting in the west, his merchandise of faith in these miraculous springs would face nights of sheer profanity: a hive of rentals and lodging businesses—places for lovers, a paradise for the daughters of Eve picking the forbidden fruit, a haven for the lustful, and a theatre for the sinful eyes of men, mouths wide open and moist with desire.

'Someone has stolen my dream!' He who had discovered these waters would certainly have been fretting these days, were he still alive, with eyes looking up to the heavens, staring in disbelief at the pilgrims' irreverent behavior.

Antipolo had been known not for one but a few other streams, although many of them branched into two, four, even eight cycles downstream. But among the many, one spring stood out for the sparse presence of people and for its pristine and unspoilt condition. Upon reaching the top of the stairs carved from the hillside, a pathway snaked towards the door of a large landscaped property bordered by a signage, 'SPRING', made from improvised bamboo slats. The ends of each letter were nailed on two cotton trees, looking as if these were planted together to become intimately intertwined, a suggestive and lusty invitation to the tourists.

Upon first coming to the entrance, the imaginative but fearful lowlander would think that he is standing on the holy grounds of a private cemetery. The hanging branches and twigs of rose apple trees, the luxuriant fruits of cashew, banana, velvet apple, native blackberries and cotton trees; some shrubs said to be 'the natural cure of rats that have survived snake attacks'. All these plants, in their splendour and freshness, could be thought of as having been fertilized by the dead people underneath. The hilly terrain, wild grass and mimosa grew everywhere, which seemed to suggest that the place indeed had been a burial site.

In the distance, a small hut looked like a cemetery chapel. On either side and at the back of the hut stood two tall huts. The fearful would think that under the ground were buried the bones of some parish priest, a village chief, or other people of distinction and repute. Ghostly memories would visit the fearful newcomer, as his eyes searched for even one small cross atop the hut, as commonly found in cemeteries.

One morning, however, a clothesline of colourful women's wear was seen hanging inside the huts. Women gracefully moved and swayed around, even as the men stood up and sat down restlessly. Some wore white, others pale red, some others fiery red, and still others green—the colour of fresh leaves.

Were they burying someone? If so, the mourners should have been in black. Were they burying a child, perhaps? But rather than a gloomy sight, the intruder might instead hear the echoes of conversations devoid of grief. Instead, in the air rose conversations filled with fun and roaring laughter. The imagined thoughts of a cemetery would vanish upon seeing five or six pretty women, running out and racing to reach one of the huts that looked, only moments before, like places where one had kept skeletons.

It was certainly not a cemetery. In the town of the dead, noise and fun would not reign. The aroma of food and the lush foliage evoked neither tears nor prayers for the dead, but rather, an invitation for sharing life and happiness with the living.

This spring was indeed the source of pride for Antipolo.

* * *

Thin needles of rain fell in the pale sunlight of the morning. It was Sunday, the second week of the nine-week feast. Indeed, the May feast was near its final day.

The cogon-grass hut with a trellis on the left had an elevated space that served as the caretaker's dwelling. It could be reached by a bamboo ladder at one edge of the hut. Under the improvised dwelling sat a centre-table with bottles of various colours and sizes, in three or four flavours; a glass container with hardened bread, caramel, and other sweets; some canned sardines, neatly atop a can of margarine; an improvised native plate of bread (if one were not favoured by luck, the bread would have been as tough as the head of the coughing tubercular man from whom it was bought); a wooden water dipper; two boxes, one for unconsumed tobacco and the other for the money from sales.

The surface of an elevated bamboo floor also served as the bed of an old hag, whose head already shone like a silver fan, with clumps of hair on her crown resembling pellets of chicken shit. Under a trellised corner was a woman nursing a baby as she stood before the stove, where she fried native cakes and ripe plantains. All of these would have been the picnic food of the crowds of bathers, had not Don Ramon Miranda rented all the baths that morning. No one could use the baths while Don Ramon and his guests were around. Everything had been reserved for Don Ramon: the seats, the merchandise sold by the vendors, the utilities, all the springs, and also, apparently, the tubercular coughing man and the old hag of a caretaker, judging by the courtesy they showed to the Master.

Three cars and a horse-drawn carriage brought the guests of Don Ramon to Antipolo on the previous afternoon of Saturday. He and two unmarried women, his daughters Talia and Meni, comprised the core group. The others included Don Filemon Borja, who could never be left out of such family occasions, Señora Loleng and her only daughter, the unmarried Isiang; the brothers, Honorio and Turing Madlang-Layon, and some other associates who were always with them during out-of-town trips. All of them came from the rich business district of Santa Cruz, except for the lawyer brothers, Madlang-Layons of Tondo, a district composed of workers and professionals.

They all stayed at the country house, which would be reserved for Don Ramon on the town's feast days. A spacious residence of unpainted wood and grass, the house might have seen better days, but it enjoyed some local prestige because it was located in front of the shrine.

Several of their friends from Manila saw them attending the early morning Mass. Don Ramon and Don Filemon were indeed rich; Honorio was a lawyer; and they all served as escorts for the women. The group was happy and they welcomed their friends who came from another town. There was no place in the world like Antipolo, where Manila's eligible bachelors would be like birds pecking at rice grains. They took their breakfast and rested for a while. Then they changed into their swimwear and charged into the spring.

Four of the bachelors stuck to each other. Two of them were Isiang's friends: Bentus and Pepito, both elegant men and scions of rich families in Tondo and Trozo. Another man was the distinguished pharmacist, Martin Morales, whom Isiang liked. The fourth bachelor was Turing's acquaintance, but maybe not for long, for now they were stealing glances at each other.

Indeed, the flock had grown.

Don Ramon swam on the right side of the pool, while the younger men took turns swimming on the left side. He then ordered the servants to roast the pig and cook the chickens in the house and serve them later at the pool side.

Don Ramon and Don Filemon entered the waters first. When they were about to finish with their baths, the women on the other side of the pool were waiting for the herbal shampoo to foam. Only Meni and Isiang had finished their baths.

'While you're waiting for the shampoo to foam, we'll look for lemongrass and lime juice,' they told the rest of the women.

'And where will you look for them?' asked Señora Loleng. 'Why not ask Petra to do that so you can change into your dry clothes?'

Petra was Señora Loleng's servant. But the two women pretended not to have heard the older woman. While whispering to each other, they went to a tree heavy with black Java plums, admiring the small, round fruits. They craned their necks and their throats dried up from salivating after the fruits, knowing that they could not get even one fruit. Isiang went to the men and asked them for help, including the widowed lawyer, Madlang-Layon.

'We must get a pole with a sickle at its end,' said Meni.

'I'll just climb the tree,' said Morales in a gesture of chivalry.

'No,' Isiang protested. 'You're still wearing your shoes and the tree is slippery.'

'Indeed, but it wasn't just a Java plum tree that we climbed during the war, when we watched our for the enemies while under the cover of the branches and leaves.'

'But you were not wearing shoes then.'

'I was and those trees had lesser branches than this tree.'

'It's up to you,' Isiang said. 'But when you reach the top, please shake the branches with vigour.'

Morales then climbed up the tree, followed by Bentus. They gripped the slender trunk and felt that they were climbing a telegraph post. They were embarrassed that Isiang might notice the shaking of their knees. Who cared about soiled clothes, anyway?

The two men later shook the tree with such vigour that the small, black plums rained down on the ground. Shrieks tore the very air. Isiang was the first to reach the plums, wiping them with the hem of her dress and then popping them into her mouth.

Meni, who was answering the lawyer's questions about her sister, Talia, also joined the crowd gathered under the tree. She also picked the small, black Java plums on the ground.

'Please don't shake the tree anymore while we're still picking up the plums from the ground,' Pepito said. He was worried that the Java plums might stain his white trousers and grey woolen suit, as well as his Panama hat.

The noise also attracted the attention of those who were still in the pools. They wanted to join in the fun and have their share of the plums. But they could not do anything anymore, since Talia and Turing were already in their swimming attires. Petra was still shampooing the hair of Señora Loleng. They could only scream: 'Hey, please share the plums with us!'

In the meantime, two men were rushing in through the gates of the compound. They wore suits and white trousers, as well as hats. They were almost as tall as each other, but the one in a hat was better built than the other. He was also fair, while the other was dark. From afar, they looked six years older than their actual ages. Their clothes were fashionable and well-cut, and they did not project an arrogant air. It was obvious that they wanted to belong to the group in the springs. They were neither lean nor obese. The darker man was more muscular, and would have been a Napoleon during the Revolution, had he more muscles. Their arms were draped around each other's shoulders, and they looked like twins. But upon closer inspection, the fair one had deep-set eyes, while the other one had wide and vivid eyes, and one knew then that they were just close friends.

The two saw the commotion of the crowd grabbing their share of the plums. Meni's heart beat faster when she saw who was coming.

'These are Felipe and . . .' she said, hesitating. Felipe was the darker of the two men.

'And who's that other man?' Madlang-Layon asked intently. Meni was taken aback and could not reply right away.

'Isn't Delfin the one who is walking toward us?' Isiang whispered to her friend. Delfin was the fairer man.

'Yes, indeed!' Meni replied as she slowly moved away from the two men near her, who were also scrambling about for the plums. She stood up slowly and made it appear that she was not part of the melee.

'Now you're done with the plums!' Isiang exclaimed. 'Is he the jealous type?'

'I don't know,' Meni said. 'But why should I care if he is a jealous man?'

While the two were teasing each other, the two men were also talking about the people a few steps away from them.

'So what are you doing here?' Felipe asked.

'We're picking plums,' Madlang-Layon answered.

'Are they sweet, Madame Isiang?' Delfin asked in a teasing tone.

'They're sweet enough for me, sir. And what about you, Meni, were the plums sweet for you as well?'

'They're bitter,' came the swift reply.

'Oh, such bitter plums,' Felipe said. Everyone tried to control their laughter, except Meni.

'She seems irritated,' Delfin whispered to his friend.

Felipe walked over to Meni and asked, 'Are you mad at us?'

A smile began to bloom on her face, and pretty soon, she was already back to her animated self.

'But why did you come only now? What time did you leave Manila?'

'It was still dark when we left,' Felipe answered. 'Where are they?'

'Oh, Father is in the springs.'

'What about you, Madame Isiang? Aren't you going to take a bath in the springs?' Delfin asked, then briefly glanced at Meni.

'I'm going there now, sir,' she said, then threw a quick glance at Meni as well.

The banter was quickly broken by the sudden rain of plums from the branches overhead. Delfin looked up and recognized the man up in the tree. He was Morales, the pharmacist, and Bentus, the smart man he had met at a high school in Sampaloc.

'So it's the two of you,' he said.

'Yes, it's the two of us,' they answered. When you came, you only had eyes on the people down there, that's why you didn't see us,' he teased.

'Not really. Very well, then, shake the branches again so I can also have a taste of these plums.'

So the two men up in the tree shook the branches again, this time with more vigour. Even the unripe green plums fell down to the ground. The farmers saw what was happening and shook their head in disgust. 'These people from Manila are like wild locusts in their hunger for our fruits,' they said amongst themselves.

Later, Felipe went to the pool where Don Ramon, his godfather, was taking a bath. Isiang, Madlang-Layon, and Pepito slowly made themselves scarce, as if they had been asked to leave. Delfin knew all of them, but he was not familiar with Pepito. And so Delfin and Meni were left and they started to talk to each other, while the others pretended to be picking up the plums that had fallen on the ground.

'Did you like the show at the Zorrilla Theatre, last night?' Meni asked with a smile.

'Oh, I don't know what was showing last night,' answered Delfin.

'You don't know?'

'How would I know? I did not even touch the door of any theatre last night.'

'Of course. And you came here this morning with such red and swollen eyes, seemingly from lack of sleep.'

'Are my eyes red?'

'No, they're vivid black. Some people say they will come, but then they go to the theatre, first.'

'Oh, my dear Meni. You don't believe me?'

'Why should I? Felipe said that the minute you got your pay from the press, yesterday, you would follow us here. But maybe you really didn't go to the theatre. To the cinema, perhaps? Are they showing a new film?'

'Not even to the cinema, Meni.'

'So you must have gone to the final day of the Feast of the Cross at Timbugan. I heard that the women who were chosen to be queens were gorgeous.'

'We don't go there anymore.'

'What virtuous men.'

'There's a snide remark there, somewhere.'

Only their eyes talked.

'Ah, so when Felipe and you retired for the night, the bells for the six o' clock Angelus were just tolling and you weren't able to watch anything.'

'You and your wild presumptions. We attended a meeting last night.'

'What meeting? You had a meeting in *her* house?'

The house of Ines, the school teacher, flashed in his mind. Ines was Meni's teacher, and she had asked Delfin to escort both of them home.

Meni then smiled, making her face look lovelier.

He said, 'You know only too well that I belong to many organizations and have meetings almost every day.'

'So what does it matter to me if you lead such a busy life?'

Delfin noticed a hint of jealousy in her voice. The two must have forgotten that they were not alone, standing under the shade cast by the tree. The two men who had climbed the tree had gone down and the people scrambling about for the plums had already moved on to the taller cashew trees. But the two remained rooted to where they stood. Meni was the first to blink.

'I'll go to the springs now. Father must be done by now.'

'Wait!' Delfin said. Then he stammered the words, 'I just want to tell you that . . . I'm happy when I see you. All the tiredness from my bones vanished when I saw you. And now we're here, together. Could there be a more delightful place than the heart of Antipolo, the dark plums and the clear streams, the green grass and this brilliant morning? But I sense that you keep on pushing me away. In your letters and in your words to me now, I haven't heard even a note of encouragement. All I get are taunts and snide remarks. Please tell me, what else should I do?'

'Nothing more,' was her laconic reply.

'Nothing more? Then why can't you give me a clear answer?'

'Look, Delfin. We're still studying.'

'So what?'

'We're still young. We have to finish our studies first. And you know my father. He'll be very disappointed if he knows we're already committed to each other. Our dreams then will come to nothing. And besides, you know that older sister will be married to Yoyong soon, and I'll be the only one left in the house.'

'Oh, Meni, there you go again. Why do you think that if you give me some hope, your father will love you less? And my studies, are you ashamed that I'm not yet a lawyer? Isn't your house already too crowded with all those men brandishing their professional degrees?'

'My, look at where you're taking this conversation.'

This made Delfin smile.

'What I meant was,' Meni continued, 'you might find it hard to focus on your studies. I didn't answer your letters because I . . . I didn't want to distract you from your studies.'

'So that's how it is. But you've no idea that the mind of your suitor is filled with nothing else except the days of waiting, hoping that one day, a letter from you would come.'

'But the time you would spend reading my letters would be better spent reading your law books.'

'Far from it, Meni. You're making my studies more difficult with your attitude. Do you think I could study hard without a Meni, the daughter of Don Ramon Miranda?'

'What? *Ay naku!*' That interjection summed up all the feelings in Meni's heart: uncertainty and misgivings and doubt. She was trying not to smile. She had remembered that when she met Delfin, she already knew that he was a bright and diligent student. In her heart, she knew that she liked him, too.

When he saw the tender look in her eyes, a boost of strength welled up inside him. 'I would rather hear you end my days of hoping, than keep me in suspicion of how you feel. And if my suit comes to nothing, then I'll offer you the ashes of the books I'm studying.'

'Bah. We women study for our own sake and not for the sake of men.'

'It sounds like a lie. The way you women speak, you make it sound as if only men are capable of lying. But I dare say that women are more interested in things other than studies . . .'

'And what might that be?' she said, irritation beginning to show in her face.

'All right. Let us sit, first, for more serious talk.'

She followed him and sat on the grass. She had already forgotten that with the noon sun rising to its zenith, she would not be able to take a bath anymore, because of the heat. Delfin sat across from her, his hands resting on his knees. He faced her, holding on to the low-hanging branch of a guava tree beside him.

Then he spoke. 'Let me make it clear to you, Meni, that not all students think that way. Some stop studying when they begin courting women, and others get better grades because of the encouragement from their girlfriends. I belong to the latter category and so you've nothing to fear. Your "Yes" will only make me study harder than I already do. Would you rather deny me this?'

'Delfin, that's not what I meant.'

The young man was about to answer when a loud voice called out from the gate leading to the springs, 'Hey, enough of whatever you're up to. You'll be late for your baths.'

The words came from Señora Loleng. Some of the young people scrambled toward the huts like pigeons roused from sleep, flying their coops. Delfin and Meni followed suit. Meanwhile, Don Ramon and Don Filemon had just emerged from the springs, their hair wet. None of the bachelors were interested in taking a dip. The two lawyers—Yoyong and Felipe—walked to the waters. But Delfin had already lost interest.

And so, those who had already taken a bath and those who had not, faced each other inside the store.

Chapter 2

Who is Don Ramon?

Amongst the people of Manila, there was hardly anybody who did not know the face, long and well-proportioned and fair, of the Spanish father, Don Ramon Miranda. His wealth came from the houses for let and he was one of the most prominent residents of Santa Cruz. Only a few places in the city had not yet smelt the acrid and smoky fumes of his car. His carriage 'on wheels', sometimes pulled by two horses from Batangas, both thickly furred, was recognized even from afar, because of the vivid paint at the back and on the sides of the carriage. Hardly a day passed by when he alone, or with his father, did not go to the Luneta—the part of the city beside Manila Bay. They would also visit the districts of Santa Ana, Pandacan, Santa Mesa and Gagalangin, especially Singalong and Pasay, where their daughters bought flowers and dried trunks for the garden back home.

Don Ramon was always found in the theatre or the horse races, in feasts and the meetings of Very Important People. His name was mentioned often in the newspapers. For example, if an expensive button fell from his suit, or he lost a beautiful dog, or a servant fled from his mansion; or if he went to the theatre in the company of Miss S, or the film star Miss M; or if he lost one or even two horses, because he always had a set of three horses, or if his car ran down a female pedestrian—all of these were written down and published in the newspapers. If these events were not reported, he would cause them to be reported, just so that he would be the subject of people's conversations.

Don Ramon could be found in the various meetings of the associations where he belonged, whether it was the group of businessmen or of homeowners' associations, amongst others. He could be found in the midst of them all, at total ease with his words.

He was not yet 'too old', he was only fifty-five years old. His wife, Aling Tanasia, the kind and famous jeweller, had died three years ago. Manila had not yet forgotten her funeral. Twelve magnificent horses from Paz Funeral Homes carried the coffin that contained her remains. And because she was a famous jeweller, Don Ramon also stoked the rumour that because he loved his wife deeply, he gave her a going-away gift of two antique rings made of the purest gold and a golden necklace of the finest filigree, along with a reliquary. If this were true, then upon entering the kingdom of Heaven, Saint Peter would ask her if he could use these jewellery as a wager for his fighting cock. We were yet to know if this news also reached the people working in the graveyard. It would be unfortunate if they had not heard of this news—at least they could have gotten a small share of the vast wealth that she had accumulated from her jewellery business.

One day, a young woman from San Miguel became the good friend of Don Ramon's two daughters. Those with sharp tongues said that the young woman's mother herself pushed her to befriend the two daughters of the rich man, so that she could be closer to him and perhaps become his next wife. The silver linings of his pocket were so thick it would make his great grandchildren's lives very comfortable. The mother and daughter from San Miguel wanted this, so the talk went around. But Señora Loleng wanted otherwise: when she visited the house of Don Ramon, she would make it a point to spit, then speak very ill of the mother and daughter from San Miguel. Why was Señora Loleng angry with them, since she herself was a married woman?

A fight almost erupted when the three met on one fine day in Quiapo, before the Holy Mass. Señora Loleng, the wife of Don Filemon, was about to leave the church when the mother and the daughter from

San Miguel were coming in. Señora Loleng spat and her saliva almost reached the sleeves of the young woman. 'What kind of a person is this?' asked the young woman.

'Why?' asked the mother.

But Señora Loleng just spat again and tossed her head. It was fortunate that there were many people coming in and going out of the church, and that was how the threat of a fire was stopped. But they stabbed each other with looks that seemed to say, 'I'll exact revenge one day,' or 'You'll also fall into my hands, woman!'

Do you want to turn deaf with irritation? Then do talk to Don Ramon.

Don't make the mistake of mentioning any one of the following provinces in the East, or Tayabas, Camarines, Batangas, Tangway, Pampanga, Ilocos, or else you would hear stories that would last the whole day long.

If ever you mention Batangas, he would tell you that he bought twenty horses there, and that all of them won in the races. During the time of Captain Berto in Lipa . . . He would relate to you the A to Z of his life as the buyer of so many horses and the winner of so many races at the Hippodrome, whether it was time of the Spaniards or the Americans.

If ever you mentioned that there was a fire in either Tondo or Sampaloc, you would hear that he had three houses for rent in Tondo as well as two houses for rent in Sampaloc, two in Binondo, and three in Santa Cruz; ten houses, all in all, which brought in a monthly rent of 4,000 pesos. He was disappointed with the fact that he didn't build two more big houses in Tondo when he last built a house there. If ever a fire would strike again, then the people who had no money to build a house would surely rent his houses.

If you talked about the lives of single men and women, then he would compare his youth with those living in the present time. He fathered one or two children in every province he had visited, and if they ever met each other, these children would not know that they are siblings because they had already grown up, while others had either gotten married or died.

He would even tell you about the difficulties he endured when, newly arrived from Europe, he lived in the town of M in Pampanga and became the rival of the parish priest on account of asking for the hand of Conchita, the only daughter of the present mayor.

The past would come back in his stories about his travails in a town in Batangas, because of one expensive horse that he had wanted to buy.

You would also hear about his exploits in the East, where he was welcomed like a true son of the town, because of a good deed that he had done for them many years ago, for which the town still had a debt of gratitude. In 1899, the enemy was still regnant and they were able to charge into town, threatening to burn houses and rice granaries, as well as the church itself. The women hid in caves inside and outside the town, because they had heard that the intruders raped the women of the town they occupied. Like an angel, Don Ramon saved the women from being dishonoured. He also became a good friend of the American colonel and was able to dissuade the American from throwing into prison some Filipinos who were mistaken to be soldiers of the revolution.

There are many other exploits that he would be excited to recall to you. An example of this was his graduating from the College of San Juan de Letran with a Bachelor of Arts degree in 1872, and his medical studies in Spain, which he did not finish on account of his many romantic liaisons with the women there, whom he claimed 'descended upon him like a flock of doves'. He also reached Paris, Berlin, and almost reached Rome and spent nine days at the Vatican, but he ran out of money when his parents stopped sending him his allowance. That was why he was forced to return to his native land. Although he did not receive any other degree or finish even one half of the requirements for any other degree and although he did not finish his medical degree overseas, he seemingly became an expert on all things European. He claimed to have seen 'all of Europe', when he was only able to visit Spain, Germany and France, and did not even take a peek at Italy.

You could say that because he had been to Madrid, he could already boast to his fellow men who had not yet heard any other booming bell in their lives, except the tolling of the bell in Saint Peter.

* * *

Before we forget, Don Ramon Miranda was also one of the rich owners of a big tobacco factory in Manila called The Progress. His investment there was worth 40,000 pesos. He and Don Filemon Borja had alternated managing the factory since it was started.

According to the scant knowledge about his origins, Don Filemon's mother had taken a 'liking' to a parish priest in Santa Cruz during the Spanish time. The said priest was so delighted when the son was born and indeed had an uncanny resemblance to him, that his delight extended to a gift of 2,000 pesos and a parcel of land in Santa Cruz, both of which were given to Filemon as inheritance, when he was already a young man.

So that the money would not just simply run out, when the inheritance was down to 1,000 pesos, both mother and son thought of starting a pawnshop. By the grace of God, the business prospered only after two years, and they also began other businesses. They lent money to the fish vendors in Divisoria and the fishermen in Bangkusay. They would lend money at a rate of 25 percent or even 50 percent, if the borrower was in truly desperate straits, and thus their business simply boomed. They also lent money to the owners of fishponds in Malabon and rice farmers in Caloocan, and when these could not pay up anymore, they simply took over ownership of the fishponds and the rice lands.

The pawnshop had taken a backseat in their array of businesses.

Filemon was already about twenty years old when they built several houses, which they put up for rent. Then he married Señora Loleng of Trozo; tongues had wagged that she used to be the mistress of a Chinese, who had lived and died in Sungsong. We did not know if this indeed was true; but what we could not deny was that Filemon's mother thoroughly disliked his wife, so much so that she died of heartbreak in 1885.

Like Don Ramon, Don Filemon did not finish his studies. He allegedly served as a village chief in Santa Cruz, and used this position to amass the wealth that he used to append before his name the honorific of a *Don*.

Don Filemon was the other big investor in The Progress. Some people said that his investment was bigger than Don Ramon's, while other people said it was the other way around. But we should not quibble about matters like these. What mattered was that Don Ramon was the director-general of the factory, while Don Filemon was its administrator, during the time when we are telling this story.

* * *

While talking to each other in the granary, Don Filemon regretted that he was not able to hire a full orchestra, or even some people from the Rizal Orchestra, or a group of native mandolin players from Trozo or Dalumbayan. He did not mind how much it would cost, as long as it added joy to their stay at the Antipolo springs.

'Were you not able to hire the players of the Grand Theatre Company?' Don Ramon enquired from his friend.

'Oh, yes. I saw Marianito last night and I heard that they would play at a house a street away from my house. It might be them.'

'That's the Reyes Orchestra, indeed,' said the pharmacist Morales. 'They are wearing the same uniform made of Barong Tagalog. But they might not be able to play here because I heard them talking on the terrace earlier. They said that after the Holy Mass, they would have to go play at another dance party.'

'Too bad,' said Don Ramon, 'our festivities would have been happier if there were music playing!'

When this wish could not be granted, their talk veered into different directions. They talked about the beautiful tableaus in San Miguel, Carpena's sweet voice, as well as the funny antics of Alianza, the laughable Molina, and almost all the other performers of the Grand Theatre Company. The names Korang Basilio, Titay Molina, Tagaroma, Lopez, Ilagan, Carvajal, Ratia and other famous performers floated in the air as the men conversed. They even thought of having a jury to decide who was the best amongst the performers. Then they talked about the other plays then showing in Manila, as well as the names of the writers, Reyes, Lopez, Mariano, Remigio, and the others.

A lovely woman named P from Quiapo bought a ticket to one of the shows and wanted to stay with Don Ramon to make her life better. But the old man refused because of the troubles brewing that day in the tobacco factory, when some workers had decided to mount a strike. All the fancy talk ceased after that.

'It's not the time for me to be somebody's patron,' said Don Ramon. 'The workers in my tobacco factory are agitated. They've been on strike for one week.'

'Why are they on strike?' asked Morales in a rash manner.

Don Filemon answered in his stead. 'Why are they on strike? You better ask Delfin and Felipe. They're the ones who know if our workers have become better people. I've heard they're the ones defending the union rights of these workers.'

Everyone's eyes were fixed on Delfin. He was seated on a bench made of bamboo strung side by side, which was usually the bench in the farm. Felipe was not there and still taking a bath. Delfin had been agitated by the snide remark of Isiang's father, and when noticed that everyone's attention was fixed on him, he could do nothing else except to defend himself.

'Please don't ask me about the strike in your factory. Even if I'm a member of the Alliance of Workers' Organizations, our sector is different from that of the tobacco workers . . .'

'Oh, so you're not aware of this!' Don Filemon said in an insulting manner. 'I thought that the workers had become rash in their demand to have higher wages because of your union. Your group must be good, your coffers are overflowing with money, and the members—whether they work in tobacco factories or not—contribute money to make us capitalists fall on our knees . . .'

Delfin felt the sharp cut. It was painful. The wounding words were said not only against the workers in the tobacco factory, but also for all the members of the organization. It was time to stand up for their rights. But he always deferred to the two old men he was talking to. Don Ramon was the father of Meni, and Meni was his life. He was reflecting on these thoughts when Don Ramon continued speaking.

'Look at how useless your union is. Look at the so-called "good" it is doing to the Filipino workers. There have been a series of strikes since these labour unions started. If the supervisor had caught them stealing and reported them to management, they would quickly ask that the supervisor be replaced. They would ask for a raise in their wages, even if production and sales were down. If you didn't give way to their whims, they would immediately declare a strike. But who would lose if they go on strike? We have 1,500 workers in The Progress factory, men and women, adults and children, yet only 300 of them went on strike, 100 women and 200 men. Even if they all joined their forces together, who would lose in the end? Could they make a dent on the lives of capitalists like us? Are we the ones who would be hungry? We have money; we will eat whether we work or not. Money is just capital for us; even if we just lie down in our beds, we will still live forever. How about them?'

'Then they would just gamble; if they have no money to gamble, then they would steal,' Don Filemon added these words, which just added fuel to the fire already burning inside Delfin.

'The cut that they've made inside me is getting more and more painful,' he thought to himself. 'They should not do this to me.'

And then he raised his face and answered the two old men who kept on humiliating the poor.

'Don Ramon and Don Filemon,' he said with a forced smile, 'you're wrong in insulting the organization of workers, simply because your factory workers went on strike. Our leadership might not agree with what they did, or might not even be aware that this strike happened. In this wise, they didn't follow one of our rules. However, they also have the right not to go to work, whether the president of our organization knows it or not.'

'And what would be their reason? What else do they want from us? What we pay them now is more than 100 percent of what we used to, years before. If you compare that with the wages at Germinal, they only got an increase of 10 percent, these past many years. At La Flor de la Isabela, not everyone got an increase in pay, and men were paid differently from the women. The same conditions could be found in the factories of La Insular, Alhambra and the others.'

'Don Ramon,' the young man answered, 'you think that the wage increase could cover the rising cost of food, clothing, housing and other needs of the workers? You should listen to the laments of the working poor . . .'

'Ah, there's no more need for that,' cut in Don Filemon.

'Please listen to me because we've a lot to discuss. The price of rice has risen many times. The food of the humble folk—smoked fish, dried fish and vegetables—have also increased in prices. We can add to that the cost of firewood, of water, of the ingredients needed for cooking, all of which have risen more than four times their original costs. Likewise with the fees for the seamstresses and the prices of clothes, hats, slippers and shoes, which are needed to avoid exposure to illnesses. How about the rent for the small house, or the cost of renovating a small house of their own? You could not repair a house for a mere fifty or 100 pesos only. How about the taxes for the house and lot, the sanitation fee, and other extractions by the State? Or if they rent a house, it's usually as small as the place where animals sleep. All of these, Don Ramon and Don Filemon, are just shadows of the real truth. What I've said about the lives of factory workers is the same as what is true of the lives of other working poor. Wherever the workers' lives turn, it all seemed to land up on capital. Capital rents their labour and the labourers also pay back to the capital.'

The two old men seemed to have run out of saliva. The others just sat silently and bit their lips. When Don Ramon saw that Don Filemon was beginning to shake with rage, he began to talk in cool and mellow tones.

'You said so many things about the lives of workers. But you failed to mention the cockfights they attend every Sunday, the games of cards that their wives attend until the wee hours of the morning, making them sleepless; their preening that was prouder than ours, whether in eating delicious food or wearing good clothes. I've seen many workers who earn fifteen or twenty-five pesos a month and yet, eat more food than I do and wear clothes that could put Captain Luis to shame. Pray tell me now, how expensive is the food, clothes, housing that they have, in contrast to their small wages? You know that you're not earning a lot of money, then why would you overspend? You don't have money in the bank, then why bring your money to the cockpit week in and week out? The poor are a thousand times prouder than the rich . . . And when they've no more money to pay for their whims, then they complain that they're not paid well enough for their work!'

Don Filemon almost applauded upon hearing what his friend had said, and then he added: 'These, these are the things that you should discuss and analyze, you who are members of the Alliance of Workers' Organizations!'

Delfin sensed that the discussion was turning for the worse. He deemed it wise to veer away from this topic. He could not have imagined that joining them on this trip would lead to this. He took a quick look at the people around him and realized that not a single one of them would understand the arc of his reasoning. Two old men whose only Lord was money; Morales, who knew nothing else but how to mix drugs; Bentus and Pepito, who knew nothing but how to wear well-cut and imperious clothes; one person whom Turing knew; two people from the Antipolo springs; people who had come and sat there just to listen to their arguments. But this was already a source of shame—it would be wrong to just take the blows passively.

'The greed for cockfights, for card games and other forms of gambling,' he answered, 'love for eating and good clothes—these I won't deny. There's some semblance of truth in what you've said. But don't think that our rules and our organization allow these. In our meetings and bulletins, we have pointed out that these traits are wrong. But the organization could not just brush these aside hastily, because we would be up against the town leaders themselves: they would say these acts are forbidden, but they allow many things to come to pass, especially those brought about by the modern times. It seems then that the only freedoms allowed are the freedom to practice religion and the freedom to gamble. But forbidding the latter only leads to hunger for other forms of gambling . . .

'Gentlemen, let us get to the point. The vices that you've mentioned are only the leaves and fruits of the workers' bitter lives. These are illnesses that cannot be healed, unless we go to their root causes. The root of all these is their poverty. And the fruits are these vices from society.

'Why won't the poor worker gamble one or several pesos, when he has no more hope of improving his lot? Why won't he gamble, when he had to meet so many needs, as father of the house and part of the community, a tier of needs that is important and necessary?

'About the good clothes, why won't he dress up well, when we still judge whether a person can be trusted or not by how he looks? Would someone wearing rags even be entertained, if he is looking for work in a factory or an office? They don't want to be thought of as "He's poor as a rat", "He looks like a thief", "This one can't be trusted", "This one should be sent to the Bilibid Prison", amongst other such vile accusations.

'And about eating well, that you said the poor should not do, but they need nourishment for the hard work that they do. What you suggest is just an extension of capital's cruelty and greed. But those who do nothing but count money are the ones who should be eating well, while those who get tired every hour, sweating and hungry, are the ones who should go hungry and should just be content with a dish of vegetables. This is the mentality of the capitalists: that the workers should get only barely enough to survive, and not that the workers should get what they need to live. This is a shameful attitude.'

Chapter 3

Capital and Sweat

Don Ramon was easily irritated like Don Filemon. But his irritation did not sharpen, for there was a dawn of truth in Delfin's reasoning. Although his wealth had covered his eyes with a layer of darkness, the learning he acquired on such occasions proved useful. The sharp thrusts of Delfin's reasoning wounded him so, although it was useless to lose one's cool in such debates. Who was Delfin compared to his knowledge on economic and social matters? How could Don Ramon, who had traveled Europe, lose in a war of words against Delfin, who might not even have sailed past Mariveles? He who had seen massive workers' rallies in Barcelona and in some provinces in France, where the worker's stubbornness only led to nothing or to the hangman's noose? He who had read on the *Political Economy* by Adam Smith, Ricardo, Neumann, Bastiat, and the easy book by P. Liberatore—why would he lose sleep over a mere student?

Oh! He never became a doctor or a lawyer, but his many books at home dealt with workers' wages and the rights of capitalists regarding labour. But we were not aware if in the enclosure of his library, Don Ramon knew the difference between tomes and wisdom, the way one's stomach grew with a banquet of food was different from the way knowledge grew in one's mind.

The reasoning that Delfin gave him was no longer mere words from a common worker. It was apparent that he had read books on Sociology. Don Ramon rued how easily such books could now enter the country. He told himself: 'Ah! We wasted the time of the Spaniards. If this happened during their time, such books now found in the Colon Library, the editorial offices, Manila Philately, and V. Castillo, amongst others, would have been burnt.'

His vexation grew and now focused itself not on the workers' strike at their factory with Don Filemon. Instead, he railed against the bad ideas of the younger man, ideas which, if not scuttled early, would erode the strong foundations of capital in the Philippines.

Delfin! Delfin! He mused to himself in a somewhat fatherly tone, 'Go slow, the path is slippery and full of thorns. Our workers are still worlds away from the condition of the workers in lands where the socialists and the anarchists are beginning to grow. The wages and conditions of Filipino workers are much better than those found even in Germany. Our workers' conditions are not poor, if you only saw the conditions in which the Spaniards, Russians and the others lived. They're the ones who could be helped by these socialists and anarchists. But look, Delfin, at how bitter the fruits are! People die in the strikes; thievery and drunkenness happen; women are raped and people die of hunger. Don't betray our country, whose people are easily swayed; stupid enough to be borne away by strong currents or by winds blowing in. If the workers hear your thoughts, they would only become more lazy than they already are . . .'

'But do you know why our workers are lazy?' Delfin countered.

'Wait a minute! These things can't be done with the impulsiveness of the young. Where will you lead the country if young people were allowed to lead? Our workers will constantly ask for their rights and will forget about their responsibilities. They're still ignorant about many things. Many of them don't even know how to eat rice, then you'll teach them these foolish ideas; give them dreams of socialism? What do young people know about socialism?'

'That is why we need to introduce it to them . . .'

He blithely ignored Delfin and faced Don Filemon. He continued speaking: 'These young people think that all that glitters is gold. Ha, ha, ha! What good did the American government have in mind when they sent these kids to the United States, supposedly to learn about the realities of life? Too bad, Delfin, that you weren't able to go to Paris, or even just to Barcelona. You would have seen the thick and bitter fruits of socialism. Even at their worst, Filipino workers never go hungry, and yet you want to introduce these ideas to them. Is that what you learnt about love of country and love of fellowmen?

* * *

Delfin's eyes widened upon hearing the torrent of words that spilt from the older man's lips. He didn't know which of them to answer first.

Meanwhile, Felipe was at the spring and now was coming out of the door. In his hurry, he was able to fix his suit when he was already outside the room, leaving behind Attorney Yoyong and the tail of the discussion. But before Delfin could answer, he touched the other man's arm and whispered: 'Will you allow yourself to lose?'

In the meantime, the other onlookers were waiting for Delfin's answers. If they were roosters in the cockpit, their tails would have been held and with hackles raised, they would have shown who was earthbound and who could fly. People thought this was just like a cockfight between aficionados.

But for Delfin, the discussion was not just mere banter or a contest. He realized that the time has come to introduce ideas of socialism in the Philippines. His two contenders were both capitalists and the other listeners were young men like him. He thought that his words might somewhat take root in their minds. Because of this, he had forgotten that he was trying to woo Don Ramon and that Don Ramon was the father of Meni . . .

'I would like to thank you,' he began in a gentle tone, 'for I have discussed this with people like you: older and experienced, who have traveled to different lands and seen so many things. I'm also aware that my scant knowledge isn't enough to change your minds.

'We belong to two sets of time: you belong to the past and we to the future and we meet here in the present. That is why what we have seen and what we are now seeing are the bases of our beliefs. The past belongs to you and the present as well, and even if a part of the present belongs to us, it's only a small part. But please allow us to prepare for the future that is no longer yours but ours.

'You can say that our labouring class has not yet learnt about socialism because it may just trouble them. But when will we prepare the Filipinos into a force that would buck the new era of the grand industries? Are we going to wait for foreign capital to settle in the country, level our mountains in their search for minerals and automate the world of labour? That is why we are introducing socialism through meetings with selected labour leaders. We teach the tenets of socialism in small bites. We do not promote laziness, but the pursuit of one's rights as a worker.

'We need not wait for the time when workers' wages go down, the way it has done in Belgium, England and the United States. I wish that we had labour laws that protect them; laws that shield them from the spiraling prices of commodities. I wish that there are also subsidies for the small stores and places of leisure that cater for the poor.

'Here, when all of these things don't exist, how can you say that the lives of the Filipino workers are better than the rest?

'Wherever there is capital and labour, landlord and farmer, lord and servant, rich and poor, there will always be a need for the teachings of socialism. In these conditions, the nest of poverty thrives and only a few suck the life-blood of the many.'

'And then what?' asked Don Filemon, who could no longer hold back his feeling upon hearing the attack on the rich, 'you will reinvent the wheel of time, the destiny that God has given to each one of us? Ever since the world began, there has always been differences in people's lives, the way red is from white and black is from yellow. Do you socialists want everyone to be rich in the eyes of the Lord?'

Felipe, who had just sat in on the discussion, could no longer hold back his thoughts. His friend is alone, dealing with the importunings of two old men. Even while he was still in the springs, he could already hear the insults being hurled at the workers by his godfather and Don Filemon. He hurried up. He was also a worker, serving as a printer at the *New Day* newspaper; also a member of the Workers' Organization that was being ridiculed by the two men; as well as a hardworking and devoted companion to Delfin in their sociology meetings. At these gatherings, he was the rashest and the most vocal about his feelings. After Don Filemon had spoken, in the heat of the moment, he took up the cudgels for Delfin and spoke directly.

'Don Filemon, that's not what the socialists want. All they want is a country with no rich nor poor, no lord nor servant, not a single slave—everyone has capital and everyone offers labour; all the lands, all the harvests, all modes of production and property belong not to a few but to everyone. Unlike now, when the rich only become richer, while the rest wallow in poverty. This is what the socialists want. On the other hand, the anarchists want not only these to change, but also for the Government to do so. That is why they are hated by the rich and the powerful. Why would these ideals be bad, when they belong to the natural rights of every one?'

The eyes of Don Ramon turned into twin points of knives directed at his godson. He said, 'So even you, Felipe, have been infected by this disease?' Then he looked at his other companions. 'Don Filemon, everyone gathered here, you should know that my godson has turned into an anarchist and a socialist, the harbinger of a new life! A new life without any rich or poor . . .'

He followed this with mocking laughter, which the other people gathered around him picked up and they laughed as well, including Morales and Bentus. Everyone else laughed, except Pepito, who could not smile or slacken his jaw at the sight of Felipe and Delfin, whose brows were furrowed.

Felipe turned pale, affected by his godfather's sharp words. He still wanted to speak, but Delfin beat him to it and resumed the thread of his earlier conversation.

'I don't know, Don Ramon, what you mean by the destitute. You said they don't exist in our country. But of the few who do, do they also include those who just simply stop breathing for lack of food?

We should give true meanings to words. The destitute should also include mothers and their children who live in tattered hovels, who lack food and medicine, who are thin and slowly dying, if not already dead.

'The destitute include babies who die on the mats of poverty, ninety out of 100 babies being born do not live beyond a few days, or weeks, or months. The destitute include those young men and women who grow up without being lit by the lamp of knowledge, unable to study for lack of food and resources.

'The destitute also include the thousands of prisoners now languishing in our jails, not because they are guilty, but because they didn't have the money to hire good lawyers to defend them, unlike the rich who can afford to hire the best lawyers in the land.

'And the destitute should also include those who are cannon-fodder for the wars that our government wages, to preserve the status quo of the capitalists. How much do we pay our soldiers who kill their fellow men? To the clear call of patriotism and love of country, our young men join the military in spite of the pittance they get and thus become destitute themselves, and later, actually die.

'Mr Miranda, the destitute also include the farmers who, in their desire not to be buried in landlords' debt would rather eat flowers from the dirty earth and rotten logs, live in the forests far away from the towns where they can get the produce they cannot buy.

'And all of them, Don Ramon, belong to the so-called "destitute", who are found in our land as in many other lands, in the past and the present, ever-growing and flourishing.'

* * *

While Delfin was winding up his words, Attorney Madlang-Layon and Señora Loleng were coming up from the springs at the same time. The lawyer reached the group a few minutes ahead. He was toweling his wet hair so it would dry up and he could part it again down the middle. When he saw Don Ramon, his potential father-in-law, the old man looked at him while swinging in the rocking chair like a man drowning. He looked at the younger man, as if asking for help from these socialists.

Señora Loleng looked like an American tank ready for war, if she were not covered from head to toe by a thick, white blanket. She smoked her cigar like a chimney, combed her curly hair and followed. Don Ramon gave her a look from head to toe. And she answered him with a glance as meaningful. Their thoughts seemed to converge: 'Oh, you have just taken a bath!' and 'Oh yes, it's too bad that Filemon is here!'

When Don Filemon saw them, exchanging sticky looks with each other, he waved at her and asked softly: 'Are the children still taking a dip at the springs?'

'Oh, these children. You're having such a ruckus here and there they are, smiling but not taking a bath. When will they ever finish? They had just started to rub pebbles against their knees to clean them.' Then she threw a sharp glance at Delfin and Felipe, before asking her husband: 'What did these kids tell you? And why do you even bother to debate with children who still have milk on their lips?'

Then she pulled from her mouth a cigar that had almost been burnt to its tip and seemingly spat, before entering a room in the cottage to change.

With this, Don Ramon's feelings also settled down, and stamped the thought of him having been defeated in the war of words by the longer time used by his opponents to speak. He lit an expensive cigar and then spoke.

'The poverty that you spoke of did not just happen yesterday or today, but even tomorrow and in the days to come. We need the rich and the poor in the land, because without capital, nothing will move and we need to pay wages to the poor so that things can be done. Those who want to live must work. Wealth comes from hard work. Capital comes from thrift. Work is the right of any person, because it's God's punishment since Adam and Eve committed a sin. If you don't want work to be difficult, will you then consider comfort a kind of punishment?'

'The socialists want,' added Don Filemon, 'a return to the time of Moses: to live at a time when manna falls from the sky. We do not have such manna nowadays!' He followed this with another round of mocking laughter, which made Delfin's blood boil.

Delfin said, 'You are all mistaken. Although not all thinkers agree on a single strand of socialism, they all agree on one point: the greatness of labour. Only labour provides the things that we need. Please don't speak of manna, Don Filemon. Even if the poor wished for that, it would not come to pass. Because from their mother's womb to the graveyard tomb, they have no burden, no mat, no bag, no carry-over, nothing, except poverty. It's but right to aspire for something more than manna, something that would give them comfort in life. But that is not what happens. The socialists go after those who live without working, who sit in laps of luxury that comes from the sweat of others. It is verily like the lives of orchids that attach themselves to the trees: those who work should live and those who don't, should perish.'

'Yes, but you only offer labour!' Don Ramon cut in.

'And capital?' added Don Filemon.

'Capital does not work, but moves people to work. And capital, like land, should not be owned totally by anyone, but should instead benefit everyone. It is like air, sea and light, which nobody can own. Whatever a person needs is already found in the bountiful sea and land. Nature is luxuriant and should be enough to feed everyone. Those who say they own a piece of nature should be called thieves. Those who claim more than what they need, kill their fellowmen. Land and capital cannot be considered as mine and yours, but ours. Land is the seed-bed of everything that we need, while capital is the means to nurture what has been sown by everyone in the land.

'You said that work is punishment and that wealth is comfort. But why is comfort only offered to a few, while everyone else is punished? You believe in what God has said, "that what you eat should come from the sweat of your brow", but does money turn into sweat when used as capital?'

Felipe controlled the urge to burst into laughter. He just walked away, so as not to irritate further his godfather, in whose house he was staying. He pretended to pick a few cashew fruits near the store room for the grains. But the others have begun to whisper.

'Money getting soaked in sweat!' said some.

'The sacks that we carry also become beaded with sweat, but they're fewer than the maize-like drops of sweat that we shed before we can even earn our keep,' said a man without a shirt, feeling ashamed by what he had heard.

But Madlang-Layon had a different take. With a cool smile, he cracked a joke: 'That was a good debate. Money and sweat: one is sweet and the other, salty. These two don't really belong to each other, except perhaps when used in a spring roll . . .'

Don Ramon laughed silently and then he said: 'Indeed, the capital I use doesn't sweat but I sweated hard, that's why it became mine. I still sweat over it, that's why it is of use to me.'

'Don Ramon, I'm not talking about any single person's money. I'm talking about money in general.'

'What I did and what I'm doing is what everybody who has capital does.'

'And my properties,' added Don Filemon, 'were not stolen, but inherited from my parents. I'm now cleanly managing them, so why should I not have comfort from them?'

'Sweat and inheritance! I'll answer you one by one, Don Ramon. While the benefits don't go beyond the just payment for the workers, after which labour won't complain, when capital moves and rents the labour of others, here lies the dangers that only a few will taste what many others have slaved for. Nobody is born to live based on the work of others; he himself should also work. If ten are needed then ten should benefit, but twenty should not be benefiting from what is only owed to ten. Everyone should sweat to produce something that will benefit other people, and they who work, should reap the just fruits of their labour. It is unfair for a few to gather these fruits only for themselves.'

'But this work is paid for!' the two older men said in unison.

'If one is paid for one's work, we cannot say that he is already fully paid and can no longer share in the fruits of his labour. Capital cannot equal labour in places where greedy capitalists reign supreme. And how about the present wages? While wages might have risen four times since the Americans came, we still need wages to rise ten times for people to live decently.'

He continued: 'Workers usually earn one peso a day. That one peso already buys his freedom and his rights. One peso for a whole family to spend. From that peso will come the food on their table for a family not of one, but of three, or four, or five, or even of eight children. From that peso will come their clothes, rent for their house and their other needs. That peso will still be taxed, and from that peso, they will wring whatever entertainment they can have. That peso separates a man from his wife and children, forms a distance between him and his parents and siblings, from loved ones who need him. Is one peso enough for all of these? It's good if one has work for that day, at all, but often, there is no regular work for them. It's clear, then, that money symbolizes a person's power over another human being and does not equate with labour at all.'

While Delfin was speaking, the two older men seemed to be swallowing their saliva, for each one of them was trying to speak ahead of the other, to counter what the young man said. But they could not butt in, for the young man just spoke on and on. However, Morales and Peping could not be bothered to listen to the exchange of words. They kept on stealing glances at the slats in the wooden walls of the bathing area, where the women changed into dry clothes. The others whispered and had their own thoughts on the discussion.

'Aside from this,' added Delfin, 'they say we have been freed from Spanish slavery, thanks to the blood spilt by our heroes. But many rich people do not know the meaning of slavery. They are angry when they cannot get people to work for them in their houses, unlike before. They say that the poor have become proud, just so they won't be called slaves. For the few who still accept household work, how much is the pittance that they get? Thousands of rich people still make more money from slavery. Two, four, or more people work in their household, often offered up by their parents themselves, to be paid four, six, eight or sixteen pesos a month, as payment for the parents' loans of twenty or 100 pesos. In most cases, such work is inherited by siblings or the whole clan. The ten pesos owed grows in luxuriance like red squash. And when the slaves break something in the master's house, living in fear and abandoned by their parents, the amount involved multiplies sevenfold.'

Like water, Delfin's words flowed. 'The master promises to clothe the slave, not because he believes that no man should walk around naked or dirty, but because he does not want to see ugliness and dirt amongst those who serve him. And lucky is the slave who has three clothes. Promises of a small pay, free food and sometimes, free education—but what kind of food and what kind of education!'

'And what do you want,' Don Filemon cut in, since he could not bear it anymore, 'that we should talk to the servants in English?'

'Wait, Delfin,' added Don Ramon, 'have you studied History? Have you read how slavery in Roman times, which is the mother of all civilizations . . .'

'I agree that the slaves in the Philippines lead better lives than the slaves during Roman times. Aside from the food, Filipino masters are different, since many of them ask their servants to eat with them and eat the same food that they eat. But when one is a servant of the house, he is at everyone's beck and call: father, mother, children, sibling, cousin, old and young, who belong to the household. And he is not tasked to do just one or two kinds of work, but he has to do everything: buy provisions, cook, draw water from the well, forage for firewood, clean the house, do the laundry, take care of the children, unroll the sleeping mats and many others. In all these various works, the slave is cursed, shouted at, spanked, or even beaten up. But it is not just that: these slaves are even asked to work in the master's factories, without added pay. Twenty or 100 pesos is enough to have slaves in the house, in Manila and its environs. Didn't this wealth grow from the sweat of others?'

Madlang-Layon was itching to speak and cut in the words of Delfin. He had noticed that the two older men's ears had turned red, especially Don Ramon, who was just hiding his vexation at this talkative young man who was a mere writer. But Delfin could no longer be stopped and heard the words whispered around him, coming mostly from the poor, who agreed with him.

He continued, 'And there is another horrid issue here that should be addressed by socialism. How do landlord treat the farmers who till the land? The slaves are ordered to burn forests and clear the land, to scale mountains stony and dense. After the land has been cleared, they will be ordered to look for others who can help them work on the land. If the new farmer has neither water buffalo nor wooden cart, the landlord will buy these things, but these are merely loaned to the farmers. And then the farmers will plant sugarcane, or coconut, abaca, coffee and tobacco and rice. But let us just talk about the rice. The farmer will be lent a sack of rice seeds. The landlord will list down the money spent on growing the rice. Usually, a sack of rice seeds, along with other necessities for growing rice, will cost from six to seven pesos. The harvest yields around thirty sacks of rice, less than the number of sacks used for the seeds. The farmers will dry the harvested rice and have them milled.'

Delfin continued, 'But how much is left for the farmer? Of the thirty sacks, several sacks are deducted and given to the landlord to pay for the seeds. Six sacks will be further deducted, to pay for expenses in growing the rice. Then three sacks are usually deducted to pay for the land tax. So twenty sacks are left: of these, ten go to the landlord and ten go to the farmer. But since this is not enough to feed the farmer and his family, the farmer then asks the landlord for a loan, in terms of seeds or money. And if the harvest is bad, the poor farmer sinks deeper into debt.

'And then the capitalists also sell jewellery and clothes, and almost force them into the noses of the farmers' wives and children, at galloping interest rates. They would ask the farmers to pay for these items after the harvest. The clan would then inherit the debts that have piled up. The farmers are even required to bring fruits and vegetables, chickens, eggs and other things, to the landlord's house, when there is a fiesta. And these farmers are sometimes cursed, too, and even beaten up by their landlords.

'In all of these things, Don Ramon, Don Filemon, can we still know without malice, who became rich through fair means? That is why we need socialism in times of slavery, on land and in the factories—to at least teach the poor the rights they are entitled to. It is time to destroy the orchids who live on others' sustenance, the leeches who become bloated from the blood of others!'

'Such are things,' butted in Don Ramon, 'but I . . . '

'My wealth has notarial documentation, wealth unstained and inherited from my parents!' said Don Filemon.

'I believe that the two of you are different from the rest. However, I cannot say if your parents' wealth came from fair means.'

The two older men stopped in their tracks, confused, especially Don Filemon, who recoiled in his seat. His gaze pierced Delfin, in the same way that Malko gazed at Pedro before lopping off the latter's ear. But to douse the hatred that was beginning to flare against him, he sought refuge in the words of Goethe.

'I was not the one who said that,' he explained, 'the wise man Goethe said that first, when he wrote down the discussion between a teacher and his student, on the subject of the origins and history of property and wealth. The teacher asked, "Please tell me, where did your father's wealth come from?" And the student answered, "From my father's father." "And where did he get the wealth?" "He stole it . . ."'

'And why do you even mention it?' said Don Filemon in a hurry, the words tumbling out of his mouth. 'Are you implying that the wealth we inherited came from foul means? That our parents' parents, and our ancestors themselves, were thieves?'

Don Filemon said this while he was standing, trembling with rage. His eyes became sharper. They could curse him from head to foot, but never ever touch the names of his dead parents. Meanwhile, Don Ramon stopped, anger boiling inside him. He wanted to lunge at Delfin, or at least throw his cigar at the young man.

'Your education was just wasted!'

'Please don't be mad because—'

But he could no longer clarify things. Don Ramon was bursting with rage. The eyes of the two angry men met, and they understood what was in both their minds.

'There, there is the man who is courting your daughter!'

'This anarchist?'

Madlang-Layon stood between the contending parties.

'Don Ramon, Don Filemon,' he said, 'don't stoop down to the level of Delfin, who is just a young man. Young people are known to be rash. You are the ones who already have maturity and reasoning . . .'

Meanwhile, Felipe whispered to Delfin: 'I can foresee that your door has been closed. You took them by surprise!'

'I think so,' said another, 'but what should we do? They have hardened their hearts against the poor.'

* * *

The bathers were bothered by the discussion. Talia was the first to come out. Thinking that her father and Delfin would quarrel, in haste, she put on a thin dress, the colour of the sea. Next was Turing, the old-maid sister of Attorney Madlang-Layon, who rushed to help Talia fix the falling sleeve of her dress. Isiang also followed suit, who was rushing such that she was not able to dress up, but just wound a towel round her head, a towel in the same colour as her chemise. And then there was Meni, squealing with delight in the water, until she came upon her father and saw her beloved throwing sharp looks at Don Filemon.

The others helped Attorney Yoyong calm things down.

Like a bell rolling, even if she were still faraway, was the voice of Señora Loleng, who did not join the group even though she was already dressed up. Instead, she went behind a mango tree near the backyard's edge. From there, she proceeded inside, taking away the fat cigar from her mouth, which in turn hit the chin of the servant who was attending to her. She then asked what the tumult was about.

'It's nothing, it's nothing,' said the lawyer.

'And why should you even debate with kids who still have milk on their lips?' Señora Loleng accused her husband. 'I even said earlier that it was foolish to discuss these things.'

Madlang-Layon went to Delfin and whispered something to him. Then he winked at Felipe, signaling them both to move away for a while. Isiang looked at Delfin, and then she tossed her head. In the long time that they had known each other, it was the first time she did this to him. Meni also seemed to follow suit, with a somewhat sharp look, but it was followed by a gentle nod. Delfin surmised it meant that he really had to take leave first, to calm down her father's anger and that of Don Filemon, who were both taking potshots at his youth, education and humble origins.

He wanted to apologize for the hurt he had caused to the two older men, but there was nothing else to be done. Señora Loleng kept on throwing sharp looks at him, followed by her snide remarks about him being their daughter's suitor.

Since Felipe also did not want to further inflame Don Ramon, to whom he owed debts of gratitude; he just poked Delfin's side and invited him to go out and leave the springs.

The two left like the warm glow of a New Day. They left behind two raging shadows now being called by dusk. Madlang-Layon, cool as usual, was like a bamboo bending wherever the wind blows. He seemed like a pole trying to prop up the falling column of the Old Town. Señora Loleng was just following the role carved out for her. A husband was a husband and this one was rich, which made her happy, since she could buy everything that her heart desired. And the young women, although still within their parents' power, managed to show their love like perfume rising in the air, a dawn of hope for these two now moving in the direction of the New Town.

It was just too bad that only two rays of the New Day could be seen, such that they still seemed to represent something weak.

Chapter 4

At the Newspaper Office

'The Fourth Estate' was the term used to describe the Press, which meant its power to play the fourth major role in any society. But according to Ernesto Bark, journalists lived in genteel poverty. Their minds are filled—they are fountains of deep and beautiful words, they are invited everywhere and eagerly received by the public, and yet, their pockets are empty. Their stomachs growl painfully from hunger and one of their feet is already inside the National Bilibid Prisons.

Such was the situation here in the Philippines, where giving leisure time to reading newspapers had just taken root. Moreover, many of the items needed by the Press—newsprint, ink, letterpress casements, and even the smallest knife kept by the journalist—were all imported and taxed heavily. The price of a newspaper could not be raised to more than a peso. In places like these, the newspaperman could hardly have a life of comfort, even if he wished to do good and help his countrymen, like someone trying to save a drowning person.

I did not know why the exiled hero, Apolinario Mabini, who was coming home from Guam, chose to practice this profession, when asked by the Americans what he would do back home. In a difficult situation such as his, being paralyzed from the waist-down and very ill indeed, why did he choose to practice this profession at all?

* * *

The worth of a country can be seen in the life of its newspapers. If the newspapers hardly survive, with subscribers of 1,500, most unable to pay their dues, the newsprint resembled nothing less than rags and the letters were like the heads of nails. This country was like a young man just beginning to grow up.

Delfin knew these dire straits. Many times he had heard the complaints and the snide remarks made by the manager or even the owner of the newspaper, when they came and asked for payment of their salaries.

'Ah!' came the reply, followed by scratching of the head and pulling of the earlobe. 'Perhaps we will just last until the end of this month. I am already sick and tired of advancing my own money for you. Look at all these letters. One collector in K said that there is still no harvest, and some farms have already been laid to waste by locusts, that's why the people cannot pay. Another from B said that the subscribers are lucky to receive four or five copies of the newspaper and that was why they won't pay for a newspaper that is usually undelivered. Another one claims that he has spent four hundred pesos for his illness, but in reality, he has collected eight hundred pesos in all. Another fellow owes me five hundred pesos . . . Ah, my head is aching from all of them!'

He sat down and continued: 'And here in the city, the rich Don Florencio of Binondo does not want to extend credit to us for newsprint. So where will I get it? I cannot give you anything. Here, take this five pesos for each of you.'

And the workers, upon hearing the laments of him who has just spoken, and worried that they would not get even a peso if they complained, would just accept the pittance. They would accept the money and sigh, wondering if they would be paid the rest of the amount until pay day comes again.

Before he left for Antipolo, Delfin heard another round of similar laments from the newspaper's manager. He was one of the writers of the said newspaper. He was lucky not to be given five, but six pesos instead, aside from money due to him for the past month. This is all

the money he brought with him when he went to Antipolo, to follow
the daughter of Don Ramon Miranda.

In a stroke of irony, it was good that he had an altercation with
Don Filemon and went home earlier than the rest. If he had stayed
longer in Antipolo, what embarrassment would have befallen him if
there were expenses to be paid and all he had were holes in his pockets
and a very short shoestring, indeed.

With Felipe apprising him that he would know all about the further
talk regarding him, Delfin was persuaded to go down from Antipolo
ahead of the group.

* * *

Four days had already passed since the dispute beside the spring waters.
Felipe had not yet gone to work at the *New Day* newspaper. He just
worked as a printer at this newspaper.

But the four days seemed to stretch into something like four
months. He was deeply bothered by what had happened. Have they
forgotten the dispute with him, the socialist? Perhaps. Antipolo was a
place for resting, a haven to soothe tired souls. Not even someone like
him could stop Don Ramon and Don Felipe from having fun with the
Grand Theatre Company, whose orchestra played music that made the
revelers in Antipolo stand up and dance. They would not just attend
Mass for nine days. Neither would they just take a bath at the springs
for nine mornings. For nine days and nine nights they would dance,
and dance with such joy.

Delfin was also bothered because he had not yet received any news
from his friend. Every morning, when he entered the newspaper's
offices, he would first ask if Felipe has arrived. 'Not yet,' was the
usual reply.

Four days had come and gone, and there was no Felipe.

He worked in a small office that had the atmosphere of a graveyard.
Only the ceaseless tick-tock of the clock, and the gentle sweep of pen
to paper on the coarse newsprint could be heard. Sometimes the jokes
and teasing of workers rose to his office on the second floor. But the
door of his office remained sealed. Inside, the six journalists worked

like soldiers, interrupted only by the noise that would make them stop
for a while, then look at each other, then return to their writing.

In the corner sat the newspaper's manager, looking troubled. In front
of him stretched the two tables placed side by side, where the five
writers worked.

'Should we put this news in the paper?' one of the journalists asked
the manager.

'What is the news?'

'Here in *Manila Times*, it says that the Supreme Court barred
Attorney Pereyra from his legal practice for cheating his clients.'

'Pereyra has been barred? Wait, don't put it yet, let's see if the
others will touch it.'

'Here's another news. Dr Barbosa caught his wife yesterday in the
house of Dr Kaligaya, and the two doctors almost killed each other.
What a fine piece of news!'

'Oh?' said not just the manager, but the other journalists as well.

'I told you that one day, someone will get his just desserts.'

'And how did you know about it?'

'Oh, right here, in the Supreme Court, where one day I heard
Attorneys Verzosa and Pamintuan discussing that very issue. That
was a month ago. Allegedly, Dr Barbosa has been seeking the advice
of Pamintuan on how to catch his wife and her paramour in action.
And that was how they were caught in the act!'

'The wife of Dr Barbosa is pretty,' the manager said. 'So it is true
that they've been caught in the act.'

'It is mentioned here in the newspaper.'

'Let us not touch this issue. We should not mention the name of
the doctor. Just a hint would do.'

'And why not?' asked Delfin.

'We should let it explode in their faces!' said the journalist sitting
in front of Delfin.

'We should. Just because one case involves a famous lawyer and the
other two doctors, we will not touch the news anymore? But why is it
that when the alleged perpetrator is a poor person who stole something
small from a store, or a housemaid who stole a watch or money from

her employer, or a carpenter's wife involved in a romantic liaison, we publish everything? Name, age, livelihood, family relations, everything?'

'Oh here comes again the lawyer of the poor,' said the man across from Delfin, in a derisive tone.

'Indeed.'

'That's why you cannot get along with your future father-in-law. You keep on dipping your finger in every pie that you can find.'

'Enough with your talk. That's the way journalists talk, a trait we got from the time of the Spaniards. Everything that the rich or the powerful do—from waking up, taking a walk, yawning, having a slight fever, a voracious appetite—is being published. When someone powerful gets caught with his hand in the cookie jar, stealing millions of pesos, it is seen as just a mistake. There was no intention to steal. And when some official begins to do his job, for which he's getting paid well in the first place, hosannahs would begin to rise from the everyone's lips. How dreadful. Why can't we censure the bad and praise the good, wherever we see them? Why do we have to cover up for the misdeeds of the lawyer, the doctor, simply because they are influential or rich?'

But Delfin was not able to add more words because Felipe peeked in from the door. With one signal from him, Delfin stood up, forgetting the squabble before him, and happiness lit up his face, as if a nail in his heart has been pulled out.

'Now here comes the news we can publish!' teased a journalist who was privy to everything. Delfin winked at Felipe, then bit his lower lip and went out, hugging his newly arrived friend.

* * *

'What's the latest? So you just arrived this morning? How about them? Does Don Filemon still remember me?'

To this barrage of questions, Filemon only said, 'Yes, and she has a letter for you!' handing Delfin a letter.

'A letter? Where is she?'

'She wrote that last night, while she was still there in Antipolo. We had decided to go home today.'

'You haven't been there nine days.'

'Yes, but they got bored because it's been raining for two days.'

Delfin did not know whether to tear the envelope of the letter. He took care of everything that came from Meni, even the mere paper that contained her letters. He would often use his saliva or water to loosen the glue on the envelope, or he would use a pair of scissors to carefully cut the edge of the envelope. After this, he would gently put his fingers inside the envelope and retrieve the letter. This is the fourth letter he had received from Meni, although he had sent a total of ten letters to her. He would also send her cuttings of his poems or essays that were published in the newspaper, a day after they had been printed. Meni was just stingy with her answers. He had to write her three letters before he got his first letter from her. She did not initiate writing letters to him, until now.

Upon retrieving the letter, both pairs of eyes raced to read its contents. Delfin read it aloud:

MY DEAR FRIEND,

I've just learnt from Felipe that you already went home that Sunday afternoon. Talia told him about it that night—I was the one who told Talia about your departure.

Up to now, my father is still displeased with you. The same goes for Don Filemon and his wife.

I will say this but please don't get hurt. Señora Loleng told me not to accept you anymore in the house because you are a man . . . (I won't say anymore here because you might get mad). However, her daughter, Isiang, shielded you—remember she had also defended you before.

But Señora Loleng was not yet done with you. At dinner time on Tuesday night, she told my father that you should not be allowed to visit our house anymore. Lawyers and journalists are at odds with each other, that is why Yoyong is also hurt.

I wrote this letter while I was still here in Antipolo, so that Felipe could give it to you and you can avoid going to our house in the meantime.

My father is easily swayed by talk and he has told me to avoid talking to you because you're an anarchist . . . It's not far-fetched that one day, you will put his life in danger. Why did he call you an anarchist? Is it true?

I have to stop here, and let me repeat to you not to meet us when we go down to Manila. Whatever you want to tell me, you can tell it to Felipe or you may write me.

MENI

* * *

Delfin could neither smile nor despair after reading the letter. He could only look at this friend and a spark of recognition dawned, that both wanted to note.

'I'm an anarchist!' he said in a confused tone after a while. 'Look at your godfather. As if he knows what he's talking about.'

'He doesn't even know the difference between an anarchist and a socialist,' added Felipe.

'He thinks I will bring danger to all of them. This is an unjust accusation. They want to paint me as a horrible, dirty and dangerous person in the eyes of Meni—someone capable of murder and is without soul. This is what they think an anarchist is.'

'Indeed,' said Felipe, 'for them, anarchy is already synonymous with murder. They do not know that not all anarchists do that. They are afraid of something that is borne by their livelihood. All they have created are ghosts and they are the first to become afraid of these ghosts. As if the poor will not rise in hatred if there is no cruelty amongst the rich. Thievery would not happen if there is no demarcation of properties. You will know guilty people: they are the ones afraid of their own shadows!'

'Such is the power of conjecture,' said Delfin. 'Accusing me of being an anarchist! Ha, ha, ha! They who want to make the world their own, they even want to have dominion over time. And what did Meni say in the face of all these accusations? Is she mad at me? What else did she say?'

'That Sunday when you went home, I talked to her in the house of the Bautista family in Antipolo.'

'The Bautistas?'

'Yes, from Santa Cruz. There was dancing until midnight. Meni and I were partners in one round of a formal dance. She said you would have been her partner in one of these dances. When other men wanted to dance with her, she would always point me out as her partner for the next dance. I even heard the children of the Bautista and Bentus family say that something must be afoot between Meni and I.'

'Maybe there is indeed something afoot?' the writer teased his friend.

Loud laughter erupted from them, a volley of laughter that reached even the newsroom.

'Please don't really be jealous.'

'So she actually didn't dance with anybody else?'

'She rarely did, and only for short occasions. It is because we were talking about you while we were dancing.'

'Really?'

'Yes, you must believe me. The things contained in her letter to you are the same things she told me. The only additional matter is the one about Señora Loleng, which I've learnt only just now. You should have seen that old woman when she danced with my godfather. She is a major flirt, that old woman! When Meni learnt that you already left, she asked me why I didn't join you on the trip back to the city. She said she pitied you. When we were leaving the springs, she was almost in tears with sympathy for you, that was why she rushed to the bathing area. She wanted me to follow you, the next day, telling Don Ramon that I need to go back because of my backlog at work.'

'And why did you not come home sooner?'

'First, we woke up late on the next morning. Then, I also had an invitation to go to Talbag. And my late departure was also good because I was able to overhear everything they said about you.'

'These people are treacherous!'

'Listen to what they say about you.'

'Let's talk about that some other time. What else did Meni tell you?'

'She gave that letter to me when we were walking in Antipolo. She took the car and took the horse-drawn carriage, and she winked at me to remind me to give you her letter. When they reached their house and I was still downstairs, helping unload our luggage, she said aloud: "Felipe, just let them do it. You might be late for work!" And then she gave me a look full of meaning. What are the other signs of love that you want to hear, my friend?'

Delfin seemed to be on cloud nine when he heard these words. But like an ill person who is served the most delicious array of mouth-watering food, he still seemed to look for the one food that was lacking. He shook his head from side to side, while biting his lower lip. Felipe seemed to sense what his friend wanted to say: 'Yes, but . . .'

'What else do you want?' Felipe just continued to speak. 'A woman's love is not only heard when she says 'yes'. Many yeses have turned into bubbles and dust. A woman will not always say outright, "I accept your love", or "Yes, you may begin hoping for my love". This is true especially of women from southern Luzon. True love is not seen in the words at the tip of one's tongue. It is seen in the eyes, in feeling what the other person also feels, and in doing everything with tenderness.'

'Yes, indeed, but you cannot take it away from me. Unless she has given me a categorical *yes*, whether in words or better yet, through a letter, a word free from cloudiness—open and pure, a word filled with the sweetness of hope . . . Whatever you say cannot calm me down. Just look at the differences between Meni and I. Add to that the conflict I had with her father, whom I cannot reconcile with. The older he gets, the more he will embrace the life of the rich. And the older I get, the deeper I shall believe in socialism. There lies our difference and thus, these roiling thoughts about Meni.'

'It's up to you, I've already told you everything. I'm leaving you with your doubts. But my friend, we have talked at length about Meni. Won't you ask me about Tentay, whom I also saw in Antipolo?'

'What happened between the two of you?'

'Last Monday . . .'

'Original! Original!' shouted the two workers from the printing press as they were climbing the stairs. 'Mr Delfin, it's already 10.30 in the morning, but we still do not have even one article as yet,' one of them said.

'Felipe, you just arrived but you have already taken a lot of time from Delfin and from us!' teased the other man.

'Already 10.30 in the morning?' both men talking said, almost at the same time, while looking at the alarm clock hanging on the wall.

'Later,' Felipe said.

And then the two friends parted ways: one went to the editorial room, while the other headed for the printing press.

Chapter 5

Thieves

'You just stand there, in front of that window. Pretend you're making phlegm rise to your throat, or pretend you're coughing. But make sure nobody but her recognizes your voice. She will look out of the window, she will see you, she will climb down the stairs to talk to you. That's what we agreed on earlier.'

'Here? At this hour?'

'Yes but be careful of people passing by, especially the police.'

'What if I'm not recognized or seen?'

'She'll recognize you. We would've finished dinner by that time. All the guests would be in the living room. Only she will be left in her room, waiting for any sound or sign coming from the window. It's almost 8.30 in the evening. I will take care of whatever happens upstairs.'

'Can she go downstairs alone at this hour?'

'This isn't the first time she's going downstairs.'

'And who else did she talk to when she went downstairs?'

The other one suppressed his laughter. Through this, he reckoned the jealous nature of his conversant.

'Don't worry, there's nobody else. Amongst all the men who liked Meni, nobody has dared to do what you will do now. Whether you admit or not, you owe me whatever luck you might have tonight.'

'But why did you say she often went downstairs, even at night?'

'She did, but often with someone else. After coming from the Night School, they would go to the garden and pick jasmines. If they could not make jasmine necklaces in the afternoon, they would do it before they slept. They would even put some under their pillows, especially when it was very hot and they could not sleep.'

'Won't the servant join her?'

'She has her own mind. She can go out of that door, come here, and even venture out onto the street—even when she is alone.'

'Who are the people in the living room?'

'The mother and daughter from San Miguel and Attorney Madlang-Layon. They had dinner here, and now are talking with Uncle Ramon and Talia. Don't you hear their laughter?'

'Yes, I've been hearing it for a while. Even Meni's brother and his wife are there.'

'They are in the dining area, playing with their child.'

'So what will we do now?'

'I will leave you and go there, to the garden. I will listen to what's going on upstairs. If something happens and someone goes downstairs, I will tell them that Meni and I are just picking jasmines in the garden.'

And the one who just left vanished under the house. The one left behind was just standing, stilled by the thought of what he would do.

The two men talking were Felipe and Delfin. In their conversation, their whispers and hiding in the shadows, one can surmise that their meeting will be followed by another, happier one.

* * *

The same day. That was the night when Don Ramon arrived from Antipolo. That morning, Delfin got Meni's letter. Felipe went home for lunch, then visited Meni, who told him that she didn't want to give her answer through a letter but in a secret meeting. She said that at 8.30 P.M., she would go downstairs and walk into their garden. Upon hearing the coughing of Delfin, she would go to the fence of their house and talk to him.

Twice, thrice, Delfin walked back and forth, as if measuring with his footsteps the length of the garden. Soft cough, loud cough . . . dredging sputum from inside him . . . but the one he was waiting for had not yet arrived. Had his friend just played a prank on him?

He stopped in front of the gate . . . He looked back to check if there was a policeman or another person. He looked intently at the lower part of the house. But no shadow of Meni, no shadow of Felipe could be seen.

From where he stood, he could hear the volleys of laughter and conversation coming from inside the house . . . He thought that he had heard Meni's voice amongst the tangle of voices.

He left the gate, paced to and fro, then stood in the corner of the house. He was now in front of the concrete wall and the fence of the backyard. And when he looked at the house fully, he was entranced by its sheer size. Don Ramon was not one to scrimp on his electric bills. The front gate was dark that night because of Felipe. That was why Delfin could stand there, in the shadows.

The house was new or newly painted. It was not the biggest house on the block. It was made of wood and stone seemingly from the last century. The house of Don Ramon, however, seemed lacking in charm or looks.

From where he stood, in the dark, Delfin had thought about the rooms and corners of the house, where Meni might be now . . . Meni, whom he had been waiting for. He looked intently at the house again, such that he could detect even the smallest mosquito.

Where the hell is Felipe? Delfin was already getting antsy with anticipation. And from nowhere, Felipe did appear, as if summoned by Delfin's thoughts.

'Just wait, my friend, be patient. She will not pass by the living room because there are many people there. From the stairs, I saw her making her way, but she had to stop to talk to Talia and Yoyong.'

'But she has not yet even looked out of the window,' Delfin said.

'Not yet? But she was really already on her way out when last I checked. She just got waylaid by the conversations with their guests.'

And then Felipe vanished again, walking into the house, and Delfin was left once more.

* * *

'She must have walked down the stairs!' Delfin said to himself. He heard footsteps in the garden.

Like the full moon herself appearing through the veil of clouds, Meni slowly appeared in the stairway. Brilliant and beautiful, she was, her image filling Delfin's mind and heart.

'Ipeng, Ipeng!'

Meni was calling. She was walking to the room under the house, where Don Ramon's driver lived with his wife.

'He isn't here, Señora,' said the wife who was nursing her child. 'He went to feed rice grains to the horses.'

'Is Felipe there?'

'I'm here,' Felipe answered, emerging from the room. The driver and his wife already knew of this meeting. They had served as couriers before, bringing Meni's letters to Delfin, and vice versa.

'Don't ask him to come here,' Meni said.

'What will we do?' Felipe asked.

'I'll just talk to him through the iron grilles of the backyard.'

Felipe cleared his throat aloud. Upon hearing the signal, Delfin rushed to the spot in front of the iron grilles.

'I'm leaving now,' Felipe whispered to Meni, 'now that you have company.'

And then he left, while muttering to himself: 'You will get more than jasmines there . . .'

* * *

'Meni?'

'Delfin?'

'I thought you would make me wait the whole night.'

'I could not leave earlier. We have many guests in the house. Have you been here long?'

'Yes, since last night!'

'You're teasing me. I saw you from that window.'

'I didn't see you!'

'Your eyes must be bad . . . What do you want to tell me?'

'Many things important, happy and sad. Everything depends on you.'

'What is that? Better hurry up now.'

'I should go there.'

'No, you can't.'

'But there might be a policeman here or someone might come along.'

'That's why you need to hurry up.'

'Yes, but what I'll tell you will take a long time.'

'Huh?'

'What if this might be our last meeting?'

'No . . .'

'That's why I want to go there. Let us go to your garden so we could sit down and talk.'

And without listening to another word from Meni, he pushed open the gate and entered. He gained access to the house and walked nearer to the shocked woman.

'Delfin, why did you suddenly enter?' her voice was quivering. 'Someone might see you here.'

'At least here I can have a place to hide, unlike outside. I want to talk to you here. If the waters in Antipolo were not witness to my happiness, then your garden could serve the purpose just as well.'

'Delfin, you must remember that my father is mad at you.'

'I know. I can't forget that, the way I can't forget you. I remember that, that's why I wanted to talk to you here.'

'What do you want to tell me?'

'Can't you tell?'

'I'm not a fortune-teller.'

'But you can tell the fortune inside my heart.'

Indeed, the night had become deeper. The garden was dark and shaded by many trees. But after Delfin had asked his question, they both looked at each other and the pupils of their eyes saw the light of love aflame in each of them.

'Yes,' the woman answered.

'Yes to what?' he asked. 'Is that your answer to what I've been asking?'

'Yes!'

'My Meni.'

With the quickening throb of his heart, in the intensity of the sweet fragrance that came from her reply, he suddenly held her hand. He squeezed it and attempted to kiss it, but she drew her hand away.

'Don't. What do you think you're doing?'

'I will sign your hand with my thanks,' he answered with tenderness.

'My hand?'

'No, your cheek!' and acted as if he would indeed kiss her. But the woman quickly pushed away his hand that had begun to cup her chin and cheek.

'Don't be so frisky,' she said.

'My Meni, please let me whisper to your cheek and lips my heartfelt gratitude.'

'On another day.'

'Oh, Meni,' he said and quickly kissed her.

'Thief! You did it without my permission.'

'Meni!'

'It doesn't matter to me. You were able to kiss me because I got distracted.'

The man stopped still at her words. What was the point of kissing her, inhaling her fragrance, when he just smelled something dead inside? He felt remorse. But he didn't want to waste those hours . . .

'Oh, my life. Why do you make light of something I did as proof of my love for you?'

'Because I didn't approve of it.'

'Then I'll just wait for your approval.'

'What else do you need, Delfin?'

'What I really want is to get your permission to kiss you again, with all your heart.'

'On another day.'

'But I want it now.'

'How?'

'I will whisper it to you, but my thanks will be voiceless. And your yes will be written on your lips, proof of two hearts and souls turned into one.'

First the eyes, then the cheeks and the lips would speak. How sweet the conversations would be . . .

'What other words of hope would you like to hear?' she asked.

'I need to hear your decision. But let us not talk here. Let us go there so that our shadows cannot be revealed by the light shining here.'

* * *

The garden was not just a source of fragrant and beautiful flowers but also a place to while away the hours. In the middle of the garden sat a *glorietta,* a resting place made of bamboo, painted to match the colour of leaves. It had a sloping roof made of thatch and around it, vines grew. It had four entrances and in the middle of glorietta was a bench with a back rest.

The two young lovers walked towards the glorietta. Delfin's hand was around the waist of Meni, while his hand clasped her left hand. It was soft and smooth, and she made sure her right hand was free, so she could use it to ward off further rash acts from Delfin . . . The flowers of the *dama de noche*, the lady of the night, filled the night with its perfume. The roses, the *conde de Paris* or the duke of Paris, as well as the many other plants, stood like guards as their king and queen strolled past them.

The two sat on the bench as if entranced. They felt as if they were the only people on earth, such was their enchantment.

'Now,' she said, 'you may tell me the other things you have to say.'

'Oh, my heaven! I wish I could bring you up into the air, so we can live there and be filled with happiness!'

'In the air?'

'Yes, I wish we were the only people on earth, so that no one could intrude upon our happiness.'

'You say so many things.'

'I fear, Meni, that you may forget me.'

'Me? Why?'

'Ah . . . I think of the gap between us. You're rich and I'm poor.'

'You may be poor, but you have a good heart.'

'But having a good heart does not always sit well with the wealthy.'

'And you also have a rich mind.'

'That's another thing that will cause all of you to hate me one day.'

'And why, Delfin?'

'Only your father knows the answer.'

'I think that if you become a lawyer one day, you'll be no longer embarrassed to ask for my hand in marriage.'

'So unless I become a lawyer . . .'

'I knew you would say that. Titles don't matter to me. Even if you have no title, as long as I'm happy with you until the end, then so it shall be. I just have to endure what my father will say. What can he do if I love you? Just now they are all there while I am here, with you . . . my . . .'

'What?'

'My . . . Delfin.'

Quickly Delfin kissed Meni, a kiss that landed on her chin.

'Oh, you're taking advantage of me, Delfin,' she said in a tone that was not angry. 'But . . . you only remember my perceived wrongs but not yours.'

Silence.

'Oh, Delfin!'

'Meni, are you crying? Tears should not flow on this happy occasion.'

'I just thought that this night that now surrounds us might become the sorrow that I'll face later, when you leave me.'

'Please don't waste your tears. I won't leave you.' Then Delfin got his handkerchief out and dried up the tears falling from Meni's eyes.

Just then, a carriage stopped in front of the gate. A man and a woman alighted.

They both carried acetylene lamps that would surely show Delfin and Meni sitting in the middle of the glorietta. So Delfin and Meni crouched and hid in the glorietta until the new arrivals had walked past them.

'Who are they?' Delfin and Meni asked almost simultaneously.

Meni recognized them. 'Aha, Don Filemon and Señora Loleng.'

'Why did they arrive at this time? It's almost nine o' clock in the evening.'

'They always come at this hour. They must have come from the factory and want to give some news to my father. It seems that the strike has settled down.'

The new arrivals were now climbing the stairs, walking as if they owned the house itself.

'I'm sure they will now look for me upstairs,' Meni said.

'No, let them look for you. Just pretend that you're in your room.'

'But they saw me going downstairs. And I've to use the stairs again to reach the house.'

'Then we should gather some jasmines first, since then you can say that's the reason you went to the garden.'

And that is what the two did. They did not bother anymore with being seen in the lights of the passing carriages, just to be able to gather some jasmines.

'How will you go out?' Meni asked.

'Things will turn out fine as long as I'm always in your thoughts.'

And then the two young lovers embraced tightly, their hearts beating as one, before they said goodbye.

* * *

'Oh,' said Señora Loleng upon entering the house. 'I didn't know you have so many guests tonight.'

As if struck by lightning, Julita was about to say something against Señora Loleng. But then she saw the other guest, the distinguished Don Filemon.

Don Ramon just stared at them and it was Talia who welcomed them both. 'Please come in,' she said. Yoyong and the rest of the company stood up to shake the hands of the new arrivals.

'Oh, what, Filemon?' Don Ramon asked. 'I've been waiting for you for a long time. I need an update from you regarding the strike in the factory. Please sit down, both of you.'

Don Filemon sat by the big window, near Julita and her mother. Señora Loleng almost turned cross-eyed while tossing her head at the two women and flashing dagger looks at Don Ramon. Instead of joining the group, she stood and went to Talia and Yoyong on the other side of the living room. Because her eyes were roving everywhere, she did not see a tin plate filled with spit, to indicate that the housemaid had to clear the table.

'Pueh! Pueh!' Señora Loleng said, looking outside the window, her back turned on everyone.

Don Filemon had not yet warmed his seat when Julita and her mother stood up to leave.

The mother said, 'We have to go ahead, now that we have two new arrivals to replace us here.'

'You're leaving now?' the company asked, except Señora Loleng, who began spitting loudly out of the window. Talia and her lawyer boyfriend were nudging each other, as if to say: 'Pretty soon, there will be a battle royale in this house.'

Talia knew that Señora Loleng was powerful. Her boyfriend had the same thoughts. Only Don Filemon seemed unaware of what was happening, as if bamboo leaves were falling on his head.

In her mind, Señora Loleng couldn't fathom why the mother and daughter had to be there. Talia explained that the mother and daughter had just dropped by for a visit because they had just arrived from Antipolo. But the rage of Don Filemon's wife could not be appeased.

'Please just tell Meni,' Julita said while going downstairs, 'that she was already asleep when we left.'

'Meni,' Don Ramon answered, 'is not yet asleep. I saw her going downstairs.' And then he called out for the missing daughter.

'Yes, I'm here, Father, I'm just talking to Berang,' answered Meni from the garden.

Then she ascended the stairs with jasmines in her hand while the mother and daughter were descending, and they met halfway.

'Are you leaving?'

'Yes, Meni, because a false queen has come to replace us,' answered Julita's mother.

Meni laughed.

'One day, she'll get what she deserves!' Julita said.

'Oh!,' Meni said, 'Don Filemon might hear you.'

To prevent a more serious confrontation, Meni touched the hands of the two and walked them to the gate.

Chapter 6

Felipe

Felipe was the son of Captain Loloy, a rich man in Laguna, but he worked as a printer in Manila. He was eighteen years old and studied Commerce at the Ateneo de Manila. He used to live in the boarding house at the college, at first, but after six months, he asked his father if he could live outside the college. And that was how he came to live in the house of Don Ramon, his father's friend.

He was in his third year when he felt dissatisfied with his programme of study at the college. The word 'commerce' became bitter, a black enemy of his soul. He himself wondered why he soured at this programme, since he would anyway graduate after only one more year. He often railed against the book on *Mercantile Economy* and crossed swords with his professor. His heart throbbed at the words 'value', 'property' and 'capital'. He railed against the notion that poverty would never vanish from humankind, since the existence of the rich and the poor was already rooted in society. The only way to help the poor would be through the charity of the wealthy.

He thought that if we only studied deeply the concepts of *Political Economy*, even *Mercantile Laws*, they might see a glimmer of light. This radiance would reveal not the theories taught in his class, but the errors and the lies collected in the textbooks.

And the days passed in such light, and in the second examination during his third year, he failed miserably. His professors and classmates were surprised. Felipe was a sharp student, so what happened? But his classmates thought—a thought that also reached his teachers—that the cause of his low grades could be his frequent visits to the house of Don Ramon. There, he would often visit Talia, the single daughter of Don Ramon, who was also his godfather.

Felipe's father was very mad, but his words fell on deaf ears. Even his mother, Aling Toyang, wrote him letters. But he did not heed them, and refused to come home to the South.

So his father sent Marcela, Felipe's sister, to study also in Manila. 'Your sister will study at the Concordia College,' his father told Felipe the day they talked, 'so that people will see I still have a child who has some sense of shame. You can't fault me. You're my eldest child and I sent you to the best school. Since you don't want to study anymore, I will send your sister to school. But from now on, mark this on your forehead, you can't expect anything from me anymore until I die. I will just spend for Marcela. If this is what you want, this is the way you will live!'

And that was how Marcela began to study in the month of June 1903.

* * *

What will happen to a son cut off by his rich father?

Filled with shame, not once did Felipe think he should just go back to college and finish his Commerce degree. It was what his father had wanted in the first place, since they had properties to manage. But at the end, he did not follow this course of action.

He thought of taking up another programme of study, perhaps Education, so he could teach. But then he had to learn English! He could be a clerk of a notary public, or a lawyer's assistant. But he thought, could he stand this kind of work? He then thought of being a civil servant, with the encouragement of his friends. But then he did not relish the thought of working for the State.

What kind of work would he do? He knew he had talent and brains, and he was not lazy. On some nights, while lying in his bed, he would think. *What have I done to my parents that it led to this?* Can't a person be what he wants to be without a Commerce degree, or any other title at hand? But the poor workers, ah! Ill-educated and of low repute, even though they are the ones who sweat, who toil even at night, who put the letters together, turn the big wheels of factories; they sew and cut and do the covers and everything else needed to make a book! Are the labours of those who print and sew the books, different from those of the ones who thought, wrote and studied those books' contents?

'Indeed, the mind can span ideas far and wide, but in this life, what will happen if only the mind reigns supreme without the work of calloused palms, hard arms, and perspiring shoulders? What will happen to an architect or an engineer who drafts the finest outline or shape of a house, if there are no bodies that would work on the wood or steel, dig into the earth and build this house?

'My father wants me to study Commerce, but what is Commerce? He said it will teach me how to manage our lands filled with coconuts, fruits, sugarcane, cacao, coffee, rice, and many other kinds of produce. He wants me to produce more from our lands, to sell not among the small people in our province, but to the big middlemen from Manila. After I have been trained, he also wants to buy new and gleaming machines, so that we could do the harvesting ourselves and sell more produce. So many plans—that was why I was sent to study Commerce. But what about our poor workers, whose bodies and souls were already deep in debt when I left, will they reap the rewards if we expand our operations and buy more lands? My father is already wealthy, yet he desires more wealth. He said that all of it is for my sister, Sela, and myself, so we can have a good inheritance. Where would my shame go if I inherit such vast wealth? I did not even sink any capital in these ventures, except for my studies in Commerce at college, or any other learning gleaned from books. For all intents and purposes, I was also born naked on this earth and the earth will swallow me up when I am dead, just like it will the children of the poor . . .

'No! I won't let my father take advantage of me. It's not my courtship, nor my aversion to studies, that led me to disobey my parents. I do not gamble, do not do anything to destroy our family's name and reputation . . . But what about me, now? I feel that even Don Ramon does not like me anymore. It's not correct that they feed me for free. It's not correct that I burden other people because I am jobless.'

And thus he looked for work that would be a source of income, and work that he liked to do.

* * *

One of his friends brought him to a printing press. There, he was taught about the wooden boxes where the letters were stored; how to recognize, link and read letters even when they were upside down. After he could already read cases and letters, he was assigned to choose the letters, even how to clean them. His hands became dirty during work, but he learnt to choose the letters that could still be used in the printer's trade.

His fellow worker used to tease him at the beginning, when he would get rattled while picking up the letters and lining them up side by side. Not once did someone shout at him because he would falter in picking up the letters and slotting them as fast as he could.

In the printing presses, you should not leave your slippers lying around. Someone would put on them a small but still-hot ball of charcoal. If not that, then some sticky glue. And you should not also fall asleep in front of the cases of letters, for you would be awakened by the loud crashing of letters on the tables.

But Felipe endured all of this. He stayed on because his friends told him to just ignore the teasing that was the wont of print workers everywhere. After only two months, Felipe was already swifter and better than those who used to tease him, and he rose in the ranks.

After six months, he was told he would receive four pesos per month. After nine months, it became six pesos, then seven, then eight after one year of working there.

'You should be thankful you're already earning eight pesos a month,' the head told him. He had asked for a raise, since the eight pesos was not even enough for lunch for a whole month. 'When we were just starting, we would even cook food or buy cigarettes for our superiors, and our own pay was not even enough to buy a new shirt or even a hat.'

Someone then asked him to transfer to a new printing press, which paid him ten pesos per month. It was later raised to twelve, and later, to fifteen pesos per month. But he was retrenched and then he transferred to the *New Light* newspaper. He started at the same monthly rate of fifteen pesos, and then when Delfin arrived, he was already earning twenty pesos per month. Because of their friendship, Delfin was able to visit the house of Don Ramon and there he met Meni . . .

* * *

Two weeks had passed since that night when Señora Loleng met Julita and her mother at Don Ramon's house. It was the middle of June, a Sunday morning. Felipe and Delfin were talking.

Felipe said, 'My friend, yesterday my mother came with my sister. My father was not there, since he had to work on our lands.'

'Is your mother already old?'

'Not really, she is only past forty years old.'

'Is she not mad at you anymore?'

'Just a little. I think my father just sways her to be mad at me. My father is like a king—he wants to have his way all the time. When my mother is here, she asks me to come home with her. But when my father gets wind of this, he scolds her. She is very careful when she comes here, especially when she brings me money or any other kind of help. Just now, before they left for Manila, my father told her not to look after me anymore.'

'And what did your mother tell you?'

'I arrived at the house yesterday afternoon, and all throughout the evening, we were talking and sometimes, we were crying. She also told me to sort out my life.'

Felipe's eyes glistened with tears. He suddenly remembered his sufferings. He gripped the handkerchief balled in his hand. Delfin noticed his eyes welling with tears. Two other fellow workers also noticed.

Delfin felt a deep sadness for his friend. He had met Felipe less than a year ago, but they had become closer than blood brothers, despite their differences. One was from Laguna, while the other was from Manila. One would be a lawyer and the other, a printer.

Delfin felt the pain hidden inside Felipe and in his friend's sorrow, felt it was his own.

* * *

'My mother asked me to come home and beg for forgiveness from my father. But when I told her that it doesn't seem like a good idea, since I am now earning my keep in the city, she burst into tears. She said that I did not need to work and earn the pittance of twenty pesos a month, since we are rolling in wealth. She kept on crying, then scolding me, then crying once more. She only stopped when I said that I plan to learn English at the night school and that I should stay in the city to take care of my sister, Marcela. She said she would tell these things to my father in the hope that his anger might subside.'

'Would it?'

'Yes, she said she will try to change his mind.'

'I hope that you and your father will repair the damage done to your relationship. However, when I met your father when he came here last December, I noticed that everything you told me about him was true: he had the stance, traits and language of a big landowner. But I also believe that a parent is a parent. Even if you are here now, on your own, think of ways to defuse his anger and heal the cracks in your relationship, bit by bit. Why not actually study English at the night school? Every night, you walk home with Talia and Marcela, you can practice speaking English with them and this would also gladden your father's heart.'

'Oh, Delfin, you don't know my father. Even if I study English, Greek, Latin, German, Russian, Japanese or all the languages on the face of the earth, he would still be angry. The only thing he wants me to study is Commerce, and Commerce alone would make him happy.'

'In whatever way, if you study English, you'll also learn other things beyond this one language.'

'So you're telling me to learn English because it will make the nation stronger? Because it is the language used by the new lords of the land? Because commerce will abound even more since world trade will begin using English?'

'Let's not go there. I just want to stay with what the Spaniards said, that learning expands the mind.'

'Yes and also the saying that time is gold. I should study first what my country needs, not what the great colonizing country needs. You are aware, Delfin, that the language of the elite will never be learnt by everyone who is poor. These official languages are chosen by the leaders and the kings, so that the country will try to understand them without them having to understand the country. And when another country takes over, we have to learn another language forced upon us by the colonizer . . . if that is the reason that you said learning expands the mind, why then I will study English, Japanese, Russian, German and Mandarin, so that whichever amongst these countries governs us later, I already know their language which I can then use to serve the new master.'

'So you even carped at me!' Delfin answered, laughing. 'But if you want anarchy that has no beginning and no source, everybody has only one country, no one is black or white, no killing will happen because your native land is being taken away from you, no taxes in the piers and harbours of all towns and islands, no sea or beach, no mountains or forts that separate one country from the next, except that the German becomes an American, when already in America; the Italian becomes Japanese when already in Japan, the Chinese is a European when he lands in Europe. In this manner, the Filipino becomes a fellowman of the Chinese, American, African and European, if he goes to their lands, and vice versa . . . Don't you realize, my friend, the need for one language for people to bond in their comings and goings?'

'One can only hope that there will be such a common language. For only then can a new day rise over the earth, and all people will become brothers and sisters to each other.'

* * *

'That's why,' Delfin said later, 'you should learn English so the powers-that-be cannot fool you.'

'English again? But I haven't even heard you speak English, Delfin.'

'Me? As if you don't know I can say "yes-yes" and *veriveriwell sengkyu*!'

'Well, I also know those words, even if I haven't studied English yet. Don't you remember what I told Teacher Ines, when we met her with Meni outside the school? I said that the "general vacation" is soon at hand and I even told her *"Gut-nay, mis Ines, ai laik yu bermitas, oh yang-ledi!"'*

A burst of laughter came from the two friends.

'And where did you learn English?'

'You're even asking who my teacher is!'

'You should have told Ines; *"Ai laik yu matrimoni".*'

'And she would have told me *"mutso loko"*, what a big fool I am.'

'Oh, Ipe!'

'Well, if you study English, I will do the same,' Felipe said.

'I cannot find time for that. Studies in the morning, newspaper work at noon, studies in the afternoon, and more studies at night? Meni might quickly become a widow.'

'But if you become a lawyer, they said that English will become the language of the courts in 1906.'

'It's up to them. They can translate into English all my pleadings in Spanish, the way English is now being translated into Spanish. But I guess I can learn it, especially if Meni and I have our way . . . she can teach me the language.'

'And you will teach her Law, right?'

'Indeed.'

'Good luck to you both as husband and wife. I hope that Don Ramon will not hound even your shadows. But then, Delfin, why did you study Law? Don't you know that is the main enemy of socialism?'

Delfin's forehead wrinkled and while he was speaking, Felipe inserted the two fingers of his left hand into the gaps of the two buttons in his suit.

Then Felipe added, 'Lawyers are the main protectors of the rich, for they are protectors of property. Here in our country, look at the lengths they went to, just to prove that the vast lands of the Spanish friars indeed belonged to them. The friars came here to teach us holiness and humility and to embrace poverty, but how were they able to accumulate such big landholdings? The lawyers defended them. And you want to be one of them, which goes against the grain of socialism.'

'Oh look at you, Felipe! Don't you remember that there are always exceptions to any rule? If a lawyer defends the property owner, then another lawyer will also defend those without land.'

'Indeed, but when lawyers battle it out in court, the other half of the battle unfolds outside, where monetary deals are struck. This is like a businessman or a middleman. He neither plants nor distributes, but just sits down and counts the profits that accumulate with him. It is also like the doctors: the more people get sick, the richer they become.'

'Half of what you said is correct, Felipe, but the other half is not. You do not know the direction I am going. I do not just study litigation. I also study Sociology, the Natural Laws, Constitutional Laws, International Laws, Civil and Administrative Laws, Mercantile Laws, amongst others.'

'Does that include studies on Political Economy?'

'Indeed.'

'Oh, please pray for us. I hated Political Economy when it was taught at the Ateneo College.'

'You are strange. How can you be a good socialist without studying all of these subjects? A small army can only conquer a big army by knowing the tactics of the bigger force.'

'But you don't need to be a lawyer to know the ills that plague society. You don't need to study all these different laws. I haven't read any of them, yet I think they are like forts that hide the lies of so-called civilization, as discussed in the book of Max Nordau . . .'

'So you have also read Max Nordau,' Delfin said with a smile. 'My friend, all the things you have said are indeed society's sicknesses. But pain and wounds are not felt by everyone, especially those who are just born. That's why there is a need to study deeply so we can analyze the situation.'

'Your so-called cure . . . But in this discussion, why do I seem to think that you have become Don Ramon, and I have become Delfin at the Antipolo springs . . .'

'No need for that comparison. What I just want to tell you, Felipe, is that you should also know the way out of everything you enter.'

'Very well, then, my friend, time passed quickly with our discussion. What about the meeting?'

Delfin fished for his watch.

'It's already ten-thirty in the morning!'

* * *

Because their voices were loud, the others began to join the two. But one of them was shaking his head, saying that the meeting cannot continue without a quorum.

'Only a few of us are here and there are ten more inside,' said a man who drew nearer to the group.

'Is it a feast day today?' asked Delfin.

'Perhaps none in the whole of Manila, but there are feast days in Caloocan, Pasay, San Pedro de Makati and Mandaluyong. Today is a Sunday, the feast of Saint Peter . . .'

One old man made this joke, which was really the truth. It made the rest of the group laugh: 'I don't understand our fellow workers who are as poor as we all are. Our meeting is just short, only at noon, and yet they could not even be distracted from their diversions. Have they forgotten that there is strength in union? Brothers, I'm also a gambler, and later, even I'll go to the cockpit. But first, I've to comply with this obligation. We want to be independent and yet we do not have unity. Will America give us back our independence if all of us are inside the cockpit?'

With these words, the two friends nudged each other and then squeezed each other's fingers, as if to say: 'And the Americans will then say that talk of independence is ripe even in the meetings of labour unions.'

'Indeed,' said one of the workers, 'we should then hold our meeting later this afternoon.'

One of the men fished for his watch. 'It's already four minutes before 11 A.M.'

'Wait, first,' said the old man. 'I will go inside and ask the leaders whether the meeting will continue or not.'

He went back after a while. 'Since we don't have enough people here, the meeting will be reorganised. Only seventeen people attended the general assembly of the Alliance of Workers' Organizations. The date for the next meeting will be announced in the newspaper.'

Felipe grabbed the hand of Delfin. 'I cannot bring you with me to the house today for you to meet my mother and sister. Don Ramon might see you there. But just be prepared because this afternoon, we will bring my sister to Concordia College.'

'Is it later today?'

'Yes and Meni will be there as well.'

'Really?'

'Yes, just go ahead and go to Paco, and wait for us there. I will then take you there.'

'What time?'

'Around 4 P.M.'

'Thank you, my friend. I hope to see Meni later.'

'See you this safternoon.'

Chapter 7

At Concordia College

Delfin was not able to take his nap at noon. He immediately took a carriage that brought him to the Paco Bridge. Because he forgot to ask Felipe if they would meet in San Marcelino or in the interior streets, he just stood on the curve on Nozaleda Street. Not once did he turn his gaze in the direction where the people he was waiting for would enter.

It was already thirty minutes after 4 P.M., but they were still nowhere in sight. Five o' clock came, and still they were not there. Maybe they had already arrived before 4 P.M.?

He was berating himself for being slow and for taking a slow carriage. Should he go ahead to Concordia College or wait here?

'Five more minutes,' he told himself, 'if they're not yet here, I will walk to Concordia College. I might see them on the way there, or even at the college itself.'

It was a hot day. Sweat streamed down Delfin's body. He faced the area in the direction of Santana, shaking his head and talking to himself. He was like a vendor who took off his hat and fanned himself with it. Irritation and anger began to well up within him.

He walked and looked and stopped.

Just then a carriage hove into view, with two black horses in front. This was the carriage bearing Meni. Delfin was already walking outside the Manggahan area, which was already near the Concordia College.

Indeed, they have arrived! His heart sang as he saw the carriage coming. But he continued walking, for they were drawing nearer behind him.

'Delfin! Delfin!' he heard someone calling from his back. Inside the carriage sat Meni, Felipe, his mother and sister. Felipe asked the driver to stop the carriage.

'Where are you going?' Delfin asked, along with a wink directed at his friend.

'To the Concordia College,' answered Felipe, 'we will drop my sister there.'

Meni pouted and looked at Felipe, as if to say, 'You two are on to something again'.

'Who is he?' Felipe's sister asked Meni.

'That is your brother's best friend,' whispered Meni.

While the carriage was coming closer, Delfin's eyes could not decide whether to gaze at Meni or the beautiful face of the newly seen sister of Felipe. They were both enchanting and he could not choose. Felipe and his mother sat in front, while Meni and Marcela occupied the seat at the back.

'Where are you going?' asked Meni with seeming nonchalance.

'To Santana.'

'Why are you walking in this terrible heat?'

'The driver of my carriage did not want to go farther than Paco because another passenger with me was going to the cockpit in Pasay.'

'But Santana is still far from there,' said the mother in a southern accent.

'It's just there over the bridge,' said Felipe.

'You should go to Santana,' Delfin said as if inviting them. 'It is pleasant to while away the hours beside the Pasig River.'

'It's you who should join us,' Felipe said.

He did not even wait for Delfin to respond. He had already asked his mother to sit in between the two single women, and asked Delfin to sit beside him.

The eyes of Meni seemed to speak. Delfin's eyes, however, were undecided. He sat near the woman to whom he had pledged his love. But if Meni's eyes were sharp enough, she would have read the thoughts racing inside Delfin. 'How beautiful indeed is the sister of Felipe!' Delfin and Felipe secretly nudged each other.

* * *

He already knew the beauty of Meni. There was no more need for his eyes to recall the shape of her face aglow like the moon; the blackness and luxuriance of her hair coiled into a bun; her ears without earrings, following the fashion of the times; her thick eyebrows and lively eyes, but skin like that of a Japanese woman, very fair with a blush ripening on the cheeks. Her nose was not flat and it hinted at the Spanish blood running in her veins. Her lips were curved into a smile, always happy and enchanting, so very like the petals of a newly opened flower.

'The only flaw is in the chin,' some people had noted, for its shape was a bit too sharp. But in the eyes of the beloved, any imperfection was only an additional source of loveliness.

She was also neither slim nor fat, but Don Ramon had remarked on how his daughter seemed to be losing weight since she had started studying at the night school.

Her face was like a slice of heaven itself. She was wearing a red dress made from textiles woven in Iloilo Province. She had neither shawl nor jewellery, except for a thin strand of gold laced around her neck, a thin ring of gold around one of her fingers, and another ring with a stone worth only around 800 pesos . . . And that was how Meni looked as she sat inside the carriage, like the moon in the morning, already touched by the first rays of the sun.

However, it was also but natural to admire someone new. Not just the eyes but also the heart gladdened at the sight of someone new and beautiful. Delfin had the heart of a poet who desired no one else but a muse. And someone new, someone beautiful, elegant and honourable, could set his heart aflame, could make him write the sweet words of a poem.

Indeed, Sela was also beautiful. The writer of our ancient songs would describe her as someone who looked like a princess. It was true that we no longer have kingdoms today, but her father, Captain Loloy, was also the king of his vast lands. Her father had given her everything that she had wanted since she was young. And now that she was already a young woman, they had decided to send her to the exclusive Concordia College in Manila.

Since then, she had followed the modern ways of the times. In her acts, ways of speaking, her thoughts, clothes, and in the way she walked and sat, she imitated everything that she saw the women in her college do. Her former friends and classmates began to become estranged from her, for she only became friends with the other students who could teach her these new ways.

If Felipe had not abandoned his studies, she would have remained in the province. Her father did not want her to study there, for he had heard that it was more dangerous for the female students to venture outside the school.

Even her father noticed the changes in Sela after a year at the Concordia College. She went home for the general vacation from April to June. She was no longer the little girl who would look out of the window when called by her playmates in the neighbourhood. She was no longer the child who ran and played with the daughters of their servants. Rarely now could you see the ways of the child in Sela.

For indeed, Sela had grown into a beautiful woman. Dimples bloomed on her cheeks when she smiled. Her teeth were white as ivory. You could see the rise of her breasts and her shoulders from her sheer chemise. Her nape, smooth and fair, was the kind of nape that would make the Spanish friars of olden days utter in prayer, 'Please save me, Oh Lord! Please save me from temptation'. You knew that Sela was beautiful even if her back was turned to you; it was the sort of beauty that could make even a priest go mad. Her mother used to tease her, even when she was young, that a prince would fall in love with her at the sight of her nape.

But in reality, Sela was not as fair-skinned as Meni. The colour of her skin was more brown, like the skin of the Tagalogs who had lived in the main island of Luzon. The women of the region loved jewellery. They would save up just to buy a ring, or a necklace, or a pair of lovely earrings. And if the poor would do that, then how about the wealthy? And the value of Sela's jewellery!

On her head, she wore a large comb made of thick and pure gold. This comb was lined with a wave of shimmering stones as large as the tears of a poor woman who could not feed her children. If this comb were sold, the poor woman and her ten children could eat well for the next 365 days.

Sela's three hairpins, also made of gold and topped with expensive stones, could feed several families for another 365 days.

The paired earrings that she wore could not only pay for the debts owed by the eight servants working in their house, it could also allow them to live in comfort for several months of freedom from bondage in the house of Captain Loloy.

And on her neck was clasped a lace of the purest gold, around one inch thick, its middle hollowed out and filled with small stones that shimmered like fireflies. Its value was equivalent to the cost of building a large school in the town where Captain Loloy lived.

The clip on her shawl was shaped like a butterfly, whose wings wanted to fly. Six beautiful stones were set in this clip, white and yellow and red and blue, each competing with the way the other shimmered under the light of the sun. This was worth around 1,000 pesos.

And what about her bracelet? It was like her necklace, made by a jeweller in Santa Cruz, and it cost 2,500 pesos.

She also wore three rings, two on her left hand and one on her right hand. They were also made of gold. One featured three pearls, another featured two, and the last ring only had one pearl, but it was a big pearl: when it caught the light, it seemed to glow like a star.

It might seem obscene, but this was the truth. I was not the one who is being obscene, but reality. And if not for this obscenity, the thread that linked the two hearts of Delfin and Meni that night in the garden would have snapped a long time ago.

* * *

Delfin was unhappy with the contrast between the beauty of Marcela and the obscenity of her jewellery. 'Too bad for this woman,' he thought to himself, 'she became a slave to material goods.' The woman's beauty now passed through him like wind, for in his mind rose the image of the typical children of the rich, whose clothes and jewellery are worth a lot of money, thousands and millions of pesos, while outside their grand mansions, in the wider world, people sleep on floor and earth, die of hunger and are buried in debts.

And then Delfin remembered that Sela was indeed the daughter of Captain Loloy, who had allied himself with the Spaniards and worked as the mayor of their town. Only God knew how he grabbed the lands of the poor and built his stupendous wealth. And these were not mere suspicions, for even Felipe had told him about these incidents.

Pretty soon, the carriage was entering the gates of Concordia College. Everybody alighted, except Meni, who had been quiet throughout the trip.

'Are you just staying in the carriage?' Delfin asked Meni, who just ignored him pointedly.

Marcela and Felipe whispered to each other.

'Who is this man whom you asked to join us?' she asked rashly.

'He is my best friend here in Manila. We treat each other like brothers.'

'And does he also know Meni?' and while asking it, her finger pointed at the other woman.

At this point, Meni was looking back and was hesitating in the middle of the stairway. She did not want to talk to Delfin. She knew that the brother and sister were talking about her when she saw the finger pointed in her direction. Her thoughts were disturbed. An anger was rising within her. She faced Delfin and seemed to blame him.

'I should not have joined you all on this trip!' said Meni.

'Oh, look at Meni! If I knew you didn't want me to join the carriage, I wouldn't have done so.'

'Phew!'

'Very well then. I will just stay here and not join all of you upstairs. I will just go ahead and leave. I might as well go to Santana.'

Meni tossed her head and gave a soft grunt.

The other three people felt the sadness in the exchange between Delfin and Meni. Marcela knew that something was afoot between them, and this was confirmed by Felipe.

'Really? Is this true?' she asked her brother. But he was not able to confirm it, because the nuns were already coming to welcome them.

'Hello, Marcelina, welcome,' said one of the nuns, and the other one greeted them as well.

Meni was also known at the Concordia College because she had also studied there. She was only thirteen years old when she and her sister Talia came to live in the college as boarders. The nuns also welcomed her warmly.

The women greeted each other in the Spanish way, rubbing each other's left cheek and then the right. They asked about each other and the nuns gave Sela an introduction to life inside the college. Other nuns soon joined them, as well as the other students milling nearby. Some of the students marveled at the beauty of Meni and Sela, while the others gaped at the jewellery adorning the body of the latter.

On the other hand, the two men with them just stayed a few paces away, their eyes roving around the reception area.

* * *

The reception area was thirty footsteps in length and ten footsteps in width. It was ill-lit and without ventilation; in the afternoons, it resembled a cave. The two stairways, one leading up to the grand entrance and the other leading down to the yard, as well as the three large windows, allowed a few rays of the sun to enter and some wind to blow in.

Upon entering through the grand entrance, you would see a large door.

Atop this large door, loomed the old portraits of Doña Margarita Roxas, between the paintings of the Sacred Heart of Jesus Christ and the Sacred Heart of the Blessed Virgin Mary. There was a big clock on the left and a large calendar on the right. On the walls also hung various portraits of several nuns as well as priests, engaged in their holy acts.

At the end of the hall, there was another door. On top of this door hung a large cross of Jesus Christ. On the left was a wooden sculpture of Saint Joseph and on the right was a portrait of a saint in red, whose name I do not know.

On the left side also loomed big portraits of the Immaculate Conception, along with a portrait of Saint Vincent of Paul surrounded by children. Further along, there was another portrait of Saint Joseph, and on the table stood an image of the Christ Child.

There were so many images of saints and miracles, along with an army of nuns, that no devil with horn and pointed tail would dare enter this place.

But there were also pedestals where potted plants sat. There was also a garden that, unknown to the nuns, must be the place where the interns and their lovers would meet. Upon entering through a door, you would arrive at the place where the students bought their things at expensive prices. There was also a space where hats could be hung. This just showed that aside from women, men could also enter this place. But this was as far as they could venture in.

If you climbed the stairs, on the left, you would see a big display stand that featured the lovely embroidery and beautiful clothes made by the students. Many of them were perfect for the salons in high society; some of them were fit to be clothes for the saints.

And on the right side were the benches, where the visitors sat. This was where tears were shed between mothers and daughters, between the interns and their friends, as well as secret intimations of love exchanged between lovers. Even the nuns suspected that some of the men who visited and claimed they were town-mates and cousins were not really who they claimed to be they were . . .

This was where Meni, Delfin, Sela, Felipe and their mother settled down after exchanging initial greetings with the nuns. What else would they talk about except Marcela, whom they brought to the college and would soon leave behind?

* * *

When Delfin and Felipe saw the portrait of Doña Margarita Roxas, they began to talk about the rich woman. Delfin told Felipe that the rich woman was the real owner of the big house with roofs made of white tiles. All the surrounding buildings, including the church, the interns' dormitories and the classrooms, were just additional construction. Margarita donated the house to the Sisters of Charity, who arrived in the country in the 1850s, to set up the Hospice of Saint John of the Cross. The nuns' congregation lived in the house and later decided to set up a school for the poor. Their acts of charity included teaching with dedication and zest. The initial funds for the school came from Margarita herself. Sor Tiburcia Ayans was the first administrator of the school. She worked hard and the school expanded. She was followed by Sor Josefa Adserias and Sor Catalina Carreras. Because of these nuns' hard work and the donations from the Roxas and Ayala clans, the school later became the Concordia College.

'And who is that Margarita Roxas?' asked Felipe.

'Here in Manila, when we were young, old people would scare us by saying "the miner is there". These words were enough to prevent us from going downstairs, playing on the streets and even caused us sleepless nights. The older people said that the miners were quick and that they would kidnap children upon the orders of Doña Margarita. The children would then be killed and their blood would be used to water the plants owned by the rich woman. These plants were allegedly made of gold: roots, trunk, branches, leaves and flowers. They were all made of the purest gold, and the fruits they bore were real money in various denominations: two, four, five, ten, sixteen and twenty pesos. They said that Doña Margarita owned these plants made of gold, in the same way that Captain Andong of Lipa also put his money on mats to dry them up. I wonder where all that money is, now?'

While they were talking from afar, Meni was thinking what could be the topic of their conversations. The words were tight in her throat.

Delfin was aware of this and just moved away. He did not want Meni to think that he wanted to go near them so he could look at Sela again.

* * *

The angelus started. One of the three or four nuns glided past them, for that was how they seemed to walk, with their feet barely touching the floor. They looked like flies buzzing in and out of people's gatherings, or at times, like eagles, with their sharp eyes judging the actions and conversations of people in a salon . . . One of them led the prayers for the angelus. Everyone stood up and some people knelt down until the prayers were finished, hands were kissed, and 'Good evening' greetings were exchanged with everyone.

Everyone returned to his or her original seat, except the two men. After the prayers, they sat down in front of the three women, and only then did they realize that indeed, a certain darkness had fallen upon the land.

'We should leave now,' Felipe said, 'Mother, I think we should leave now. The sky has already turned dark and it might rain soon.'

'I think Ipe is right, Sela,' said the mother. 'We should leave now. Just do your best, my child, and behave in the most appropriate manner.'

And then her face contorted and she began to weep. Sela's eyes also filled with tears but they remained unshed, unlike the first time when they brought her to the college.

'Oh,' Felipe said them in a teasing tone, 'you should shed your tears now because you might not be able to see each other again. You have decided to bring her here as an intern, and then you cry.'

Meni laughed at this joke. Then she added that even if her parents were in Manila, when they brought her here, she would also shed tears and could not eat well for a few days.

'When will you visit me, Mother?' asked Sela.

'Next month. Your father and I will visit you.'

'Please bring young coconuts and other fruits from our yard, and sweets made in Laguna. Please also bring me perfumed oils. I want to give some of them to Meni as well.'

'But can you eat all of those young coconuts, Sela?' asked Felipe.

'Why not? And I will give some to the nuns. They eat a lot of young coconuts.'

'Oh, do they?' asked Delfin suddenly.

At which, Meni shot him a sharp look and a hardened jaw because she was gritting her teeth. Delfin saw these cues and fell into silence, as if his tongue had been cut. Nobody else noticed this, except Sela. And thus she confirmed that her friend and her brother's best friend were already in a relationship.

Meni could not understand why she was filled with anger at Delfin. She even regretted knowing Marcela. But even she felt that her show of anger had been excessive. To do more would show her to be a woman of coarse character. There would be other hours, other days. And these thoughts calmed her down.

The other nuns and students milled again around them. Tears, laughter, more stories were exchanged, prolonging the farewell. Sela kissed her mother's hand and later, rubbed her cheek against Meni's.

Delfin was at a loss whether to say goodbye to Sela by shaking her hand or not. But he thought that Meni would not mind it. Saying goodbye formally was the mark of a civilized person. He was about to go to Sela, who was then still talking to Meni, whose hand was around her. But Meni did not take her hand off Sela and Delfin just walked down the stairs instead.

Delfin walked downstairs, his head bowed down, like someone a snake had bitten. Upon seeing this, Meni's heart was filled with pity. Sela also felt the same. But when Meni smiled to cover her anger, Sela felt better and sighed, a sigh she had directed at her mother and her brother, who were now leaving her.

'Felipe,' she called out to her brother, 'when will you come back?'

'You ask Meni,' he answered.

'Ah, Meni. She won't visit me again.'

'Why not? Just wait and see. She will be back next week,' Felipe promised.

'Thanks to all of you. Goodbye, Mother.'

But the mother could not answer anymore, for she was tearing up again, regretting that they had decided to send their daughter to study in the city.

Then they climbed into the carriage and it moved away. Upstairs, Sela, the two nuns, the old guard, and some students watched the carriage leave. Inside it, Sela's mother and Meni sat beside each other, while Delfin and Felipe occupied the other seat.

Upon reaching Santana Street, Delfin asked the driver to stop.

'Why?' asked Felipe.

'I'll go now to Santana.'

'You should do that tomorrow. The rain is about to fall.'

But Delfin could not be dissuaded. He saw that Meni, who was silent except for a few grunts, showed her disapproval at his departure. But Delfin said that he had already arranged an appointment with a classmate there and he should go even if it was already night.

'Hey, Felipe,' said Meni, 'just let him be, since he still has a meeting to attend.'

'No, it's already night.'

'Yes, it's indeed night,' the older woman added, 'and it might rain.'

'If night overtakes them,' said Meni, 'and the rain reaches them, then they can walk and wait out the rain at Concordia . . .'

The two men exchanged looks, their eyes in the darkness like two shining swords, but still, Delfin left.

Chapter 8

Conversing Letters

13 June 1904

MENI,

I was waiting for you to write to me. I think it is you who should explain why were you mad at me yesterday. However, I cannot wait any longer. I cannot help but remember your wrinkled forehead, your wounding look, your words that could put a lump in my throat and your pained heart because of me.

Please believe me when I say that I could not sleep last night because of this. What did I do yesterday that made you hate me so? Were you irritated because I joined you without asking permission to do so? You should know that Felipe was the one who invited me to join. He told me that you will be there with them, to convey his sister to Concordia College. And I told him to tell you that I am coming along. Felipe and I even agreed to meet you in Paco. He didn't tell you all of this? If he forgot to do so, then it is not my fault. I didn't intend to do this without your permission.

You hold our future together in your hand. And nobody can snatch that future away from us, unless you move your hand and let it be gone.

I still believe that your words of love will be like webs around me when I die, and likewise on my part.

Let us learn to know more about each other's traits. This is so that when you see me act or hear me speak or crack jokes, you will not get the wrong impressions. Please do not think that I like someone else. One writer has said, 'There is no poison in love more powerful than jealousy. It is like a small animal roaming inside the body of a sick person, which may not immediately strike, but will slowly kill that person.'

Do you know, Meni, that your heart is now filled with poison and microbes? If we want to live in love, then we should set aside all jealousy.

I am only yours.
DELFIN

TO DELFIN,

I read your letter five times. I do not have the duty to write first. It is you, since you know I am mad. But do you still have to ask why?

I am no longer angry now. But I do not want to hear that you went again with Felipe on his visit to Concordia College. If you really want to see me truly and deeply angry, then do pay another visit there.

It is good that you were not able to sleep the night before. On the other hand, I slept so soundly and well. Do you know why? Because I remembered the beautiful face of Marcela. If you ever taught me how to write a poem, which you have long promised to do, she would be reading tomorrow a poem about her, published in the *New Day* newspaper.

Last night, I had a dream. I dreamt that I was a man named Delfin. Two days ago, I brought a young woman to the college. She was a woman whose beauty was beyond compare. I just can't remember any more if Marcela was her name. While inside the carriage, I felt I was enchanted and saw no one else except her beauty. I looked at her from head to foot, my eyes dreamy. And likewise, she was with me: she could not answer when the other people with us were asking her questions. Our looks and smiles became more intense when we reached the college. The nun seemed to have noticed us: she asked me go to downstairs, that was why I failed to shake Marcela's hand . . . (Now, now: the young man was ashamed!)

That was my dream. Did you also have the same dream?

I will end here, Delfin. The words you are saying about jealousy are not true: to be jealous means to be in love. Look it up in the dictionary and check, and if you do not believe it, I will explain to you at a later time.

Your *Concordiana* named
MENI

P.S.: Perhaps you can write a poem about Sela on my behalf?

* * *

20 June

DELFIN, my dearest:

Nobody noticed, don't worry about it. Only the driver of our carriage noticed it, but my father was unaware of what was happening. It is true that I almost fainted when my father hollered: 'Why is there no light on top of the big door?' I thought that he had sensed your presence and was going downstairs. He just noticed the lack of light because it was a Sunday, and he was with Don Filemon and the Americans in his carriage. He left for the races at lunchtime and only returned at night. He was sore because he lost.

I just pretended that nothing was happening. From the garden, I just slipped quietly into the kitchen.

Were you scared?

Felipe did not know what to do last night when I had not yet returned to the house.

I cannot say for sure if we are still going to go through with our studies at the night school. Yoyong does not want Talia to study anymore. He said that if we want to learn English, then we can just hire an American teacher to visit the house. What about you, have you made any decision?

Please accept a letter attached to this: this was sent to me by Pepito Serrallo of Tondo, and I was not able to give this to you last night. Read about all the foolish things he wrote there. He dared to write in Spanish, even if he could not do it well. See if you could already hire him to work for your newspaper.

I will end here. One loud . . . for Delfin.
MENI

PS: Please do not come here this week. You might be spoilt by the beauty of our glorietta. Just come back next week, OK?

* * *

(Pepito's Spanish letter to Meni translated into Tagalog)

IN THE HANDS OF MY HOPE

To the peerless *Filipina Judit:*

This is the third time I am touching my pen from which nothing flows but the ink of love, so that I can offer my perfumed words to your peerless beauty—you who are like the angels and seraphim—the fragrance of my love, words that you have not yet answered, while I await the hope that would come from your lips.

Those who do not profess love for you cannot exist on this earth, you whose beauty God has ordained to be the Queen of the Flowers and the Extreme Orient, the ideal of the Filipino race, just like the heroes Burgos, Rizal, Mabini, amongst others.

Please do not refuse me some words that would be like water for my heart, which is thirsty for love.

When I first saw you taking a bath in the springs of Antipolo, I could not control anymore the stream of my love for you, in this my happy days of single-blessedness. While we were picking the plums, I did not know what to do because I wanted to kneel in front of

Your Majesty. But somebody came and stole the thunder from me. Now I know who that person is, but if he is indeed lucky to have your hand, please know that I am not afraid to offer my life against someone who is blocking the spring of love gushing from my heart, whomever he might be!

I kiss the traces of your footsteps, oh great star of the East! I await your sweet response to my holy desire!

Farewell, lyre of my love!
PEPING SERALLO

MENI, my dear,

Thank God that nothing happened. Do you know where I got out of? Not through the door, but rather, I clambered atop the fence. If there were a policeman patrolling outside, he would have thrown me into jail and I would have had to spend the night there. But nobody can compare that with what happened between us on the first night at the garden, the night when Señora Loleng came.

So that Serrallo has even threatened me? Perhaps he brought contraband with him? Why don't you answer his proposal? Poor man.

Yoyong also talked to me earlier. He told me of his misgivings about all of you going to night school. I also think it is better to have a tutor teach you English at home. Why don't you transfer to the Philippine Normal School? They are still accepting students right now.

Don't you notice something about Felipe? It was a Sunday yesterday and yet, he just stayed at the house the whole day. Don't you see him looking sad these days? I feel bad for him since this morning, when he came to me. He had more sighs than words. He was on the verge of tears. Let us check on what is happening with him, it might be something important.

Do you know Tentay, whom he would visit at the San Lazaro in Santa Cruz? Tentay was also there when you were in Antipolo. I am not sure if you met or if Felipe introduced you both to each other.

But I do not think that could've happened, since Felipe is so secretive. He barely told me about her and his visits to her place. He never even took me with him: he just said 'one day'.

Tentay had several siblings, and her parents were still alive. According to Felipe, their family was neck-deep in debt. The father was ill, and the mother was still nursing a baby. A brother older than Tentay had been gone for six years, and no one knew where he was, since he had left the Philippines in 1898. Someone said he was working as a servant on a ship. I do not know how that came to be.

Felipe met the father at a meeting of the Alliance of Workers' Organizations. It was the mother who disliked Felipe. And Tentay, who loved her father more than her mother, had to stay in the middle. Felipe did not know where he stood in Tentay's heart, although he had been courting her for a year.

There were days when Tentay would be all sweetness and light to Felipe, filled with promises and bringing peace to our friend. Those must have been the days when she followed her heart and the advice of her father. But there were also days when the light blurred and dimmed. She would sometimes say words that shook a man's sense of hope (the way you sometimes were, before). In tears, she would even tell Felipe to just forget about her, so that her mother would leave her in peace. At times like these, Felipe would just leave the house with bitterness on his tongue, worry in his heart and sadness filling his whole being.

But these are not the present sources of Delfin's sadness, since he can very well deal with these. What he cannot accept, which he confessed to me today, is that for the past week, Tentay has been angry with him.

Tentay's father had known about Felipe's real situation in his hometown. He had learnt that Felipe was extremely wealthy and was only living a poor life in Manila because his father got mad with him for not studying well. Tentay's father was old, and when he coughed, blood would be mixed with his spit. He was getting weaker and weaker, and had no more strength. Because he knew of Felipe's good character, and perhaps in his dreams that one day, soon, his wife and family would have a good life, he wished that Felipe would marry Tentay.

But the mother and the daughter were not aware of the sick man's wish. The mother only saw Felipe as another poor man. She also seemed to have lost all hope with Tentay.

Felipe gave them no inkling about his wealth, whether in word or in deed. He would just tell them that he came from the South, that his parents were still alive, and that he had a sister. That was all he told them. He even told them an additional lie: that because of his work at the printing press, he was able to send money home to help his family.

On the other hand, Tentay could not care less whether Felipe was poor or not. His poverty was not one of the things that endeared him to her. For she felt that only a poor person could understand another poor person. And a rich person would just turn her into a slave.

But Tentay also knew that she was beautiful. Men with money and learning would kneel in front of her. The only thing she would tell Felipe was, 'Oh, Ipeng, I chose you over the men courting me even if you are poor and not so good-looking.'

You can just imagine, Meni, the effects of these words on someone like Felipe.

However, the old man's illness took a turn for the worse in the past month, such that the children feared they would be orphaned. Even though it must've been difficult, they still went on a pilgrimage to Antipolo.

Felipe visited them last Saturday and found the house as lonely as a graveyard. The children were weeping; the mother and daughter sat on a bench, whispering to each other with their tears falling and chests running out of breath. The sick man was leaning on a bench made of bamboo and spat weakly into a trough filled with ash. He waved at Felipe and bade him to come in.

Tentay motioned Felipe to sit near her, while her mother continued nursing the baby.

That day, Tentay asked for Felipe's forgiveness. She told him not to court her anymore but to treat her just like a sister. Tentay said that her father had talked to them, telling them about Felipe's real station in life. He wanted Felipe to take care of Tentay because of his good heart. When she heard this, the mother neither agreed nor disagreed.

But it was Tentay who disapproved of it. When she heard the news from her father, the love vanished from her as if it had been cleansed out of her. She wept and told her parents that she would not mind marrying someone as poor as their own family. She was afraid of marrying into wealth if it might mean maltreatment from the rich husband's parents. This made the father feel bad and bitter tears were shed. The children noticed this and began to weep themselves.

Tentay related all of these events to Felipe. Then she added that any word or consolation from him would not change her mind.

A black sadness followed Felipe all the way home.

Look at Felipe's restraint. This happened yesterday and he only told me about this today. If I had not noticed his sadness and asked him about it, he would not have told me what had happened.

I am sorry I had to tell you, Meni, what happened to someone who lives in your house. I felt as if I have just written about the life of another man. But I think you should know about this now. You and I can learn something from this, can't we?

I will now end here.
DELFIN

P.S.: What are you saying, that seeing you would spoil me? Oh, Meni! Even if I do miss you terribly—it is next week then, if it's next week.'

* * *

MY LOVE,

You did not do anything else yesterday except write me a novel! You are indeed a writer. Because your letter was so long, my answer will be short.

Two days from now, on Thursday, there will be a show at the Zorrilla Theatre. One of the artists has sent us complimentary tickets, but I will not join them to watch the show. Can you come here?

What contraband are you talking about in the letters of Pepito? The letters are here. I just kept them with me, just to test if, indeed, 'jealousy is the poison and microbes of any relationship'. Now you see that it is not only women who know how to ask for loyalty in love . . .

We can talk about my studies in the Philippine Normal School later. And the same with Felipe's situation. What a pity!

What is it you are saying about there being something we could learn from what happened between him and Tentay? That because you are poor, you also want to give me the same reasons that Tentay gave him? Just wait until you come here . . .

MENI

Chapter 9

The Wealth of the Poor

It was near the end of August 1904 and they were having lunch, when Felipe saw Lucio, Tentay's brother, coming towards him. He was only twelve years old. His eyes were filled with tears when he came near Felipe. The latter felt as if a fist had been struck into his gut. Lucio had never been here before. Felipe quickly stopped eating and greeted the boy.

Without any word, the boy gave Felipe a piece of paper, which he quickly read. 'Where is your older sister?' he asked.

'She's outside, waiting for you.'

Felipe was not even able to wash his hands. He just grabbed a piece of paper and cleaned his hands with it. He got his suit and hat, and quickly put them on.

He did not mind the jokes coming from his fellow workers. He asked the boy, 'Are you the only ones here?'

'Yes and my sister is on the other street.'

'How is your father?'

The boy did not answer. He just looked at Felipe, then bowed his head. He thought that the father must have died, for Tentay's note had asked him to take a leave from the printing press as soon as he could.

Even though he was hesitating, Felipe asked, 'Has your father passed away?'

'He is not dead, but he is looking for you.'

They saw Tentay standing at the curve of the road. They went to her. Her eyes were not just red, her face was stained with tears, and she sobbed when she saw Felipe.

'Oh, Felipe, I hope you can see my father alive,' she said.

Then the brother and the sister cried, and Felipe was so taken with their sorrow that he almost shed tears himself. But he restrained himself, feeling that if he joined in their sorrow, it would be like wood being added to the fire. Not many people were up and about on the street, but one or two persons did notice them.

'Then let us get a carriage so we can go now,' said Felipe.

It was a hot day and carriages were nowhere in sight. Finally, one hove into view and they hailed it. Tentay and Felipe sat at the back, while the boy sat behind the driver.

They reached Bilibid Street without speaking. Her dying father's condition filled Tentay's thoughts. She was also suddenly shy at being with Felipe, for it was the first time that they had sat closely beside each other. She was worried about what people might say, especially those who knew both of them.

'I was supposed to just ask Lucio to fetch you,' Tentay said, 'but he didn't know where you work.'

'And why do you know where I work?'

'Have you forgotten the day when my mother and I came from San Miguel? We were passing by your printing press when you suddenly came out of the door.'

'Oh yes . . . But does your mother know you are coming here?'

'She was the one who asked Lucio to accompany me.'

'And does your father know?'

'No. He was having hiccups when we left. He had been asking for you, that's why Lucio and I quickly left the house. There was no one else who could fetch you.'

'How is he now?'

'He's all right when there are no hiccups. But when he stops hiccupping, that's when he begins to run out of breath. It looks so frightening and it would be hard to talk to him when he has these attacks.'

Meanwhile, the carriage was already near its destination. Tentay's house was in one of the interior streets in front of the San Lazaro Hospital.

* * *

When they were near the house, screams rose in the air. 'Oh my God. Dandoy, Alejandrino . . . please do not forget the name of Jesus, Mary and Joseph.'

This wail was followed by the sound of two children crying. Felipe's head seemed to swell and his heart was torn by sorrow. He thought that he was not able to make it in time to see the father still alive. But he had to restrain himself.

'Tentay,' he told his fiancée who was kneeling in front of the bamboo bed where her father lay. A curtain separated this space from the rest of the house. 'Please go to your siblings and take them away from this. Your mother and I will just stay here. Bring your sister who is still nursing her milk and you may go to the neighbour. Hurry up!'

'Felipe! Let us all stay here and die!' was Tentay's answer. Her words seemed to go deeper than bone. 'I want to see my father until he closes his eyes.'

'Aling Teresa,' Felipe whispered to the mother, 'please let me stay here and say the prayers for him . . .'

'Yes, my son, you better do it. It won't be good for me to do it. Oh, Felipe!'

Then she drew a very deep sigh and restrained herself from crying again. She grabbed the arm of Tentay. Pretty soon, there was only Felipe and the dying man. But before the mother left, she gave instructions to Felipe.

'Ipeng, please say the prayers to Jesus Christ. Do not forget! Please have mercy on the soul of my husband.'

And thoughts rushed inside Felipe's head. Of death's majesty, a person's life, a father dying, the woven mat on which the poor slept, the fate of a woman who would soon be a widow, and the children who would be orphaned, the reward or punishment that awaited in the other life, the body that used to be strong, that worked tirelessly for other people and will now soon be gone, to be buried and disintegrate . . . all of these thoughts raced inside Felipe, as he watched the face of the man who was about to die.

It seemed as if there was a thread beneath the bamboo bed that was pulling the life out of the old man. He wheezed horribly and kept his eyes closed. When he opened his eyes, only the whites would show, for he was having difficulty breathing.

Felipe did not know by what name to call the old man, since it would be disrespectful to call him by his name, 'Alejandro', since the sick man was older. But for the sake of the old man's soul, he put tradition aside and began to pray.

'Alejandro, in your heart of hearts, please don't forget to call the name of Jesus, Mary and Joseph. Alejandro . . . Jesus . . . Mary . . . Joseph. . .'

Felipe said this prayer, as well as other prayers for the sick. The old man must have recognized Felipe's voice uttering calming words to him. He opened his eyes and said in a hoarse voice, 'Felipe,' then he demonstrated with his right hand his wish to have a glass of water. 'I'm thirsty.'

Felipe parted the curtain and talked to Tentay. 'Your father is thirsty. Do you have meat soup to nourish him?'

Tentay and her mother looked at each mother, and Tentay shook her head grimly.

'What about congee or water from cooked rice?'

Tentay rushed to the kitchen to look for congee, but it was not edible anymore. It was cooked last night precisely for the old man, but he never asked to eat until today, for he had been ill the whole night.

The old man then told Felipe that he only wanted to have a glass of water. 'What sharp ears he has!' the mother told Tentay. 'He must have heard our talk that we no longer have soup or congee, that's why he only wants water to drink.'

Tentay and her mother restrained themselves from crying. The daughter immediately got a glass of water and returned to her father. 'Father, here is your glass of water. Should I use a tablespoon to help you? You don't want any soup?'

The old man shook his head and opened his mouth. Tentay put the tablespoon of water near her father's mouth, her hand shaking.

'Let me do it, Tentay,' offered Felipe, when he noticed that Tentay was nervous.

'Oh, let the daughter do that,' said two female neighbours who had come in and parted the curtain.

The father took in five tablespoons of water and no more. Then he spoke, 'Thank God. Felipe, where is Teresa?'

The mother came closer. 'My wife,' said the sick man. 'Where are the children?'

'They're all here. We're all good. Don't worry about us. We're all healthy, by the grace of God.'

'Always take care of them.'

'I will. Don't worry.' She almost cried, were it not for the nudge from one of the female neighbours beside her.

'I'll just sleep for a while,' the old man told Felipe. 'Don't leave . . . And please take care . . . of my family, for me.'

Felipe was speechless. The old man slowly roved his eyes at everyone gathered around him. Then he leaned his head on the right side of the pillow, and closed his eyes. Everyone began whispering and their hold on the curtain loosened. Only Tentay and Felipe were left.

The mother, as well as the neighbours, Aling Marta and Old Woman Toyang, sat on the bamboo stairs and began to talk.

'Why is there no single image of Jesus Christ in the place where Felipe prayed?' Aling Marta asked.

'We have one. We borrowed an image from Santa Cruz, a big one. But when Andoy's condition became better, the owner took it back from us. He said he will lend the image to a dying man in Quiapo.'

'Who owns that image of Jesus Christ?'

'Hermana Barang owns it.'

'Oh, her image is very powerful. Too bad it isn't here anymore.'

'I know of another image of Jesus Christ. This one is also powerful,' added Old Woman Toyang. 'But it's in Timbugan and I don't know who amongst us can go there and borrow it right now.'

'I have four children and cannot leave the house,' said Aling Teresa. 'Tentay is here but I can't just send her out on errands anywhere.'

'Why not Felipe?'

'Oh, he has just arrived. And I'm not sure if the owner knows him.'

They called Felipe, who also didn't know the place. So it came to pass that Old Woman Toyang was assigned to borrow the image of Jesus Christ. She would also look for another image, if that one wasn't available.

'Felipe,' said Aling Marta, 'don't allow Andoy's head to lean on the right side. That is the side of the devil. He should lean his head on the left, which is the side of the angel . . .'

Felipe ignored such superstition and went back inside.

'Another thing,' said Old Woman Toyang, 'do you have blessed water here?'

'We don't have it,' answered the sick man's wife.

'What kind of people are you? May God have mercy on you . . . Has Andoy done his confession of sins?'

'Yes, he did that last week, in the house.'

'But did he already take the Communion?'

'Not yet. He wants to take it in the Church, when he's well. He said that he isn't dying yet.'

'Oh my God! Now it will be hard for him to take Communion. It's as if you don't care for a person's soul.'

'Maybe that's why he is suffering,' said Aling Marta, 'with his head leaning on the left, then on the right!'

'This only happened today,' said the wife. 'He always leaned his head on the left. He also gazes at the picture of Jesus, Mary and Joseph.'

'Well, that's good. That will save him from the temptations of the devil,' said Old Woman Toyang, who then uttered a short prayer.

Because she wanted to check on her husband, Aling Teresa stood up and walked to his bed.

'Is he asleep?' she whispered to Felipe and Tentay. Felipe answered 'yes' while Tentay nodded.

The mother said, 'Thank God to the Blessed Virgin Mary and to Jesus Christ,' then carried her young child and went out of the house again.

Old Woman Toyang bade them goodbye, so she could go and borrow the image of Jesus Christ, while Aling Marta was left with Aling Teresa.

* * *

Aling Marta was a widow with no child, since her child had died. Her husband used to gamble sometimes, leading them to quarrel. Aling Marta resorted to chewing betel nut, smoking and gambling as well. Sometimes, she would even join her husband in the cockpit.

'And that is my life,' said Aling Marta. 'Like unwanted cats. We don't have a house of our own. Our in-laws, although comfortable, are angry at us. You should be thankful, Teresa. Even if you become a widow, you have your children with you: they are treasures. How many children do you have?'

'Eleven in all, including one who was stillborn. But only six children survived . . .'

'You still have six treasures. The wealth of the poor lies in their children.'

'Good if all of them turn out to be fine. But one of them, Ruperto, has been missing. I don't know if the sea has reclaimed him . . .'

She could not speak anymore and burst into tears. Then she sobbed loudly, as if not aware of someone very ill inside their house.

'Oh, my son, Ruperto,' she wailed, 'we haven't seen him in six years. What if he comes back much later? He wouldn't be able to see his father alive.'

Upon hearing her mother crying, Tentay went out. But when she learnt that they were talking about her missing brother, Ruperto, she also began to shed tears.

The six-year-old Amando then toddled over to the sick bed of his father. He looked at his father, examined him as if he were not a child. Then Amando toddled to his mother and embraced her.

This was followed by Victor, who was born three years after Lucio. Victor just stood in front of his father. He was the stoic one, who just looked at the event unfolding before him as if no ill wind could touch him.

Six children! One less—he who was stowed away on a ship and must have been swallowed up by the sea by now. One daughter who was eighteen years old, Lucio, Victor, who was nine, Amando, who was six, and Julian, whom she was still nursing . . . These were the so-called jewels that her husband would leave her. The precious treasures of the poor!

* * *

The weeping outside made Felipe leave the side of the sick man. He reminded the family that their weeping would only worsen the situation of the sick man.

He said, 'Hearing the name of the missing Ruperto, along with your weeping, might just snuff out whatever life he still has left within him.'

Aling Marta reminded Aling Teresa. 'You should not think of your missing son but of the ones who are here. Ruperto is a man. He's already grown up and can very well take care of himself.'

That calmed down everyone. When they heard a rustling behind the curtain, they all rushed in. But the sick man only moved his hand, touching the curtain, and fell asleep again.

Tentay said, 'Ipeng, you should sit down first. You've been standing for a long time and your legs might be tired.'

'That's OK, I'm used to standing for a long time. And I already rested earlier by sitting on that chair,' he said, pointing to a nearby chair.

'Yes, but come near me and I'll tell you something.'

The bench that she offered to Felipe was less than four footsteps away from her father's bamboo bed. This bench could be seen from the outside, where Aling Marta, Aling Teresa, and the children sat. The house was indeed small. It had no bedroom. It was just a rectangle that was three arms' length in width. On one side, stood a small, dirty kitchen.

If you were walking outside and happened to glance inside, you could see the whole house at once. There used to be a room, especially for the single daughter, but this room was in disuse. It became a space for the sick father, who coughed blood and wheezed throughout the night.

Tentay spoke. 'I'm so ashamed to have had to fetch you, earlier. People might think something was afoot between us. And . . . what did your fellow workers say when you just left them? Did they see us? Did they see Lucio?'

Felipe knew that he would lessen her sadness if he gave her a balanced answer. Tentay was now smiling shyly, her eyes red from weeping earlier. Her face looked like a summer day lashed by rain, once happy but now sad. But beneath this, Felipe saw a woman with a fine character, a daughter who loved her parents, and a woman who was truly in love. So he decided that it was his turn to be honest yet tender with her.

'Don't worry about fetching me earlier,' Felipe said. 'Don't worry about it. Nobody in the printing press saw you. And what if they did? Their comments should not bother us, because they don't know what is within us. Besides, we'll do everything for the sake of your father.'

'Yes, Ipeng, because of my father, we suffered and I did things I shouldn't have done.'

'And what are these things that you shouldn't have done?'

'You haven't been here for several weeks . . . Perhaps, you got mad at me or my mother. . . And then it was I who had to go there and fetch you.'

Tentay seemed like a melting candle while she talked. Her gaze was downcast, her head bowed low.

'But you came for me because your father was looking for me. We should give all the wishes of a dying man. Let us not even bother discussing why you fetched me. What I want to know is why your father asked for me and what he wants me to do.'

'Indeed, Ipeng, my father is dying . . .'

Then she could not speak anymore. She remembered the times she hardened her heart when her father was talking to her amiably about Felipe. She only followed his advice to accept his suit because the old man was gravely ill and indeed, dying. There was no more time to say 'no' to the request of her father.

'I don't blame you,' said Felipe, when he noticed that Tentay had become speechless, although he could guess what she would say. 'When I first met you, I already felt that you were cold to me. Your father had not yet even told you about my family's wealth in the province, but you already had scant feelings for me. But your coldness turned to hatred when you knew I'm rich. I've told you many times that I bring no wealth with me, since that wealth belongs to my family. I also cannot accept something that is not even mine. I even told you about my beliefs regarding money. I added that you would get to stay here with your family, you need not come with me and live with my rich family in the province. We'll live here and we'll help each other out, even if we live a life of poverty. But—'

Tentay kept her peace and just listened.

'But Tentay, you never trusted me. Even I became a burden on your family. Other people become happier when they come to know better the one who loves them. But you . . . you just wanted to push me away. Only now did I feel some kindness towards me from your mother. And then, even you and your father had your disaffection for each other. The three times that I visited between last July and August, you didn't even greet me. Now, Tentay, place yourself in my shoes. It pains me not to have visited you and your father in the last three weeks. But what can I do? I don't want to burden you anymore with my feelings for you. I just hoped that one day, you would change in the way you regard me.'

Tentay could hardly speak while listening to Felipe. Her gaze was downcast, yet at times, she would raise her face and look at Felipe. A smile was beginning to form at the ends of her lips, as if she wanted to say, 'Oh, why do you have to remember everything?' But since death was knocking on their door, it was not the proper time to open her heart to Felipe and tell him that he shouldn't worry anymore. She wanted to tell him that she already loved him, that she would no longer treat him with coldness nor show him the shadow of her doubts. Such was the mystery of love!

'But now,' Felipe continued, 'because of the sadness that now fills all of us, since we're waiting for your father to pass away, I'll just shield these feelings. I only opened up to you because you asked me questions.'

Tentay could also not speak. She realized her mistake. Why had she allowed her father's good wishes to make her turn Felipe away? Why had she insulted a love that was pure and true? Felipe had been courting her for one year and shown nothing except respect and kindness towards her parents, fondness for her siblings, and humility and love towards her. He was never haughty during his visits. But she was worried about the fate of her mother and siblings, if ever she got married to a rich and powerful man like Felipe.

Chapter 10

A Father's Last Wishes

The shadows of everything that had happened and was still happening flitted about in Tentay's thoughts. She was worried that her stubbornness regarding her father's request might have worsened his situation. She blamed herself.

Two nights ago, she remembered that her father was already bidding them goodbye. Wracked by terrible coughs, he asked forgiveness of his wife for not loving her enough. Her mother and Tentay had wept copiously, and her mother had embraced her father.

Her father told her, 'Tentay, if you can't really love Felipe because of his wealth and possible mistreatment from his family, it's up to you to decide. But amongst the men who are courting you, I really favour Felipe. His kindness will be his redeeming factor over his wealth. I liked him not because of his wealth, but because of his kindness. His salary at the printing press and his family's wealth will help you live a good life. Unlike me, who since I was young, until now, had to work hard day and night, even if sick. But there were still days when we had nothing to eat, and now I'll die without leaving you anything except poverty and debt. If you don't love Felipe, then don't get married until Lucio has grown up to be a teenager, or your brother, Ruperto, has come back to us.' At the mention of her brother's name, tears again glistened on her father's sunken cheeks.

After a while, her father had slept again and her mother had resumed talking to Aling Maria. Tentay took this occasion to talk to her father again, if only in her thoughts. She told him not to worry anymore. *I'll follow your advice regarding Felipe. Don't leave me with sad thoughts in your heart regarding this. I don't want you to be sad, even in the afterlife. If you so wish him to be my destiny, then so be it, my dear father, everything is clear to me now . . .'*

Later, she recalled all this to Felipe, and even added that when her father woke up, she told him these things. Some kind of happiness had descended upon her father's face, and asked that Felipe be fetched so they could talk. That was why although it might seem unseemly of her, they had had to rush to Felipe's place of work to fetch him.

'And what will he tell me?' asked Felipe.

'I don't know. But I guess he will talk to you about my family and I.'

'But what you told your father . . . did that really come from your heart?'

'Yes, and I can repeat it in front of God.'

Felipe did not expect such happiness that day. In the midst of so much sadness and grief, Tentay's words were enough to drive away the dark clouds.

For her part, Tentay was so relieved. She followed her father's advice, and also followed what her heart held true. Felipe thought to himself, 'I'll also die if Father passes away with ill feelings about me.' And at that moment, Tentay urged Felipe to come to her father and tell him with all humility what his intentions were.

* * *

At that point, Amando, Tentay's kindest brother, came to them. He put his arm around her waist and looked up at his older sister. By his gaze alone, Tentay knew that he wanted to say something but could not say it out loud. So she put her ear closer to Amando and asked, 'What is it?' Tentay was disturbed by what Amando whispered. She looked outside, then at her mother sitting on the stairs, but she did not say anything. The boy did not leave her, and she told him to wait. Felipe asked what the matter was.

'What did Amando tell you?' asked Felipe.

'Nothing,' she answered softly, while looking at her brother who was then walking toward their mother.

'Please tell me what's wrong,' said Felipe.

'Just wait here,' answered Tentay, then she stood up and went outside. He was surprised to see through the door that the stove was burning and Lucio stood in front of it. What was he cooking? Rice? Tentay went to the stove and lifted the pot of clay. Indeed, it was rice.

Even if she were an inveterate gambler, Aling Marta had a heart of gold. She would help others quickly if she had the wherewithal to do so, especially if she had won in gambling. At times like these, her hands were outstretched towards those who borrowed money from her or sought her help . . . She knew that Aling Teresa's family sometimes lacked food to eat for the day. Aling Marta could tell that the family had not yet eaten their lunch. It must already be 3.30 in the afternoon. But Aling Teresa could not confide in her about this directly. Her eyes just filled with tears while her young son sidled up to her, whispering about the burnt rice.

But who amongst their neighbours would help them this time, since they had become inured to the family's asking for help? Aling Teresa had a sister in Tondo, but she was married to a cruel man. He would drive away anyone from Aling Teresa's family who would go there and ask for help.

It had been two months since Tentay last worked at the tobacco factory in The Orient because the wages were small. She would be lucky to take home two pesos, which was not enough for her fare and food. Since her father fell ill, both mother and daughter had decided to accept dresses for mending or sewing at home. Some people would bring them textiles to be sewn into clothes, dresses, shorts and Chinese-style T-shirts for men. They would sew the clothes with the sewing machine at the house of Tentay's friend.

But they had not done any sewing in the last three days, on account of her father's terrible illness. Whatever money had been paid to them, had already been used to buy their food and medicines for the sick man. A woman who was married to an American asked them to sew two dresses in flaming red, but she could not yet get them, even if one month had already passed. She said that her husband had not yet been paid and she had no money to pay for the dresses. One day, she came back and said that she would just get one dress first, then return to pay for the two dresses. She never did. Neither did they see even the shadow of the American husband. Aling Teresa had thought of selling the suit out of desperation, but she never did it. She did not want to be accused of selling something that she did not own. If it were only the mother and the daughter, they could live without eating a lot, but what about the children and the sick man?

Finally, she was able to offer it for sale to a female neighbour, who balked at the colour of the dress. It also did not fit her. Out of pity for the poor Aling Teresa, the neighbour gave her two pesos, which was enough for them to buy food for the whole day and the next day as well. But what was two pesos for six people, including a sick man who hardly ate and needed medicine?

What about Lucio, what help did he give? When his father fell ill, he joined Tentay at the tobacco factory. There, he learnt how to make cigarettes, he hauled bales of tobacco and poured the shredded leaves into the machine. The foreman would order him around and he would sometimes hit Lucio on the head. They also did not feed him, even though they ordered him to get their food, gather the dishes and wash them. Twice a month, he received three pesos, and when his sister left the factory, he followed suit. Along with other kids, he carried packages and pieces of luggage belonging to people taking the boat at Escolta, from morning till night. But what did he earn there? He earned four, eight, or sixteen pesetas daily, but sometimes lost them in gambling. When he lost, he would tell his mother that the day's pickings at the pier had been slim. Perhaps Lucio, like the other young people working there, had also developed the habit of pulling something from inside the pieces of luggage that he carried, if the owner happened to look somewhere else?

That was why Aling Teresa asked her son to stop working there, for fear that this would just be an added burden to her already manifold problems.

And what about Victor, who was only nine years old? He had caused a lot of problems for his parents. He was always out on the streets, stubborn, frisky, always immersed in play and could not care less about the poverty of the family. Since his father had fallen ill, it would be a lucky day when he could be found at home for even an hour. In the mornings, he would leave and go to Trozo, where he would bathe the horses in the sea or the river, for a fee. More than once he had fallen from a horse or was chased by cops on the streets. The eight pesos he earned from this was not even enough for food.

Mang Andoy was indeed right in looking for someone who would help his family after he had passed away. This must be what was giving him strength as he now lay asleep, so that when he would wake up later, he could talk seriously with Felipe and tell him his final wishes. He saw Felipe as someone who would protect and take care of his daughter.

But Felipe must have forgotten that he did not ask permission to leave the printing press. His fellow workers saw him leave, but they were not sure he would return later. But this did not matter to him. What mattered was to hear the sick man's final wishes, to see the woman he loved, to be able to help this family broken by so much poverty . . . All of these mattered more to him than the lash of words he might receive back at the printing press.

Felipe thought of himself as stoic, but his tears fell at the sight of the children happily eating the food given to them and the mother eating morsels of rice, so she could have milk to feed to the baby she was nursing. The children were delighted because this time, they were not eating watered-down congee but pure and real grains of rice. That was why Aling Teresa could not scold Lucio who, when given the money by Aling Marta, bought rice but did not cook it with lots of water, for congee, as instructed. The young boy must already be tired of eating watered-down congee every day.

Tentay did not want to eat. Even if invited again and again by her family to eat, she did not do so. 'I'm not hungry,' she said. And in reality, she could not feel hunger anymore, used as she was to giving her share of food to her family. She just entertained him to avoid

Felipe from noticing how her brothers scooped the rice and greedily ate it. But Felipe also asked her to eat.

Aling Marta had already left by then.

Felipe noticed the glaring poverty in the hut, even if the mother and daughter tried to hide it. Inside the house, he told Tentay about his feelings.

He said, 'You don't even consider me as one with you—one with you in feelings, one with you in dealing with your problems. So what if I know that you don't have money for lunch? Tentay, you didn't even think of my situation earlier, when Aling Marta was here. Why am I here if I can't help all of you?'

'Please don't blame me,' the woman answered gently. 'Was I the one who welcomed Aling Marta? And my mother is surely embarrassed that you would notice that we didn't have food today.'

'Yes, Tentay, both of you are right. Now I am thinking that I'm the one at fault here . . .' He stopped and seemed to be listening to a voice from within him. 'I'm aware of your poverty and I should have offered my help.'

And then the two kept their silence. Tentay did not want to speak anymore. Felipe even more so. He blamed himself for not noticing that there was no food for the day because he grew up rich and had never had a day without food in his life. And then he remembered Tentay's secretive nature, she, who still treated him like a stranger. But he put it down to the fact that only recently had they talked about their feelings . . .

Their silence was broken when the sleeping man turned on the bed. They thought he would stand up, but he just lay on his back and wheezed, as if running out of breath. He looked so tired, as if he had walked for a long, long time. Both Tentay and Felipe did not know what to do.

'Father! What happened to you?' asked Tentay.

From outside, Aling Teresa shot inside like an arrow. 'Andoy! Oh, my Andoy!' she said, screaming out his name as she rushed to his bed.

The children, who had just finished eating, were also shocked. Even the nursing baby woke up. Felipe calmed everyone down.

'Everyone, please keep quiet,' he said. 'Your father is like that because he just woke up.'

And that seemed like the truth. The sick man's breathing evened out. He opened his eyes, scanning the faces around him: his wife, children and Felipe, all gathered around his bed. Then he looked at Felipe and nodded at the young man. Felipe drew nearer and put his ear near the mouth of the sick man. But his voice was not soft: Tentay and Aling Teresa also heard the sick man's words. He was telling his family not to grieve and not to weep. He asked the children to go with Aling Teresa and Tentay. He told them to keep quiet and to leave for a while, since he wanted to say something to Felipe.

They drew the curtain and went outside.

'What time is it, Felipe?' the sick man asked after a while.

He spoke with clarity, even if his voice was hoarse and his breathing came in fits and starts.

'It must be around 4.30 in the afternoon,' the young man answered gently.

'Oh, it's still early. I forgot . . .'

'Do you feel better now?'

'Oh, my son! I feel a little better now. But it will be like this. All my strength . . . is gone . . .'

'Do you want to eat congee?'

The old man shook his head, raised his hand and pointed at his throat. In a hoarse voice, he said that it was difficult for food to pass through his throat.

Felipe was listening to the sick man's answer when Tentay came in with a cup of hot rice washing and a teaspoon. Upon hearing the word 'congee,' mother and daughter ran to the kitchen and retrieved the washing from the boiling rice that Lucio had set aside. This would be good for their sick father. Lucio was giving his sister a cube of caramel that came from their mother.

But when offered the cup, the sick man's face turned into a grimace. It was a grimace more of sorrow now that he could no longer enjoy the taste of food. But Felipe was able to persuade the sick man to open his mouth and take in some spoonfuls of the rice washing sweetened with caramel. The ones feeding him were delighted, because the sick man finished half a cup. Overnight and through the day, he had not eaten or drank anything, except the water he had drunk earlier. His family thanked God and thought that their father would soon be well.

Afterward, everybody left again, leaving Felipe alone with the sick man. Aling Teresa shushed the baby Huleng and gave her to Tentay. She then sat near the curtain so she could hear the conversations on the other side.

'Is your chest still painful?' Felipe asked after a while.

'Oh yes! It seems to have gone . . . Shattered . . .'

The young man did not speak for a while. He looked at the chest of the sick man, and knew that his days were numbered. Mang Andoy resumed talking.

'Felipe, thank you for coming here . . . Did they fetch you?'

'Yes, they did.'

'I want to talk to you . . . before I pass away . . . Teresa will say something to you . . . something we had already discussed . . . Oh! Please take care of my family . . . when I go . . . you're the only one I can depend on . . . I have been sick for a year . . . I have already taken too many medicines . . . But this illness seems to be my fate . . . The longer I stay, the more I suffer . . . It's better for me to die . . . so our life will not worsen . . . I won't be a burden anymore to my wife and children . . . This is such terrible poverty, Felipe . . .'

Then the sick man stopped, as if wanting his heaving chest and tongue to take rest.

'It might do you good,' said Felipe, 'if you just rest for a while. We can just talk later when you feel better.'

'No,' the sick man said, shaking his head, 'I'll leave the moment darkness falls. When I fall silent, it will be forever. Felipe . . . are you still a member of our Alliance of Workers?'

'Yes, I am.'

'Is it better now?'

Felipe hesitated on whether to tell him the truth or not. But then, why hide the truth from the sick?

'No, it's not.'

The sick man sighed. 'It seems I'll never see that Alliance turning out as well as it should . . . They cannot fix it . . . Is it all we have to expect, especially from someone like me who is sick? In the past months, I asked Teresa three times to go to our headquarters . . . But there was nobody there . . . When there was someone, he said they could not do anything for me . . . the Alliance has no money . . . and was also mired in debts . . . So if I die now, the ones I will leave behind will have nothing for themselves . . . Too bad for our Alliance. I joined it even though I was already weak, on Labour Day itself. I thought that, with all these people around, the Alliance will be a success . . . It turns out they cannot even help an ailing member like me . . .'

Chapter 11

Talia and Yoyong

It was announced by four newspapers: two Spanish, one Filipino-Spanish and one American, which was then followed by the other newspapers that came out of Manila, even in the pages of the ones published in Tagalog. Although they did not come out simultaneously, and even though you could notice that those that followed got sentences and extracts from earlier news, all of them appeared to be an invitation card from Don Ramon Miranda.

And what was the invitation about?

Natalia Miranda and Honorio Madlang-Layon were going to get married in the afternoon on the forthcoming Saturday. It would be held at the cathedral, so the invitation was sent to prominent people living near the cathedral, all the way to the neighbourhood of Don Ramon.

It was already the middle of November.

The silliness of the newspapers came to the fore again. Aside from the letter of invitation from Don Ramon that blazed like lightning, the newspapers also featured letters that were flowery and dripping with sentiment. Indeed, there was a caveat at the bottom of the page that the readers could not attend the wedding on the basis of the invitation printed in the newspapers. However, the newspaper owners hoped they could attend; indeed, the invitation letters said that the event was open to the press, whose members could even enter the interiors of the house. Thus, there was no more need for individual invitations to be sent to everyone in the press. A general approval came in the wake of this sweet invitation, so that the members of the press dipped into their memories, and even consulted dictionaries to find the frothiest words, to be attached to the name of Don Ramon Miranda and the couple to be married.

For Don Ramon, they were deciding whether or not to use 'rich and landed', 'the wise investor', 'the adviser of Philippine capitalists', 'happy', 'honourable', 'noble', 'old bachelor', 'tireless Managing Director of The Progress', amongst others.

For Talia: beautiful, fragrant flower, demure, great, the elder of the two stars in the Miranda family of Santa Cruz . . .

For Yoyong: young and handsome, famous writer and legal expert, artistic and rising politician, the winnable lawyer and bright Professor of the Law, 'one of our dearest friends' . . .

The newspapers of Manila released a steam of their usual, boxed phrases announcing the wedding in the family of Don Ramon Miranda. They sounded like hired workers playing with drums and cymbals to announce a different show in the theatres.

The godfathers suggested by the young man's family were distinguished, and it included Commissioner W. The godmothers suggested by the young woman's family were distinguished as well, led by the rich widow of Lafuente. Don Ramon had wanted Señora Loleng to be one of them, but Talia thumbed it down.

The invitation and the announcements from Don Ramon could also not be missed in Delfin's newspaper. Everyone said, 'I'm coming to this wedding,' 'I'll join the Director,' 'I'll write the news myself.' Several of them kept on reading and re-reading the letter of invitation, but they did not read the names of *Natalia* and *Honorio*. Instead, they read Meni (for Filomena) and Delfin; snide remarks for a fellow worker whom they wanted to tease and whom they thought would be envious of the grand wedding of one of Don Ramon's daughters . . .

Loud laughter followed their readings of the names. All their gazes fell on Delfin, who just sat without speaking, and everyone continued with their mean remarks and taunts.

'I'll join Delfin,' one of them said. 'I've nothing to fear if I'm with him.'

'Were you also invited?' one of the directors asked Delfin.

'Me? I might even receive a kick from Don Ramon if I go.'

'And why?' someone asked in protest, 'you're going there as a member of the press, like all of us here. But if Don Ramon turned his back and you kept on pinching Meni from the first moment you see her there, then your father-in-law would indeed kick you.'

'Ssssshhh,' the director hissed in a joking manner, so the laughter subsided. 'Pinching is something we don't do here at work. Hey, go back to work.'

'But wait, dear Director, let us clarify who would attend the wedding.'

'Me, just me,' the Director said in a teasing tone.

'No, that can't be. All of us should attend.'

'Seang and Reynoso would be there, without a doubt,' one said happily.

'And those from Sampaloc?' added another. 'Oh, I would endlessly dance with either of the women.'

'From Sampaloc?' asked someone else, and followed this with laughter and a teasing look at the one who had spoken earlier, as if to say, 'Are they from Lardizabal?'

The earlier speaker understood this, and both of them burst into laughter.

'And without doubt, you would find there Julita, Maestra Ines and the whole family in Makapugay as well . . .'

'Oh, really? Then I'd want to dance with Julita.'

'I'll dance with Maestra Ines.'

'Well, you can be with Ines and be irritated,' another added.

'I'll dance with Meni!' said the director.

'Hey, I'll dance with her,' countered another.

'I'll dance with Meni in the two-steps,' added another.

'I'll dance the *waltz* with her.'

'And I'll dance with her when the following dances begin: the *rigodon de honor*, the valse, and the two-steps,' said the director.

And they all spoke together like a group of noisy Chinese. They were only numbered six, but the racket they made was impossible.

They were arguing about who would dance with Meni, even though it was still three days until the wedding and the dancing, on Saturday.

'And what would happen to Delfin?' asked one of them, finally, in defence, 'if we snatch Meni from him?'

'Delfin is a communist,' the Director said, upon seeing that Delfin was just smiling and keeping to himself. 'He won't complain when our *community* . . .'

'Hey, hey, my communism doesn't include that!' said Delfin, who could not contain his annoyance anymore. 'A woman isn't like a chicken, whom the whole public can peck at.'

'And why not?' asked someone else, 'true communism should be open to all. It can't be done in half-and-half, or even in pieces. In property, capital, intelligence, those whom you court, and even your wife . . .'

'Hey,' interrupted the director. 'The wife isn't included anymore. That kind of communism is only for barbarians, not for civilized people like Delfin and I, right? Delfin? I think only the two of us have the right to dance with Meni.'

'It's not right,' the four other workers said in unison. 'All of us! All of us!'

'All of you should just shut up!' Delfin said aloud. 'My nose is turning narrower . . . You don't even know if you can attend without a proper letter of invitation, yet you're already choosing your dance partners.'

'Okay, that's it,' the Director cut in. 'Go back to work. Let's talk about this later. It's already noon and nobody has written anything yet. Let me just write the news myself . . .'

The noise in the newsroom slowly ebbed. Like blacksmiths who had picked up their hammers and iron again, they returned to their respective anvils. The echoes of laughter were replaced by the scratching of ballpoint pens on paper. Someone would a make a noise, someone would whisper, someone would argue, someone would lapse into silence. Such a small thing had stirred them, yet the sharp points of their pens could wake up a country that had long been asleep, could banish the heavy burden from those who govern, could cause trouble to the whole of humankind. And that was the worth, whether expensive or cheap, of the hours that ticked by every day in the world of the newspapers.

* * *

Saturday was fast approaching.

The single women of Santa Cruz seemed as if they were getting married themselves, going by the preparations they were making for the wedding, choosing the gowns they would wear to the dance. They did not like clothes they had already worn. 'This dress is expensive and pretty, but I already wore it during the Saint Rosary. This dress and handkerchief have been seen before, during the feast day of Our Lady of Del Pilar. This color is now too common; that colour does not fit with this dress; that colour is ugly at night. The bride will wear white in church, light blue at home, and red during the dance. Therefore, we should not wear the same colours. We should have different colours, cuts and designs, so that we don't look too bad when compared to the bride and the other guests . . .' These were the thoughts that filled the minds of the single women of Santa Cruz who were Talia's friends, as well as those from Quiapo, Trozo and Binondo, who had received the invitation to the wedding. Those who had the means bought new dresses, while the others made do with adding new designs, new earrings, and other things that would give their dresses a sense of newness in the eyes of the other guests.

So they bought, sewed, measured and tried on dresses in a flurry at the houses of the single women, during the last four days before the wedding.

But amongst all of them, Isiang was the most anxious. She was accompanying Talia to the party in her honour on Saturday afternoon, and she would put on Talia's veil during the wedding. Martin Morales was Yoyong's best man—the pharmacist who loved Isiang, who bravely climbed and shook the plum tree near the springs of Antipolo. What great choices! Both of them had worked on this. Isiang planned to be the maid of honour to Talia, while Morales asked Yoyong if he could be the best man. They told each other that someone who put on the veil would one day have a veil put on her head as well . . .

Because of this, Señora Loleng, Isiang's mother, felt even prouder. Mother and daughter had roamed around the city, had been to the shops of Paris, Manila, Islas Filipinas, Ricart and Soler, La Bella Filipina, Nueva Siglo, Siglo XX and even the Almacen of Velasco, and upon reaching home and trying on the clothes, were still unhappy with them. Isiang had had three sets of clothes made, as if she had wanted the guests to mistake her for the bride herself. If confusion filled Talia and her sister, as well as their designers and dressmakers, the same confusion also filled the minds of Señora Loleng and her daughter with the sewing of their clothes for the wedding and the dance.

And how about the men? They were also preparing, what else: new shoes and new ties were enough for a single, old, black suit, which was fine, since the event would be held at night.

As Saturday approached, the lack of time deeply troubled those who had invited and those who had been invited. The anxiety about the preparations had reached even the cathedral on Saturday noon. What Miguel told Julia in the musical play, *No More Wound*, seemed apt: 'all the churches would be lighted, and the bell in the tower would be turned . . .'

* * *

Don Ramon summoned twenty-four male workers at The Progress on Friday: some would help in cleaning the house and decorating it as well as the garden, while the others would help in cooking and storing the food. Six women who were also working at the factory were asked to help with hanging the damasks and curtains, as well as with rolling out the different carpets. They were also asked to hang the sashes on the doors and the buntings from the windows, as well as put on the cloth covers on the chairs and draw the design on the platform. Two days were lost for them, Friday and Saturday. They would get their weekly salary for four days on the coming Monday, because Don Ramon never thought about having to pay out the salaries of more than 1,000 people on that Friday afternoon. They usually received their salary on a Saturday but Don Ramon told Don Filemon that the salaries should be given on the coming Monday, this time. 'My stomach, just endure this day,' the workers in the tobacco factory seemed to mutter to themselves, upon hearing the instructions of the owner of the factory. They had no work on a Saturday, but they had to help at the wedding of their patron's daughter. That was why the workers whom Don Ramon did not choose to help with the wedding just stayed home for two days, scratching their bellies.

Thanks to the twenty-four men and six women, along with the others already in the house of Don Ramon, its exteriors and interiors, visible from near and far, even if it was only Saturday noon, already looked like 'a palace in a kingdom in Albania', if we were to believe the plays of old. It could have been a palace, since it was indeed beautiful and grand. Plants grew in luxuriance in front and on its sides, very much like the vaunted gardens of princesses. However, it did not have a tower of seven tiers, since this country was prone to earthquakes.

Strung on the walls made of stone and iron were Japanese paper lanterns of such gorgeous colours, announcing to the people, even if they were still far away, that this was a place where a great celebration was going to be held. The Japanese paper lanterns also abounded in the gardens, the doors, and even in the space under the great house, hanging from windows and even behind the house. Just the Japanese paper lanterns must have already cost this wedding hundreds of pesos. It could have caused some improvement in the lot of the Filipinos if these paper lanterns that decorated feasts, made by the Chinese and Japanese, were instead crafted here. The money would have been made here and stayed here . . . But when would people like Don Ramon think like this?

The sellers of plants in Singalong and Pasay also had some relatives working at The Progress. They offered various flowers and plants, beautiful leaves and coconuts, palm and banyan trees, and other decorative plants and shrubs for the house, where the feast was going to be held. Many of these were offered but only a few were bought. When it came to the giving of gifts and currying of favours, the poor Filipinos could be compared to the rich who never suffered the pangs of hunger.

But it rained when afternoon came. The Japanese paper lanterns and other decorations outside the house got wet. But this did not dampen the liveliness of the feast. The couple who was about to be wed, their parents, witnesses, bridesmaids and best man, and many others, arrived in the cathedral when it was not yet five o'clock in the afternoon. The rain caught some of them as they made their way to the cathedral, where rites and rituals for the wedding of the rich would take place at five thirty. Some people were already waiting in the church, while others wended their way to the grand house.

Money ruled in the rites and rituals performed in the church. Some parts of the ceremonies were shortened or lengthened, but whatever happened, it still only boiled down to this: three priests, sacristans, those who lit the candles and held the small but brightly burning fireworks, brilliant lights on which much money had been spent with sheer abandon, expensive curtains and fresh flowers, thick carpets and smoke from the censer, bells, organ music, orchestra, songs, prayers, blessings, and other empty and useless rituals for the wedding to appear respectable and expensive . . .

'You, woman, do you take this man to be your lawfully wedded husband?'

'Yes, I do.'

'And how about you, man, do you take this woman to be your lawfully wedded wife?'

'Yes, I do.'

'Man, I am giving you a wife and not a slave.'

'Woman, you came from a man's rib, love him and follow him with all your heart . . .'

'May you both live together and live well . . .'

These and other things were spoken in Latin and Spanish, and thus was the grand wedding performed.

The carriage bearing the newlyweds led the convoy going home and it seemed to have descended from the clouds. It was pulled by two black horses with eyes the colour of charcoal and movement like that of kings, as they raised their feet and stretched their necks and trotted.

It was followed by the carriage bearing Señora Loleng and Isiang, a rockaway carriage with shining windows also pulled by a black horse with fur like that of a deer.

Next was the carriage of the godfather, Commissioner W, beside the carriage carrying Don Filemon.

It was followed by the carriage of Don Ramon, beside that of the godmother, the widow of Lafuente, which irritated Señora Loleng when their eyes met. Isiang did not want to be far away from the carriage of the newlyweds. Señora Loleng wanted their carriage to be near that of Don Ramon, so that she could see how he acted around the other godmother . . .

The carriage bearing the pharmacist Morales and Celso Bentus went hither and yon: it went ahead, then slowed down, moved beside another carriage, wanting to be near the carriage of Isiang, who kept on looking behind at them. But it could not insert itself in the path of the other carriages, because of the distinguished personages inside those carriages.

After this were fifteen other vehicles that were of mixed build: carriages pulled by horses, box-like vehicles drawn by a native pony, two automobiles bearing those who attended the wedding in church: men and women, most of them single; some people working in government; some businessmen and factory owners; friends either of Don Ramon or the newlyweds.

From the cathedral to the house in Santa Cruz, the whole entourage, when one looked at it the first time, resembled a cortege for the dead, but a cortege for someone who was rich. But this thought would be banished upon seeing the couple sitting inside the lead carriage as well as the expensive clothes of the women, none of whom wore the colour of mourning, and had not a trace of sadness on their faces.

* * *

While they sat together, Talia and Yoyong remembered no death: no grief, no horizon of the sky looming before them; no tears, no bitterness, no suffering, no thorns of life. Everyone was smiling, everyone looked fresh, everyone was fragrant, pleasant and good-looking. Honorio, who should have been used by now to the sight of a star falling from the sky, a partner in life and bearer of happiness, having experienced all of these before, now seemed new to the ways of love. He did not know what to say to Talia. And when he looked at the people staring at them, he seemed to see only earthworms, while he felt fortunate, indeed, and a thousand times happier because of this.

But it was more so with Talia. She knew that every young lady was filled with envy. She felt the swell of sentiments in the hearts of those who believed in the blessings of the sacrament that had been newly received by them with much faith. Pure soul, the wind blowing, fire of love, marbled hope, chest of iron, a being like water, silky presence, perfumed words, love and affection . . . Yoyong had everything!

* * *

Even before the first carriage could enter the gate, in the air had already floated a happy song from the Rizal Orchestra, which was waiting by the grand staircase of the house. From the windows, in the space under the house, on the stairway, inside the house, the friends of Talia and the friends of Yoyong—aside from the many guests already waiting in the house—welcomed the newly-weds and offered their sweetest and most profuse congratulations. Such happiness, such noise, heaps of gladness and rejoicing!

Some of the women in the gathering, after greeting Talia, began whispering to each other. They looked at her dress, made snide remarks about it and laughed amongst themselves.

They said, 'The Spanish-inspired dress doesn't look good on her. Even if she were wearing all silk, it would have been better if she wore a Filipino-inspired dress!'

'Why, Talia is a *mestiza*, a half-breed!' said another.

'What if she's a mestiza? She is only the granddaughter of a Spaniard, while I'm the daughter of one. But the Filipina-inspired dress really looks better for mestizas. If I get married, then I will no longer be able to wear something like that.'

On the other side of the living room, a flock of women, including Señora Loleng, who had just sat down, were praising Talia's beauty: the dress looked good on her, they said, because she was fair-skinned and tall and not too fat, with a high-bridged noise, thick eyebrows and hair done in a bun—the Spanish way.

In yet another gathering of women, the talk centred on whether the jewellery shimmering on Talia's fingers, arms and chest, neck and hair, were bought in Estrella del Norte and the others bought from Felix Ullman and Zafiro, and which of those were given by Yoyong as gifts.

Meanwhile, in the gathering of men, talk drifted from Honorio being a lawyer, his character traits and those of Talia, what the newlyweds must be thinking now, in the midst of so many guests. Some went to where Yoyong was sitting and whispered something which lead to a burst of laughter from both Yoyong and the guest, and the others would follow suit. These must be the usual jokes made at newlyweds . . .

And alongside all this laughter and talk, the orchestra kept on playing. The guests drifted in and out of the salon, they would sit down or stand up, like sticky and sweet delicacies made of coconut milk, brown sugar and glutinous rice, that was continuously being stirred. Many were just arriving, although it was already thirty minutes past six o'clock.

Meanwhile, Talia who was already getting dizzy from the heat, scanned the crowd and then went inside the room to change her clothes. Turing, her new sister-in-law, as well as her parents-in-law, helped her and fanned her while she walked.

But where was Meni? Where was the youngest sibling who should have met her and kissed her, hugged her and be filled with the same gladness that now filled her heart? Where was the Meni who had helped her with sewing the dress she would wear, who even helped her put on the dress before she left the house for the wedding; the Meni who was happy and teasing her saying, 'Talia, if the time comes for me to get married, I hope you will also help me.'

But where was she? She did not join them in church, and she did not welcome them back home, either. She was nowhere to be seen in the living room, nor in any of the rooms of the house. Talia did not really mind Meni's absence, because she was busy earlier, talking to the many guests and receiving the fragrance of their good wishes. And when Turing was helping her put on the dress, she said, 'Meni doesn't want to enter, she is there outside, weeping.'

It was as if a fist had hit Talia's chest. She just remembered that she still had a sister. But who had the right to feel bad and to cry? She, who had momentarily forgotten because of the newness of her marriage, or Meni, who did not even welcome her and wish her well since her father and her sisters had all agreed to her marrying Yoyong . . . In the scales of reflection, she decided that it must be her own fault. She immediately repented. Tears sprang to her eyes. She asked Turing to hurry up with taking off her jewellery. Then, when she was only wearing her dress, without any ornaments at all, she went through the doors of the two nearby rooms, without passing through the living room, and went straight to the kitchen of the house. Someone told her that Meni was in the bathroom. She went there . . .

And indeed, Meni sat on the white water tank, her feet resting on one of the three steps of the stairs, her head bowed low. She sat in front of one of the sealed doors, one elbow planted on one thigh, her eyes speaking only to herself, filled with sadness. Her face was washed with tears, not the tears brushed by Delfin's lips that night at the garden, but tears of love for a sister who would be separated from her from now on—even from the mat and the blanket they had once shared! Was she envious? Or was she filled with remorse? Was she anxious? Or was she filled with fear? Where must Delfin have been at that moment?

'Meni!' Talia called out as she poked her head inside and slowly opened the door. Her voice was tender yet sad, filled with wonder at what happened to her sister, whom she had finally found.

The one who was called was surprised. She raised her head. It was Talia! She ran to her sister and asked, 'Why are you here? Why are you sad at my coming?'

Meni could not speak clearly. Her voice was choked in her throat as she embraced Talia, her heart filled with confusion.

'Why do you feel bad?' continued Talia. 'Don't all of us like Yoyong? You were even the one who often told me that Yoyong was kind and you would be comfortable with him if ever I got married to him, and that even Father as well as our other siblings would like him.'

'Yes, but . . .' and Meni began to cry again. Through this, she seemed to show that she could not avoid feeling sad. She liked Yoyong for her sister, but Talia was tied to her as if by an umbilical cord; and yet, it was Yoyong who would steal her and be with her from now on, night and day.

'If I only knew,' Talia said, now feeling sad herself, 'that in the end you would not like me to marry Yoyong, even if he courted me with so much patience, I would not have given him my word and my promise of love.'

'How about me, Talia? I would now be alone here.'

'We won't leave this place. You've nothing to worry about.'

'You'll leave later on. Yoyong has a house of his own.'

'So what? We'll only leave after you've gotten married.'

'You're making fun of me!' Meni said in a hurt tone. 'Will Father be lax with me, now that you're married?'

'But what if it's your time to get married?'

'Oh . . . that time won't come. Father said that I'll join him on a visit to Japan, after you were married.'

'So what? You'll also come back here. If Delfin cannot follow you, don't worry, I'll watch over him. You can send to me your letters for him and I'll bring the letters to him.'

Meni had not yet heard her sister speak like this before. Talia knew that Delfin was Meni's lover. She had read some of Delfin's letters to her, but these were the ones written before the rendezvous in the garden of their house. She was also aware of her father's terrible anger toward the relationship, and this must have caused her to feel some displeasure as well, at first. But they were sisters, both single, and they liked each other immensely. So Talia, even though she was not in complete agreement with her sister's relationship with Delfin, just let her be in the same manner that Meni did not interfere in her relationship with Yoyong. But now she felt the sense of isolation and sadness that enveloped her sister. While at first she had doubted her sister's words, she now knew that Meni was sincere in her offer of help.

Just at the moment when their hearts were calming down, Yoyong, Turing, Isiang and the others arrived. They must have sensed what was happening and so they followed suit. There they all clustered together, with Meni's eyes still red from crying, and so they all cheered her up and brought her inside, even to the point of almost carrying her.

The discomfort and tears shed between the sisters spread like wind inside the whole house. Those inside the salon exchanged whispers and snide remarks, some of which were shallow and the others, deep. But like all things, this also came to pass. Meni was already happy when she went out into the salon. The bright light only showed a few traces of the sadness that had clouded her face, moments before. One by one, those present whispered to each other about the vast difference between the beauty of Meni and Talia. And indeed, this was true. All of Talia's dresses were cut as if they were for a matron—not just her wedding dress but also her house dresses. Word got around that this was what Señora Loleng and Don Ramon had wanted . . .

So instead of adding to her beauty, her clothes just diminished it. For her part, Meni wore dresses inspired by the native Tagalogs; her dress was pleasant to the eye, it was cut well, and did not clash with the colour of her skin. From the way the two sisters dressed up that day, the female guests saw how funny and ugly it was to borrow clothes from other lands, and how beautiful it was to wear dresses that belonged to one's own people. They learnt that not all that was good in Europe or the United States should be borrowed and imitated by the Filipinos. Whether in clothes or character traits, we should only borrow those elements that would not destroy what was beautiful in our own country and race. In other words, those that would not warp or destroy the very soul of the native Tagalogs . . .

The men shook Meni's hands, while the women either shook her hand or kissed her cheek, as if she were the one who had just got married. The guests were happy to see her, and many of them had seen her beautiful face for the first time.

Peping Serrallo was also there, and while in the company of his friends, Morales, Bentus and a few others, was dumbstruck at the sight of Meni's beauty. Bentus flicked him on the ear. 'Hey! An ill wind might blow your eyes and render you cross-eyed.'

But Peping just ignored the sharp words. He just touched his newly flicked ear but did not take his eyes off Meni. He had written to her several times, but his letters were ignored. When Meni smiled at something that her new sister-in-law had whispered to her, Peping talked to Bentus in Spanish. '*Chico, mira me adorada tormente: es una verdadera angel caida del Eden . . .*'

Bentus and Morales almost burst out into laughter upon hearing Peping declare that his heart was being tormented by an angel from the Garden of Eden.

'My friend, you cannot do anything anymore. Meni's tormented heart now belongs to a newspaperman,' Morales teased him in a soft voice.

'Who? Delfin?' And he let loose a laughter filled insult, believing himself superior to Delfin.

Meanwhile, the sounds of plates clattering and spoons and forks tinkling rose outside as dinner was prepared, while in the salon, beer and other drinks were already being served by hovering waiters. This followed the new custom amongst the Filipinos, not only amongst the rich but also amongst the poor, that beer, ice cream and different kinds of pasta should be served at feasts and even at small gatherings. Oh, beer that had crossed over to the modern times!

Don Ramon always stayed in the company of the commissioner, who sat between him and Don Filemon. In front of them sat the widow of Lafuente and the newly arrived Señora Loleng. Don Ramon invited all of them, especially the members of the press, to join him in his library that contained the many presents for the newlyweds. Many of them followed suit, to admire the wealth added to the already wealthy.

The room was big. Meni had the key to the room and she opened it. There were three beautiful shelves, taller than a human being and wider than an arm's span and a half. They contained various books, some of which Don Ramon had inherited from the Spaniards, who had died here in the Philippines; the others were books he had read at the College of Saint John of Letran and at the university in Spain, when he was still interested in taking up Medicine. The other books were bought from his various trips to Europe, while others were bought in Manila, including the new novels that were beginning to be popular and sold at the club, which had just closed because the members had quarreled amongst themselves, thus leading to the sale of the books. In the middle stood two long tables and near the windows sat two round tables, covered with tablecloths made of white silk.

If Señora Loleng were to be believed, all the gifts to the newlyweds that were contained in the library must be worth around 100,000 pesos! But if we parse this statement, it would be more likely that the gifts must be worth around 50,000 pesos.

And who gave these gifts? Don Ramon was Don Ramon, and wealth begot wealth. He had many friends in the whole of Manila—money begot money, and gifts begot gifts. Don Ramon loaned money to friends and also gave lavish gifts to their events. Yoyong and Talia also had their fair share of friends. And the fact that their godfather was the commissioner himself and their godmother the widow of Lafuente, ensured that the gifts from the guests would indeed be expensive.

The crows gaped at and admired all the gifts. But did anybody amongst them, even one person, think that the room that they had entered at that moment had no value except as a mere container of sleeping wealth hoarded due to the ill ways of the rich?

* * *

In the programme that Don Ramon had prepared, the *rigodon de honor*, the traditional formal dance, would be danced after everyone had had dinner. With one signal from him, the orchestra segued into music. Fleas seemed to have crawled on the backs and thighs of the men, and they looked like earthworms squirming in boiled rice with anchovies, as they stood up from their seats and went nearer to the women!

The early birds who already had their eye on their Dulcinea amongst the ladies did not join anymore the rush of men standing up from their seats. They just exchanged sticky looks with the women they liked, or winked at them, and they were all set, 'Be prepared, because this will be a conquest!' But those who had no initiative were seemingly roused from their sleep when the orchestra began to play. They darted looks in different directions. Some of the beautiful women were also choosy; some of them stood up in the middle of the salon, and from there, the men coming looked like an invading force looking for a route to reach them faster. And when they reached the women, the men looked like bees buzzing as they spoke to them. If the women liked them, they let the men take them by the right hand to start dancing, and if they did not like the men, they invented all sorts of excuses. Thus, the act of choosing a partner became somewhat coarse, since Don Ramon forgot to ask his guests to get tickets since there was going to be dancing after the dinner.

The salon was indeed grand. The round tables were filled with such fragrant flowers, thin and shimmering conch shells and other items from the sea, as well as albums pushed to the sides to make the space even bigger. It was so spacious that the dancers could be divided into two groups, but our attention should be fixed on the group where the newlyweds belonged. This group was composed of eight pairs. It was led by no less than Don Ramon, whose hand was draped around the shoulders of the willing widow of Lafuente; they were in front of Meni who was in the company of the imperious Commissioner. Amongst those in the lead were Yoyong and Talia, in front of whom were Turing and Simeon (a friend of Turing whom we did not see at the Antipolo springs). On the sides were Dr Alejo Bravo and Julita (the woman from San Miguel), in front of the mestiza were Generosa de Vera and the lawyer Barbaro San Benito (a friend of Yoyong's), as well as the teacher Mr Morgue and Miss Ines, who were in front of Señora Loleng.

When she realized that she was merely placed on the side, Señora Loleng glared at the rich widow of Lafuente, who had been laughing ever since she was still in the carriage at the cathedral. She was also horrified to see the woman from San Miguel, who she had long wanted to shame. And in front of her was a man whose long neck resembled that of a long-legged bird, as well as a Miss Filipina who did not want to speak in Spanish and Tagalog, but only in English. She would be embraced by this woman's old husband, who had grown antique from dancing this stupid ball dance. Oh, angry gods!

And these were not the only words that Señora Loleng wanted to expel from her heart and her throat. If only she could become the lead star in a traditional play, she would have uttered: 'Why, dear heavens! Why breathe life to this unhappy existence of mine? Why not just kill all the traitors and scoundrels in our midst?' Señora Loleng felt all of these emotions at the beginning of the dance, so she just went through the motions of the dance and called to her daughter, Isiang, to replace her in the second part of the dance. But Isiang refused, complaining about the tightness of her new pair of shoes. So Señora Loleng had no choice but to finish the second part until the chain of dancers became confused.

To calm her feelings at the people and the dance that went haywire, Señora Loleng just entered the room where the women changed their clothes; she was looking for her daughter, who was not there. Somebody told her that her daughter went outside to do something, entering the rooms that Talia had entered earlier to go to Meni. Why did she have to go outside when the changing room already had everything that the women needed?

So Señora Loleng followed the route earlier taken by Talia. She was beginning to think that her daughter must be doing something bad outside. She thought of Morales. She went back through one door and checked if he was part of the men in the salon who had not yet danced. But he was not there, as well as in the other groups. *These traitors! Where are they?* The hair on the skin and nape of Señora Loleng stood on their ends as they had never done before. She had earlier detected something in the acts and the sticky looks between the two. She had scolded her daughter more than once for her indecent treatment of her chemist suitor. She knew that they were in love, that was why he was allowed to visit their house and was treated well. But to do this in another person's house—leaving behind many people inside and vanishing without asking permission, this was unacceptable behavior, even for an only child.

The mother's doubts were proven true. She first went to the bathroom where Meni was earlier seen but Isiang was not there. She went to the stone stairs of the kitchen and heard people whispering on the terrace. Her blood began to boil. It was a dark place, with hardly any light at all. Only the tails of light from the kitchen and the bathroom went through the doors and illuminated the dark terrace and the stairs. There were still pots of flowering plants that were not brought down to decorate the stone stairs and the interiors of the house. There was a space there filled with flowers and leaves where people could only be discovered by someone who had suspicions.

'Isiang? Isiang?' the mother called out rapidly in the semi-darkness.

There was no answer. But the mother saw someone moving in the shadows.

'Dionisia? Dionisia?'

'Yes, mother?'

At the sound of her daughter's voice, Señora Loleng drew nearer and shouted, her voice filled with fury.

'What are you two doing here? And what are you doing here, young woman?'

She pinched her daughter, who could not voice her pained protest because of shame and surprise. She wanted to shrink into the corner of the terrace and hide behind the potted plants, but her mother had already lunged at her. She was caught by the hair and afraid that the bun that took her half a day to fix would be ruined, she had stood up. As she was standing up, she hit a potted plant that fell and crashed into the unused well below that was covered by a plank of wood, following the orders of the sanitation authorities, who said that such wells might be sources of microbes.

Morales did not know where to hide, and he also did not want to abandon Isiang to her mother's fury. He tried to intervene and calm the old woman down. But as the woman was straightening herself up, Isiang said that 'I only asked him to help me pick some flowers!' Upon hearing this, the mother faced Morales.

'You shameless man!' she shouted. 'Your education is wasted on both of you.'

'Please don't shout, Mother,' Isiang pleaded.

'Huh? So now you are ashamed?'

'Señora Loleng,' Morales slowly said, 'I'm the one who's at fault. I followed her here without her knowledge. Please don't create a scene here. You can do that in your house and you may even kill me if you want!'

'And you feel shame now?' Señora Loleng was shouting and did not care anymore if people could hear her.

'Mother, please,' Isiang said in a gentle voice, although she was almost in tears.

'He! You shameless woman!' And she aimed a slap at her daughter. Her palm hit the young woman's earlobes and she fell on the tiled floor. Then Señora Loleng faced Morales again and hit him repeatedly.

Her loud voice and the sound of her fists hitting Morales caught the attention of the people coming and going into the kitchen, as well as that of the two cooks. Someone ran to Don Ramon and Talia to inform them of the trouble on the terrace.

Don Ramon was still able to hear the words of Señora Loleng. 'Is that what you would do to us in return for our kindness, you shameless man? And you are even a chemist!'

'What's happening, Loleng?' Don Ramon said even while he was still afar.

'Don't meddle here!' she said. 'You deal with your partners there and leave us here!'

The words of a guest to the owner of the house! However, the servants of the house already considered Señora Loleng as part of the household.

Don Ramon was able to calm her down. He asked someone to bring Isiang inside, and he scolded Martin Morales, berating him for having no respect for the owner of the house who had invited him to a party, and drove him out like a person of no importance. He was asked to take the stone stairs from the kitchen itself, and not the stairs in front of the grand house.

Morales descended the stairs without even remembering to get his hat. Like someone bitten by a snake, he just went downstairs, entered the space under the house and left through the door that opened onto the street.

Meanwhile, upstairs and amongst the people working outside, what they saw when the mother discovered her daughter's rendezvous with her suitor was like honey and milk of coconut. When Meni, Don Filemon, Yoyong and few others were following Don Ramon and Talia, it was the time when Isiang and Morales had just walked down the stairs. But could something like this be hidden? There were just too many witnesses! The river would rather clog, because its rising could not be controlled. A whisper was louder than a scream. And with this, the whispers outside and the furrowed brows of those who had entered, even if Isiang had already gone to the room with Meni, also entered the ears and came to the knowledge of the other guests.

'What an early dessert!' some people said.

'After all, they are young,' said the others in Spanish.

The mythical figure of Mandarangan seemed to have sat on the nape of Don Filemon when he heard all of this. He rushed downstairs and chased Morales. But the young man had already vanished. He was already outside; like a stunned bird, he sat in a corner, his head bowed low.

All gladness and grief must pass, especially in celebrations like these, in which everything was new, when everyone wanted to be noticed and become the apple of everyone's eyes. Moreover, it was already dinner time: many stomachs were already growling and people were already licking their chops. What happened between Isiang and Morales was soon forgotten by many, while a few others, who were eating later, continued whispering about what had happened and were even laughing about it.

Señora Loleng and Isiang were not able to have dinner. They just wanted to reach their own house. While the guests were having dinner, the mother and daughter just let Meni and Turing calm them down. Then later, they went downstairs and left, without even saying goodbye to Don Filemon.

Felipe was not there while all of these things were happening, even though he was a member of the household.

But he was not missing. Don Ramon had asked him to fetch Marcela from Concordia College that afternoon. But she was not able to join him, for she was ill. Beside this, she also did not know how to dance, and it would be such an embarrassment to turn down an offer to dance.

Felipe invited Delfin to join him in fetching Marcela, but his friend refused. He was worried that his wife-to-be might hear about it. Felipe just laughed when he heard Delfin's refusal. He was aware that Sela had been the source of Meni's jealousy. As for himself, Felipe also told Delfin: 'Your refusal to join me now and in the future shows that you're just avoiding to be in the presence of the young and beautiful Sela.'

From Concordia, Felipe went to Delfin again, to discuss the reasons why he did not join him. They also talked about why Felipe's mother and father could not leave that day and that was why they had just had their lavish gift and financial contribution to the wedding ceremony sent, as proof of their kinship even from afar. Felipe also asked his friend to attend the wedding celebration and not mind Don Ramon anymore. There would be many guests there, including the people from the newspaper, and it would have been improbable his presence would still have been noticed.

But Delfin flatly refused. Meni, who had also asked him to attend the wedding celebration earlier, had now told him just to skip it. During the last conversation between Don Ramon and Don Filemon regarding the invitations sent to the newspapers, Don Filemon had said the name of Delfin in a degrading manner, while talking about the newspapermen of *New Day*. Delfin just endured everything in silence. His mind was tormented by the wedding celebration, the petal-like softness of Meni's hands that would touch the arms or drape over the shoulders of another man dancing with her. A pinch of envy and a pinch of jealousy. And then why would he say that only women suffered from jealousy?

Felipe also was home alone in the house. It was already evening, and the newlyweds were already there when he arrived. He informed Don Ramon of the reasons why Sela could not join them. Then he spent thirty minutes looking at the good-looking people assembled in the salon, seeing the heaps of lavish gifts and offerings, shaking the hands of a few people—only a few, since a mere newspaperman like Felipe could not have many friends in such rich and distinguished company—and after coming inside and going outside the house, climbing the stairs and going back under the house, he finally retired to his own space, while above him, the newlyweds and the guests were enjoying a feast. Up there were people like him who were serving at the dinner table, who could not even close their eyes during the whole night of the celebration. How many days of tiredness and how many nights of sleeplessness would they endure, all for the wedding of the lord's family?

He sat for a while on a wooden chair that was the only furniture in his place. Then he unrolled his mat over a piece of plywood and lay on it. But he was filled with anxiety while his body lay on the mat. So he sat up and decided to shut the door so that he would be in complete isolation and there would be complete silence. Should he turn off the light? Not right now, he was not sleepy anyway. And in the light of that old gas lamp on the table, one could read one great lesson in life, a sweet smile of the future that he was waiting for, an invitation for him to reflect on the explosion of joy upstairs, while he was there under the house, the root cause of it all—at the gap between his beliefs and character traits, relative to the character traits of those who were heedlessly wasting money upstairs.

He could not abide by what was happening. He could not understand how thousands of pesos just fly when the rich get married and how not even a single peso is there for the poor who were dying.

In his mind drifted again the thoughts of Tentay and her poor family, especially during those days when Mang Andoy lay dying. Again and again in his mind, he saw the looks, the shapes and acts of Tentay's brothers when he offered them food; the halting way that Aling Tere ate, not thinking of her own nourishment but that of the baby that she was nursing; Tentay's tears streaming down her face when she had neither soup nor rice broth to offer to her father—all of these were like sad flowers threaded together that reminded him of the smell of a corpse, of a house, of a poor and broken life . . .

Meanwhile, upstairs, in the house where he lived, at that very moment, people were not quarreling over morsels of rice; there was no Teresa feeding herself to extend the life of her baby, there was no Tentay weeping because she could not offer comfort to a dying father, no sadness, no life filled with thorns . . . Everything was in excess, everything was happiness, even grief and strife were happiness still, all the food delicious, all the decorations beautiful, everything was sheer abundance and luxuriance! All created by Capital!

But why? From whence did the difference between one and the other come from, when everyone was a human being who had a right to live in comfort?

His reflections dove even deeper. He tried reaching the very roots and reasons for the differences between people's lives: of the wealthy and the poor, of the powerful and those without power, of those who command and those who follow, of the lord and the slave, nobility and servility. . . and in his mind returned the debate that had flamed between Don Ramon and Delfin in Antipolo. He believed, deeper in his heart, the reasoning given by Delfin. The clarity of Delfin's thoughts, the proof found in the books that Delfin had read regarding how the rich and the poor lived in other countries, and the truths shown in the lives of the poor and their children as seen in Mang Andoy and the lives of the rich like Don Ramon, Don Filemon, and Captain Loloy, who was his father. All of these cohered inside him, stoking his hatred for the wretched condition of humankind and the way the Philippines was governed.

Unlike Delfin, Felipe was just beginning to reflect on the human condition. He did not believe that we should probe the very roots of what ailed the country, look for the nits that cause the wounds of the poor to fester. It was enough for him to see and hear the lamentations of the poor, not just in the Philippines but elsewhere, to drive him to think of ways to heal the conditions in the shortest time possible. And these solutions, in Felipe's rash mind, should not be slow but sudden: cut the core or pull the roots that cause the harmful plant to grow; slash the young bamboo shoots of cruelty that harm one's growth; banish those who are cruel and oppressive, so that they would not infect others and mutate; bring down the hierarchy so that everyone would be on equal footing, equal in class and ways of life. He knew that some people were born in the mountains and forests, while others were born in the plains or beside the sea. Everyone would have his or her own characteristics, skin colour, height and shape. But these differences should not detract from their basic humanity. His wide readings and keen observation of things that delineated people's differences proved that poverty was not natural for human beings; they did not come with it when they born, but were made up by people themselves—the bitter fruits of those who governed the country.

Who was born not naked? Who was born with a ring shimmering on his finger? Who was born already rich and powerful, or powerless and poor, already owning land and a house, and other kinds of properties? Not a single one. They only acquired this after birth. But how? And here came the riddles and rot of society, rottenness that led only to more rot, heaped on the heads of the weak and the poor, the smell of it all festering in the whole world. That was why the socialists, especially the anarchists, wanted a world where people would be well-fed and clean, with enough weight and solidity of character. And this could come only if we cure the rot, according to the socialists, and if we throw away the rot, according to the anarchists . . . Felipe preferred to discard the rot and not just to heal it, because according to him, even if what is rotten is cured, it would still be rotten: later it would just infect other people with its weakness and smell.

His reflections just went deeper and deeper. In his mind's eye, he recalled the hard and similar truths expressed by Kropotkine, whose books he had read, especially *The Conquest of the World*, as well as Juan Grave's *The Future Society* and *The Moribund Society*, Sebastian Faure's *Universal Sadness*, J. Proudhon's *La Proprieda es un robo*, Karl Marx's *Das Kapital*, Eliseo Reclus's *Evolution and Revolution*, Bakounins's *God and State*, Tolstoy's *Resurrection*, amongst many anarchists who had written about society's rot, as seen in governance, the laws, capital, labour, inheritance, property, warfare and all the other benefits that accrued only to a few people in society. At that very moment, he remembered everything that he had read from all those books, which he bought at such great cost to him, considering his penury.

This was the flame of his thoughts. He had always been passionate about the human condition. Delfin also knew about corruption and felt passionately against it, but cold reason also told him that there was still goodness remaining and people should be saved. In his mind, only when you weigh both sides of the issue could you see an idea grow and bear fruit in the right time, and according to the scheme of things.

Felipe was wallowing in his thoughts. He could barely feel what was happening upstairs. His thoughts seemed to have led to dreams. Outside, dinner was already finished. The guests had entered the salon again and rushed to the dance floor for an all-night celebration. The orchestra and the piano hardly paused from playing, as well as the sound of voices singing. Some guests who could not fight off their sleepiness anymore began to leave. All of these things happened without intruding upon the stream of his thoughts, until the end, when he forgot and fell asleep, sinking deeper amidst the images of the life he was living, and when he woke up, it was already morning, and the sun was at its zenith in the sky.

It was very quiet upstairs, as if nothing had happened the night before. The echoes of music playing and voices raised into song were gone, as well as the shuffle of feet and laughter ringing. The feast was finished. The newlyweds were in deep sleep, entwined in each other's arms.

Chapter 12

The Bitterness of Captain Loloy

At midday on December 7—the day before the Feast of the Immaculate Conception, the patroness of Concordia—Captain Loloy left for Manila. He took with him a young man and a young woman, and he went straight to the guest house of his friend, Don Ramon.

Just like before, it was not Felipe whom Captain Loloy looked for upon arriving, but his son's godfather at confirmation. He would ask him about what his hard-headed, disobedient son had been up to. If the father and son had a chance to talk, it would be brief, and it would be a miracle if it were not full of curse words that Felipe would bitterly remember. Captain Loloy was not quite over his disappointment with the boy, whom he expected would succeed him in managing his vast wealth.

But Don Ramon was not at the guest house. He could have been at the factory, the house of Don Filemon, The Progress, the house of the young woman from San Miguel, or at a hotel with some friends. It was only Meni and Talia, both taking their siestas, whom Captain Loloy caught at the house. His other friend, Attorney Madlang-Layon, had left that morning for a trial at a provincial court in Pampanga.

A servant girl informed Talia and she hurriedly wore a kimono before peeking through the door. She recognized Captain Loloy seated in the living room, cooling himself with a Japanese fan.

'It's you, sir!' Talia greeted while peering through the door.

'Why, Talia!' Captain Loloy responded. 'Where's your father?'

'He's not here, sir. He took his lunch out.'

'Oh no! What about Yoyong?'

'He's in Pampanga.'

'In that case, just continue resting,' said Captain Loloy.

'Please take a rest, too. You must be tired. Have you had lunch?'

'Yes, on the ship.'

Talia, before retreating into her room to sleep, called for a manservant and requested him to prepare a room where Captain Loloy could rest.

Meni was asleep in a room near Talia's.

Both of them did not see Captain Loloy later that afternoon. He left a message that he had gone to Concordia College. He told one of the servants to tell Felipe upon arrival to wait for him.

Felipe, from the press, typically went to San Lazaro to check whether there was a meeting that he and Delfin could attend. That afternoon, he went straight home, although he only passed through his rental room to get something. No one noticed him and no one was able to tell him that his father was around.

He was soon back on the street. He would usually reach San Lazaro at sunset and would usually hear a conversation between Tentay and her mother. The daughter would be sewing something on the machine that Felipe had saved up for, out of the small sums that his mother sent to him. The conversation would be about him.

'There's nothing more to ask of him, by the way he presents himself. I thought that Father liked him because of that, not the money of his family.'

'And your siblings agree with you,' Aling Teresa replied. 'All I can say is that you must take care of your body. Whatever I've done to care for you won't matter if you don't care for yourself. Our purity is all we have. If you give yourself too early, the man might show his true self. He won't be worshipping you then, but he'll be only worshipping himself.'

'Felipe has never spoken about that.'

'Don't trust just like that. A man is a man, and we are forever women. We may be firm at times, but we turn into rags in the face of love. Any refusal can be softened by a promise.'

The sewing machine started rumbling again.

Felipe worried that he might be noticed. He looked around and peeked into the window. He noticed Tentay seated on the floor with the sewing machine, and Aling Teresa also sat leaning on the wall made of bamboo strips. He hesitated to go in right away for fear of being seen and caught eavesdropping on their conversation. But he also did not want to miss out on the conversation. He might learn how to live with their family from what he would hear.

'A man, after getting what he wants from a woman, can easily look for reasons to leave us. If he sees another man looking at you, or notices a bad action, he finds a harmless letter for you from someone else, or a handkerchief or another object, he'd argue with you until you fight and he makes that his reason for leaving you. They turn the tables around when they find someone new. When a problem arises because of your relationship with Felipe owing to this, there would be no family worse off than ours. You might as well be careful with your father's words because Andoy will just suffer more in the afterlife if he sees that your purity has been soiled.'

There was silence between mother and daughter, as if they were about to pray.

Then Tentay spoke. 'Felipe really hasn't done anything like that, or spoken about it. I think he'll behave properly with our family, although I wonder about his parents. His mother and father are high up there in the social classes and his sister is also used to luxury. Sometimes, I wonder about following father's last reminders. When Felipe is here, we talk about the customs that are observed for mourning and Lent, but I can't help but think of his parents. Won't he be a chip off the old block? And shouldn't someone like him marry someone of his own stature?'

'How can you say that? You haven't met his family yet.'

'One of Felipe's officemates told me that they only mingle with their kind. What if they find out that someone of our stature will marry their son?'

In the ensuing silence, Felipe moved away from the house and then walked back, coughing to indicate that he just arrived.

He paid his respects to Aling Teresa, then said, 'The night has caught up with your sewing!'

'This handkerchief is a rush job,' she replied.

Aling Teresa called out for Lucio. She asked her future son-in-law, 'Isn't Lucio in the fields?'

Mother and daughter looked at each other, possibly thinking that Lucio and Victor should play in front of the house so that they can warn them that Felipe was coming.

Tentay said, 'They might be playing with the ball that the Americans had introduced.'

'They don't get tired of playing games,' the mother sighed.

Felipe wasn't sure if he was going to be let into the house.

'Why, come in and sit,' the mother said.

The three of them helped out with putting things in order, while Amando played with the youngest one, Huleng.

The sun had already set behind the mountains.

* * *

That night, Tentay and Felipe spoke for a long time until dinner caught up with the family. The two of them said that they would follow.

'Why do you look sad?' asked Felipe.

'Me, sad? You're the one I'm paying attention to.'

'Just checking if you remember your father's reminder to you.'

Tentay's heart seemed to have been pierced by a lance.

'Why are you asking that, Ipeng? Don't you know that the memory you bring up is bitter for me?'

'I'm just joking, Tentay! I'm sorry. It's just that that memory keeps on coming up in my mind.'

'Isn't it the same case with me? I still wouldn't bring it up like you do, out of respect for the promise that I'd made to my father and to you!'

Felipe fell silent.

'Will you ever ask about that again?'

'No,' promised the man.

'Really?'

'Promise.'

'What time did you leave the press?' Tentay asked with a smile.

'Around 5 P.M.'

'Why did you arrive just now?'

'I dropped by the house.'

'The house?'

'Why, where else?'

Tentay gave Felipe a wondering look. He replied with a naughty smile.

'Is it true that you didn't see Lucio by the door?'

'That's what I said. Did you ask him to be on the lookout?'

'Yes. You might drop by the house of the pretty neighbors . . .'

This bantering continued until after dinner, when the rest of the family had already joined them. As usual, they played several card games. Lucio already knew how to play, and even to cheat! He teamed up with his mother, with Tentay and Felipe on the other side.

They played until midnight, without the two noticing their hunger. Anyway, there were no classes because of the Feast of the Immaculate Conception on the next day.

When Felipe went home, the gate was already locked. As usual, he just climbed up the fence.

Ah, the new man's life.

* * *

Felipe lighted a match after entering a hallway. He saw three people snoring. He recognized the one lying down without a mat on the floor: Gudyo, one of their manservants in the province.

The first match ran out, so Felipe lighted another one. The two woke up and were surprised to see Felipe. They woke Gudyo up by rocking his shoulders.

'You're here!' Felipe said. 'Who's with you?'

'Felipe!' Gudyo said groggily. 'I'm with the captain.'

'Father?'

'Yes, and Andang as well.'

'The two of you, are you with Gudyo?'

'They'll pick up Sela today, not on Christmas.'

'And Mother?'

'She was left behind in the province.'

'What time did you get here?'

'Late in the morning, we took the boat.'

'Early today? But I didn't see you early in the afternoon.'

'We were probably upstairs. Captain went to Concordia College. He asked us to wait for you and tell you to wait for him. That's why I fell asleep here.'

'Is Sela already here?'

'Not yet. It's the Feast of the Immaculate Conception at the college tomorrow. I think we'll take our return trip on Saturday.'

'What did Father say when he saw that I was out?'

'He was upset, wondering where you were. He and Don Ramon spoke loudly upstairs. I think he told your father that you were courting someone in Dulumbayan.'

'You heard that?'

'Yes, while they were having dinner. Don Ramon said that you were courting a beggar, that's why your father was so angry. It seems that there were more things said about you . . .'

Felipe was not able to speak right away. *Beggar?!* 'Are you sure that's what he said?'

'Yes. Don Ramon was laughing as he said it, and the captain was not able to answer . . .'

'Ah! Didn't they even think that 'beggar' is someone who has suffered and has been aggrieved, someone has a pure heart and a sense of honour?'

Gudyo was stunned at what Felipe had said. From the time he was little, when he started to live at Captain Loloy's to replace a brother of his who had passed away, he already had a debt of 200 pesos. He thought that he would always be in debt to the man until death . . .

'Oh, son of slaves! When will I be able to return to you the freedom that my father took from you?'

Gudyo could not speak at all.

'Why did Father ask you keep an eye out for me?'

'I don't know.'

The two of them agreed to go to sleep. Gudyo was snoring again soon after, while Felipe took a moment, cradled by his doubts into sleep until morning came.

* * *

Captain Loloy woke up early, before everyone else in the house.

After waking up, he went into the living room and took a seat while finishing a cigarette. After this, he went down to the first floor to see if his son was in his room. He pushed the door open and there the son was, awake and writing at his desk. Only Gudyo was with him, still lying down. The other two were already upstairs. One was wiping the floor while the other was helping prepare Don Ramon's clothes for the day.

'Felipe, come here.'

Felipe, stunned, turned around. He approached his father like an accused approaching a judge.

'What time did you get here?'

'11 P.M., I think.'

'And where were you for most of the night?'

'I got carried away . . . playing card games at a friend's house.'

'A friend! And why, are you still taking English lessons? You told your mother that you'd go to night school.'

The father noticed the boy's hesitation.

'How good you are!' he continued when is son could not say anything. 'You've lived up to the image of the shameless one, and still you treat us like fools. It would have been better for you to die than to shame our family. I could have disowned you. If others asked about where you were, I could just say that you died here in Manila. Go! Marry that beggar's daughter. Tell our townsfolk about what you've really learnt here: you'd rather bring home another mouth to feed instead of studying! And you brought shame to this house where you live. One day, I'll be forced to bring you to heel. Even God won't be able to blame me if I exercised my authority as a parent.'

Felipe could not say anything. His good manners prevented him from answering back. He was very upset about Don Ramon's accusation that the woman he loved was a beggar. Yes, they did borrow money and are sometimes at the point of begging for food, but it was not their fault. They were not like those who blatantly ravage all available resources for their own benefit, taking even the workers' very skin. But how could he tell his father this?

'Tell me, what do you intend to make out of your life with that?'

'Nothing,' Felipe was barely able to say.

'What do you mean, nothing? Do you just plan to board here for the rest of your life? Oh God, why did you give me a shameless son?'

Felipe refrained from saying anything more. Captain Loloy eventually took pity on his son. The father, seeing how big he was, noticed how his son had made himself small. There was no other way but to take Felipe out of this place. He found out from Don Ramon that his son was fond of going out with friends who teach him crazy ideas of socialism and anarchism. These words that ended with '-isms', Captain Loloy barely understood. But he associated anarchism, thanks to what he had heard, with the idea of killing a president. He eventually decided to take his son home, so that under his watchful eye, his good manners could be restored as well as his sense of hard work; so that later, he might find someone to marry who belonged to the same social class as them.

Captain Loloy and Don Ramon had kept the plan to themselves, not wanting to tell Felipe right away. The father lowered his temper and refrained from cursing.

'Well, we'll go to the college after breakfast, and we'll watch the procession of the Immaculate Conception. Marcela will be all prepared and beautiful today. Look at how she does everything to make us proud, unlike you!'

The calmness of what was said bothered Felipe. His father did not just calm down that way. But he just agreed with everything that the old man said.

* * *

They went to Concordia College that morning, but they could not speak to Sela. One of the nuns had assigned her to be an angel for the procession. When Captain Loloy, Felipe and Andang, the servant girl, saw her, they were amazed: she had a silk veil over her face, and her hair was covered with strips of thin Japanese paper. An angel did not have curly hair. All of the angels had to look like children of Spaniards: no one dark, no one ugly, no one with curly hair, no child of the native Tagalogs.

The three returned in the afternoon, this time with Talia and her siblings, who also wanted to watch the procession.

They were able to speak to Sela for a while. She did look like an angel, because her brown skin color was covered with five layers of white powder.

Meni was grateful that Delfin was not there to see it.

Captain Loloy almost got a lump in his neck while craning to see Sela during the procession. The way he saw it, his daughter was the most beautiful angel in heaven.

That night up to the next day, nothing important happened. Felipe could not think of a reason to tell Tentay why he was not around on the feast day.

Felipe was able to go to work the next day. He had to ask permission to go home at midday because he was expected to help buy things to bring to the province. Sela would be picked up that afternoon so she could join them on the trip home.

All of these things gave Felipe a feeling of unease, but he never suspected any of his father's plans.

'Who knows what that might be about?' Delfin said. 'Your father has probably thought about things, so anything that you might do will just make him angry.'

'That's what I thought, but I'm not sure.'

'What if he takes you home along with them?'

'Takes me home?'

'Who knows? If that happens, what will happen to me and your friends? How about Tentay? Why don't you say goodbye to them first, so that they know you're going home?'

'Oh, Delfin, please don't talk to me about going home! I don't need to let them know; you know they feel bad about my father, and rightly so! And I'm going home? Father will have to overcome struggle before I go with him. That is the farthest thought from his mind. If this ever happens, I'll surely dry up his blood when I'm there.'

'But you can't say that.'

'Tomorrow, the ship *Passage of Perez* will leave the pier. Go there. If nothing bad happens to me, I'll be taking Father there. Sela will be joining him, too. You'll get to see my sister and we'll go to work together.'

Felipe left the press at midday to buy various things for the trip home. In the afternoon, the father and son picked up Marcela, and they arrived at the house of Don Ramon at night. His father seemed gentler. There was even singing and dancing to piano music, a hearty dinner and a roaring good time upstairs. Aside from a few side remarks between him and Meni about what he and Delfin had spoken about, Felipe was of good cheer, face-to-face with Don Ramon, his father, as well as Señora Loleng and her daughter, Isiang, whom Talia had invited because a friend was going home to the East.

His father woke Felipe up at dawn. He was ordered, rushed, forced to prepare himself for the trip home, without any room left for disagreement. He was indeed going home.

'Oh, if only I could fight my father!' Felipe told himself, unable to do anything as his father railroaded him into joining them. 'Why do I need twenty more years to have a firm resolve, even when I think better than my father and know that I would never want to inherit neither his manners nor his wealth?'

'Are you coming or not?'

Felipe hesitated until he heard Marcela coming down the stairs, to calm him enough to agree to his father's plan. He intended to return back to the city with his sister after Three Kings' Day in January.

Sela was the one who opened the chest, folded the clothes, and placed the books and other things that Felipe might use while in the province.

They had no more time to have breakfast, for the ship would be leaving soon. One of Don Ramon's grand carriages brought all of them to the pier.

Delfin was already at the pier on time. Even if the carriage was still far away, Delfin could already see the sadness in Felipe's face. Even Sela, who was usually a picture of joy, looked like a wreath of funeral flowers.

The bridge to the ship was about to be pulled out when they arrived. Felipe was not able to say much to his friend: 'You're right after all. I can't believe my father . . . Take care of the press and my family in San Lazaro. I will write to them immediately!'

Captain Loloy, who was minding the servants loading their baggage onto the ship, paid no mind to Felipe, Sela and Delfin, until later when he had to rush the siblings to enter the ship because it was about to leave.

Delfin did receive a letter after five days. Aside from the circumstances of his arrival, Felipe had asked Delfin not to tell Tentay anything about what took place between him and his father, lest this should worsen the situation. He would be coming home before Christmas. By the time he wrote his next letter to Delfin, Felipe would have saved up a bit of money to send to Tentay.

Felipe described the situation at home and in his province. It was the same, or even worse than before. His father, who is also the current town mayor, continued to behave like a king who had not lost his grip on his subjects. He still had many servants attending to his every need, both men and women, including those who were already serving him before Felipe left for Manila.

Delfin, on the other hand, fulfilled his friend's wishes. Although he was careful with his words, Tentay just sat quietly, waning like a candle. She could not believe that Felipe just left without saying goodbye. She thought that he was still in Manila and just avoiding the burdens of her poor family. Aling Teresa was also dumbfounded by what she had heard. It was the first time that Felipe had done such a thing.

The mother and daughter whispered to one another. Did Felipe hear what they were talking about that afternoon?

'That must be it,' Aling Teresa said. 'I can't believe this.'

The mother and daughter then asked Delfin about where Felipe truly was, and what had truly happened. They trusted, especially Tentay, that Felipe was in Manila.

Delfin could not stop himself and he showed them Felipe's letter. Tentay read it carefully, but still persisted in thinking that he was in Manila. Delfin showed her the stamp from Laguna, but what did she know about the postal system?

* * *

Delfin wrote to his friend in the province. He described the sorrows of the mother and daughter, and asked Felipe now to write to them directly, that if he wants to send money, it would be best to route it through him. Delfin would just bring the money to them.

The next day, Delfin was about to go to the post office when he saw something around lunchtime, something that he could not imagine Tentay doing.

After he wrote his letter, he peeked out his window that, being higher than street level, gave him a view of what was taking place on the street. Toward the right, he saw a woman, wearing a tattered shawl the colour of a rotten egg, along with a child.

Based on how Tentay looked, it might have been that she was really testing if Felipe were not in Manila. Delfin looked at the child who went into the press. After Lucio saw Delfin, the boy's complexion turned ashen. Tentay had asked him not to show himself to Delfin at all costs.

'Why, Lucio!' the writer greeted the boy. 'Why are you here?

The boy could not speak right away. 'Nothing.'

'You're not looking for me?'

'No.'

'Is it Felipe?'

'No.'

'Where did you leave your sister?'

The boy could not stand the questions anymore. Shyly, he said 'Goodbye' and went through the door.

So Delfin went to the door and peeked out when he thought the boy was already far away. And indeed, he was right. Tentay was with her brother to buy food from the stalls in Santa Cruz, but they dropped by the press to check if Felipe was there.

That afternoon, unable to stand the situation anymore, Delfin went to San Lazaro. Given that the family did not believe that Felipe had really left, he took with him the draft of his letter.

Tentay was not at home when he arrived. According to her mother, she was with a woman in Tondo. Lucio was home, but he was with the other children. Delfin felt that they were not telling him everything, but he tried to hide his suspicion from them. He did not expect that he would get nothing from that visit.

On the Tuesday of the following week, he received another letter from Felipe with twenty pesos in bills enclosed. The letter contained ideas on how to make Tentay believe the circumstances of his departure, and his request to hide the details of why he left. He wrote about his sister playing the piano and providing entertainment to everyone, about how he would leave the town and would visit the farmers. His father just let him be. He was also able to tell his father that he would continue to send letters to Tentay.

Delfin brought the letter to the mother and daughter. He expected to get nothing out of this visit, once again. He caught them and they had already accepted that Felipe had left Manila, but not the idea that he had left Manila against his will. 'It's not acceptable,' according to them, 'that there's something that would cause this to happen, except the breaking of a promise, aside from the possibility that his parents took him back, never to return.'

Delfin then handed the letter to Tentay.

'Are we such children,' they said 'that after we're hurt, we can be comforted by a piece of rice cake? With God's mercy, we'll survive despite the sufferings that we now endure.'

Delfin's throat dried up, trying to convince them to accept the twenty pesos. Even the children to whom he was giving a peso each, shied away and hid in the room after seeing Tentay bite her lower lip.

Delfin left without achieving anything.

Chapter 13

Flowers and Their Thorns

Meni was a flower that, for a few weeks, had already wilted because of too much sun.

Talia, deeply concerned for her sister, noticed the changes. They were mostly together since childhood, sleeping beside one another and living within the same house. After Talia got married, she promised that she would never be too far from Meni. Her affections were now divided between her husband and sister. The younger one, surely, could not accuse the elder of failing to keep her promise.

Before her marriage to Yoyong, Talia noticed that some of the clothes that Meni typically wore could not be found in the laundry pile. She wasn't entirely sure because it was Meni who took care of handing over, listing and receiving the cleaned items from the laundrywoman.

As the months passed by, Talia noticed more changes in her sister. Even her husband must have noticed some things because one day, when Don Ramon was out, Yoyong asked her about it. Yoyong and Talia had been sitting by the window.

'I've a bad feeling about this,' he said.

'Do you think it's true?' Talia asked.

'Weather predictions might go awry, but never my hunches!' Honorio Madlang-Layon answered.

Talia seemed to bear a mountain on her shoulders, even while seated. She looked in the direction of Meni's door. But she only caught the cast of a shadow.

'Who do you think it is?' Talia asked her husband.

'Why do you ask me?' Yoyong tried to avoid the question. 'You're the one with her for most of the day. You know her actions. You must know who comes up here to see her!'

The truth was that Talia knew who it was. Even before her marriage, her younger sister could be read like water. Delfin was a well-known young man, present in the meetings typically attended by lawyers. He and Attorney Honorio Madlang-Layon were not just acquaintances: they were also good friends, and usually spoke to each other. Even at work, they could be found talking about topics and bills presented before the city of Manila, sometimes agreeing, sometimes not. Yoyong knew something about Delfin and Meni as well. That was why he stood in between Delfin and Don Ramon during the outing by the Antipolo springs.

Notwithstanding these thoughts, Yoyong said nothing. He tried to ensure that Talia was all right. Aside from this, he did not think the relationship would bear fruit, given Don Ramon's dislike for Delfin, as seen during the outing.

'I can't say much about anyone who's been here recently. Bautista, Peping, Dr Limpoco . . . I haven't seen anything suspicious about them.'

'Are you sure you don't know?'

'No. Really.'

'Is there anybody else who's courting her?'

She thought about it. Try as she might to identify another suitor, only Delfin's name really came to mind.

Both Talia and Yoyong skirted around identifying Delfin. In the end, she was forced to say it.

'There's . . . Delfin!'

'What are you really thinking? Is that just your hunch?'

Talia could not answer. Anger for Delfin rose in her chest. She regretted what she had promised to Meni on the night of her wedding, that she would bear all of their father's anger, in case the

younger sister ran away. She said that out of pity. Now, if she knew that
Meni was running away with Delfin, Talia would have turned a deaf
ear towards her younger sister's tears and told her off.

'Look, I think that the best thing to do is to try and feel what
Meni's going through now and to talk to her . . .'

'Really? In case she does it, I'll kill her. I'll ask Father to kill her!'

'Don't do that!' Yoyong teased her. 'Is she just a mere chicken
whose neck you could just wring?'

'Well, how do you think she is?'

'In case it's true, well, I'm glad that they did things ahead of
time . . .'

'Oh, why don't you just sleep, Yoyong?'

'Don't you want a writer nephew? Doesn't Father want to have a
grandchild now from one of his daughters?'

Talia stood up, ready to burst into Meni's room.

'Hey! Don't talk to her now. Wait until it's just the two of you at
home. And don't lash out at her.'

'Should I be cheerful with her?'

'Not cheerful . . . just remember that once upon a time, you were
a young girl, too.'

'I wasn't like that at all!'

'Really? I just forgave you, that's all. If I had courted you better
then . . .'

'What would you have said?'

Yoyong gave a loud laugh, trying to calm Talia down. She did
relax a bit. The couple resolved to talk with them—Talia with Meni,
Yoyong with Delfin.

* * *

Yoyong went shortly to their reading room. Talia noticed someone
looking out of Meni's window. Meni was not moving as she looked
down, seemingly gazing at the hanging plants.

Talia approached her quietly. It was dim in the garden, with only
the moon providing light.

'I'm here!' Talia said, surprising Meni.

'I thought it was someone else!' the younger sister replied.

'What are you looking at?'

'Nothing. Just trying to get sleepy.'

'And why is it that you want to go to bed so early?'

Talia eyed her sister from head to toe. She focused on Meni's chest, then on her face. Meni was never like this. Meni could not stand her sister's stare.

'Forgive me. I can't stand this anymore. Please kill me now.'

'I think I will, Meni!'

Meni did not show even a bit of shock.

'You promised that you'd help me.'

'What's happening to you, Meni?'

'I don't expect anyone to take pity on me. Only you.'

They started to talk, but one could barely hear them behind the door. One could only sense Meni's desperation, and Talia, despite her anger, felt sadness and pity for her sister. Meni wished she had told her sister earlier.

'Meni!' Talia said. 'Father will kill you for this! I regret not getting married earlier and leaving this house.'

'Why?'

'Because Father will blame me. He'll kill me if something happened to you!'

'I'll take the blame and punishment.'

'Oh, that won't do for him.'

'In that case, you really can't help me.' And a tearful Meni held back her sobs. Talia felt guilty, but the weight of what would happen seemed heavier than her promise.

'You've no right to feel bad! Oh, the shame and worry that your thoughtlessness brings to me and our family! What else do you want from me?'

'Nothing more,' said Meni in sobs. 'You should just kill me . . .'

'What?'

'Don't blame yourself for not marrying early and leaving. Tomorrow, you won't see me here anymore. Please forgive me, Talia . . .'

Meni embraced Talia, drenching the latter's shoulders with her tears.

'What? Meni!'

'In case Father looks for me, just join in the search. Please tell him that you don't know that I had left, why I left . . .'

'Stop it, Meni! Where will you go?'

'Just let me be!'

'You're not even sure if Delfin will profess his love for you.'

'Oh, if you only knew him!'

'Of course, I know he's a good person. But how will you end up if you go with him?'

'I don't want to be with a rich man, Talia!'

'Yes, yes, but we won't be able to stand seeing you in misery!'

'It's too late now. I've already fallen for him.'

'What have you agreed upon?'

'We'll do what's best for each other. But how can we do that without the support of my family?'

'I don't refuse him because he's poor. I don't want him for you because I just want what's best for you.'

'That's why you'll no longer see me.'

'Oh, come on, Meni!'

'Don't worry. I'll write to you after two days . . . Yoyong must be looking for you now.'

Thinking of her husband, Talia excused herself from the garden and went into the living room.

* * *

Yoyong tried to listen in on the conversation from the reading room. When Talia approached the reading room, he was already gone. She went to the bedroom and saw him seated on the bed, yawning as if sleepy.

He asked Talia about the rush to talk to Meni. Talia asked Yoyong if she could sleep in Meni's room, but he did not answer. So she just waited until he was asleep, then she went to her sister.

But Meni was already deep in sleep. Talia brought her ear closer to the younger one's heart, and then to her stomach. If they were kids once again, Talia would have already peppered her sister's stomach with kisses.

It was not yet late. At the neighbouring Rogacianos, the husband and wife were still playing dominoes. Don Ramon was not yet home. People were still on the road, some of them going to the Zorrilla Theatre to check if a movie was showing.

Talia was consumed with the thought of her father arriving. Still, tiredness overcame her as much as it did her sister. Wanting to keep a watchful eye, she slept on one of the lounge chairs in the living room.

She did not see Meni wake up and begin packing her clothes and jewellery. The clock struck midnight. Meni waited for the coming of dawn. She looked for her sister, thinking that she must be tucked in bed with her husband.

Meni had to wait two more hours for no one to notice her on the street. It would be very safe to be out at 4 A.M., when people would be on the way to the *Misa de Gallo*, one of the novena Masses that was held in preparation for Christmas.

She and Delfin had no definite agreement on how they would meet. Still, Meni felt the deep urge to elope. If worse came to worst, she would just go to a common friend's house in Quiapo. There was no one there except her friend and her friend's daughter. Meni trusted that Delfin would see her there.

All these were Meni's thoughts as she arranged her things. Suddenly, she saw Talia through her door, lying down on one of the lounge chairs. In a few seconds, Talia was suddenly up and approaching her.

'What are you doing?'

'Nothing. Why are you there? Where is Yoyong?'

'He's asleep. I really intended to be with you.'

'What if he looks for you?'

'Let him be then.'

'Does he know you're here?'

'He knows. Yoyong sensed something was going on before I did.'

Meni turned pale. 'You didn't tell him?'

'No.'

'What does he know?'

'Everything.'

Talia saw the luggage on the bed. 'What is this?'

Meni said nothing, but her sealed lips told her everything.

'Please reconsider. You don't want to see me angry, do you?'

'Talia! Please let me go! Father will just kill me if he sees me!'

Yoyong slept lightly and was awakened by the sound of the voices. He considered intervening, but thought it better not to.

Talia took some of the items being packed, and Meni grabbed them. Back and forth this continued, until Meni's jewellery box dropped on the floor.

'I can't believe you!' Meni cried.

'It's your fault!' retorted Talia.

While picking up the scattered pieces, Talia asked Meni if she was indeed going through with leaving the house, but she received no reply. Talia, despite her anger, persuaded her sister to stay. The elder would be the one to talk to their father. She would ask for Yoyong's help, also their brother Siano's, so that Meni and Delfin could be wed in peace.

'But that's impossible!' Meni said.

'Come on. We'll take care of it.'

'If Siano finds out, he'll kill me!'

'I'll ask Yoyong to vouch for you. You know they listen to him.'

Despite her doubts about Talia's offer, Meni found comfort in the thought that Talia would support her.

'And what if Father says no?'

'Then you can elope.'

'When will you discuss this with Yoyong and Siano?'

'Tomorrow, I promise.'

'When will you tell Father?'

'Let's see. It will have to be when he's just with us at home and when he's in a good mood.'

The sisters embraced. Talia kissed her little sister on the cheek, brow and on her hair. They were not able to sleep anymore, nor go to the church for the Novena Mass.

Yoyong was drifting in and out of sleep while thinking of what was going on with the sisters. Later, he felt Talia's cold kiss on his cheek and her cold fingers on his nose, as he sensed the sunrise.

Chapter 14

Delfin's Personality

Sitting down, writing, nodding at the place where he was seated. Sometimes whispering, his words were in tandem with the words he was counting on his fingers. Then he would raise his face; suddenly, his eyes would focus on a photograph in front of him, the image so vivid and beautiful—the photograph of Meni. He would look at it while he was writing, the muse of his poetry . . .

That afternoon, Delfin was not able to leave his house. He was finishing a poem he was writing for Meni, as well as for the baby in her womb, and he was entranced.

His heart brimmed over with a mixture of gladness and grief: gladness that he would soon be a father; grief that before that would come to pass, they would have to go through a thicket of suffering.

He was anxious night and day. He wanted to be with Meni every single moment. But because of his restrained personality and secrecy in word and deed, nobody in his family and office knew about what was happening. No one except Felipe, but everything that Felipe knew, he had only intuited, because neither Meni nor Delfin, even though the three of them were so closely knit, had told him of their fate so far.

As for Delfin, he knew he was prepared for what would happen. He was willing even to give up his life if that would be the price of victory.

Meni made him aware of all these things—and then, there was the marriage of Talia—and they discussed nothing else when they met and in their writings, except what they would do in the face of the troubles that were going to befall their relationship. They had planned to elope several times, but Meni could not finally decide and agree. She kept on saying 'later' or 'let things be', and so they could not push through with their rash plan. He understood the sorrows that a woman in a similar situation had to go through; the things she had to balance in her life. And because he could not persuade her to stay away from the thickets that surrounded her, Delfin just made sure that Meni's trust for him deepened. That was why he would send her letters or write poems that would be published in the *New Day*, with a secret title that only Meni understood, giving her pleasure and calming her thoughts.

That afternoon, he was finishing a poem; a poem that mirrored his fondest feelings, a poem for Meni that made her feel she was not alone in carrying the burden of her sadness and anxieties.

FOR YOU
Blessed land on which I sowed
The seed of my one and only life,
The seed that in you wasn't wasted
For now it has grown into a plant,
Look at me and I
No longer want anything else
But to see from that particular plant
The fruit of our shared life.

*

To you who kept my fragrance and sap
In your core that is pure and sealed,
Your core that when it unfurls
Your fragrance and mine begins to rise
Look and I am
Always excited and want nothing else
Except to have you, my fair flower!
In reality, or even my dreams.

*

Smooth mirror on which is imprinted
The image of my own face and heart,
My face and heart whose colours,
I promise, would never fade.
Please know that
I am troubled and unhappy
While we hide and cannot show
What we tirelessly long for.

*

Your heart that has accepted mine,
Which secretly linked your life to mine.
The link that has sealed our fates,
A bond that nobody could sever:
I am here,
Ready to add vividness to your colour.
Make me your defender and your core:
I will hold you in the plate of despair.

*

Name of my name completely twinned,
Alive with attraction and trust,
Do not be sad, do not be troubled,
Cover your ears from the noise of the crowd;
I am here
Who gave you my noble word,
A promise that will never waver
And which you can bring to the grave.

*

In our moments of suffering,
Please sing the song I always sing:
'If we could endure the pointed thorn.

Then we would be consoled and never suffer',
The suffering would be wiped away.

He only needed a few more lines and the poem would have been finished, but he heard someone calling from the stairwell: it was the former coachman of Don Ramon, and he had a letter from Meni.

'She asked me to wait for your answer,' the coachman said.

'And where is she? Didn't you drive them this afternoon?' asked Delfin, while opening the letter.

'No, sir. I also wondered about that. Even Señorita Talia did not bother to go down. It's also good, since I don't have to clean the carriage tomorrow.'

'How about Don Ramon?'

'He didn't have lunch at the house today. He just told me to bring the three horses to San Lazaro this afternoon. I think the horse of Mr Yoyong will be in a race today. Both of them are still at the race tracks and will go home when it's already dark.'

While the coachman was still speaking, Delfin started reading the letter. The coachman noticed Delfin's furrowed forehead and the anxiety on his face while the reading the letter. Delfin was not content with reading it while standing up—he returned to his writing table, his right hand on his forehead, elbow on the tabletop. The letter seemed to bear some grave news of a terrible event.

We all know that terrible event contained in the letter, but Delfin only learnt about this now. Herewith:

18 December 1904

DELFIN—

If you're still quiet, you should be bothered now by what is happening to me, since this might be the day that I was telling you about, the endpoint of my life.

The whole night long and up to this afternoon, Delfin, if you only knew the shame and suffering I have endured.

My condition, Delfin, was already noticed last night by Talia, after we had dinner, and not only by her but also by Yoyong. My sister almost killed me, if not for the fact that I was all humility when she was already really angry.

Oh, if I had managed to eloped with you at dawn, what would you do now? And what about the troubles that would have erupted in our house? And all of this is because of you, Delfin. If you abandon me at this point in my life, you won't see me again, even if I've one thousand lives; you won't even get to see my shadow anymore!

I had already packed my clothes; I was determined not to stay till morning, but Talia was checking on me the whole night long. I was about to leave when she stood up and confronted me, and both of us cried. She stopped me from leaving and said she would be in charge of our father. She would also ask the help of my brother-in-law, even that of my brother, to ask my father to calm down and forgive me and allow me to be with you. Both of them know it is you, since how can I deny it?

Talia also asked me to write you this letter to tell you that before they and Rogaciano talk to my father, they want to talk to you first, in Yoyong's house in Tondo, tomorrow, Monday afternoon. Don't forget to be there. Please be humble before them, even if my sister curses you. They will ask you questions and probe how you really feel toward me. It's now up to you! If you abandon me in my moment of shame, if I can learn to kill myself, I can also learn to kill someone else! Mark my words.

I've to go now, Delfin, and I fully hope that you'll meet with them and talk well with them, and please do consider your beloved, who now knows the taste of tears every hour because of her love for you.

MENI

Delfin read this letter more than twice. He even repeated those parts where Meni's words cut like shards in his heart. If he did not consider that the coachman would have to go home late, he would not have written an immediate reply.

So he answered her with a letter. It was filled with reassurances that his heart commiserates with hers, is twined with hers forever, and would not be clouded over by anything else. As proof that she was on his mind, he attached the unfinished poem to his letter. He also promised to visit Yoyong's house at the appointed time.

On the afternoon of the next day, the husband and the wife, as well as Delfin, almost arrived at the same time at the designated house in Tondo.

While there, even at the very beginning, cold words were already exchanged, mostly on the part of Talia's queries and accusations. It could only be expected: a sister was a sister. In front of her was he who she thought made light of the dignity of her house; who dared to get to Meni, who came from the same umbilical cord as she; who caused Meni to face the wrath of her father—all of these combined in Talia's being, that was why she could not be anything else but cold toward Delfin. But Delfin decided not to meet her head-on. He answered her humbly, even if her words were hard and cold. She spewed the words 'no shame, does not know any sense of honour', and issued the threat that 'one day, he who upended our house will get his just desserts.' But Delfin just swallowed these words down into his gut. He knew that these harsh words could come from her, and he had already steeled himself. But Talia ended her raging words when she saw his humble response. She left Yoyong to deal with Delfin, and she hastily left the living room.

Yoyong was not a hot-tempered person. Being only the brother-in-law, he had let the sister let loose a stream of angry words, while his demeanor was firm but also considerate, and Delfin responded likewise.

While there, Yoyong finally knew about Delfin's background. He learnt that the man was a native of Manila, the only child of a family that could otherwise be considered well-off, except that their fortunes were ravaged by various illnesses and deaths. Delfin was left alone at the age of ten and raised by the sister of his mother. He grew up with his auntie and his two cousins. The family pinned their hopes on Delfin, who gratefully considered them his own family. Delfin earned forty pesos from the newspaper, an amount that could hardly cover all the family's expenses. His Law studies were occasionally interrupted by lack of funds to pay for his tuition and books. The amount of forty pesos that was paid to a newspaperman who was also studying, a member of various organizations, and like a parent to two young cousins was just small change for the reckless ones.

'It's all there,' said Yoyong, after Delfin had revealed to him his background, 'the things that would alienate you from Meni's father and siblings. I had come to know of their character traits more than once. I was not only wearing a plain shirt and pair of trousers when I began courting Talia, but they knew that I didn't have the means to match Talia's wealth, and thus, I was also treated with indifference. Even before we got married, they were already doubting if my title as Attorney was genuine, and Don Ramon and I were not fully comfortable in each other's company. Don Ramon has the habit of making snide remarks, and from this I inferred that he only looked at money, and nothing else.'

'As I told you,' Yoyong continued, 'you can just imagine how bitter will be the venom in Don Ramon's heart if he knows that you're the father of Meni's baby. He's not yet aware of Meni's condition, but one day, he will be. And if that time comes, I don't know what fate will befall you and Meni. That was why we needed to talk to you first. We wanted to know your thoughts on this matter.'

'Oh, Mister Madlang-Layon,' Delfin said with sorrow, 'since you've opened your heart to me and told me everything, all I can honestly say is that I've nothing to offer except one assurance: that I'll preserve Meni's honour, even if the spear of death crosses my path. I'd like to thank you for calmly intervening between us. Please do not think that your time is wasted in calming Meni and I. I'm indeed a poor man, with no solid title to my name nor great wealth, but please tell Señora Talia that her sister wouldn't suffer so if she would be with me.'

'If it was only Talia,' said the lawyer, 'it would have been an easy matter. I'm talking about her father. The gap between the chances of him accepting our side over his own is wider than the distance between the earth and the sky. You and Meni will have to pass through the eye of a needle. Oh, with Don Ramon?'

'I think it will be better if Meni and I just go far away from him.'

'That was what Meni had also thought. But whichever part of the earth will you go to where he cannot find you? Moreover, why do you have to leave your work with the newspaper?'

'I'll just take my chances.'

'That's an immature way to decide, Mr Delfin! As for Talia, now that she knows everything, she won't allow her sister to simply leave. She promised Meni that she'll talk to their father. But she only wanted to know what's on your mind, because if Don Ramon comes around and agrees, would you also take responsibility for Meni? If it comes to this, then it's better if you just kill yourself!'

'As I've told you, Mister Madlang-Layon, I'm offering my life and soul to this issue.'

'If that's the case, then I'll now call Talia . . . But before I forget! Before I call her, I've to tell you something.'

'What is that?' asked Delfin, whose hopes were beginning to rise.

'You've got one thing that Don Ramon truly hates. More than your poverty, there's something about you that he doesn't like and won't accept, even if the very eyelashes of Meni give birth to a child.'

'What is that?'

'Do you remember the words you had exchanged at the Antipolo springs?'

'I can't forget that. That's the reason why until now, I can't visit Meni's house when before, I could go there in the company of Felipe.'

'Felipe and you, according to Don Ramon, are like bitter gall to him. This will be the main reason why both of you won't see eye to eye. The socialist doctrines that you had told them will only bear this fruit. You attacked the logic of private property. Could we now tell our people not to aspire for wealth, while we teach them the virtue of hard work and remind them every hour that the lack of money and wealth leads to lack of comfort for humankind?'

'Oh!' Delfin answered in amazement. 'I didn't mean to say that the Filipinos should not aspire to wealth. What I said was that we should not just sleep and allow wealth to accumulate in the hands of the few; wealth should belong to everyone. I said that many people become wealthy not from their honest labours and decent work, but from drinking the blood of the poor, grabbing that which others have worked hard for, just because they are bound by a small rent or a humble loan. What I meant was that because some of our people are now wealthy, they use money to do whatever they want—indulging in sheer luxuries, buying extravagant houses, excessive clothing, lifestyles, and others, while here and there, you can still hear the cries of the poor and the echoes of suffering from all over.'

'But could we simply change them now? I don't fully agree with Don Ramon, but what I can say is that, those issues are now being discussed in countries more developed than ours, and will be discussed in the days to come. The time has not yet come for us here to discuss these issues.'

'These were the very same things that Don Ramon had told me,' answered Delfin.

'That's true,' agreed Madlang-Layon. 'I didn't respond then because I didn't want your discussion with him to go on any longer. But since then, I 've long wanted to talk to you, to inform you in a calm manner that Don Ramon has a right to feel bad and be hurt, especially Don Filemon, with the words that you had told them. Your revolutionary theories on private property all lead to Communism, which should not yet be discussed, given the present state of our country, or the present character traits of our workers. The ashes in the two men's cigars were still hot, that was why they were not able to clearly say these thoughts. But what does socialism want in the developed countries? That in the hands of the State should go all lands, all seeds and harvests, all machines used in production, all capital, property and their administration, and that the State—or its representatives—would run the whole scheme of things. In this way, there would be no more division between the poor and the rich, nobody would grab someone else's property, because everyone now owns everything. But that is pure utopia! A mere dream that will never happen.'

'It's not impossible,' said Delfin, 'it will be done in stages so that—'

But Madlang-Layon just continued to speak. 'To reach those goals, the Socialists will want to be the majority in the parliament, Congress, or any other national assembly, so that they hold the reins of power, the way they now do in Belgium. But what will happen? It will be the same. The moment the Socialists hold the reins of power, they will also lord it over the country. And what has socialism done until now?'

'Why do you say that?'

'Can you compare, with your eyes closed, the comfort in socialist countries like Belgium and Germany, for instance, with the comfort in countries like the United States, which does not follow this belief?'

'So you're telling me that there's no socialism in America?'

'There is, but what I mean is that the beliefs of the socialist party aren't the ones that give comfort to America, nor to other countries.'

'My friend, Madlang-Layon, indeed the socialist party is not a major party in America, but it does follow some of the tenets of socialism. The Constitution of the United States is filled with socialist tenets. These include the State's takeover of the railway industry, socialized housing, giving away of lands to the poor, the opening of public schools, providing water to the people, the opening of public libraries, recreation houses, health centres, orphanages . . . All of these are signs which show that the light rays of socialism have begun to shine on the United States—'

'You must understand, my friend, Delfin,' answered the lawyer, 'if America is now pursuing the so-called socialist ideals, there are two other more powerful forces at work in that country: trust and syndication. Their capitalism there lords over everything, even the so-called socialist ideals. While the workers organize themselves and solidify their ranks, the capitalists are doing likewise, helping each other survive the workers' strikes, bribing those who govern, lobbying for the passage of laws that would bolster their ranks, harvesting the grain and the fruits of Capital. While your so-called socialists strengthen themselves, so do the big capitalists.'

'On the other hand, Mister Honorio, instead of weakening socialism, that only makes it stronger,' said Delfin.

'And why?' the lawyer asked in amazement.

'Because money is now just concentrated in the hands of the few; and therefore, the socialists will face just a few enemies when the hour of reckoning comes and the social revolution arrives.'

'A few but still a lot, my friend, Delfin. Don't you know that the so-called trust is an organization of different capitalists? This means already powerful interests linked to each other to become stronger.

The social revolution that you're talking about and the violent upheaval desired by the anarchists . . . all of that won't change the natural course of things. These trusts, however bad they seem, also bring some good. Thanks to the various capitals, we could discover and tap the many resources underneath, hidden by nature itself.'

'All that capital will lead to more good for everyone if it is in the hands of the State,' Delfin butted in, 'in the name of everyone. Everyone will care for it, because everyone will benefit from it. But if capital is only in the hands of the so-called trusts, they will just lord over the land and not know what the people want. They will be mere lords of capital, feeding from the ranks of the weak and the poor. This is what's happening now in the United States. What the trusts can do, the people forged into one can do better, for the socialist State is nothing else but the group of people that needs the resources and the very same people who were meant to benefit from them . . .'

Honorio Madlang-Layon stopped in his tracks. He thought that Delfin and him would just go deeper into discussion. He suddenly remembered Talia, who must be getting annoyed while waiting for him. At that point, Turing entered with two glasses of cold beer and placed them atop the wooden table between the two men. But Talia was not annoyed; she was with her sister-in-law in the room near the stairwell. They could hear the two men talking about things that they never understood. They just told each other: 'These learned men. When they talk, their discussion goes everywhere.' But they were entertained while listening to the talk.

The two men inside offered the beer to each other. Yoyong drank half of his glass of beer. Delfin just sipped a bit, since he was not used to drinking beer. After wiping the foam from his lips and moustache, he answered Delfin's last argument.

'Look at this,' he said. 'I don't agree with either of these two systems—the individual system and that of the socialist. I dislike the first because it gives inordinate importance and power to the individual, something that he does not have and cannot have. Individualists contend that there should be complete freedom, that no one should be forced to do something or follow someone that he doesn't believe in. As for the

second, I also don't believe in socialism, which as far as I can see, is what
you espouse. Socialists believe that the individual is for the group, that he
should do something for the benefit of the group to which he belongs.
It believes that no one can live alone, that the individual should be a
social being. The smallest morsel of food that he eats comes not from
his own sweat, but is the product of a process that involves many other
people. A person's weakness can be bolstered by the strength of others,
so that all would arrive at the common good . . . In this manner, the
socialists give the highest power and importance to the State.'

'But both individualism and socialism,' continued Madlang-
Layon, 'in my own opinion, have their own respective weaknesses. For
the humanist, the regard given to individual turns him into a kind of
god. And for the socialist, they surrender everything that they have to
society. The first wants individuals to be free to work and fend for their
needs, while the second wants society to do these for the individual.
Both are mere dreams. It's because the individual is really part of society
and the State, even if he works hard in his own capacity. On the other
hand, the group should not hinder the dreams of any man.

'My friend, Delfin, we should stick to a system that straddles the
two: we should not enshrine completely the rights of the individual,
nor should he be allowed to lean entirely on the power and capacity
of society. They should both be respected and given importance, and
neither should aim to decimate the other. This falls under a new theory
in Economics called interventionism. In this wise, the State is sometimes
socialist and sometimes individualist, depending on the circumstances.
The people will be taught what they need to learn to earn a livelihood
and pursue their dreams, and then they are let go. The State owns the
collective land, business, property, amongst other things that all people
should have; but it also allows individuals to own a small parcel of land
and other kinds of property, as long as this doesn't harm the general
collective. So the State in the interventionist system is not run by society
as socialists want it to be. It is run by an organization composed of
people and those who govern them, which maintains order, gives justice
to all, balances the conditions of everyone. This society isn't an obscene
one; it is not built on mere dreams but is based on solid reality and

what really happens and should happen in the lives of people and how their affairs are managed.'

Delfin understood what interventionism was about—where the State sat in the middle of what the individual wanted and what the collective wanted. He agreed with the benefits it could give, why not? Even if he was an idealist, he also read books and knew reality. But in his mind, things had not yet settled. The clouds of knowledge had not yet parted before his eyes. A storm of doubts still filled him. What he believed in now, he would later doubt. And what had been settled for now, would be undone later. He knew the importance of socialism, but he was also aware of the difficulties in establishing it. He also believed that the present scheme of things was bad; the system and its governance allowed the poor to be gobbled up by the rich. A solution is needed. Delfin was looking for new ways of healing. Interventionism looked good on paper, but has it been successfully done anywhere? Not even in the United States, or England, or France can you see its shining examples; there where the many poor also suffer at the hands of the few who are rich. What else could Delfin say to this lawyer who was arguing with him with reason, unlike the old men with whom he contended in Antipolo?

'Mister Honorio,' he finally said, 'the system in which the State or government stands between the governor and the governed is already being implemented in several countries, but the comforts that everyone wants haven't come there as well. Things even took a turn for the worse. This happens because the forces of capital, intelligence and official duties drown the ordinary people, who are generally unlettered. When the State intervenes, it only allows the wealthy to govern further. This, in turn, allows only two kinds of people to swim: one who are already tired and hungry, and another who aren't, and both kinds of people are racing to the shore of progress.'

'Your assumptions are wrong, my friend, Delfin, the State won't allow such a thing to happen. The State is mandated to protect the weak . . .'

'But that isn't what happens,' stressed the writer. 'The government today just pretends it's no longer a monarchy and works there to administer to the needs of everybody. But when the poor make a mistake, the full force of the government crashes down on them, in the name of the protective State. We don't know where the hand of justice is, the hand that should punish those who oppress . . .'

'It's there,' cut in the lawyer, 'in the decision of the people.'

'And who will tell us about what the people want?'

'The press.'

'The newspapers and the press that are also influenced by the power and force of the oppressors? The press that caters to the interests of business, the moneyed, and the powerful?'

'But,' insisted Madlang-Layon, 'when the press reveals the mistakes of those who govern us, they become mere saints with feet of clay, and they slowly melt away and disappear.'

'And is that enough punishment for the wrongs they've done? Moreover, it would be fine if the government would listen to the exposés of the press, but what usually happens is that they just turn a deaf ear to them and then sue the press.'

The lawyer Honorio thought for a moment before he piped up again. 'Look, here, my friend, Delfin, since you're a newsman yourself, it's good we're discussing this. When the press reveals the truth about the scheme of things, it can cause cracks and destroy the foundation of anything, however stable it might seem. And here lies the difference between the State and government. The first is composed of the people themselves, while the second is the group of people and bureaucracy that administer the affairs of the State.'

'Let me tell you this, Madlang-Layon, my friend,' said Delfin, 'that what you said is also a pipe dream. The true force of a nation lies not in the figment of one's imagination. The true force of a nation only shows when there's a revolution that would alarm the State and cause it to crumble. We could not deny the French their revolution in 1789, nor the Americans theirs in 1774. We also could not deny our own, when in 1896, we came together as one and separated from Spain. And the same is now happening in Russia, where the people are rising in revolt. The power of the State in an interventionist system is just a whisper in the wind. The government controls everything: the armed forces, the police, the arms of war, the natural resources, the laws, the justice system, as well as the penal system. Nothing is done for the country without using the threat of bullets. Those things are happening even in the United States, where things are not fair, as they seem to be, to the uninitiated. So you're telling me that if the rich is guilty, then he should also be punished?'

'Indeed.'

'And how will that come to pass, given the way the justice system works in this country?' asked Delfin. 'How will that happen when the lawyer of the rich can just do a cross-examination of the poor and plunge him into the hole of illogic?'

'Here,' said Madlang-Layon, 'we have free lawyers under the Public Attorney's Office. The courts assign them to take up the cases of the poor.'

'Oh, those public attorneys!' said Delfin with a bitter smile. 'The free lawyers, those who are not for hire.' But he did not continue what he wanted to say, recalling that he was talking to another lawyer, who might feel bad about what he would say. With the words 'free lawyers,' he was already able to pointedly say what he wanted to say. Instead, he just said: 'I should be thankful, then, if the lawyers appointed by the courts to give free service to the poor are not just fresh graduates but seasoned barristers. Let us return to our original topic. I've yet to see a law that bars rich people from making money from the sweat of their brow, from turning poor people into slaves in the form of unjust wages for workers and unequal distribution of harvests with the farmers.'

'But slavery isn't allowed by the law!' Yoyong exclaimed.

'Not allowed? But I haven't heard of a wealthy man going to prison for oppressing his servants, imposing usurious interests on debts that, like snakes, just become bigger the more you notice them. No one has gone to jail for having servants who are ill-fed, badly clothed, lashed with commands here and there, cursed, wrongly accused and bearing the brunt of violence from their lord and his family. The same injustice goes for the poor farmers toiling in the fields.'

'Why will the rich go to the jail when no one files a case against them?'

'But that is the issue,' said Delfin. 'Why do we wait for the poor and the weak to file a case against the strong, when such a case will be decided by the mayor or friend of the rich?!'

'We can't do anything about that!' Madlang-Layon said, 'if the cowardly poor don't bring a case against the rich, then they should just suffer in silence. That's why they need to study and learn their rights and duties as well.'

'Oh, Mr Honorio, to study. How can they who inherited the debts of their dead parents ever go to school? And how many rich people have sent their servants to school? Where will he get the money to pay for his tuition, except to sell his body and soul, again, to the master? How can the poor study when, even if they work hard day and night, what they would bring home would barely be enough for their daily sustenance. What happens is that even if they're still young, the children of the poor begin to work just to help their parents with the daily grind.'

'We can't do anything, Delfin, my friend. Not all of us can be masters so there will be no more slaves. Not everyone can be rich so there will be no more poor people at all.'

'But socialism can wipe out slavery and lordship. Everybody will work, without demanding obedience from anyone. We'll have lesser people killing themselves by working so hard only for the very few, who live in such comfort.'

'And what?' asked the lawyer in a snide manner, 'should we all become farmers then? Fishermen? Factory workers? Will there be no more lawyers like me and law students like you?'

'Perhaps, we won't need lawyers by then,' the young man said with a smile, 'because there would be no more tenancy of the land, nor concerns about private property, since the courts will render judgments in a manner different from today. We'll then follow the judicial system in Switzerland, the United States and other countries.'

'But that will only happen to developed countries.'

'That's why in a socialist State, everybody will study what he prefers to and learn to do what society needs. Nobody has to steal because property already belongs to everyone. There will be no more treachery against the government, because there is no government that would be the object of such an act. All troubles will be decided upon by a body handpicked to discharge such a job. The wars between races and countries will also vanish, because there will be no more greed, and if such exists, it can be easily extinguished by an international junta.'

'Dreams. Utopia,' said the lawyer. 'But do you really think that the socialist State is the promised land? Will there be such a condition when no one will want for anything else?'

'It doesn't end there,' the writer explained. 'You can think of something better than socialism. What I'm saying is that we should change the scheme of things in our country because no one system has yet healed the ailments of the poor and the injustice done to so many. In a socialist State, some people will still face a lack, but unlike what we have now, when we have those walking wounded on the streets, whom the carriages of the wealthy pass by; sometimes there is a feast, and sometimes, there is a famine . . .'

'Very well, then,' the lawyer said, 'it's all up to you. If you don't want to believe me that what you're saying is all a pipe dream.'

'A dream today that will become a reality tomorrow. The discoveries of the last century were not even in the figments of the imagination of people two centuries ago. But look at what we have now, we have ships and the printing press and electricity, amongst many others. The rule of kings before is slowly being replaced by the rule of the people; the power of the few is now being handed to the many. And all of these will continue because, inevitably, everybody is waiting for socialism to dawn.'

'So you really expect this to happen, given the conditions of the Philippines right now?'

Delfin glared at the lawyer, then slowly answered. 'When I defend socialism, I don't mean that it will just happen overnight. I considered the benefits of the interventionist system, which is now being implemented in some other countries. It will be still difficult for socialism to take root here, given the current conditions of the country and the way it's governed. I'm also aware that the poor people also have habits that should be corrected. I'm also aware that socialist doctrines spread better in the free and developed countries, administered by their own children and not by foreigners. I'm also aware that the capitalist system here isn't as deeply entrenched as it is in the United States, Spain and France. Nor that the difficulty of working here is one-fifth of what it is in other lands, where workers daily encounter the jaws of death, or go deeper into the earth in the mining pits. I accept all of that, Mr Madlang-Layon.'

The lawyer was listening with rapt attention.

'But I also believe that we should allow the radiance of a new day to shine on this land, so that we can begin helping the poor. We should stem the hapless violence against them, inflicted by the capitalist enterprise. That day will certainly come when our factories will be bigger, the machines shinier—and it's all starting with our printing presses, where printers are being shunted aside in favour of the newly arrived linotype and monotype machines, run by a burst of electricity. One day, we will be sovereign and free, and the foreigners will leave us to run our own government which, even if they do not give willingly, we will certainly have one day, the way the branches wither, when the time is ripe. The punctual defeats the agile. Our workers should not remain asleep while the capitalist kingdom fully reigns. They should have the force to wrestle with the greed of that kingdom. They should realize that the lives of men and the fate of countries need not end up like this. The poor should now realize that they are poor not because it's natural or ordained by God. They are poor because of the way they are governed, by the laws that burden them, the system that helps only the shrewd and the powerful . . .'

While the writer was harping on this, the lawyer was just shaking his head. Just then, he saw Talia winking at him, biting her lower lip, her forehead furrowed. She already looked annoyed from having waited for so long.

Talia and Turing had regaled each other with their stories. They had shed tears when Talia narrated what happened to Meni, whom Turing also considered as her own sister, friend and confidante. Their whispers and storytelling had all but finished, while the two men were still engaged in their hot debate.

When Yoyong noticed his wife's annoyance, he returned the discussion to the original agenda of their meeting. He now knew how stubborn Delfin was, a quality that Don Ramon would not accept even if Meni and he tried their best to pacify the two parties.

'If you're like that,' Madlang-Layon said, 'then you and your father-in-law will never see eye to eye.'

'Oh!' the young man said with confusion. 'What I've said is just between the two of us. But I won't engage with Don Ramon in such a discussion.'

'So what shall we do?'

'I'm not expecting anything, Mister Honorio, except your help. I'll offer my own life if that is needed to save the honour of Meni and Don Ramon.'

'Oh what! Are we going to wait for night here?' Talia asked in a sharp voice, as she entered the living room.

'Yes, my dear, we're almost finished,' Yoyong said in a gentle voice.

And right there and then, they decided both the husband and wife would talk to Don Ramon about Meni's condition, and they would later call on Delfin to tell him what happened.

Delfin knew that he could trust Yoyong to do his best in front of his father-in-law and brother-in-law, because of Yoyong's great estimation of him.

And it was only then that they said their farewells to each other, when the day was already turning into dusk.

Turing joined the husband and wife in going home.

Chapter 15

The Dignity of the Rich

Talia and Yoyong fulfilled their promise to Meni and Delfin. They even spoke to their brother Siano, soon after, despite Talia's fears about his temper. Moreover, they even got Siano's wife on their side, and on the same night, they decided to speak to Don Ramon. They were having an amiable chat over dinner when the lawyer brought up the subject.

Meni was trying to see what was happening in the dining room. She was pacing to and fro in her room because Talia had informed her that they would speak to their father that night. She could not hear much from where she was, so she peeked twice. On her second try, her eyes unfortunately met with those of Don Ramon, who was soon spewing anger as Yoyong tried to hold him back.

'How dare you all!' the old man screamed. 'I'll kill her!'

Meni's body shook and she went cold.

'Meni! Meni! Where are you? Come here!'

Meni felt like she was ready to die. She looked at the windows of her house, contemplating whether she would rather jump and die than be killed by her father.

'I'll kill all of you!' exclaimed Don Ramon even while Yoyong and Siano had already secured the arms of the old man. 'This is your fault, Talia. This wouldn't have happened if you didn't connive with her!'

'Father, it wasn't my fault,' Talia tried to explain.

'I want to see her!'

No one could answer.

There was no chance anyone could beg Don Ramon for mercy. Talia's face was already awash with tears, while Yoyong and Siano tried to reason with the old man.

'We'll lose face with other people with all this noise you're making, Father,' said Yoyong.

'What do you mean, losing face? Just bring her here!'

Talia could not stand it anymore. After the second scream, she went straight to Meni's room. The sisters embraced in tears.

'How come you still brought it up?' Meni asked.

'This is your fault!' Talia cried.

The two almost slumped onto the floor. 'Hide!' Talia said. 'I'll just tell him you're not here.'

'Where will I hide?'

'Under the bed, in the ceiling? Pass through the window. You can get through to the other room.'

The two were stuck in their confusion. The old man screamed again. 'I'm coming!' Siano rushed into the room, followed by his wife.

Don Ramon escaped from the hands that restrained him and rushed into Meni's room.

'Where's the shameless one?'

Meni struggled to stand.

Yoyong rushed to help, but he was too late. Don Ramon had already slapped Meni and then stomped on her as she fell to the floor.

'Mother!' Meni cried before she finally fainted.

* * *

The house was silent as a grave. Don Ramon's eyes blazed with tears, but he was not able to repeat what he did earlier, because Yoyong and Siano again restrained him.

No one was able to approach Meni until Talia screamed and rushed to her sister. Siano and his wife followed, leaving their father, who was breathing heavily.

'Losing a child doesn't matter to me if she'll just bring me shame!'

Meni regained consciousness after being ministered with ether, water, and bites on her thumbs.

She was carried gently to her bed. Her ragged body seemed to have no bones and Talia did not leave her side.

But then, Meni's cheek began to quickly darken. She put Talia's hand to her chest, letting her feel the frantic beat. She was dizzy and numb all over, even in the feet, especially the thumb that her sister-in-law had bitten to wake her up.

The siblings thought of calling Dr Borja, the family physician, but did not dare, for fear of shame. They thought of other doctors, but Don Ramon would have known all the doctors in Santa Cruz, where they lived.

Talia and her sister-in-law kept watch over Meni, while the two men stayed with Don Ramon.

Later, the two women fell asleep, and Meni found herself awake in the dark of night. She thought of Delfin and missed him. The slap of her father's heavy hand and the stomp of his feet she could bear for the love that she felt for Delfin. She knew that she could die for him.

Meni eventually fell asleep. Don Ramon, according to a servant, had slipped out of the house, wearing only his house clothes, after Yoyong had left him in the room.

While walking in the half-dark, Don Ramon seemed to see the faces of his friends and acquaintances; he thought they were jeering at him. He felt dejected among those who lived in Santa Cruz, in Manila, in the whole of the Philippines. Even Loleng, whom he thought would understand him best, seemed to look at him with spite. She must be thinking that Meni should be thrown out of the house now. Since all the other children were married, there was no reason for Loleng not to visit him, nor for Don Ramon to not give her all the things that she wanted.

Talia and Yoyong checked the old man's room. And indeed, he was gone. Don Ramon did not go out and walk the streets at this hour, except when he would go to Mass, because whatever you said about him, Don Ramon was still a Catholic, after all.

* * *

Meni woke up when the sun was already high in the sky. She woke up fully rested. But what worsened were the wounds inside her, the anxiety running riot in her heart over the fate that awaited her and Delfin, who had no intimation of the hatred unleashed upon her by her own father.

She wanted to rise from her bed but her body still felt weary, even though her sleep was deep, though fitful. She eventually sat up to take the food that Talia was offering. But she had no taste for food. Her throat and chest seemed to have tightened, refusing any nourishment. Her sister's eyes beseeched her to eat just a morsel of food. Both of their faces were awash with tears.

'Aren't you also mad at me, Talia?' Meni asked.

'Why would I be mad at you?' Talia answered. 'Come on, please eat now.'

She ate a morsel of food.

'What did Father tell you this morning?'

'He is not here today.'

'Not here?'

'Yes, when we woke up, he was already gone.'

'Where did he go?'

'Maybe he just went somewhere else to calm down his feelings.' Meni sighed deeply.

'How about you, Talia? Will you also abandon me?'

'Abandon you? Is what I'm doing now an act of abandonment?'

'Oh, my sister!' Meni said in a sweet and gentle voice, and put one of her arms around her sister's shoulder. 'I was afraid you would also change your mind about me, because of the shame I would bring upon this house if ever people know about the sin I've committed . . .'

Talia was silent for a while. Her chest constricted when she heard those words. 'Why are you saying that? Even if what you did was not good, have you seen me turn my back on you?

'You're right, but . . .'

'What else do you want?'

It was Meni's turn to lapse into silence. The two sisters just looked at each other and changed the turn of their conversation when Talia's sister-in-law entered the room. The sister-in-law was not yet aware of Meni's condition. She collected the unfinished breakfast and pretty soon, the two sisters were left alone again.

'Talia,' Meni resumed, 'I want to ask a favour from you.'

'What is that?'

'If only it can be done.'

'It will be done.'

'Will Father come back soon?'

'Why would he come back soon, in this situation? But Siano is looking for him.'

'So Siano is also not around?'

'No, I asked him to go to Dr Gardula.'

'A doctor!' Meni said with surprise. 'And why would you fetch him to heal me when I'm not sick at all?'

'Your face is still swelling and darkening. You said that your body also aches and your heart seems to be palpitating, maybe . . .'

'I'll bear all of this, Talia. Since Father isn't here yet, I am requesting you to have someone fetch . . . him.'

'Who? Delfin?'

Meni nodded.

'And what if Father returns and sees him?'

Meni thought for a while, and then she spoke again. 'We will ask him to hide. I just want to talk to him now; I want him to see my condition. Please find a way for this to happen.'

'But you should not talk to him here!' the other answered.

'And where? I cannot go downstairs . . .'

'Let's just write to him and tell him everything that happened.'

'No. I want to talk to him. I also want you to see what he would do.'

Talia was still expressing her disagreement, but Meni sweetly pleaded with her until she finally agreed to send a letter to Delfin, asking him to come to the house as soon as he could and not to worry about any harm being done to him, because Father was not there.

* * *

But Madlang-Layon did not look too kindly upon this. He heard about it from Talia herself, who had whispered it to him while he was reading a newspaper in the living room. He asked someone to go after the servant bearing the message, and fortunately, they were able to retrieve the letter.

Madlang-Layon explained that asking Delfin to come to the house at that point would not be in the best interest of anyone. If the old man sees Delfin, or someone whispered that he was allowed entry into the house, everyone would be in trouble. And that would certainly include him, Madlang-Layon, who was still trying to get in the good graces of his father-in-law. And if Siano should ever see Delfin in the house, it would not be too farfetched to imagine he would lose his self-control and harm the man who had taken his sister away from all of them.

Meni considered these explanations. She later on agreed that it would be more dangerous if her brother or her father would see or hear that Delfin had indeed entered their house. Yoyong also promised that he himself would seek out Delfin in the newspaper office, to relay to him everything that had happened in the house.

Meanwhile, Siano was just arriving with Dr Gatdula, whom he had been sent to fetch.

The doctor took Meni's pulse, examined her face, looked at her bruises as well as the pain on the sides of her body, and then asked Meni what else she was feeling and where else the pain was. Afterward, the doctor asked Talia, Siano and his wife about their relationship to Meni.

Dr Gatdula was a medical doctor from the province, who had just recently moved to Manila and was just establishing his practice. He still did not know a lot of people and did not have rich patients like the family of Don Ramon. That was the first time that he had entered their house.

The intelligent doctor already knew the real cause of the bruises on Meni's face as well as the small swelling on the side of her body, even if these were not serious conditions. Nobody in the house would dare admit the real reason, except that Meni did something wrong and her father slapped and kicked her in fury.

'Oh, she also has another condition!' added the doctor, who was now smiling and trying to detect if anyone who was in front of him already suspected Meni's other condition.

Talia pretended she knew nothing.

'You should be careful with her,' the doctor said, 'because the pain on the side of her body and her refusal to eat, as well as the palpitations in her heart and her sadness, might lead to more serious ailments.'

And then the doctor wrote down the medicine for the bruises on Meni's face as well as the side of her body which was still red from the kick delivered by Don Ramon. He also gave her medicine for the palpitations in her heart and the tightening of her chest. And then, like a priest listening to a confession, he brought his lips close to her ear and whispered something while the others were preoccupied with reading the list of medicines that Meni would have to take. The doctor said something that took Meni by surprise, telling her to be careful with herself so that her condition would not further worsen. Meni could not answer with denial . . . She just lapsed into silence, but the words of the doctor filled her heart and flowed through her veins, reached her face and filled it with the pale colour of shame. But what else could she do? It was a doctor who was telling her about it. She just silently blamed Siano for fetching the doctor. It was good that they did not know this doctor, and that Don Ramon was also not there.

When the doctor was about to take his leave, he just left instructions that he need not return anymore for a check-up, as long as they follow the medical regimen that he had given. But should something come up, they could fetch him anytime.

Meanwhile, Yoyong also climbed down the stairs. He meant to fulfill the promise that he had given to his sister-in-law, whom he pitied. He was able to see Delfin in the newspaper office and they talked in one corner.

Delfin was told everything, including the recent visit of the doctor. A storm of sadness filled the heart of the writer. But this was soon replaced with anger at Don Ramon. If he was not thinking of Madlang-Layon, he would have flown into a rage and began hurling curses and threats at the old man who was belittling his very person.

But Madlang-Layon seemed to possess a potion that calmed down Delfin. He explained that Don Ramon might indeed be wrong, but they should also consider the treachery they had done to the old man, as well as having dishonoured the good name of a family.

'That is true,' Delfin said, 'but would we resort to that if we were not subjected to Don Ramon's strictness and insulting words?'

'The old man was only strict with you,' said Yoyong, 'when you had a debate at the Antipolo springs. But earlier, you were even allowed to visit Meni in her house.'

'But I didn't go there to court her. I was always in the company of Felipe.'

'But Don Ramon already knew that you were courting one of his daughters.'

'Be that as it may,' said Delfin, 'didn't they also go through the life of a single man, and thus had to resort to acts like these?'

Madlang-Layon laughed before he answered.

'Do what I say and not what I do. Do you still remember this line of reasoning?'

Even Delfin smiled upon hearing this.

'What I can tell you,' added Yoyong, 'is to calm down so we can discuss things in a more reasonable manner. I think we can still get the old man to turn around. Let us allow a hurt father to go through a wave of anger. I'll give you an update on whatever happens. Just be careful with Don Ramon and his anger. Don't worry about Meni, I think this is the last pain that she will endure . . .'

Delfin mellowed down upon hearing the agreeable and caring suggestions of Yoyong. At that moment, he looked at Yoyong as a blessing. What other kindness could a friend give? If he could, he would have kissed the hand of Yoyong in gratitude. And when they were about to separate, he could not help but give his great friend a hug.

Chapter 16

Señora Loleng

The birth of the Messiah in a crib in Bethlehem, which used to be the focus of so much celebration in the house of Don Ramon, seemed to not have entered the minds of anyone. Where is the happy and hardworking Meni who would decorate the manger? Could Talia even be bothered to do this chore?

Every child or adult who came and wished the family a Merry Christmas that day left the house scratching their heads. Don Ramon could not be found at any time in the house. The exteriors and interiors of the house looked as sad as a graveyard and as disorderly as a jungle, unlike Christmases past. All the windows were closed, as if there were no people living inside. The servants all told whoever visited that there was nobody there, or else, that the residents of the house had gone elsewhere for merriment.

Everybody was surprised at this sudden turn of events, which was contrary to local customs. But how would things remain the same when Meni had changed, Talia had changed, and even Don Ramon had changed? He no longer had a single daughter and the number of people living in his grand house had changed as well. Don Ramon used to know only one Delfin; now there might be a smaller one, who would be a source of shame . . .

191

And indeed, Don Ramon hardly stayed in his grand house anymore. He found an excuse in his friend Don Filemon, in whose house he sometimes slept and whiled away the hours. Don Filemon just let him be. When Don Ramon did not go to The Progress factory, he would just take over the work for the day, thinking that his friend needed consolation for his griefs. And this source of distress was also well-known by Señora Loleng and her daughter. The old woman did not relish keeping secrets and having secrets kept from her. Don Ramon was delighted with the consolations offered by the family, by the warm greetings of the mother and daughter, who welcomed him whenever he visited.

The house also had a piano, and Isiang, like Meni, played the piano well. She also knew some songs whose beauty would be swallowed up by her big voice, but it provided a source of entertainment for all, especially for Don Ramon and Señora Loleng, who sat at the back.

And that was how Don Ramon spent the days and nights of the Christmas holidays. If Don Filemon was not at the house, he played the role of Don Filemon; and if Don Filemon was there, then there were two Don Filemons.

Isiang did not mind all of this. She owed a lot to her mother and to Don Ramon, who entertained themselves inside or outside the house, while she did likewise with Morales, the pharmacist. While Señora Loleng and Don Ramon talked about The Progress factory that was being run by Don Filemon, Isiang played the piano and sang with Morales. While the two older people must have conversed about the sadness that had descended upon the house of Don Ramon, the two younger ones must have tasted the pleasures of heaven and inhaled the perfume of blooming flowers . . . It was amusing to think that while the two older people were about to die upstairs, the two younger ones were like children playing underneath the house . . . Morales was no longer scolded when he visited the house. The discord he had sowed had long healed.

'My daughter must have gone down again,' said Señora Loleng to Don Ramon, whenever she noticed that the piano had stopped playing in the living room and the voice of Morales had gone as well.

'Oh, let them be, since they're young lovers,' the old man would respond.

This would be followed by the sound of their laughter, and this was how the day slid past the mother and the daughter.

* * *

If Don Ramon did not visit his mistress in San Miguel for two, three or even four days, nothing would be amiss. But if he did not visit for a week or even two weeks, especially on nights when it would be pleasant to go out at night and take a stroll in the fairs of Quiapo and the Luneta, or in another part of Manila that they used to visit in his carriage with Julita, it would be a source of wonder, suspicion and anger.

Julita began to feel annoyed. She waited during the midnight Masses, on Christmas Day, and even the days afterward, but nothing happened. Don Ramon did not even send her a rotten fruit or carriage. Julita would ask someone to look for the old man in his house or in the factory, but he could not be found; even when she and her mother looked for Don Ramon, they could not ascertain his whereabouts.

'He might be sick,' the mother said.

'What other illness would befall that old water buffalo?' answered Julia, anger rising within her.

'Then where else would he go?'

'Where else, but wallowing in the mud, there with the old hag in Santa Cruz!'

Julita's anger was worsened by the fact that her finances were dipping. She did not really mind Señora Loleng and her affair with Don Ramon. What riled her was that she and her mother were not being provided what they needed. News had reached her that Don Ramon was indeed staying in the house of Señora Loleng, and would even sleep there at noon and at night.

Julita wondered at this. To take a nap at someone else's house after lunch would be all right, but to sleep there at night? What would Don Ramon's daughters think and say?

She was not aware of the troubles that had befallen the house of Don Ramon. Ever since Talia had gotten married, she had not set foot inside the house. So they visited the house on the day that King Herod had ordered the decapitation of the babies. But when they visited, only

Talia seemed to be there. Meni, who used to give them such warm welcomes, had only taken a peek from one of the sealed windows. It was not yet eight o' clock at night, and yet, Talia claimed they were already sleeping. When they asked where Don Ramon was, Talia said: 'Oh, I don't know. Maybe he's in the house of Señora Loleng.' Whether Talia had intended to say this or not, hearing these words fed the suspicion growing inside Julita, and she began to get agitated again . . . *With Señora Loleng!*

They had entered the house with high hopes and left it with a heaviness in their hearts. Instead of going straight home, they wended their way to the house of Señora Loleng. They stopped in front and heard ringing laughter inside the house. Julita immediately recognized the deep voice of Don Ramon, a voice in seeming unison with the shrill voice of a woman, a voice that, like a vine, entwined itself around her ears. She even heard Don Filemon laughing aloud.

'You beast!' Julita told herself.

Both mother and daughter were shaking with anger, but what could they do? They could not just go up the house. If she could only do it, the mother would have reported the incident to a policeman, but in the impotence of her rage, the mother planned revenge against Señora Loleng instead. They would vent their ire on Don Filemon and Señora Loleng, and not as much on Don Ramon.

Like people who had lost at gambling, the mother and daughter went home filled with distress. While walking, they kept on talking about the best way to get their revenge. They wanted Don Ramon to stop his liaison with the old woman, Señora Loleng. Julita could not understand why she was being abandoned to fend for herself, when she was the younger woman and single, at that. The other woman was not only old, but she was also married—a rabble-rouser with a mouth like a chimney, with her cigar smoking. She was also beautiful, but the difference with Señora Loleng was that the older woman was a mestiza, but did skin color determine one's goodness and beauty? Señora Loleng had met many men before, the Chinese from Trozo and the other men from Santa Cruz, before she got married to Don Filemon. And who knew? Aside from Don Ramon, maybe she had other men as well?

Julita began to have an affair with Don Ramon because of her mother, who had been blinded by Don Ramon's wealth. Julita realized that Don Ramon was not paying her attention anymore because she was poor. The wealthy only deserved to be with other wealthy people. She recalled Don Ramon's promise that if Talia ever got married, he would marry her after four months. But where, when and how would this promise be fulfilled, since she had already been abandoned?

She began to feel sorry for herself and said to her mother, 'It's your fault why this happened to us!' The mother just kept quiet and changed the topic of the conversation.

They kept on walking around Santa Cruz, and arrived at their house after many hours.

* * *

It was a custom in the house of Señora Loleng that when the clock struck twelve o' clock, whether Don Ramon and Don Filemon had arrived or not, they would begin to eat. During those days, Don Filemon did not go home for lunch and just stayed at the factory to cover for Don Ramon's absence. But that noon, the mother and daughter had no inkling that it was Don Filemon who would arrive, and not Don Ramon.

Morales was already there since ten o' clock in the morning. He was teaching the two-steps dance to Isiang, and she taught him how to play the piano, afterwards. Since Don Filemon had not come home and Don Ramon had not yet arrived, she just allowed Morales to stay for lunch.

While they were eating, a messenger arrived to say that Don Ramon would not have lunch there; he would just have his lunch at his own house. But which house? Don Ramon was in San Miguel, since earlier that morning, he had unfortunately met Julita and her mother in Santa Cruz. They were about to board a carriage that would take them to Santo Cristo, when Julita's sharp eyes saw Don Ramon walking with his cane, from Enrile Street and going in their direction.

Julita poked her mother and pointed at the old man in the distance. They did not enter the carriage, nor did they wait for the old man to come nearer to them but they rushed towards him. Even if she was single, Julita had the tendency to act like a married woman, loud and angry, and did not mind if the other people would know that she was the mistress of Don Ramon, since the old man was a widower and rich as well.

Many people in Santa Cruz knew Don Ramon and while he walked, they greeted him and he responded in return. But he was not able to respond to Attorney Villaruel, who had greeted him, since he already saw the mother and daughter charging toward him.

'Now I'm doomed,' he told himself. 'I finally fell into the hands of the mother and daughter who are like the soldiers of the State!'

'What happened to you, you old loafer?'

She was still three feet away from Don Ramon when Julita's outburst began. But Don Ramon was not surprised by these words, the way a seasoned diver was not surprised by the attack of a small fish. The colour did not drain from his face. He even managed to smile.

'Oh, where are you going, Juleng?'

'Where?' the woman answered. 'Wherever!'

The old woman did not say anything. She just took several steps back, smiling and winking at Don Ramon, letting Julita do the talking.

'And how about you, where are you going?'

'I came from the house and I'm now going to the factory.'

'Factory? Which factory?'

Julita said all these words with a certain nervousness in her voice. Her eyes were beginning to film over with tears, but they seemed to be crocodile tears, for Julita was not in love with the old man.

Don Ramon felt like a rooster gazing at Julita. She seemed prettier now, even if he had not seen her only for two weeks.

'Don't be mad anymore,' he said in a sweet voice. 'You just don't know the troubles I've had recently, that's why you're accusing me of these things. Let us go. Where do you want to go?'

'Why would you care where we're going?' Julita said in a haughty tone. 'We're going to that old woman whose house you sleep in at night . . .'

'Oh, come on. I'm not going to the factory anymore.'

It was the old woman who answered. 'We're really going to Divisoria.'

'Okay, let's go to Divisoria then. What do you want to buy?'

'Ah!' Julia said. 'Enough of that Divisoria.'

'So where do you want to go?' asked the mother.

'To an old piece of hell!'

Don Ramon laughed and then he said, 'Whether it's an old piece of hell or a new one, I'll come with you.'

'Oh, don't come with us anymore. Just join your old—'

'Don't be too noisy, my dear. We're on the streets. You can make this kind of talk later in San Miguel. I'll come with you.'

In short, the young woman toned it down and they all took a carriage bound for San Miguel.

While en route, Don Ramon noticed that the mother and daughter were winking at and whispering to each other. They were even smiling secretly at each other. He asked them what the matter was, but the two women just kept to themselves.

Lunch was served for the old lover boy in the house of Julita and after eating there, he also rested. There, he listened to Julita's accusations and suspicions, just letting her vent all her frustrations, and later, he listened to her make a litany of everything that she needed. Everything returned to normal—love of money and love bought by money slept beside each other fitfully in bed.

But the rest afforded by noontime did not descend that day upon the house of Isiang.

Don Filemon went home that day, at noontime. Without any warning, he quietly climbed up the stairs, whereas before he would call out, 'Loleng!' or 'Isiang' while he did so, today there was only silence. He did not immediately push the door open. First, he listened to the sound of conversation and laughter interspersed with the tinkling of the utensils, the clatter of plates, the sound of the servants' footsteps as they served the group that ate oh so quickly. The male voice belonged to Morales, while the female voices were those of his wife and daughter. He did not hear the loud and booming voice of his friend, Ramon. He fished for a letter from his pocket, which he quickly read as if he were playing a part in a play. After reading the letter, he put his ear again to the door; then he folded the letter and put it back in his pocket. Then he fished for his watch and checked the time: pretty soon, lunch would be over. It was almost one o'clock in the afternoon.

'Why is Ramon not yet here?' he wondered to himself. 'Or maybe he has finished lunch and is already resting inside?' Then he pushed the door a little bit, and through the gap, he surveyed his house. Ramon was not there; he also felt nothing. 'Maybe this letter is just full of lies!' he told himself. He knew that Ramon often had lunch in his house, along with his wife and daughter, in his absence. Earlier that day, Ramon had asked him if he were coming home to have lunch and he said 'No,' he would just have lunch in the factory. So Ramon would surely be here. 'Or maybe he had lunch in his own house?' he wondered. He could not bear days like this, because that morning, Ramon had told him about his problems at home and the boredom that had begun to settle on him, because of Meni whom he forbade from marrying Delfin.

Don Filemon stayed in that position and place for a long time. When he could not hear the voice of Ramon whom he was looking for, he vented his ire on Morales. 'And why on earth is this Morales here even at lunch time?' he asked himself. 'So are these two women now conniving against me?' The three had finished lunch and were now standing up. Loleng went to the kitchen, while the two went inside, perhaps to play the piano or to sit down and converse. The old man was intently listening to them on the other side of the door. Don Filemon heard Morales talking, as the two young people were sitting down near the staircase. 'Your mother might have had a bad day, her partner is not here!' This was answered with 'Oh, you are wicked!' along with the sound of her laughter. And then the two went inside, their hands joined with each other's, and sat on the chairs in the living room.

One servant came from the kitchen and was rushing toward Isiang, walking on her tiptoes. She was making motions to Isiang with her hands and lips that somebody was outside. This servant had seen Don Filemon when she was throwing the morsels of food outside the window. But the two young people could not understand what the servant was saying, and their chests tightened when she motioned to the door she had been pointing at. There was a gap in that door, and Isiang thought she espied the face of her father. Without saying anything, she moved away from Morales, and drew her hand away from his clasp. 'My father is here!' she whispered quickly to the pharmacist, who almost fainted with surprise.

But Don Filemon could not bear it any longer. He pushed the door with force and shot inside the house like an arrow. The two young people had thought it would be their last day on earth, but Don Filemon was not prone to slapping people and beating them up, unlike his friend Don Ramon. He was indeed a loudmouth, however, and released a volley of curses like someone who was mincing fermented food. He did not go to Morales but to the daughter, whom he did not hurt but lashed her with his words.

'Where's your mother?' he asked in an angry voice.

But she was not able to answer such a quick question; neither was Morales able to say anything. He might be a tall and big-boned man, lusty even, as shown by his acts at the terrace that night, but on that day, he just stood rooted to the floor.

'Where is your shameless mother?' Don Filemon repeated his question.

His eyes were like twin points of knives, his jaw and teeth were chattering, his fists balled tightly and when these fists moved, Isiang thought it would be her judgment day. She was finally able to answer: 'She is outside.'

'Loleng!' Don Filemon called out in a loud voice.

But Señora Loleng had already been apprised of the situation. The servant rapped repeatedly on her door, and when she opened it, she was told that indeed, Don Filemon was back, and was in a foul mood. She knew that the source of his anger was Morales.

At the sight of her, Don Filemon threw a torrent of curses and hurtful words. But Señora Loleng, who had never shrunk from her husband or anybody else's anger, answered him back, curse for every curse, shout for every shout, the vilest word for every vilest word she had heard. She even tried to outtalk Don Filemon. But this time, the man did not just let her be. When Don Filemon blamed her for what Morales was doing to Isiang, she answered back that he could not do anything indecent to her because she, the mother, was always present. But this only inflamed further the coals of Don Filemon's anger. His mind darkened. He grabbed a chair and threw it at her and she avoided the chair flying in her direction with a scream of her own. The chair hit one of her feet and she fell to the floor. Morales was about to help Señora Loleng. Upon seeing him, Don Filemon ran to his room and grabbed his revolver atop his small table. Like an arrow, he flew back into the living room but was met by Isiang. She was about to help her mother rise from the floor when she saw her father running into his room, and she knew he would get his revolver. Morales was about to flee but Don Filemon had already cocked the revolver at him. She embraced her father, and with all her might, tried to wrestle the revolver from him but failed; she clung to his neck so that her father could neither move nor walk. 'I'm going to kill you' he said. Her father shoved her aside and she fell near the feet of the table fronting the mirror.

But Morales had vanished by the time Don Filemon was able to free himself from his daughter's grip. Señora Loleng did not know where she would go. She was about to run away when she saw her husband's revolver pointed at her. She was not sure if he would indeed kill her; what she was sure of was that if Don Filemon had reached Morales, the young man would have been dead by now.

Isiang stood up and grabbed her father from behind. She was gripping her father's hand while her mother was screaming, 'Filemon! Filemon!' She suddenly grabbed her father's right hand, and the revolver almost fell from his grasp.

'Come here,' he said to Señora Loleng in a powerful voice. 'Come near me if you want to live!'

Señora Loleng did not know what to do. Should she come near, as he was telling her, or should she make a dash for the door? Isiang had already knelt in front of her father and was asking for forgiveness for her mother's sake. But her father just pushed her away.

'Where is that man?' he demanded at Señora Loleng. 'Where did you hide him?'

'He's already gone,' she said, thinking that Don Filemon was looking for Morales. But because she did not want to approach him, her husband came to her and her daughter screamed. Isiang thought that her father would shoot her mother dead, or strike her with the revolver. Señora Loleng ran away but Don Filemon caught up with her. He was gripping her so tightly that the sleeve of her dress was almost torn.

Even the servants, along with the carriage drivers living underneath the house, began to shout. Some of them came from the kitchen, while the others climbed up the stairs. But Don Filemon just shouted at them, and then he closed all the windows and doors.

When it was only the three of them left in the living room, Don Ramon resumed his questions. He fished for a letter from his pocket, gave it to Señora Loleng, and asked her to read it.

With her hands shaking, Señora Loleng got the letter. She read the letter, her eyes filming over with tears.

'Read it aloud!' Don Filemon said, 'so that your equally shameless daughter will also hear what it contains.'

The paper was folded twice and the letter was typed. It began in this way: 'Oh, poor Don Filemon With Two Horns!'

If you want to know why we now gave you the surname 'With Two Horns', you should spy on your house every day, and there you will see two horns. The first horn comes from your wife, while the other one is from your daughter and when you come home at noontime or at night, they put on these two horns on your head without your knowing.

Do you know who are helping your wife and daughter crown you with two horns? None other than your business partner, Don Ramon Miranda, and your son-in-law, Martin Morales.

And do you know what time they make your horns? Every time you leave in the morning and sometimes, when you don't show up for lunch at noon time.

Go home at noontime today or tomorrow, and then you will know that you owe me a debt of gratitude for telling you the truth.

SOMEONE WHO PITIES YOU

'So, what did you read?' Don Filemon demanded when he saw that his wife had finished reading the letter.

'Why would you even believe such a letter?' Señora Loleng said blithely, to revive her self-esteem.

But Filemon just slapped her, and he also slapped his daughter. 'And why would I not believe this letter? I've been suspecting both of you for a long time. And what better proof than what I saw today . . .'

The old man's tongue and body were quivering with rage as he spoke. But one could see in him someone who did not want to kill anyone, the hatred of one who feels disappointed with the object of his hatred—and that was why he could not completely discharge the revolver that he was carrying.

'And where did you get that letter?'

'You don't have to know where. What I want you to tell me is, where is Ramon?'

'I don't know! I'm sure he is with his woman in Santa Cruz.'

'Did he say he was coming here for lunch?'

'No. I told him that if he wants to come here, then he should come here. If not, then he should not.'

'Shut up!' Don Filemon accompanied his words with his revolver aimed at her, as if to strike her.

She screamed and said while crying, 'Why are you doing this to your wife and daughter?'

And she lost it and began to weep without consolation. Isiang also began to weep, such that the mother and daughter seemed to be mourning for someone who had just died. Señora Loleng punctuated her tears with her words, saying why would she do such a thing in her old age. She even implied something about Don Filemon's own indiscretions, saying philandering men become violent towards their wives and suspect them of doing what they themselves were doing.

Don Filemon stood stock still. He was not used to hearing such sad words and such sharp accusations before. It entered his mind that someone must have written that letter just to make a fool out of him. He might have teased other women before, but he never really entered into any relationship with them. Once, Señora Loleng visited The Progress factory and chanced upon him teasing the beautiful female workers, and this had led to a quarrel when they had reached home.

His anger slowly subsided, but he did not show it. He wanted to prove to her that he was still the man of the house and head of the household.

'I want you to call for Ramon now!' he said with all the power he could muster.

Señora Loleng hesitated.

'Write him now and ask him to come here so that we can talk man to man!'

'And why are you asking me to write? Why don't you just do it?'

Isiang, who used to be talkative in the presence of her father, was now reduced to shame and just eyed her parents in silence.

'I'm ordering you to call him!' he said, his eyes beginning to sharpen again.

When Señora Loleng saw that the anger was rising within him again, she immediately called for Teban, one of their servants, and asked him to find Don Ramon at his own house or in San Miguel, and to fetch him in her name.

'But I don't know where to find him in San Miguel.'

'There on Novaliches Road. Ask them where Julita lives.'

And thus the servant left as told, as if he were about to fetch a doctor or a priest.

In the meantime, the accusations inside the house had died down. Don Filemon paced about without letting go of his revolver; sometimes, he would place it atop a table or a chair, and later, he would pick it up again. Many things ran riot in his mind. Meanwhile, Señora Loleng felt regret the moment the servant left. She should have given a signal to Don Ramon about what was happening. The look and mental condition of her husband was that of someone who was ready to kill anyone else. She and her daughter still cowered in fear of her husband, whose recent actions they had never seen before. They just contented themselves with stealing glances at each other. From the way Señora Loleng looked at her daughter, she was blaming the latter for what her husband must have seen when he arrived home and found Morales with their daughter. And Isiang, who seemed to understand that look from her mother, was communicating that she was not doing anything indecent to cause such an uproar from her father. When Don Filemon turned his back, the mother and daughter were able to speak to each other. 'I wonder who wrote that letter?' Isiang asked. 'I don't know!' answered the mother.

If that letter had caused confusion in the minds of the two women, it also did so in the mind of Don Filemon. He was wondering who had sent that anonymous letter to him. He did not know whether to thank the person or to exact revenge from him, given the present condition of his family. But he was resolved to finish the business with Don Ramon that afternoon, and he was ready to face death if needed, as he waited for the other man to arrive.

* * *

Don Ramon arrived, leaving behind a confused Julita. She thought that there was indeed trouble, but it was a domestic one that involved Don Ramon and his daughters. She was not aware that the servant who had fetched Don Ramon was working in the household of Señora Loleng.

He arrived at a house shrouded in the sadness of a graveyard. The three members of the family who sat apart from each other, hands on chins, resembled family members visiting the plot of a dear departed in a cemetery. We did not know whom Don Ramon resembled when he entered the house—whether an angel or the devil, man or beast. Truth to tell, Don Filemon felt his anger rising again the moment he saw the other old man; the sight of a formerly respectable and dignified man whittled down to that of an ancient and grey-haired enemy who had long betrayed him behind his back. In Señora Loleng's heart flitted the dark wings of fear, anger and a strange kind of happiness: the hair on her nape rose at the sight of Don Ramon fighting with her husband, and there was anger at the thought that he had to be fetched from the house of his mistress in Santa Cruz; and finally, she felt happiness that in the midst of their domestic troubles, someone had come to help them.

Don Ramon did not know whom to talk to first, for the three just met him with stares that were either sad or filled with other secret meanings. Nobody amongst the three could speak. The revolver was no longer in the hands of Don Filemon. Without intending to, it fell from his hand a while ago, landing on a chair at the back. But the man who just arrived had already eyed the revolver, giving credence to the statement of the servant that Don Ramon should come, otherwise blood would be shed in the house of Don Filemon. It was Don Ramon who finally spoke.

'Why, what's happening here?' he said, while looking at the three family members, one after the other.

But no one spoke, so he repeated the question.

'Filemon, what's happening?'

Don Filemon did not answer, but just fished for the letter from his pocket and gave it to the other old man, who put on his eyeglasses and began to read. Upon reading the first line 'Two Horns,' he muttered silently to himself and felt a foreboding coming to roost in his heart. He was already thinking of what to say and how to act while still reading the letter. All this time, he was acutely aware of the revolver lying on a chair behind Don Filemon. After reading, he took off his eyeglasses and fixed his clouded eyes at Don Filemon.

'So have you now read it?' the other man said in a taunting manner.

'Yes, but . . . why would you even be swayed by a mere letter like this?'

'Ramon, there's no smoke without fire,' Don Filemon answered with barely contained fury.

'If you believe something like that, then you're someone who has lost his marbles.'

'No, Ramon. If the one who wrote that had not witnessed things, he would not have written that letter.'

'But we should not believe everything that we see. This is no longer the time for . . . Where is your faith? As Saint Thomas himself has said: "Only believe in something after you've felt it."'

'I saw something and I felt it as well, Ramon. If not for the fact that I just restrained myself earlier, this matter would have been exposed much earlier for all the world to see. But now that it has been known even by an anonymous person, who has written this letter to me, it's time to exact my revenge from my friend, my wife and my daughter who have all betrayed me . . . I'm here as an aggrieved man, this is Filemon who has borne witness to all these things!'

He said all these words while his heart boomed. Meanwhile, Don Ramon was controlling his laughter at the sight of Don Filemon, laughter mixed with pity at the other man's stupidity. Don Filemon was the one who should be the active party here, but he was only reacting to what the suspect, Don Ramon, was saying.

'Filemon, don't say these things to me,' Don Ramon answered with a certain hardness in his voice. 'We are two men talking here. But I've no intention of quarreling with you over a matter that has no beginning and no end.'

'No beginning and no end!' said Don Filemon.

'I said that because you're accusing me. We know each other not only now, but have for a long time. You know what I've done and where I've been, my life's twists and turns, my mischiefs and desires. I didn't keep any secret from you . . . And now, you're accusing me of something that is beyond me? I'm not asking you to cast aside your doubts, but to not believe any malicious intent borne by that anonymous and cowardly letter. If we suddenly become mad at each other and part ways, people will ask questions. And if people knew that the source of our discord was just a letter like this, don't you think that the letter-writer will just laugh at you and whisper nastier things about you, for falling for their letter?'

'I don't care who wrote that letter,' Don Filemon said, 'because I'm not blind. Do all of you really think I'm that stupid?'

'Nobody is accusing you of that, Filemon.'

'When I arrived at noon today, I heard one of you talking about the exact contents of that letter.'

'Who? Morales?'

'Yes, and I saw him with my good daughter here, inside . . .'

'Well, if that is what you're saying, then you can blame even me. But I don't know with these kids. All I can tell you is that we also went through what they're going through now. When we acted before with our girlfriends, our acts looked real indeed, even if we just made them up. And yes, I would visit your house often, and I would look at them here: they were just talking, having fun, playing the piano and singing. Their looks, action and words are those of young people who are indeed in love with each other, and I'm sure both you and your wife are also aware of this. And I cannot say anything else to prove what that letter contained. I know I won't just sit here and say or do nothing if your daughter and Morales would do something indecent. Morales would sometimes have his lunch here, but he only did so upon my invitation, because we were happy to see him play the piano while your daughter sang. We were delighted, and you would be, too, if you were here.'

But Don Filemon seemed unmoved by the words of his friend. While listening, he was shaking his head and showed his disapproval. In his mind, he felt ashamed at the man who had sent the letter, as well as the others who could have known about this and would look at him from now on with disdain.

'Ramon, Ramon,' he continued, 'we are now well in our years, although I'm younger than you, that's why it will be wrong to betray or fool each other. All I can say is that from now on, I don't want to see in my house the person I'm suspecting of betraying me. And he who doesn't follow my wishes will get what he deserves!'

He said this in a cold and hard manner, then looked at the revolver atop a chair behind him. But Don Ramon, who was not used to being the water to douse a flame, who was not used to giving way to other people, showed no hint of nerves. Bold and unafraid, he met the stony words of Don Filemon with his own words of steel.

'And why do you speak like that? Do you think you can scare me?'

Upon hearing the turn of the conversation, Señora Loleng wanted to stand between the two men. But she restrained herself when she saw the fury in her husband's eyes. Even Isiang was reduced to paralysis; she just looked and listened at the two old men before her.

'You should remember,' Don Ramon said, 'that I wouldn't be here now in your house if I was not fetched and invited to come here.'

'But I didn't invite you, Loleng did,' Don Filemon answered, and then took one step backward.

Don Ramon looked at Señora Loleng without meaning to, and she also looked at him with a mixture of surprise and a seeming toss of her head, her lips pointed at her husband, as if to say, 'I wasn't the one who wanted you to be fetched, but him!' It was fortunate that Don Filemon did not catch the look between the two parties.

'If you're not the one who had me fetched, then there's no longer any need for me to stay here a second longer,' said Don Ramon, 'if you want to prove your manhood and engage me in a duel, then don't do it here. Come to my house, or we can do it elsewhere, but not here!'

Don Filemon did not utter any word after that. His cheeks betrayed the chattering of his teeth. Don Ramon did not wait for any other action. He walked backwards to the stairway, afraid that Don Filemon would betray him and shoot him in the back. He was able to descend the stairs without any hitch at all. Don Filemon was left stewing in his anger. And the man who had left finally reached the road.

He did not return to San Miguel anymore, but to his own house. As the middle of the afternoon descended into nearly dusk, the old man kept on walking, seemingly unaware of the heat and his perspiration. While walking, he was thinking of who must have written that anonymous letter that caused the erstwhile courteous and kind Don Filemon to act the way he had, that noon. While ferreting out possible suspects in his mind, he suddenly thought of Julita, who must be angry because he had failed to visit her in San Miguel in the previous weeks. She also wanted to seek revenge from Señora Loleng, whom she openly disdained.

His suspicious were proven to be correct. If he could only remember the whispers, winks and looks exchanged by the mother and the daughter on the carriage en route to San Miguel, then the suspicion would have solidified. That very morning, Julita had dropped at the post office the letter for Don Filemon as her revenge against Don Ramon and Señora Loleng. In the whispers exchanged between the mother and daughter, Don Ramon had heard the mother's query: 'How about the letter that you just dropped in the mail?' And the daughter had answered: 'This old man is now in our hands. Well and good. As for the husband and wife over there, let them taste the bitter fruits of their discord.'

Chapter 17

The Conspirators

Before Christmas, before he was allowed by Talia to enter the main house, Delfin received a letter from Felipe. It bore news on important things and of grim events and disasters, and of Felipe's impending departure for Manila.

My dear friend, did you know what made my father angry? He had forbidden me to go down to the farm to hunt or to mingle with our workers. He even refused to let me accompany him whenever he'd go out on his daily errands. One of our workers had told my father that I have been indoctrinating our farmers with ideas on their inherent human rights and how they should be treated with dignity and respect by capitalists and landowners. Absolutely true. I have been planting the seeds of socialist ideals in the minds of the poor lowly farmers toiling on my father's land and of those from neighboring towns.

When asked how they and their ancestors became servants, they would say, "We don't know". It had been that way for as long as they could remember. All of them are in debt, and forever will be, if things don't change. I urged them not to pay their dues anymore, for their forefathers had long settled their debts. They should break their bonds and refuse to serve the interests of their greedy masters.

The middle-class men who heard me preach dismissed me as a demagogue and rabble-rouser to an angry crowd. They even called me a false prophet leading the blind to destroy themselves. I have been teaching the workers the benefits of a socialist society and its benefits—a land without lords, a society free from capitalism. I even told them that I, none other than the son of their master, Captain Loloy, refuse to take any part in this long history of exploitation. I think they believe me to be genuine and sincere . . .

And so it seemed that because of my teachings, my father had a row with one of his workers. He beat up the worker with his walking stick just because the poor man failed to complete his work for the day. The worker left my father's service, and soon he will be joined by my constant companion, Gudyo, who also wants leave to depart with me for Manila . . .

Father heaped the blame on me. I've been here barely half a month and I've been severely scolded four times. Mother just sat and cried in a corner as she watched my father lash at me with curses and expletives . . .

What am I to do, Delfin? Should I just turn a blind eye to the acts of injustice and oppression unfolding right before me? If those who are enlightened just stand back and do nothing, then surely darkness would descend upon our land and consume us all . . .

That's all for now. Father just can't wait to get rid of me, so I'm leaving. I'll be there before the New Year. Please relay the news to Tentay and Meni.

This and many other things were what the extraordinary Felipe had to say, and Delfin promptly replied. Delfin had not much to say about the lectures on socialism and the incident with Captain Loloy's servant. He just gently scolded Felipe for being too brash and impulsive, if only out of respect for his weeping mother.

Delfin's mind kept wandering off to Meni. He did promise to Felipe that he would break the news to Tentay when he got the chance. Since the afternoon he was humiliated and refused the twenty pesos sent for them by Felipe, Delfin had been avoiding visits to the main house.

At the end of his letter, Delfin told Felipe to just stay with him instead of Don Ramon, upon arriving.

Since the day when Madlang-Layon sent Delfin to the post office, and Delfin heard the sad news that Meni had mysteriously fallen ill, Delfin had been visiting the lawyer in Escolta. He was desperate to gather more news, and pleaded with the lawyer to help arrange a meeting with his beloved Meni.

Meni had been doing exactly the same thing. In a letter she received, she found out how Delfin had been suffering as well. She kept begging her sister to let her see Delfin, and even sought the lawyer's help to intercede. But it was not meant to be.

All that crying and moping worried Talia, who was worried that Meni's already frail condition could only get worse since it was clear Meni didn't want to get better. Not only did Meni hate her coldhearted father, but she had also begun turning away from the rest of the family. She had stopped eating, didn't take her medicines and refused to see her doctor.

Talia could not decide whether to scold her sister or to shower her with more affection. Her sister's tantrums had begun to annoy her. She baited Meni with news that Delfin would soon visit, but Delfin never came. She thought of sending Meni with Yoyong to Tondo, so the lovers could get a chance to meet. But the fear of her father stopped her. She knew there were spies amongst her father's servants, and she didn't want to risk being caught in the crossfire.

One afternoon, Talia decided to have lunch with her sister. She asked the servants to bring food inside the room, and she sat down beside Meni to feed her. At first, Talia gently prodded her sister with a spoonful of hot soup, but Meni simply refused to eat. Talia then decided she'd had enough of Meni's tantrums and she just snapped. She threw the spoon on the floor and quickly stood up, almost knocking down the bedside table. She took a few steps to the door, then turned back to her sister and said:

'Go ahead and kill yourself for all I care! You really are trying my patience with all your childish nonsense!'

The words she uttered pierced her own heart, and she felt as if poison were coursing through her veins. Talia had just stepped out when she heard the sudden, loud sounds of china and cutlery crashing on the floor inside Meni's room.

Talia rushed back inside, shocked to see Meni stiff on the floor, half her face soaking in what looked like a small pool of blood. She must have hit her head on the wooden floor, or the corner of the chair seat, when she rose from her bed and collapsed. She was not breathing. Within moments, the servants had rushed in to revive Meni.

Siano sought Dr Gatdula and by the time the doctor arrived, Meni had already begun to regain consciousness. She was back in bed, breathing laboriously, her head wound neatly bandaged by the servants.

When Meni opened her eyes, she saw not the angry face she had seen before she lost consciousness, but Talia's eyes and cheeks glistening with tears. The sisters looked into each other's eyes, and there was a silence like that between resentful lovers unexpectedly crossing paths after a long separation.

Dr Gatdula knew what had happened between the sisters. He kept clicking his tongue and shaking his head while tending to Meni. The sisters took it to mean that he was disturbed and displeased by the situation.

'It's really up to you if you choose not to follow my medical advice.' He felt for Meni's pulse. 'Why wouldn't you eat?'

Talia gave the doctor a surprised look. Then, she realized the doctor must have already learned what happened from the chattering of the neighbours and servants. She just nodded quietly, and directed her gaze down to her sister, as if pointing a finger at the silent culprit.

Dr Gatdula, who by this time, had already gained intimate knowledge of the household's affairs, gave a prescription and spoke to Talia in private. The doctor knew that Meni's illness could not be cured just by medicine alone. As a doctor, he could only give advice on how to avoid Meni's condition from taking a turn for the worse. He frankly told Talia that if the family would not allow the lovers see each other again, they should just send Meni away from Manila. He recommended a lovely and remote place where she could, in time, forget about Delfin.

The doctor's advice deeply troubled Talia.

* * *

As soon as the supplies arrived from the drugstore, Talia sat down again beside Meni to give her the medicines.

'Why do you still bother to treat me?' Meni objected and pushed the medicine away from her lips.

'Don't be silly. Come on, take your medicine, please.' Talia insisted, and again took the spoon to Meni's lips.

'Oh, my sister! I no longer wish to live! All of this is pointless.'

Talia gave her sister-in-law, who was also in the room, a knowing look. Without uttering a word, she quietly stood up to let her sister-in-law take her place. She sulked in a chair far away from Meni's bedside, staring blankly at the wooden floor. She wondered if her sister-in-law could coax Meni to take her medication! She knew Meni wasn't just being hard-headed. Talia could hear Meni's silent pleas for help even as she refused to gulp down her medicines. Talia couldn't quite decide whether her sister was just being dramatic, or if she really wanted to end her miserable life.

Meni sat up, propped up against two large pillows, and motioned for Talia to come to her bedside. Talia nervously followed.

'Feel my chest. I've difficulty breathing. Do you feel it?'

'Don't be silly. It's just your heartbeat, like mine. Here, feel my chest.'

Talia took Meni's hand and put it on her chest.

'Yes, but my heartbeat is not as strong and steady as yours. I think I'm dying.'

'Stop that silly nonsense! Take your medicine now, and I'll call for him.'

'Who?' asked the sister in-law with seeming indifference.

Meni, upon hearing those words, turned to look. She stared at Talia with disbelieving eyes that seemed to say, 'seriously?'

'Yes, him. Take your medicine and Delfin will be right here in front of you before you know it.' Talia turned her attention back to the spoon in her hand.

'All right. I will drink that only when Delfin is already here, in flesh and blood.' Meni felt excitement for a moment, but she was held back by doubt as this wouldn't be the first time her sister tried to deceive her with lies on Delfin's return.

Talia wasted no time and called for their coachman to fetch Delfin. Right in front of Meni, Talia gave specific orders for the coachman to look for Delfin either at the post office or at home, and that he should not return without Delfin.

'But what if Siano finds out?' asked Meni.

'No need to worry about that.'

'It's already two in the afternoon. Siano has already left. Very unlikely for Siano to find out.'

'What if he catches Delfin here?'

'All good, as long as they don't cross paths.'

'What if Yoyong finds out? 'Meni said once again.

'I'll take care of it!' Talia said.

And just like that, the three women in the room felt as if thorns were pulled from their sides. Suddenly, all the despair that tightened their chest and cast a shadow in the room was gone. The room and their once-sad faces were now aglow with excitement and hope.

Meni was puzzled by her sister's change of heart. Talia had finally taken pity and caved in. Meni felt pleased, thinking that her antics had worked. She was sure she would finally get through to Talia, as she had always known Talia to be a loving, dedicated sister.

On the other hand, Talia thought she could no longer stand seeing Meni suffer. She was fed up when she threw the spoon on the floor earlier, but when she saw Meni lying stiff on the floor, her head soaked in blood, she wept and immediately regretted what she had done. As she watched her sister-in-law tend to Meni, she realized that the only way to help Meni now was to let her see Delfin. She didn't care anymore if their father found out that Delfin had come to see Meni.

Siano's wife, their sister-in-law, like a dutiful servant, just obeyed the orders of the mistress of the house, Talia. She behaved like water taking the form of its vessel. She was one with her sisters-in-law, in joy and in suffering.

* * *

The gate was already closed when Don Ramon returned. It took a while before a nervous attendant, the coachman, came out to open the gate for the waiting master. Don Ramon nearly scolded the pale-faced servant whose hands were shaking as he fumbled for the keys. The old man wondered why the gate had to be locked, as he started walking to the main house. But before the coachman could usher him into the house, the master had turned to his servant. He ordered the servant to turn back and close the gate.

Don Ramon was accustomed to all the windows of the house being shuttered. What he found strange was that as he was entering the main house, his arrival startled the housemaid who was sitting in a chair across the main door. The maid didn't know whether to stand up and hurry back to the kitchen, or to just sit still. She was pale as white vinegar. Don Ramon thought: Oh, she must be worried that I'm in a foul mood, or shocked that I came home unexpectedly, perhaps?

'Where are the others?'

'They . . . they are inside . . . sir,' the maid replied in a timid voice.

'Are they sleeping?'

Her eyes roved to the interiors of the house, and then she answered, 'I think so . . . sir.'

'Did Meni eat anything?'

' . . . I don't know . . . sir.'

'Did she go out?'

'No, sir.'

'Who brought her food?'

'It was Miss Talia, sir.'

'Is Yoyong around?'

'No, sir. He hasn't returned, sir.'

'And Siano?'

'He went out, sir, earlier today.'

This interrogation was very quiet, hardly audible from inside Meni's room. The maid did not dare to speak up, as that would have been disrespectful to the master of the house. She just wished she hadn't been caught unawares by the sudden arrival of the Don.

Don Ramon walked to the grand living room of the house. There you could see all the four doors of the four rooms of the house: Meni's bedroom, Talia's bedroom, the study and the storage. Don Ramon and Siano lived in rooms outside the main house where it was cooler.

Meni's and Talia's doors were slightly ajar. Don Ramon could hear faint footsteps and hushed voices from inside Meni's room. He stood outside the door to listen intently, but then the room fell silent. He walked to the windows at the far end of the living room. As he made his way back to the couch, his daughter-in-law walked out of the door. She looked flustered and nervous, hardly able to speak, looking as if she had just been pushed out.

'What's wrong with you?'

'Oh, nothing!'

'Nothing? Who's in there?'

Because she could not answer and she looked scared out of her wits, Don Ramon grew suspicious. The gatekeeper was fumbling with the keys, the housemaid's face was entirely drained of color, just like his daughter-in-law standing before him now. Then there were hushed voices and faint footsteps inside Meni's room. He didn't think it was Delfin; he was more concerned that something bad must have happened to Meni. Since that day he beat up Meni, Don Ramon never entered her room again. But this time, he couldn't resist the urge to peek inside to see what was going on. And so he did. In that room where light and dark seemed to be pulling at each other, all he could see was Meni sitting in her bed, turning to the door that just opened. Then, their eyes met. As Don Ramon withdrew from the door, he felt a curious blend of rage and pity and suspicion. Meni felt nothing but immense shock and fear.

Don Ramon moved to Talia's room. As he peeked inside, he was outraged to see Talia shoving a strange man under her bed.

'Talia!'

Talia froze as if someone had just shot her in the back. Don Ramon rushed in and ducked to see who that strange man was. It was Delfin, dressed in white, all curled up in a far corner under Talia's bed.

'What the hell are you doing? Why are you here?'

Talia grabbed the old man by the waist and pulled him away just as Don Ramon reached under to drag Delfin out. 'Stop it, Father!'

Don Ramon, strong for a man his age, broke loose, and Delfin struggled under the bed to evade capture. A wild goose chase had been set in motion. Talia summoned all her strength to pull the old man away. Meni jumped up from her bed, squealing. And Siano's wife threw herself and joined in the fray. The three women struggled to keep the old man's hands from wringing Delfin's neck. As Delfin bolted for the door, Don Ramon hit Talia, who was trying to block his way, flung Meni who desperately clung onto his coat, and bumped Siano's wife as he chased Delfin.

* * *

Delfin never made it past the closed gate. As soon as he stepped out of the house, the coachman who heard the commotion upstairs pulled him aside and told him to hide.

'Where is he?! Where did he go?!'asked Don Ramon, breathing heavily like a raging bull, as he descended the stairs.

'I don't know, sir.'

'*Sinverguenza*! Shameless man. What do you mean you don't know? Cohort!'

Don Ramon slapped the coachman so hard the poor thing heard a ringing in his ears.

'Believe it or not, I don't know where he went!'

The old man decided to ignore the servant and ran for the gate. But the gate was untouched, so he figured that Delfin must still be somewhere inside. The wild goose chase continued as the Don scoured the grounds, cut through the shrubs in the gardens, circled the basement and searched the stables. It was a while before he realized he was alone in this wild manhunt. He saw his servants just looking on, staring at him as if he were a mad dog chasing his own tail.

'What are you doing just standing there, idiots! Go and search for Delfin!'

Thinking Delfin might still be inside the main house, the Don grabbed the horsewhip hanging in the carriage and rushed back to the main house. As soon as he came back inside, the servants who seconds ago were passive onlookers suddenly turned agents who sprang into action.

Don Ramon thought to himself, 'Traitors! Cohorts! This is outrageous! Servants conspiring against their master!' He felt that killing his servants and their bloodlines would not even come close to dousing the flames of his anger.

He called all of his servants, one by one, starting with the coachman, and asked them about their role in this grand conspiracy. But who in their right minds would ever admit that they willingly joined in such a plot against the Don? Not a single soul, despite the cruel words, the crack of the master's whip, the violent beatings by a merciless lord.

And so the old man turned his wrath on Talia, for he was convinced a transgression of this scale could not have happened without her knowledge.

'Talia!'

In the end, with his masterful skill in interrogation and extortion, Don Ramon got the three women to confess to their sins.

It was already sunset when Yoyong returned. He was just on his way home when he met one of the servants who reported what was happening at Don Ramon's. As he entered the house, he saw the sad faces of Talia and the coachman, Meni trying desperately to catch her breath, and Siano's wife, pale as a ghost. And then he had to hear all about what happened from the sore party himself, Don Ramon. Yoyong was furious with Talia. But he knew he had to defuse the situation, so he calmed everyone down.

'Where is Delfin? How did he escape?' Yoyong asked his sister-in-law when the others had already left the room.

'I have no idea. But I heard Talia and the coachman whispering earlier. Delfin hid under the stairs, and when your father returned to the house, he took his chance, ran for his life, jumped over the fence, and scurried out of sight.'

'Daredevils, you all are!' said the still furious Madlang-Layon.

Chapter 18

When the Dust Settles

So, what happens now? What am I to do next?

These were the thoughts running inside Don Ramon's head as he went on with his daily affairs. He struggled for the answers to these nagging questions, but he felt defeated.

He kept mumbling to himself and staring into empty space, like a solemn novice going through some sacred spiritual exercise. He no longer felt the urge to go out and about on the grounds outside the house. He had abandoned his pursuit of Loleng and Julita. He just sent a letter to Julita explaining why he had stopped seeing her.

And as for Loleng, well, he simply cut ties with her. Even the factory workers noticed the uncanny coincidence that on one fine day, both women failed to show up for work. He asked Siano to run the operations at the tobacco factory in his absence. He also did this in case Don Filemon did not show up, which he suspected would likely happen.

Everyone in Don Ramon's household was uneasy. They were cautious around him, tiptoeing on broken glass, as it were. They began speaking in hoarse voices, taking pains to prevent any noise that could stir him. They shrivelled like the mimosa within a mere foot of Don Ramon. In a matter of days, the entire house had turned into a graveyard haunted by ghosts that dared not speak, or a prison house terrorized by a cruel warden.

Yoyong, who used to be close to Don Ramon, shed his old cheerful self and kept his distance. Talia behaved like an imprisoned wife caught in an act of adultery. She was still so afraid of her father that she isolated herself in her room.

And Meni. Oh, poor Meni! She was the only living soul who still defied the old man. As if to spite her father, she would cough loudly and often took long gasps of breath that could be heard from every corner of the house. But this was no longer an act. Meni's condition had turned for the worse. Dr Gatdula confirmed it and so did the other physicians, whose second opinion the Don sought. The old man's heart was crushed, but he was too proud to let any sign of emotional weakness show.

Indeed, the sight of Meni just wasting away pierced his soul. He was now uncertain whether it was wise to get in the way of his daughter's happiness. He thought he had only himself to blame should this illness take his daughter's life.

Oh, to sentence his own daughter to death! The thought just shook Don Ramon to the bone. He was mortified by what he had done. A deep regret gnawed at him from within. And shame. Surely, what Meni did was nothing compared to what he had done to Loleng, the wife of Don Filemon, and the lovely and innocent girl, Julita. Or even to all the nasty things he had committed in his young days, to all those poor, innocent women whose tender hearts he had broken.

If Yoyong were to approach him now and negotiate a truce for Meni and Delfin, he would likely surrender and agree to let his daughter marry the man he despised. He just wanted to dispel this heavy atmosphere of despair and allow life to return to the house.

But the old man still could not shun his dark thoughts. He still could not wrap his head around the fact that Delfin was poor and had nothing to give but everything to take from him. Delfin scorned him for his wealth. Delfin marrying his princess would surely bring him shame, turn him into an object of ridicule. He believed that Delfin was a shady character, an orphan, an anarchist, a starving student, a penniless writer—a far cry from the likes of a Carnegie or a Rothschild suitor to whom he would gladly betroth his daughter. And so, Don Ramon convinced himself that he was right to reject Delfin.

Out of frustration and desperation, he thought that if Meni were to die, he would leave the country and flee overseas, far away from the unforgiving townsfolk who would surely blame him for his daughter's death. Or he would pack Meni's bags and take her with him to Manila. He thought of carrying a gun so he could shoot down Delfin if he ever saw him again.

What should I do? What a miserable life this is!

He'd been asking himself the same questions over and over again for the last three days. But he was nowhere near a resolution. All these thoughts and worries were beginning to push him over the edge.

✦ ✦ ✦

It was one of those late afternoons that Don Ramon was in a better mood, when Yoyong had the chance to talk with the old man. The Don was having a quiet stroll in the garden, smoking a big cigar. When Yoyong saw the old man settle in a garden chair, he went to sit beside the Don.

It was small talk at first, about the weather, then they spoke about how they needed more funds to build a new site for The Progress, how the increase in tariffs on tobacco had affected production, and how plans were underway to generate more capital for the business.

Before long, the conversation landed on the recent unfortunate events that had befallen Don Ramon.

'All our business plans would surely come to fruition if I weren't so distracted by recent tragic events. They're all meaningless at this point. I prefer to die in peace now, rather than put up with all these travesties by my very own daughters,' said Don Ramon.

'But why dwell on such dark thoughts of death? You still have a life ahead of you,' answered Yoyong.

'Yoyong, my daughter has tarnished my good name. Your union with Talia brought great pride and honour to our family. But Meni's affair with Delfin has caused shame and disgrace. How can I face my peers now? And I have only Talia, your wife, to blame. I'd rather die and take my daughters with me to the grave, than live a life without dignity. That, or I would go to jail for killing my own daughters.'

Don Ramon's woes unsettled Madlang-Layon. Yoyong suddenly realized how the Don held a distorted view of his so-called honour. He found it odd that Don Ramon had lost his bearings over his daughter falling in love with a penniless but bright and decent man, but thought nothing of how he had violated the likes of Julita and Doña Loleng. He was now convinced that Don Ramon let him marry Talia only because he was a famous lawyer, a prominent political figure, and the scion of a rich family. He was, in every respect, the complete opposite of Delfin. These musings, Yoyong kept to himself. He steered the conversation to his agenda of brokering peace in the household.

'Let all of that go, Father. We cannot undo the past. No one blames you for what happened to Meni. What we should worry about is preserving Meni's honour. Unlike in America, here, when there's talk of a woman having been disgraced by a man, the only way to restore her honour is to have her marry the culprit. It doesn't matter whether the man is ugly and poor, or that the woman is beautiful and rich. Once a woman has been taken by a man, the only way out is for them to get married. We are unlike the Americans, who prefer to file lawsuits that always end with the woman being paid off in court. Our women's honour simply can't be bought. To avoid public scandal, let us not press charges against Delfin.'

'There's no need for that,' Don Ramon said.

'As you wish, Father. I only wanted to give a word of caution. Let's stop for a moment and put ourselves in the shoes of Meni and Delfin. Undeniably, they're young and reckless, all too willing to sacrifice themselves in the name of love. If public shame is all we're worried about, whether they get married or not, the damage has already been done. It won't hurt to conform to society's norms. Not to mention, I fear that Meni's condition is getting worse. It seems to me that she is dying.'

'What better fate than death befalling her or any one of us!' Don Ramon said.

'Death seems to be more desirable for someone like you who loathes shame and ridicule. But we have an opportunity here to redeem ourselves. News of what's happened to Meni hasn't spread outside this house as yet.'

Don Ramon rebutted, 'Ah, but you're forgetting how our servants love to gossip, Yoyong. And do you think Delfin wouldn't speak to his friends about this?'

'We need not worry about the servants. I've warned them not to tattle about Meni's condition. And as for Delfin, he wouldn't dare, as he fears you more than he fears God. In fact, it has been months and we still haven't heard of any rumor spreading around.'

'How would you know?' Don Ramon insisted. 'Haven't you noticed how every time I step out of the house, people stare at me? They whisper to each other, their ears already burning with juicy tales about what's going on inside this house! Some would dare greet me with bold questions like, "How is Meni doing? How come she is rarely seen outside? What illness has befallen her?" Yoyong! May God forgive me if I kill a neighbour, or myself, for that matter!'

'I'd caution you not to let your emotions rule your actions. Fear and anger can only bring you more suffering and turn friends into enemies. Besides, it's normal for people to be curious about a neighbour they haven't seen in a while. I was like that when I was courting Talia. I'd rush here after a week or so of not seeing her or hearing from her, just to make sure she was all right. Often, we only have ourselves to blame for all the hardships we face.'

The conversation seemed to have calmed the old man a bit. Madlang-Layon, it seemed, was succeeding in coaxing the old man to finally follow his suggestions.

'By all means, have it your way. I leave it all in your hands now, despite my objections. I'm leaving the country for Japan, and there, perhaps, I'll end my misery. Tomorrow, I'll make arrangements. I'll leave you in charge of this household. Siano will be running the factory in my absence. Please help him in managing our rented properties. Aside from Japan, I will tour America and Europe as well. I'm never coming back. I'm now free of the burden that are my daughters, so I'll go wherever I please. You're free to do as you please with the estate I'm leaving behind. If you wish to send me some money abroad, thank you.'

Yoyong just listened to the old man's flow of words. He was speechless.

'Honorio, I've long wanted to do this, and the timing couldn't be better. I'm grateful that Talia has you as her husband, for you're a wise man whom my daughters can depend on while I'm gone. My only request is that you tell no one of my plans, not even your wife, at least not until I've left. Just tell them that I went on a business trip to Japan and other countries.'

Yoyong was delighted after listening to the old man's plans.

'Are you serious about your plans?'

'Absolutely, and they're final.'

'In that case, shall we go ahead with the wedding plans?'

'I don't really care, Yoyong! Don't ask me anymore. I don't want to see Delfin or Meni ever again. Once they're married, I don't want them to ever set foot in this house again. Never let them take anything from this house! Tell Talia to send me a full inventory of all the jewellery and fineries in this house.'

And so it was that Yoyong finally got the old man's blessing.

* * *

That same evening, Yoyong told his wife about how the old man had allowed the wedding of Meni and Delfin. Talia broke the news to Meni, and the sisters were aflutter as they spoke about the preparations. The news reached Siano and his wife, and it wasn't long before the four were huddled in Meni's bedroom, like ghosts on the eve of All Soul's Day eagerly awaiting their ascension from purgatory.

Don Ramon lay awake in his bed as he kept mulling over his plans. He was now filled with conviction about his plans to leave for Japan, and then stay in America until his dying days.

Madlang-Layon kept his word and did not speak of the old man's plans.

Everyone felt at ease as they imagined the excitement and delight of the coming days. Except for Meni, whose heart overflowed with happiness after being liberated from agony, and Talia, who shuttled to and fro to attend to her sister's needs.

'Talia, please get some sleep,' Yoyong said.

'Yes, dear, I'll go to bed shortly,' Talia answered.

'It was a bad idea to break the news so soon. I should have waited until tomorrow.'

'Oh, don't be angry, please.' Talia planted the sweetest of kisses on her husband's forehead and lips. 'All right, let's go to bed now.'

It didn't take long before Talia again spoke.

'Dear, could you excuse me for a bit? Meni is surely still awake. I'd like to go and see if she's okay. She's all alone in her room.'

'Fine. Go.'

And the two sisters stayed up all night, all fired up by thoughts of a brand-new day that was to come at the break of dawn. The morning after, Yoyong arose to greet the old man, but Don Ramon was gone. Yoyong wondered if indeed the old man had planned this all along, and that he had already left the country. If that were so, surely the old man must have had all his travel arrangements in place. Yoyong looked around inside the old man's bedroom and saw nothing out of the ordinary. But he couldn't shake the feeling that something had gone wrong with the old man. Yoyong rushed out to ask the servants if they had seen the Don leave the house earlier that morning. The coachman living in the basement said he had heard someone open the gate, but he thought it was just the groundskeeper.

Madlang-Layon kept his worries to himself and set out to look for Don Ramon.

* * *

Night had already fallen when Don Ramon returned. All arrangements for the wedding had already been made. It was agreed that it shall be held at a friend's place in Quiapo, where Meni would soon be staying, as per Don Ramon's wishes. Meni thought it would be quite a scandal if she moved in with Delfin in Sampaloc.

Meni, already six months on the way, had already shown early signs of recovery from the bruises left by her father's beating, the countless sleepless nights, the self-inflicted starvation, the constant tug-of-war with her sister, the emotional and psychological toll of having been separated for so long from her beloved. All of it suddenly seemed like a distant memory. It wouldn't be long before she and Delfin were finally joined together as husband and wife.

Meni waited for Don Ramon to retire to his bedroom before she rose from her bed. Assisted by Talia and an aide, she took a carriage and left that evening for the house in Quiapo. The wedding ceremony didn't take place until the afternoon of the following day. Don Ramon had decided to be uncooperative, and Madlang-Layon had to put up with the old man's tantrums before he got the required signature on the parental consent form.

It was already sundown when the Capuchin priest arrived to officiate at the private wedding ceremony. Delfin wore an old linen suit and white trousers, and Meni was garbed in her everyday clothes that were far more elegant than the holiday garments worn by workers and farmers on New Year's Day.

'What a pity, a rich girl marrying a penniless writer,' the woman who owned the house in Quiapo whispered to her daughter. 'Now, you know what it's like to marry someone against your parents' wishes. This is nothing like Talia's wedding. Nothing at all. So, my dear child, when the time comes, choose your husband wisely.'

Talia and Yoyong, the godmother and godfather to the newlywed couple, stood as witnesses, along with Siano and his wife, and a friend of Delfin's, who was also a writer.

At long last, after crossing a vast ocean of sadness, the lovers Delfin and Meni were finally one as husband and wife.

Chapter 19

Clear Skies

Meni found herself alone in her new house, finally freed from the clutches of Talia and Don Ramon. She was no longer daughter nor sister; she was all wife now to Delfin. She felt the pain of separation, which Delfin could banish. But Delfin was a gentle soul and a kind-hearted husband—he was no master nor lord to Meni. He didn't take Meni as a slave, but he was exhilarated that she was now captive in his love. He was still the same man who promised to be forever faithful and true to Meni, until death did them part.

Delfin's only desire now was to peel from before Meni's eyes the thick veil that shrouded the skies above them. This was no longer a time of grief or suffering; he wanted Meni to gaze upon the sun now ablaze with their love.

'My dear Meni, I devote my whole being to you now. Take all of me and leave no remains.' Delfin muttered as he held his wife in his tender arms.

'No, Delfin. Let me give all of myself to you.' The still-fragile Meni struggled to get up from bed.

'Be still. Rest upon my chest and lay your head on my arms. Let me ease the pain of your illness.'

'How am I to give of myself in this sorry state?'

'I am your husband. Keep me within your heart. Never fear that I will ever leave you.'

'But you are inside of me.' Meni pointed to the child growing inside of her.

'Ah, indeed!'

'There's nothing that can keep you from me now.'

'Oh, nothing. Nothing, indeed, my dearest Meni.'

Nothing could ruin their happiness now. Meni no longer feared her wrathful father, nor the slanderous townsfolk, as her dignity had been made whole again by her marriage to Delfin. She was no longer troubled by talk of her bearing a child out of wedlock. And she had her ever-doting sister, Talia, to rush to her side in times of need. She had detached herself from the old luxuries she once had—the jewellery and the fine clothes of old were nothing compared to Delfin's love and devotion as her husband and would-be father. She couldn't care less that her husband was a poor man, or that she didn't marry a lawyer or a physician or some other professional with deep pockets. She took pride in the fact that Delfin was an admired writer, a law student who would someday become an important statesman. All her father's wealth and influence were now overshadowed by the coming of a newborn, whom they would shower with love and affection beyond any measure.

Meni felt intoxicated by the happiest of thoughts. She was finally free from fear, sorrow and despair.

* * *

It was a Saturday afternoon when Felipe, accompanied by Gudyo, arrived in Manila to see Delfin. Delfin rushed out to greet Felipe, whom he hadn't seen for a year. Upon learning of the wedding, Felipe couldn't wait to see his best friend's wife.

'Where is she?'

'I am inside, Ipeng! I'm coming out in a while!'

'Oh, Meni, you don't have to,' Delfin called out to his wife.

But Meni was already at the front door, reaching out to clasp Felipe's hands. Felipe was struck by Meni's unrecognizable appearance—sunken eyes, pallid cheeks, shrunken nose, quivering mouth, pointed chin, veined neck, protruding collarbone, shrivelled limbs.

'What happened in the last month? Delfin, this was not what I imagined from the letters that you had sent me.'

'Why, certainly not. The last time I wrote to you, her condition was not yet that bad. I didn't write anymore because you said you were coming before New Year's.'

'What's the matter, Ipeng? Do I look horrible?'

'God, Meni, you look seriously ill.'

'Don't be ridiculous. I am very much alive, just like you are. Though you seem to have put on some weight, if I may say so. How fortunate you are.'

'Oh, you are the fortunate ones, for your woes are over. Unlike me! Delfin, have you heard from Tentay? I have been dying to hear news!'

'I will tell you all about it. But for now, come inside and rest a bit.' Delfin turned to whisper to his wife to have some refreshments brought out for the two guests who had just arrived. But as soon as the servant went about to prepare supper, Felipe politely declined.

'There's no need, since we already had snacks on the ship. Earlier, the ship we were on had problems docking and we were unsure if we could make it here before sundown. Let's just sit down and talk. Tell me all about what had happened while I was away. Oh, and do have some of these treats we brought for you. Meni, have some of the young coconuts I brought. I hope it's okay?'

'What about Tentay? What did you bring for her?' Meni asked as she drank the juice from the young coconut that Gudyo had cracked open for her.

'Nothing.'

'Nothing? Take some of these treats with you and give them to Tentay. You mustn't go and see her without bearing gifts, you know.'

'Oh, no. I won't be going to see her until tomorrow.'

'Go and see her now. Don't wait until tomorrow. Delfin tells me that Tentay's family is going through a rough time now. You have been neglectful!'

'I sent them money, but she refused to take it. What was I supposed to do? Delfin told me he was turned away several times.'

'Of course she would. If Delfin abandoned me like you did Tentay, I would burn all the keepsakes I was given by Delfin.'

'You would burn them?' Delfin teased.

'Absolutely.'

'You women have such a temper!' Felipe said.

'And you men are so heartless!'

'Okay, well, Felipe, perhaps it is best that you bring all these gifts to Tentay. No one here is going to eat them, especially that whole jackfruit. They're certainly not good for Meni.'

Felipe decided it would be wise to follow Delfin's advice. He had just run away from home, and he certainly didn't have time to buy more gifts for Tentay when they arrived in Manila. He couldn't bother his sister and mother, since they wept every time he told them of his plans of leaving for good. He was heavily guarded by the servants, who were instructed by his mother and sister to watch his every move. His sister, Sela, was grounded by his father and couldn't go back to school in Manila. His father was afraid that Sela would learn the same stubborn ways that he had taken up while staying in Manila.

It was one midnight when Felipe ran away. He only had four pesos as pocket money, since he didn't earn wages during his entire stay at home. Four pesos was a measly sum for two people taking a half-day walk from a remote town in Laguna to the docks by the bay, to get on board a ship that would ferry them to Manila, where they would have to find a place to stay. By the time he reached Manila, Felipe had no money left for Tentay's hard-up family.

The three friends chatted until Meni felt nauseous and asked to take their leave. The sun had long set, and the conversation had gone on about what had happened during the time that they didn't see each other—the sorrows, the pains, the joys of the days past. But they were all feeling hopeful now, as they faced a promising future.

'I shall speak with you again, but for now I have to rest.'

'Felipe, have dinner with us before you leave.'

And so they had an early supper. Felipe and Gudyo were just leaving, when Talia, Yoyong, Siano and his wife came to visit. Felipe stayed on for a while to catch up with old friends. It was already eight in the evening when Delfin said goodbye to his old friend. More laughter and cheers filled the house as the new visitors came to learn that Felipe was off to see his beloved Tentay.

* * *

Not much had changed in San Lazaro. Felipe saw the same old Aling Teresa, Tentay, the kids Lucio and Amando, and the nursing Julian. Curiously missing was nine-year-old Victor, who had been sent away to live with an aunt in Tondo. The family had agreed to give him away, so he could go to school and help out in his aunt's household. As a token, Aling Tere had received eight pesos, which she had used to buy new clothes as Christmas gifts for the children—a small price to pay in exchange for Victor's schooling.

At first, there were warm words of welcome and greetings between Tentay and Felipe, but the exchange turned sour when Felipe mentioned his letters and Tentay's refusal to take the money he had sent through Delfin. They began to have a heated exchange of words and made grave accusations at each other.

'I never expected you would do something like that, Felipe.' Tentay was shaking her head, obviously still hurting, as her mother turned to catch the toddler, who was about to bump into the wall.

As the couple continued arguing inside the house, the children outside were fighting over the young coconut. Amando already wanted to eat the coconut, but Lucio warned that it would give them a stomach ache. They decided to go for the delicacy made with coconut milk, sugar palm and honey. The two children went at it like starved kittens snarling, hissing and pawing at each other. Gudyo looked on, occasionally breaking them up, undecided whether to be amused or to feel pity for the hungry children, for he knew exactly how it was for poor people like himself.

Aling Teresa felt ashamed that a stranger such as Gudyo would see her two children fighting over food like hungry animals.

'Lucio! Amando!'

The two children froze in shock. Lucio dropped the half-eaten candy he was holding, and the two turned to their mother glaring at them through the door. Like foot soldiers, the two children stood up at once, dropped their candies, and quietly marched off to clean themselves up.

'It was my fault. I gave them the candies,' Gudyo apologized.

Aling Teresa put down the toddler she was carrying and went to scold and spank the two erring children. 'Have you no shame? Acting like starved beasts! In front of a total stranger! Shame!'

Meanwhile, the couple inside were oblivious to the commotion that went on outside.

'No, you and your mother got it all wrong.' Felipe smiled after hearing Tentay's long lament over the events that had happened during his absence. 'If it were entirely up to me, I wouldn't have left Manila. My work is here . . . my studies . . . Oh, heck! This is where my Tentay is!'

'Your Tentay!' Tentay scoffed. 'You have the nerve to say that after running away with nary a word to me or even to my mother. After living for so long in your hometown, and being told by your parents not to court a poor woman like me? "My Tentay"! Did you really think it would be okay to just come and go without somehow hurting our feelings?'

'No, it's not like that at all. Such harsh words. Even if I did go away for a month, you were always on my mind.'

'Oh, so you were worried about us here? And you thought the best way to show your concern was to send us money, worried that we're probably dying of starvation? Did you really think we were so shameless that we would just accept your token donation?'

'Tentay, please!'

'Did you really think that just because we are poor, you could humiliate us like that?'

Tears streamed from Tentay's eyes as she choked on the hurt feelings that she had suppressed for so long.

'If my father were still alive, you wouldn't treat us like that!' Tentay broke down completely and sobbed.

* * *

Felipe was dumbstruck as he watched Tentay weep. He gazed at her tears that glistened like crystals in the warm light of the gas lantern, and he felt pain in his chest. Tentay's last words, 'if my father were still alive . . .' rang in his ears.

'Out of respect for your dearly departed father, to whom I made a solemn vow, Tentay, I ask that you never speak such harsh words ever again. My conscience is clear and I was not untrue to the words I gave to your father. Never would I ever dare to insult you for being poor. It wasn't just money I gave. In the three letters I sent, I wanted you to know why I had to leave all of sudden to go back to my hometown . . . Why are you so angry?'

'You would be so angry as well, if you were in our shoes!'

'I know, Tentay. I understand why you were hurt when I left without saying goodbye. But there was no need to be offended by the money I sent. And you should never think I'd ever insult you for being poor. I'd never do something like that.'

'Not to our faces . . .' Tentay answered.

'Oh, so now you're saying I'm untruthful.'

'Don't you turn things around! You acted like a totally different person when you turned your back and ran back to your parents!'

'Let's not go there again.' Felipe gently pleaded. 'True, my parents are not very keen on me finding a partner here, and that they want nothing more than a daughter-in-law from a rich family. But they don't know you, and I'm sure they will like you, once they get to know you.'

'On the contrary, your parents will surely scrutinize me and once my flaws are exposed, they will certainly forbid you from ever seeing me again.'

'I don't care if they decide you are an unfit bride! In matters like this, I will always make my own decisions.'

'But they're already pulling your strings!'

'No, I'm just being a dutiful son. You did exactly the same thing. You were just obeying your father's wishes when you took me as your suitor. I'm sure you wouldn't be in a relationship with me if your father were against it.'

'Should we be talking about that now?' Tentay objected.

'And why not? You brought up my parents' disapproval of you. You seem to have forgotten how your mother used to dislike me, and you dated me only to please your father. Why shouldn't we talk about these things?'

'But that's different! I entertained you even before my father asked me to take you as my suitor. I didn't tell you, at first, that I actually liked you because I was afraid your parents would object if they found out that we were a couple. From the beginning, I knew it would be impossible for your parents to like me, since they thought too highly of themselves. I didn't want to give you any false hopes. All I wanted was to be with someone whom my parents and siblings would gladly accept as one of their own.'

'And who might that be?'

'Well . . .'

'Really, who might that man be?'

'Wait, I was talking about then, not now.'

'Then . . . now. It doesn't matter. Who's that man?'

'There's no man.'

'C'mon. Why wouldn't you say?'

'He's not here in Manila, at the moment.'

Felipe was flabbergasted. For a moment, he fell silent. Then, without a hint of a smile on his lips, he replied, 'Who is he? Where is he from?'

'Oh, he comes from a province somewhere in the East. His parents forbade him to see me because they wanted him to marry a girl who comes from a rich family.'

Felipe realized that Tentay was playing him, and he burst out in laughter. 'Nice one! But that man is right here in front of you, body and soul! He never really left because even when he was away, his heart and mind were right here with you.'

'Oh, no. You're not the man I was talking about!'

'Who is it, then?'

'I told you, it's not you.'

'Then I'll seek him out.'

'And if I told you it's you . . . ?'

'Then, I will tell you, I'm your man, indeed!'

Ah, such sweet words! Tentay had abandoned all pretenses at this point. She and Felipe sat in silence, gazing lovingly into each other's eyes.

'I've always feared that your parents would hate us if we ever got married.' Tentay sighed.

'Just tell me when, anytime you want. You're the one who's holding back. You and all this talk of sorrow and despair. Look at my friend, Delfin. He's now happily married to Meni. And they're living on their own now. Meni dared to go against her father's wishes, and because of that, she got what her heart desired most. If Meni could do that, so can I! She's a girl and I'm a man. There's nothing my parents can do to stop me from marrying you. I won't let them.'

'But Meni and Delfin were destined to marry. The wife may be rich, but the husband is a talented man. They're so unlike us. Look at me—a fool, an ugly woman, unfit to be any man's wife.'

'Unfit? Ugly? Not at all! Honey, you're twice as pretty as Meni!'

'Oh don't you go mocking me like that! You always do that to me!'

'I'm not mocking you, or teasing you, even! Women like Meni are as pretty as finely cut gemstones. But you, my dear, your beauty is innate, all coming from within!'

Tentay sat back as if embarrassed by Felipe's words. Felipe knew then that Tentay would never speak again of how ashamed she was of being poor. It was already late, but the two just kept on talking. Aling Teresa had already fallen asleep with the children, and Gudyo at some point, could not keep up anymore and decided to leave the two and retire for the night.

* * *

Sleep eluded Tentay that night. She kept thinking about her conversation with Felipe. Felipe had decided to stay in Manila for good and keep his job in the city. If they were to live together, they would not consider staying at the house of Felipe's parents. Instead, they would live with Tentay's family. Felipe did not want any wedding ceremony, since he considered matrimony to be an instrument of slavery under the religious institution. He would rather do away with all the pomp and circumstance, since all he cared for was being free to love. But Felipe's idea of free love deeply disturbed Tentay, for that notion went against the dictates of faith and the norms of society. She knew that her mother would not like the idea, and she loathed the idea of being scorned by the public for being immoral.

Tentay thought they could easily approach any religious priest to officiate at their wedding, because that was what a devout Catholic was supposed to do. But Felipe thought that there was no need to have mere mortals, just like themselves, bear witness to their union. There was no need for a complete stranger to bear witness to their profession of love and devotion to each other. And he hated the idea of having to pay for the ceremony. The money for the wedding would be equivalent to the money that three poor families would need to support themselves for a year.

Tentay could not bear the thought of living in sin before the eyes of God, if she were to become a mere domestic partner. But Felipe reminded her of the importance of virtue and fidelity, that it should not matter whether or not they were blessed by the sacrament of matrimony.

What about her mother? 'Surely,' Tentay thought, 'she would disapprove.' Being a devout Catholic, her mother would vehemently protest. 'That's not how we were raised by our mothers and fathers. That goes against everything that we were taught to be true and good.'

Tentay was utterly confused, since she could not decide whether Felipe's plans were good or bad. As with any moral dilemma, Tentay drew up all the pros and cons. As dictated by her faith, it would be immoral to go with Felipe's wishes. It was a bad idea if only because she was uncertain of Felipe's sincerity. It would seem like a marvelous idea, if one were to consider that Felipe would still be forsaken by his family and peers no matter what, so there was not going to be any real damage there. And should it turn out that Felipe was a bad husband, she could easily leave him.

It was almost daybreak, but Tentay was still wide awake. She still had not arrived at a peaceful resolution.

'Here's hoping against hope. Perhaps, if I talked to him again . . .'

And finally, Tentay fell asleep.

Chapter 20

Money Makes the World Go Round

One week passed before Don Ramon set his plans in motion. In that one week, after Meni had left the house, he had not left his room and had spent his days wallowing in despair.

Several times, he had thought of ending his own life and contemplated all sorts of ways to do so. Should he shoot himself in the chest or blow his brains out with his revolver? Hang himself like Judas did or drink poison? Jump off a bridge, or run amok and challenge anyone to death? But he decided it was not his time to die just yet. He dreamt of traveling overseas, leaving his hometown that had become a bitter source of shame, and live in bliss in a land far away until his dying day.

He thought to himself, 'When I'm gone, they can say whatever they want about my family. I won't have to hear any of it.'

Now and then, he wondered about Julita and Señora Loleng. Loleng was a married woman, and he just could not take her with him on his trips. On the other hand, Julita was a young single woman who had only her mother, a presentable woman who would just follow her daughter around. Surely a long journey would be tiresome if he did not have a woman for a companion. He toyed with the idea of taking Julita with him, but then decided to forego anything that would weigh him down. He reminded himself that he was going on a leisure trip, born of a desire to hide from everyone he knew. He wanted to seek adventures until his final days. Surely in Japan, America and Europe, he would easily find a replacement for Julita that suited his taste in women. All he needed was money. The twenty grand he had initially set aside would not be enough, so he thought of withdrawing all his money, leaving just the estate and all his assets to his children.

'With all this money,' Don Ramon mused, 'I can go around the globe! And there will still be all my properties and capital funds to leave to my children. They would get their inheritance when I die.'

But who was the 'them' who Don Ramon was referring to?

He had already disowned Meni and banished her. That left him with only Talia and her husband, and Siano and his wife.

'I'm the patriarch and I'm still alive. I'll decide what to put in my last will and testament!' Don Ramon thought as memories of Meni and her right to his estate rose in his mind.

As far as he was concerned, his life in Manila was over. He went about finalising his last will and testament like a dying rich man would have done. And for this, he asked his son-in-law, Attorney Madlang-Layon, to help him. The two men were inseparable, working tirelessly as if they were building Solomon's temple.

Talia began to suspect something was odd with her father. She tried asking her husband, but Yoyong did not break his oath to the old man. And on several occasions, she espied on her old man in his room, rummaging through documents and packing his clothes. Still, Talia had no clue what was going on. The old man kept his room under lock and key whenever he left the house. The only person Don Ramon spoke to was Yoyong, who seemed to be the only important person in the house.

That was the frequent topic of conversation during Talia's and Siano's visits to Meni. On the one hand, the siblings were grateful that through Yoyong's help, Don Ramon had finally calmed down. On the other hand, they were bothered by the fact that the old man now seemed to love and respect Yoyong more than his own children.

Meni took it the hardest: she had all the right to feel angry and resentful. Nonetheless, she was grateful to Yoyong, for had it not been for him, she would surely have died from illness and despair by now.

Still, their faith and trust in Yoyong remained unchanged. They were grateful that Yoyong was there to calm the ever-volatile Don Ramon.

* * *

Indeed, Madlang-Layon had the old man under his spell. He had gained an intimate knowledge of how Don Ramon's mind worked. The old man had begun spilling his previously heavily guarded secrets—the properties, assets and liabilities that were unknown to his children. Don Ramon had long resigned himself to the idea that he could not rely on his children, not even Siano, to handle his affairs if something unexpected were to happen. Madlang-Layon had always been Don Ramon's trusted counsel in all the legal battles he had faced. When Madlang-Layon spoke, Don Ramon listened in rapt attention.

Madlang-Layon knew all the reasons why Don Ramon wanted to leave the country. It was not just about Meni's love affair with Delfin. The old man needed to get away from Don Filemon, who had become his sworn enemy. Rumours about him and Loleng had reached the ears of Don Filemon, and after that fistfight, the two men were no longer on speaking terms. There was no doubt in Madlang-Layon's mind that this was the best time for Don Ramon to leave Manila for good.

But coming up with a good alibi for Don Ramon's departure posed a great challenge. What sort of excuse would friends, relatives, neighbours, and business partners accept? They would think that Don Ramon was going to just import equipment for the tobacco plant and visit Japan, America, and Europe to study global trends in the tobacco business. He could also be negotiating with diplomats to reduce tariffs on tobacco and lower taxes that had become a threat to local businesses. Moreover, he could also be seeking treatment for a serious illness, abroad. Surely, these would all be logical reasons that no one would question.

This time around, Don Ramon chose to forego the usual fanfare from the press. 'We'll let them know only when I'm already on board.' Don Ramon's children would surely object to him traveling all alone for whatever reason. Fortunately for Don Ramon, Julita had already refused his offer to travel with him to Japan. But Señora Loleng was another matter: despite the ruckus between Don Ramon and Don Filemon, Loleng still kept on sending messages and letters to Don Ramon.

Nothing stood in his way anymore, except the last will and testament, which he entrusted to Madlang-Layon. Yoyong had taken care of everything, and he had assumed the power of attorney to preside over the estate in Don Ramon's stead. Yoyong had been chosen to become the new master of the house, not Siano, the son whom Don Ramon had never trusted to handle important matters.

* * *

On the eve of his departure, Don Ramon had dinner with his children and spoke to them about his plans. He told them it would only be for a few months, and should he die overseas, he had drawn up his last will and testament for his children.

Anyone who knew Don Ramon knew better than to oppose when the old man clearly had full conviction behind his words and decisions. But Talia and Siano, upon hearing of their father's ghastly intentions, voiced their objections. The children suddenly realised what had been going on between Don Ramon and Madlang-Layon. Talia mumbled to herself, silently reproaching her husband for not telling them what was going on. Had Yoyong told them, they would have foiled the old man's plans, which at that point, were already final and absolute.

It was not long before Talia, being unable to grapple with the things she had heard, stood up and left the dining table. Followed by Yoyong, she went to her father's bedroom and saw his luggage and briefcase, all neatly prepared. The two argued a bit, but Madlang-Layon's sweet words and deft manner prevailed, and Talia, in resignation, quietly drowned her objection and sorrow in silent and bitter tears.

Siano and his wife quickly regained their composure after hearing the shocking news. It wasn't hard to convince Siano on the wisdom of his father's intentions. He had no objections to managing the payroll at the factory, or to his inheritance as stated in his father's last will and testament. He did not mind that he would not oversee the rented properties, or that Meni would receive absolutely nothing from their father, or that his brother-in-law would be the executor of his father's estate. His father's wish was their command, and there was nothing they could do to change it.

Compared to Talia, Siano was nothing: she was more of a man than Siano ever could be, when it came to matters like these. Talia was more vocal in her protests and spoke of her suspicions openly.

'If he was really going on a trip, why the last will and testament?' Talia asked Yoyong as they sat in the living room while Don Ramon, Siano, and his wife were still chatting in the dining room. Talia feared that she would never see her father again, that he might die in a faraway country.

'And if he really needed to rush his last will and testament, why did he leave out Meni from his will? Poor, poor Meni! I cannot allow that!' And Talia sobbed. 'You knew about all this. Why didn't you say anything? You're a lawyer and her brother-in-law! Meni wasn't some illegitimate daughter, she was born out of holy matrimony. Why would you do that, and what's your excuse for not leaving anything for Meni? That cannot be!'

'I had nothing to do with your father's plans,' pleaded Madlang-Layon. 'You know him, what he says, goes. It wasn't my place to tell him what to do with his wealth and properties. It was his wish to leave Meni out of his will. He's the father and I've to follow his wish. For justifiable reasons, a father may disinherit his child, and that's something only lawyers would understand. And more importantly— and this is the reason I didn't go against his wishes—your father resented what happened to Meni. I'd rather he removed Meni from his will, because otherwise he would have taken all his wrath out on her. He would have murdered Meni and Delfin with his own hands, if I hadn't been around to rein him in. And it's not all bad that his money and belongings will still go to his own children. He did tell me that if you object, he will put the last will and testament on hold and just spend all his money on luxuries and leisure. If that happens, none of you will get anything. You may not know it, Talia, but your father almost gave away thousands of pesos to Julita and Señora Loleng. Good thing I was around to stop him. And as for Meni, do not despair. She's still family, after all. We won't abandon her, no matter what.

Meni doesn't need to know anything, if we continue to help her and give her anything that she needs.'

Talia could not think of any other objection to raise to her lawyer-husband. Although she was educated, she knew nothing about the legalities of inheritance and estates. She trusted Madlang-Layon's competence and loyalty. Besides, she did not know how to legally argue Meni's case. She had to accept defeat. All her sorrow, she just blamed on her father's cold and cruel heart. She took comfort in the fact that Yoyong cared for Meni and he would never abandon her sister in times of need.

'What exactly did he tell you? That he's leaving and never coming back? Thus, the last will and testament?'

'He didn't say for how many months or years he'll be gone. It's all uncertain for now.'

'Why don't we tag along, then? You said you also wanted to visit Japan.'

'Now's a bad time. Russia and Japan are still at war. And if we leave, who will take care of your father's estate here? We certainly cannot rely on your lazy brother, Siano. He will surely just let things go if the tides were to rush in.'

Talia couldn't help but agree with Yoyong.

'Yoyong, I've a bad feeling about father's departure. I'm afraid he'll die at sea, or die alone in a distant place.'

'Oh, your intuition and gut feeling. Death follows us no matter where we go. And there's nothing we can do to change the mind of your hard-headed old man. I think it would be best for him to leave the country, especially since Don Filemon still holds a serious grudge against him. Did you know about what happened?'

'No. What happened?'

And so Madlang-Layon told Talia the story he had gathered from Don Ramon, about what happened between him, Loleng and Don Filemon. Soon, they were joined by Don Ramon and Siano, and the conversation went on about Don Ramon's departure the next day. Talia, still feeling sorry for her sister, broached the subject of the family heirlooms that Don Ramon had stashed away in one of his suitcases.

'I'm taking them with me!' Don Ramon objected. 'If you wish, you can give her all the simple clothes and accessories, but burn all the fineries that are left behind. The fine jewels that belonged to your mother, those are your mother's and she has no right to anything of your mother's. Your mother, if she were still alive, would surely have strangled your sister for what she did.'

'Father, I don't think Mother would do that. Mother loved Meni so dearly when she was still alive.'

'Nevertheless! If your mother were still here, this wouldn't have happened. She would have blamed you. You were the older sister, and yet you let this happen! I don't want to talk about this anymore. It's getting me all fired up again.'

Talia felt as if a cat had got her tongue. Her father's words pricked a festering wound. She was speechless.

'What do you want should happen? Do you want to see me mocked by that bastard who, after stealing my dear daughter, would be rewarded with riches stolen by his kin? Those who disobey me, I no longer consider my own children. She chose to be with the poor, so shall she live amongst them! That's their own burden to carry now. They've already disgraced me. I won't stand to be an object of ridicule!'

Madlang-Layon could already feel the tension rising. He gave his wife a warning look, as if to tell Talia to drop the conversation. But Talia persisted.

'But Father, since you've already disowned her, please let her have these fine clothes. It would be a pity to leave these to waste. I've no use for them. And mother's jewellery . . .'

'Fine, she can have the clothes. But the jewellery, absolutely not! I'm taking them with me wherever I go, to remind me of the treacherous daughter whom I've punished. That's it. End of discussion. I'm getting all riled up again. My decision is final. Do as I say!'

Everyone in the room bowed their heads upon hearing the old man's words. The tense atmosphere began to subside. After a while, the conversation ended and they all stood up, yawning, ready to retire to rest for the night.

The following morning progressed according to plan. There were no farewells, except friends who were convinced that he was leaving to take care of some business at the factory. He did not bother to see Don Filemon at all and just left him a note sent by post. He sent a memo telling his factory workers to help his son in managing the day-to-day operations while he was away.

He was accompanied by one of his manservants, a young orphan from Pampanga, named Tikong, whom the old man had grown to like very much because the boy was obedient and subservient. Nothing was more endearing to Don Ramon than a slave all willing to do as the master pleased. Tikong had sworn an oath to follow Don Ramon wherever he went, even to his death bed.

Meni, whom Talia had not seen for a week, was clueless about had happened. Talia still had not come to grips with their father's abrupt departure, and she still could not accept how Meni, the rebel child, their own flesh and blood, had been disowned. Talia was afraid her sister might already have heard the news, and she did not want any emotional conflict with Meni. As she was never one to betray her sister or lie to her face, Talia kept her distance from her poor beloved sister.

However, Delfin had known for days that Don Ramon Miranda, owner of The Progress, had left the country. He found it odd that there were no reports about it in the newspapers. This was quite uncharacteristic of Don Ramon, for the wealthy man loved media attention. But Madlang-Layon assured him that the old man was travelling on business. Delfin thought nothing more of it and decided that Meni did not have to know.

But the couple had started wondering why the siblings had stopped paying their daily visits. They thought that Don Ramon, whose wrath knew no bounds, had forbidden them. They had not dared to visit the Mirandas, since they did not want to get into any more trouble with the old man. Besides, the physician, who, at Talia's behest, made regular house calls, discouraged Meni from going outdoors until she had fully recovered.

For several weeks, Madlang-Layon and Delfin had been bumping into each other on the roads, in council meetings, or wherever their duties took them. The two would exchange warm greetings and pleasantries, and when asked why Siano and Talia hadn't visited for days, Madlang-Layon would apologise that he had been busy and that he had been holding them up. In their chance meetings, they never spoke about Don Ramon, for the mere mention of the name only opened old wounds for Delfin, who had not forgotten the pain caused by the old man.

Chapter 21

Meni in Isolation

It had been said that not all illnesses could be cured by doctors, that medicines could not heal the lovesick, that happiness was the only antidote to pain and suffering, and that a woman willing to die for her love should just be allowed to settle down with her man. Such was the case with Meni.

Dr Gatdula had always been able to treat all sorts of illnesses, be they bruises, concussion, nausea, palpitations, ulcers, and the like. But when it came to emotional problems and heartaches, he was of no use. After all his attempts to treat Meni failed, he jokingly suggested that a witch doctor might be the only one who could cure her. He understood that the only way for Meni to get better was if she wanted herself to heal.

Undeniably, it had been Dr Gatdula's advice that had made the family relent and reconsider the marriage of Meni to Delfin. His insistence that the root cause of Meni's illness was her heartache moved Don Ramon to finally grant his daughter's desire.

Meni's condition had been steadily improving, thanks to her new 'physician', 'Doctor' Delfin. It was as if Delfin had found a miracle ointment that washed away all of Meni's aches and pains. Meni was now tucked away, safe from her father's cruel ways, spared from public shame, and full of hope for her unborn child.

She felt totally at peace in her isolation. She was now sharing a home with Delfin. It didn't matter that she didn't have a beautiful bedroom, or a lavishly decorated living room. She didn't care about having a grand piano, huge wardrobes, vanity mirrors, a courtyard full of fragrant blooms, or the other luxuries showered upon her by her father. All of those fine things did not measure up to the joy and warmth she felt in the arms of Delfin. Now, more than ever, she felt truly blessed and she didn't want anything more.

In the morning, feeling ever so light, she would get up and help Delfin's aunt prepare breakfast. But the aunt wouldn't let her soak her fingers, get soiled handling pots, sit in front of the hot stove, handle smelly fish, set the table, or clean up after meals.

'Oh, you're not used to this, my child!' the aunt would tell her whenever she'd offer to help out. 'Menial tasks like these don't suit you, my dear!'

Meni was constantly barred from doing chores. Her aunt-in-law doted on her, repeatedly rushing to her side to ask what she would like to eat or if she was feeling unwell, tirelessly cautioning her to be extra careful with her movements, reminding her to untie her hair when going to sleep, and warning her not to go outside at night. The old woman would make her wear a pouch full of crushed garlic cloves to ward off the evil creatures at night, and Delfin would complain of Meni smelling like spring rolls.

Meni was given round-the-clock care and protection to make sure her labour would be without complications, and the baby would turn out all normal and healthy. The aunt would always scoff at the doctor tending to Meni's pregnancy. 'Back in the day, my mother never relied on doctors and medicines in her pregnancy, or when she went into labour. Look at me and my siblings, we're all still alive and well, even now. I bore several children, but never did I see any doctor at all. All we needed were herbs and roots, and thank God, we're all quite well.'

Thus were the teachings and words of wisdom from Delfin's aunt. The woman had been a widow for years, raised a full-grown man by herself, was now married, and was still raising two young children at her age of forty. Indeed, the aunt was old-fashioned and quite superstitious. Delfin would tease her for blindly holding onto ancient beliefs and notions, and his aunt would always reprimand him for questioning the old customs.

Nevertheless, Meni, who didn't share the old woman's beliefs and notions, quietly obeyed her aunt-in-law and took every medicine that she gave. In this new home, she didn't have to lift a finger at all. She relished this newfound motherly love from Delfin's aunt, a love that for a long time she had never felt while living in her father's house.

Meni didn't feel alone anymore. She had house guests—friends and colleagues of Delfin's, and some old friends who came to see how she was doing—and they would all indulge in cheerful banter until dark.

* * *

During daytime, the only ones in the house were Meni, the aunt, and the two small children. Delfin, Felipe at the publishing house, and even Gudyo, who had rented his own place, would be out at work.

Meni began to worry that she hadn't seen her siblings for a week. Talia had sent all the clothes her father didn't want to give to her, and gave word that she would be visiting again, as soon as Yoyong had free time. Talia's excuse made Meni uneasy. She didn't think Yoyong was reason enough for Talia and Siano not to come and see her. She was worried that something bad might have happened to her siblings. Or did their father forbid them to visit her?

Meni felt the urge to ask Delfin and Felipe to snoop on the house in Santa Cruz to find out what was going on there. The two men willingly obliged and set out, one late afternoon, to spy on Don Ramon's house. All the windows were shuttered, and the house was just as dark and gloomy as it had been when Meni had been gravely ill. The shrubs had gone wild in the courtyard, and a thick dust coated the leaves. The servants, it seemed, had abandoned their tasks and duties.

The two men would have abandoned their mission if it weren't for Tino, who came out to buy something at the Chinese store. Felipe called out to Tino and motioned for him to come closer. Tino was elated to see his old friends: Felipe whom he had not seen for a long time, and Delfin, who was the root cause of the chaos that descended upon the house of Don Ramon. It was from Tino that the two men learnt of Don Ramon's flight, how Meni's name might have been removed from the old man's last will and testament, and how Talia had wept and wept over Meni's plight. Delfin and Felipe were deeply disturbed by this news. On their way home, the two men wondered how they would break the news to Meni.

'I was just thinking, what was that last will and testament that Tino mentioned?' Felipe wondered aloud.

'That Meni's name might have been removed from the old man's last will and testament,' Delfin supplied.

'And if that were the case, did you want your wife to inherit something from her father?'

'Felipe, you know my stand when it comes to such things. You need not ask me at all. My concern is about the old man's legal basis for striking Meni off his last will and testament. What rule book did he use to justify absolutely disowning his own flesh and blood?'

'Rule book!' Felipe blurted mockingly. 'I was fortunate enough not to lay hands on such a rule book! But from the little I've read and heard, such rule books are nothing but an inverted pyramid of rights and obligations, where the bottom pointed part refers to the rights and privileges of the poor and the weak, while the top, fat part pertains to the rights of the rich and the mighty. These rule books are all laws heaped by masters upon slaves. And don't forget, Don Ramon had a brilliant lawyer, his son-in-law, by his side. Surely, those two found a way to circumvent the laws governing inheritance!'

'I don't know, Ipe,' Delfin said, shaking his head. 'They can have their way with the laws. They really didn't have to draw up that last will and testament. Remember that one time I had a heated argument with Don Ramon and Don Filemon, when I quoted Goethe and raised my objection against inherited wealth? Didn't I say that passing on amassed wealth through inheritance only breeds lazy and apathetic offsprings?' And what right do parents have in passing on to their children wealth that was certainly ill-gotten, anyway? That's exactly how prodigal children have proliferated!'

'Indeed,' Felipe agreed. 'And it would be such a sight to behold, the children fighting tooth and nail to get a lion's share of their parents' riches. That's when we get to see the ugly truth that blood is not always thicker than water, playing out. That's when all the stench comes out. All because of the wealth that they never really worked for.'

'It reminds me of the old superstition that when rich people pass away, their souls are sent back to earth to haunt the children they left behind, to urge them to return all their wealth and belongings to the poor.'

'Ah, I know of similar stories,' Felipe said. 'And a lot of them mention the Church, how aside from giving back to the poor, departed souls ask that part of their wealth be given to "the house of God".'

'Yes, that, too,' Delfin agreed. 'The Church always receives inheritance from dead rich people. She could act as an executor presiding over the dead rich people's wealth and belongings. She would have been the perfect model of a truly communist society, following the communist ideals of Jesus Christ. But then, I'd already lost all faith in the Church. The clergy are no longer the austere holy men of the old days, for they have become greedy and corrupt. Felipe, it is people like Don Ramon to whom such old stories and superstitions should be told, precisely because of the values he adheres to. Men like Don Ramon and Filemon, and even your own father, Captain Loloy, they worship money and wealth as their god. Heaven for them is right here on earth, not in the afterlife.'

Felipe quietly mused. Men like Don Ramon, Don Felipe and his father, Captain Loloy, were raised to be decent rich men by giving alms to the poor, donations to the families of the deceased, and doing charity. These men had been moulded to think that was what decent rich men should do; that by doing so, they will give back to the poor some of the wealth they never really earned themselves.

Delfin guessed what Felipe was thinking. 'I don't know about your father, for I have no personal knowledge of his affairs. But Don Ramon! The little Carnegie! Ha!' And the two men laughed heartily.

Then, Delfin added, 'If he disowned Meni just because she chose me, a man he absolutely hated, do you think he would bother throwing away his money to the poor, whom, I am quite sure, he truly disdains for lacking the same ambition and drive that he has?'

'But do you really think Don Ramon would disown his own daughter, just like that?' Felipe argued.

'Oh, I have no doubts about it. That's totally in sync with Don Ramon's character.' Delfin confirmed. 'What I am wondering is, what did Madlang-Layon have to say about that? Did he give his consent?'

'I already told you, Delfin. Madlang-Layon is a "good boy". He must have done exactly what a good lawyer would have done.'

'But would he, on his honour and dignity, agree to the old man's wishes?'

'C'mon, Delfin. Honour is laughable. That's money talking, my friend. Surely, he would set aside his honour and dignity in the face of gold coins and treasury notes? If Meni were to be removed from the old man's last will and testament, to whom would Meni's share go, then? Of course, to the two other children. Surely, Talia would be receiving more. Remember, what is Talia's is also his.'

'I don't think Yoyong is capable of doing that. Perhaps, Don Ramon took Meni's share with him when he left? But Yoyong couldn't . . .'

'Believe whatever it is you want to believe, Delfin. I really wouldn't know any better. But somehow, I cannot shake off this feeling that your benevolent brother-in-law must have put the old man under a spell, or he must have performed some trickery of sorts. We both have seen many times how every time Madlang-Layon said no or that cannot be, Don Ramon would immediately back down. You've seen how close these two men have become. Besides, Madlang-Layon is quite aware of your socialist leanings . . .'

'What a way to take advantage of my socialist principles!' Delfin said, laughing.

'We shall soon find out!'

The two men were standing outside Don Ramon's house. Dusk had already set in and darkness had shrouded the four corners of the sky, and was now descending upon the house that stood far away from the street lights.

* * *

Delfin and Felipe decided not to waste time in breaking the news to Meni, although they chose not to tell her that her father had left the country for good. Meni broke into heavy sobs and started choking and catching her breath. Again, she fell unconscious.

Perhaps it was a bad idea to tell Meni, even though at first the two men tried to withhold that bit of information about Don Ramon not coming back, ever. But Meni already had a bad feeling about the situation at home, and so Delfin was forced to tell her the truth.

Meni regained consciousness momentarily, thanks to the medicines that were always at hand at home. They had reason now to fetch the doctor for an urgent house call. Delfin wrote a letter to Talia to tell her of this most recent mishap, without telling her that he had found out about their father because he and Felipe were spying outside their house. It was just hours after the letter had been sent that Talia came to visit Meni, once again.

Chapter 22

Madlang-Layon's Intentions

'Father wouldn't have left if it weren't for you!' Talia scolded Meni after she was criticized for not preventing their old man from leaving.

'Fine, blame me for him leaving.' Meni answered. 'But you could have told me! I could have had the chance, on the pain of death, to beg for his forgiveness and plead for him to stay. But you didn't care about me. It seems to me you no longer regard me as a member of this family.'

Meni broke down in tears, which prompted the people in the room to rush to her side to calm her down, lest she fainted from the distress.

The exchange of heated words stopped at once. Delfin and Siano interceded to banish the tension between the two sisters, who clearly harboured ill feelings toward each other. They began to speak to each other in a calm manner. Talia, upon seeing Meni becoming more receptive, told her all she needed to know. She didn't withhold a single morsel of truth, including the bit about Meni's name being removed from their father's last will and testament.

Meni was not bothered by her father's last will and testament. Talia was worried Meni would accuse her of conspiring with their father, but this was really farthest from Meni's mind. The news did not shake Meni even a bit.

'I would always respect your wishes,' Meni said. 'I followed my own heart's desires, and I would willingly accept Father's decisions, and that of my brother and sister. Especially you, Talia, to whom I owe everything, even my life. I'm not bothered by Father's decision at all, if that's what he wanted. Delfin and I, by God's mercy, will survive without the inheritance. My only request, my sister, is that you do not forsake me in my time of need. I worry that I may not overcome my delicate situation at the moment.'

'Oh, please stop that!' Talia cut her off, sighing heavily, tears streaming down her cheeks.

For a moment, Talia imagined a very dark butterfly fluttering around Meni, as if to confirm her sister's fear. She willed the image out of her head and decided it wouldn't do Meni any good for all of them to be gloomy and wallow in despair. She thought she should cheer her sister up, instead.

Siano's wife, who was listening to the sisters' conversation, went out to get Delfin, fearing that the atmosphere inside the house was once again thickening with tension.

'What's with the two of you?' Delfin said with a smile. 'It has only been minutes and here you are, crying your hearts out again. Why don't the two of you speak of how to love each other, for the sake of the children you are carrying in your wombs?'

The sisters' faces brightened upon hearing Delfin's words, and they began to smile. It was now evident that Talia was also pregnant and would most likely deliver not long after Meni.

'There's no reason for you two to be sad, now that you're both expecting.' Delfin added. 'You two will have a lawyer and a journalist, you'll see.'

'Ah, Delfin.' Talia answered. 'If they were to become a lawyer and a journalist and end up in the same situation we are in, I'd rather they died before they even became adults! Let the Grim Reaper take them away upon their birth.'

'Oh, you're just saying that,' Delfin teased. 'I'm sure that once they're born, you will pay no heed to any mishap. You will want them to survive, and you will definitely rush to their aid.'

'Be that as it may, ' Talia argued, 'now that our family is going through this terrible crisis, how I wish death took us when we were just little children. We may be wealthy and living in luxury, but we are far less fortunate than those born in poverty.'

Talia's words awakened in Delfin's mind some of the socialist thoughts that had lain dormant inside him for a while. Here was an enlightened, privileged woman, not a socialist by inclination, uttering the truth that happiness in life does not come from material wealth; both the rich and the poor suffer from despair, harbour deep feelings of regret and resentment, and experience sorrow and misfortune. Delfin thought it ironic that a wealthy woman could easily succumb to hardship, that someone with access to great wealth could easily drown in sorrow, and that those who are ruthless toward the underprivileged could be weak in the midst of poverty.

Delfin knew what Talia and Meni were arguing about—Don Ramon's flight and Meni's disinheritance. He knew Meni didn't care about her father's wealth, as he had long indoctrinated her in socialist ideology. He had professed that he married her not for her family's money. Delfin taught Meni that a man's wealth should be passed on not only to his children or loved ones; instead, the bulk, if not the whole of it, should be given to cooperatives, or charities, or the town's treasury, for the benefit of the general population.

These and other teachings were no longer new to Meni. Although she may not be as hardcore as Delfin, a true socialist, Meni clung to these ideals as she argued with Talia about the inheritance.

* * *

Talia and her sister-in-law decided to stay for lunch at Meni's, and Siano and Yoyong went on their way home. Later in the afternoon, Yoyong began to worry whether he should go back to fetch the two women. He was tormented by doubts every time he thought of Don Ramon and the children he had left behind, and especially Meni and Delfin. He couldn't deny that he played a big part in excluding Meni from Don Ramon's last will, and in being assigned as the executor of the old man's sizable wealth. Despite having been an exemplary husband and brother-in-law, people would not put it past him that he may have been corrupted by greed for power and money, which he would never have gathered from just being a lawyer.

Recalling the days when he was just courting Talia, it was clear to him that his ambition for power and wealth had pushed him to get close to Don Ramon. He would not have met the old man if it weren't for the legal battles they had won in court. They wouldn't have bonded intimately—and this was during the time that Madlang-Layon's first wife was still alive—if it weren't for their mutual love of horseracing and other pastimes. In fact, money brought them together, just as well as the thirst for greater wealth and luxury. And after marrying Talia, Madlang-Layon gained greater access to lucrative opportunities. Surely, nobody would doubt that he used his status as the son-in-law and lawyer to achieve his lifelong aspirations.

Nonetheless, Madlang-Layon had always held himself as a man of honour and dignity. He was a man of good heart, because if that weren't so, he would never have misgivings about reaching his goals and ambitions. He wouldn't be feeling the pangs of guilt at all for the secret dealings between him and Don Ramon. He would shun dirty linen from ever touching his otherwise unblemished skin.

Such were the thoughts going through his head when Yoyong came home to find that Talia and Siano's wife were still at Meni's. He was torn between wanting and not wanting to go and fetch them. He felt like he had a star branded on his forehead that he didn't want Meni and Delfin to see. It was as if the cat had got his tongue, even though he hadn't spoken to Delfin about these matters. Delfin, although still young, was quite accustomed to lawyerly things; a man who was quite familiar with the inner workings of treachery, someone skillful enough to detect any sign of betrayal. Nobody could outsmart Delfin with hollow promises, for just like every other journalist, he possessed an intimate knowledge of worldly affairs everywhere.

On the one hand, Madlang-Layon knew Delfin to be a socialist who held strong objections against inheritance and personal wealth such as Don Ramon's, but that didn't mean Delfin would passively accept Meni being disowned by her father. Delfin, undeterred by the fact that Talia was Meni's sister, would surely raise hell for having been denied their fair share of the old man's riches. Meni's share was by no means meagre. For a socialist like Delfin, one hundred—or even fifty—thousand pesos was already a huge sum of money that could be used to build an enterprise that would deliver the working class from their misery. 100 grand! That would have been enough to build a modest house, a good library, and a medium-sized processing factory, all for the benefit of the proletarian society.

It would not do Madlang-Layon any good to feign innocence and lay all the blame on Don Ramon, since it really was the old man who had the power to prepare his last will and testament. It would be hard for anyone to believe he was merely acting as a mediator and a pacifist to Don Ramon. If he were to wash his hands off this whole mess, he would stand to lose a lot more. He wouldn't be able to present the signed agreement as proof that Don Ramon willingly designated him as executor. If the affidavit were to be disposed of, then he would have no power to execute anything at all.

Madlang-Layon, out of due diligence, did counsel Don Ramon on the ramifications and legalities of excluding Meni from the last will and testament. In his mind, he could readily cite several law books, none of which made even the slightest mention of something to this effect that 'a father is well within his legal rights to deprive an offspring of his wealth, solely on the basis of the offspring marrying the wrong spouse.'

But Don Ramon is an extremely stubborn man, and it was this stubbornness that led to Madlang-Layon standing to benefit greatly, and Delfin and Meni getting absolutely nothing.

'Find a way to circumvent whatever laws stand in my way,' Madlang-Layon recalled the old man saying. 'Bottom line, I don't want that traitor child of mine to get anything from me!'

'But Meni is a legitimate heir whose only mistake was marrying the man you didn't approve of,' Madlang-Layon had counselled the old man.

'That marriage is precisely what I despise!' Don Ramon said. 'If my daughter had the courage to go against my will, why should I be forced to honour her as my heir and beneficiary?'

'Oh, but that's not reason enough,' Madlang-Layon answered. 'A child's right to the parent's estate is immanent, and such right cannot be taken away just because she married the wrong man. Even her right to marry anyone she chooses is inviolable.'

'But she wasn't of the right age when she got married, and she disgraced herself by getting herself pregnant before she even got married!'

'It doesn't matter, Father. Didn't you give your blessing?'

'That's your fault!' Don Ramon answered.

'That's not my fault. My wrongdoing was having the desire to bring peace to this household as quickly as possible. It was clear that no amount of fighting and arguing could change the fact that your daughter was miserable. It was inevitable that the couple would end up together.'

'In that case,' Don Ramon said, 'your law degree is useless! Couldn't you find a way to deliver what I want? Sure, I'm no lawyer! But don't you think it's utterly humiliating for a father to give in to his rebel daughter's wish to marry a starving vagabond, a socialist and anarchist?'

'Don Ramon, your words are too harsh! I would have you know that the intelligence of lawyers is governed by the dictates of the law.'

Don Ramon scoffed. 'Pfft, so what? What if we can justify depriving Meni of her rights as heir, on the basis of her marriage to a socialist–anarchist?'

'That would be unprecedented here in our country.'

'Then set the precedent! Make this the first case to add to your reputation as an esquire! Then everyone in government would know that such travesties happen in the country!'

'That line of argument will not stand in the court of law!'

'And why not? I would assert that it is justifiable to deprive an errant daughter of her inheritance, and it is equally justifiable to withhold my wealth from a socialist! Don't you see? These socialists are bent on opposing the wealthy and the ruling class!'

'I beg your pardon?'

'They don't like money, they hate rules, they reject reason; they're far worse than prodigal sons and daughters!'

'Assuming those things were true . . .'

'They're absolutely true!' Don Ramon stood his ground.

'But Meni is your child, not Delfin, no?'

'That is immaterial! What would be Meni's would be Delfin's as well, now that they're legally married!'

'You could stipulate certain conditions for Meni to be eligible to claim her inheritance. That you could do.'

'Like how?'

'When she gives birth and the child survives and grows up, then she can claim her inheritance. That way, the beneficiaries would be her and her child.'

'And who might this child be that I would want to nurture and care for? The offspring of the one who had the gall to go against my wishes! You know the apple doesn't fall far from the tree. Meni's already been brainwashed by Delfin and I am pretty sure the same would happen to their child. Meni would not have disobeyed me if it weren't for the influence of Delfin.'

'I agree, Father. But . . .'

'You never run out of buts.' Don Ramon was infuriated. 'So, you're saying there's no way for me to get out of this shameful mess? This is absolute humiliation, Honorio! Don't even think . . .'

Madlang-Layon, already running out of words to refute the old man who desperately clung to his wicked line of reasoning, scrambled for the copy of the *Civil Code* to show to the stubborn Don Ramon. He showed the pages where the law outlined specific conditions for disinheritance. The old man shook his head at what he was reading. Then all of a sudden, he exclaimed in excitement.

'Here, look at Article 853, second and third clauses. Can't we use these as our basis?'

Madlang-Layon struggled to contain his frustration. 'No! It's not like Meni physically assaulted you, nor did she ever utter disrespectful words toward you. On the contrary, she was all humble towards you.'

'That's the second clause. What about this, the third one?' The old man insisted.

'But Don Ramon, that would be to accuse Meni of having committed immoral acts.'

'Yeah? What moral acts has she done lately?'

'This clause refers to prostitution, solicitation for sex. That's about selling your body and your dignity.'

'Not only did she sell my honour, she tarnished it, crushed it, completely destroyed it! And . . .'

Madlang-Layon was at a loss for words. It was impossible to reason with the old man whose mind was already blinded by wrath. He fell silent and no longer said a word. But the old man, who had grown impatient with Madlang-Layon's lack of cooperation, issued a final declaration to end the discussion.

'If that's the case, so be it. I will still do as I please. Let them squint in the dark. And you can be at ease. Just let me do this alone then . . .'

This was how Madlang-Layon's conversations with Don Ramon often ended, before the old man left the country. Madlang-Layon would not stop reasoning with the stubborn old man. In hindsight, he thought it might have been best to just let the old man have his way. That way, he would have had nothing to do with the fine print of the old man's last will and testament, and he wouldn't have to hide in shame from Meni and Delfin.

Unfortunately, that wasn't how things turned out to be. He was named as the executor of the old man's will and testament, the one person who stood to gain the most from the secret arrangements with Don Ramon. He went with the flow and feigned ignorance of the stipulations of the last will and testament, signed in the presence of Don Ramon's closest allies as witnesses. He no longer resisted. He would hold custody of the last will and testament until the old man passed away, with the hopes that when that day came, Meni and Delfin would not file a lawsuit to question the legality of the document. And should Meni and Delfin win their case, he would just simply wash his hands off the case and deny any part in the making of the last will and testament. After all, the document would clearly show that everything that was written there was the old man's wish, and his alone.

And so it was that Madlang-Layon decided not to go and fetch Talia and her sister-in-law. It was already dusk when Talia and Siano's wife, who got tired of waiting for Yoyong to pick them up at Meni's, decided that Madlang-Layon had no intentions of coming to get them. And so, they left Meni's house and went home.

* * *

Since that day, all they could talk about at Meni's was how Don Ramon callously left the country and disinherited Meni.

Delfin and Felipe were in agreement that the last will and testament was drawn up under the guidance of Madlang-Layon. They suspected that Madlang-Layon had turned his back on friendship and loyalty. They were yet to see the actual last will and testament, but Talia had sent them an abstract, as the official last will could only be read upon the death of Don Ramon. They also found out that all the livestock, vehicles, and equipment were given to Madlang-Layon as per a duly notarized statement signed by Don Ramon himself. It was the same notary public in Escolta that revealed to Delfin the excerpts of the transcript of the agreement. Delfin and Felipe concluded that, indeed, Madlang-Layon and Don Ramon had clearly conspired to come up with these horrible machinations.

When Meni found out about these things, she was so ashamed and she felt so betrayed by her siblings and Madlang-Layon. She never imagined Yoyong would willingly work with her father to disown her, as she thought her disobedience was not reason enough to be mistreated in this way.

Meni was in disbelief at first, but after a while, she decided to take the matter up with her siblings and discover the truth about Madlang-Layon's involvement. But Delfin discouraged her. Talia came by one day to invite Meni to their house, but Delfin refused permission. He quietly asked Meni to refrain from stepping foot in her old man's house, and to never take any of the disputed wealth that belonged to her father.

The siblings began to grow apart; gradually, Talia and Meni became cold toward each other. The money and the gifts and the medicines that came from Talia dwindled, and Meni stopped asking for financial aid altogether. Talia, upon her doctor's orders, had been forced to stay indoors in order to not contract any illness that might affect her delicate pregnancy.

What made matters worse was when Talia found out that it was Delfin who forbade her sister from coming over to their house. She was so furious, she didn't care anymore what Delfin's reasons were. She began to feel resentful that Meni married Delfin, whom they never approved of. She started resenting Meni as well, for she thought that Meni was such an ingrate to be blindly following her husband's wishes. Negative thoughts and emotions began to grow inside Talia. 'They have nothing on me. I am not one to give in to their emotional blackmail, if that's what this is about. Fine, if she doesn't want to come over, as I surely am not going to visit her either.'

The two sisters stopped reaching out to each other. Even Delfin and Madlang-Layon had had a falling out and were no longer on speaking terms. Such a fallout was not without financial setbacks for Meni and Delfin. Delfin's earnings at the press, plus Felipe's contributions, were hardly enough for their growing needs. Delfin was in danger of quitting school as he could no longer pay for the costs of his education. What complicated the situation for Delfin was that his membership in all sorts of councils and organizations obliged him to keep shelling out money for contributions. Delfin was forced to cut down on his expenses and stopped taking the horse-drawn carriage and abandoned his old habit of buying new books at his favourite bookstore.

Meni also had to do her fair share. She quietly endured their impoverished conditions and kept reassuring Delfin with a smile on her face. But no amount of pretending could hide the naked truth from Delfin, for he could see how much his wife was suffering. Several times, Meni offered to pawn or sell her precious jewellery, but she would back down upon seeing Delfin's remorseful tears streaming down his cheeks. Many times, Meni professed she would endure any hardship, but she could never bear to see her husband weep. Once, they even had an argument, but who was to blame? Who between them was at fault?

'Delfin, what if we contest my father's last will?' Meni once suggested to Delfin, when they were talking about the hardships that they were facing.

'Why?' Delfin asked. 'Can't you endure our poverty and suffering any longer?'

'No, it's not that. I feel guilty that you're toiling so hard, all because of me! What with my frequent visits to the doctor and all the prescription medicines. Why do we have to endure so much pain and suffering when there's a solution at hand? Here we are, scraping the bottom when others are benefitting from what is rightfully ours?'

'Ours, you say! Ours is that which we worked hard to earn. Let them relish the wealth that they did not earn. We do not have to take any of that. We are far more blessed and honourable than they are.'

'Yes, indeed, but . . .'

'Let us honour your father's wishes, Meni. If it is true that he refused to give you any of his wealth, then so be it. For us Filipinos, we strive to honour the wishes of our parents, especially that of our dearly departed parents. We already went against your father's will by getting married; let us obey him now if he doesn't wish to give you anything. We may have the right to persecute them, but you know the kind of person I am and where I stand on these things. Be one with me in suffering and hardship, and you will find blessings and joy that are beyond your siblings' reach.'

Meni, upon hearing such soothing words, felt at peace and buried her sorrows in silent tears.

Chapter 23

Thanks to 'Mr Fiend'

Tentay had many other admirers, aside from Felipe. More so when Mang Andoy passed away, and when Felipe was away for more than a month. On several occasions, driven by lust, Tentay's suitors made attempts to sexually assault her.

She might have come from a poor family, but Tentay always presented herself neatly and decently. She had an attractive face that lured picky suitors. It wasn't surprising that her olive-skinned beauty and gentle demeanour often elicited praise from other women: 'Oh, if I were a man, I would court Tentay!' or 'If I had a younger brother, I would have him marry her.' But even as women profess their admiration for a fair lady, it is unsurprising for them to suspect that beneath that veneer of earthly virtues lie dirty secrets.

Certainly, 'Mr Fiend' was one of the men who lusted after Tentay!

'Mr Fiend' was the type of guy whom nobody could tell if he was married, or single, or widowed. Despite their efforts at digging up the truth about him, Tentay and her mother failed to find any clues as to his real identity and origin. He just turned up one day at their town, on a December morning after Felipe had just returned, and had stayed on since. He introduced himself as Juan Karugdog, and whether or not that was his real name, people in the town called him 'Mr Fiend'.

Since he had met Tentay, he had lingered all day and night outside her hut like a fiendish creature on the prowl—as if waiting for its prey to come out. Like a hound, he would tail Tentay wherever she went, keeping his distance and never establishing contact.

Nobody knew what his occupation was. It was said that once he was seen carrying a holstered gun tucked under his shirt, thus spurring rumours that he was some secret agent. People stayed away from him and shunned him like a black snake—feared by many, befriended by a few, and despised by all. Speculations flew about him because of his secretive manner and how he spoke in innuendos at times and with brutal frankness at others. He acted as if he wielded power and authority, was a force to be reckoned with, and therefore, a man whom everyone should respect and love. Tentay's neighbours had warned her never to let Juan Karugdog into her house.

Nonetheless, Juan Karugdog kept visiting Tentay and dogged her on the streets. He didn't seem to know how to properly court a lady and kept showing up at her doorstep at unholy hours and tirelessly bragging to Tentay that he was a fearsome man who was always brutal to those who wronged him.

What was Tentay to do with him? They were all women in the house, and they felt utterly powerless to deal with his arrogance and fend off his threats. Out of fear of being raped by Mr Fiend, Tentay began carrying a pocket knife in her purse when she went out, in case she needed to defend herself against his advances. She would politely entertain him at home, but whenever he behaved threateningly, she would leave and lock herself up in her room, or go out and pretend to take care of household chores.

Juan Karugdog, indeed, was a man so full of himself. He would let the coins in his pocket jingle as if to make himself utterly irresistible to people who had no money. Aling Tere, who had known the man for barely a month, was already fed up with Mr Fiend, but was too much of a proper old lady to shoo him out of her house. She told Karugdog that Tentay was already set to marry a man who was out of town and would be returning from the province soon. The revelation further emboldened Karugdog, who declared that he was willing to die and to kill another man who would foil his plans. The women instantly regretted telling Karugdog that Tentay already had a boyfriend.

* * *

It was just before Felipe returned that Mr Fiend committed a grave act of transgression against Tentay. He came to Tentay's house on one late afternoon, just as the sun was about to set. That evening, Tentay did not invite him to supper. It was already late, but Karugdog acted as if he had no plans of leaving. It was already ten in the evening but he was still there at Tentay's. Tentay went out of the house as Aling Tere was putting the children to bed, and Karugdog followed her. He circled around Tentay, mumbling words that she couldn't make out.

'What is that you're saying? 'Tentay blurted.

'Quiet!' Mr Fiend shushed her and pressed the palm of his hand against her mouth.

Tentay was overwhelmed by shock and rage at the man's bold move. She could not shout out to her mother for help, but there was no need, as Aling Tere, who had heard her cry, was already at the door, peering out to investigate what was happening. The old woman could see Karugdog bent over her daughter as if whispering something to her. Aling Tere did not make a sound. She steeled herself and prepared to shout out to the neighbours for help. Karugdog was still mumbling words that Tentay could hardly understand.

'Why would you be aggrieved?' Tentay uttered when she understood what the man was trying to say.

'You already have a boyfriend. What about me? Why didn't you tell me the day I first came to visit you? Why did you lead me on?'

Tentay uttered to herself, 'The nerve you have! Why should I even tell you I have a boyfriend?'

'So that I didn't have to fall in love with you!'

'Oh, how easy is it for you to be smitten! I've only known you for a few weeks, and you expect me to let you in on my secrets?'

'You kept secrets because you wanted to deceive me!'

Tentay cut him off, shaking in anger. 'Mr Juan, don't you go accusing me of wrongdoing in my own house! What motives do

I have in deceiving you? Watch your words. You're not talking to an ignoramus!'

Tentay thought this man would be choking on his own blood if she were a violent woman. She realized she didn't have her pocket knife with her, so she motioned to go back inside the house, but Mr Fiend stood in her path.

'Don't you dare leave if you wish to settle this matter amicably!'

Tentay froze in fear at the man's threatening words.

'You know for a fact that I wouldn't hesitate to kill or be killed, so don't you humiliate me. I ask you, is it true you already have a boyfriend?'

After a moment of silence, Tentay admitted. 'Why would I deny the truth?'

'Who is he?'

'He is not here.'

'Where is he?'

'Why do you want to know?'

'I want to know if he's a worthy man.'

'He is a fearless man. But he's not here. He's somewhere in the East.'

'He can't ever set foot here again!'

Tentay thought Karugdog had gone mad.

'I swear to make every effort to get to know this man!'

'I will introduce you to him myself when he's here!'

'Don't you mock me!'

'I do not wish to mock you, but . . .'

'What else have you got to say?' Karugdog again pressed his palm hard on her mouth.

Tentay resisted and pried his hand away from her mouth. Burning with rage, she screamed at Mr Fiend.

'Leave now, Mr Juan, if you do not wish to be harmed!'

'That's all it takes for you to get angry?'

'Leave, now!' Tentay commanded.

'Fine, I'm leaving! But not without a token from you . . .'

'What token?'

'A little . . . kiss . . .'

Karugdog moved in to plant a kiss with his dirty lips on Tentay's pristine right cheek, but Tentay countered with a loud smack and screamed for help to her mother, who came rushing in, cursing at the vile Karugdog. Mr Fiend reached for his gun, the women shrieked, and within moments, the neighbours, roused by the commotion, came to their rescue. By then, the cowardly Mr Fiend had already fled the scene. Before scurrying away, he left a stern warning: 'One day, you will all die at my own hands!'

After that incident, Mr Fiend did not leave Tentay alone. He never went back to her house, but he lingered around her house like a bat in the dark of night. Tentay and her mother were so terrified that Aling Tere no longer allowed Victor and Lucio out of the house. They found solace in their kind neighbors who had volunteered to chase off any intruders.

Rumours started going around in the vicinity of Timbugan that a fiendish creature had been terrorizing San Lazaro. Some said that it was an American outsider working at the local mill. The rumors struck fear in the hearts of the locals, especially the pregnant women and little children. Others believed it was a dog-like creature with a short tail, except that the tail was actually a revolver. Some thought that it was a wild boar that snarled upon sensing people nearby as it disappeared into the dark.

Even in San Lazaro, where people had known that the rumors sprang from the incident with the suitor whom Tentay had scorned. Word started going around that, indeed, a fiend roamed around at night. But they knew that the creature of the night was Mr Fiend, not some American outsider.

The tale of the night fiend reached even the towns of Mayhaligi and Oroquieta. The townsfolk believed one could hear someone walking around in chains outside their house at night, but nobody actually ever saw who or what it was. They speculated it was an escaped convict, thus the sound of ball and chains being dragged around. Such a rumour frightened the locals, for they believed it was a dangerous criminal who had been sentenced to life for murder, a monster who would slaughter whomever he chanced upon at night, drain the blood and devour the hearts and feast on the organs of its victims. This fiend would break into people's houses, looking for cooked rice for his cannibalistic feast, invading kitchens, upending clay pots, wreaking havoc when his search turned up nothing. Victims would be fortunate if their lives were spared in this case. Nobody could say for sure where this escaped convict was hiding during the day. Some said he must be seeking refuge in the tombs of La Loma; others would say that he came out of the forests of Diliman and Masambong, while there were some who said that he returned to the Bilibid Prisons before daybreak.

All these rumours and tales reached Juan Karugdog, who felt mildly amused by it all. Fearing that his life might be in danger, he decided to stay away from San Lazaro for a week. He sent word to Tentay that he was no longer in Manila and that he had gone to a distant province on a new assignment. Karugdog's disappearance put the neighbours at ease. Then, just as the neighborhood watch had stopped, Mr Fiend stood at Tentay's doorstep, one Saturday evening, politely and meekly asking to be let in. He came bearing gifts of snacks and food for the little children, and he asked for forgiveness for his acts of transgression. He implored that if Aling Tere would not accept him as Tentay's suitor, then he would like to be accepted at least as one of her own children and Tentay's younger brother.

Of course, Tentay and Aling Tere could not be fooled by such silly antics. Nonetheless, Aling Tere feigned acceptance and muttered, 'Of course, if you're truly remorseful and sincere about becoming part of our family'.

Juan was so elated that, in his old, arrogant manner, he let himself in. He was so egged on by Aling Tere's mercy that he felt emboldened to ask if he could stay for the night, since he was tired from his trip.

'I'm afraid that cannot be,' Aling Tere politely said. 'People would talk if they found out that you stayed here overnight.'

'Then I'll leave before sunrise.'

'Even so, I cannot let that happen. It will be highly inappropriate.'

'But I won't be making any trouble . . .'

'Be that as it may, our neighbours hate you so much. They might attack you if they ever found out that you were here.'

'I'm not afraid.'

'Ah! But I had already told you that I cannot let you stay!'

Upon hearing this, Mr Fiend no longer objected. Tentay, who was eavesdropping from inside her room, was getting impatient that her mother had not yet sent the crazy man away. Karugdog finally left, feeling glad that he had been received well by the old woman, but disappointed as well for not being allowed to sleep over. He just walked to the gate mumbling to himself. In the dark street outside, he surveyed the house to estimate the height of the windows. He said to himself, 'You just wait, Tentay . . . tonight at midnight!'

Karugdog strolled along the street of Cervantes, occasionally pausing to glance back at where he had just come from. As he drew close to the Opera House, he saw a big man standing in the middle of the road. It was an American constable, which made him nervous, prompting him to take a detour, much like a cowardly thief running away from persecution. He went past the officer without trouble, although the American did stare long and hard in his direction, upon realizing that he had deviated from the main road. The streetlamps shone on the road, and since it was just ten in the evening, many people were still out.

Mr Fiend just continued walking until he reached Libertad Theatre. A live show was still going on there, as well as in the Zorrilla Theatre, but he did not go in to watch, since it was already late. He just stood outside, looking at the posters plastered near the theatre doors. He could read, although with difficulty, as he squinted and went up close to decipher what he was reading. He was almost enticed to buy a general admissions ticket upon hearing the sounds of singing, the live band playing, and the audience laughing inside the theatres.

But he decided against it and instead went to a stranger and asked what time it was. 'Not long now,' he mumbled to himself. He went to the women selling nuts and boiled eggs and what-not, bought peanuts which he stuffed in the pockets of his suit and trousers. 'I wish I had brought my wristwatch!' he told himself. Now and then, he would go and ask passersby about the time. He did not want to risk carrying his watch anymore, since it was rare and expensive. 'Should I wait until the live shows are over? Or maybe not. Better that people are still out

on the streets at this time. No one would suspect I am up to no good.'
He decided not to wait any longer and started walking back to San Lazaro.

The gate to the house was not properly secured; all that he needed
to do was insert a finger, untie the knot, and very lightly push the
gate to get inside the yard. Karugdog knew his way very well around
the premises.

Through the cracks in the windows and the holes in the walls of the
house, he could see the faint glimmer of the gas lantern. The occupants
normally put out the light at night before they went to bed, but since
the incident with Tentay, they had the gas lantern lit all night.

'Well, I'll take my chances,' he thought to himself as he tried
to figure out his next move. 'I'll climb this window near the lantern.
I'll snuff out the light, or if I fail to do so, then I'll just have to do it
with the light on. I'll shoot whoever makes a sound or resists me.'

He felt for his gun tucked in the back of his trousers, and he also
carried a dagger with which to silence his victims, if needed.

He took the short ladder lying nearby and set it just below the
window. Quietly and slowly, he climbed without making the slightest
sound, slightly lifted the window panel, and peered inside. Tentay was
not in the living room, and he thought she might be sleeping in her
room. He saw Julian and Lucio sleeping beside Aling Tere and thought
that Victor must be with Tentay.

In the faint light inside the tiny house, he could see Tentay's feet
and Victor's head as they slept in her room.

He wondered how he could cut the wire that secured the windows.
The dagger would be of no use. If he were to enter through the other
window, he would not have a way to put out the gas lantern.

'I might have to break in through the other window!'

And that was what he did: he moved the ladder and climbed to the
other window, which was also tied with a wire, but even more tightly.
This family, in the absence of a grown man, had nothing but a wire to
protect themselves.

But there was no way he could get in. Neither was it a good idea to
break in through the main door and get past the living room. It seemed
that Karugdog's plans would be foiled!

'What if I just sneak in through the bamboo slats from underneath the house?' Mr Fiend wondered.

The underside of the house was just a few feet above the ground. He could slash an opening through the floor of the room big enough for his head and body to go through.

He concluded that this was the best move.

'Yes, that's it! From underneath the floor!' Karugdog was now filled with excitement.

The darkness of the night served as his accomplice. It so happened that the house was situated deep inside the neighbourhood, a good distance away from the town's main street, far from the reach of the streetlights. He could surely carry out his plans without trouble, except if the sleeping occupants were roused from sleep.

Like a clever and skillful burglar, he first cleared a path for his escape by removing the obstacles around the house. He imagined Tentay might surrender out of fear, or put up a fight out of sheer rage. In any case, Aling Tere would surely wake up and scream for help. And there was a good chance that the neighbours, who had guarded the house, would come to the rescue in no time at all. And even if he could make an opening from under, it would be quite another matter to escape from his attackers through the same hole. He imagined all these scenarios in his head and thought he would need to clear the window for a clean escape.

So he crawled underneath the house, not minding hitting his head twice as he moved toward his prey. He stopped at where Tentay was sleeping and began to cut the wooden slats loose. After dismantling sixteen slim pieces, he attempted to squeeze in, but the opening he made was still too tight. It took twenty slim pieces and a few floorboards before he his large body could fit into the hole in the floor. He was determined to see his plans to fruition.

He poked his head into the hole and surveyed the room. He froze in fright upon seeing the low light that illuminated the house. He looked at the sleeping Tentay, then turned his eyes on the locked window, nervously gulping like a prison inmate frantically eyeing his surroundings for a way out.

As he knelt underneath, he pushed his shoulders in, wiggled his right arm through, then the left. He began to stand up to climb through the hole. The floor made a creaking noise as his hands pressed against the boards, which could not rouse Aling Tere, who was gritting her teeth, nor the little children who were sleeping like logs.

He stood in the room and debated whether he should first loosen the wire that secured the window.

'Ah, no need! I don't want to move now that Tentay is already within my grasp.'

He walked over Victor, almost stepping on Tentay's foot. His hands and limbs trembled so terribly that he dropped the dagger, which landed with a loud thud on the floor. Tentay was awakened by the noise and saw Karugdog lunging at her.

'Who are you!?'

Juan felt as if he was shot in the chest. He forgot about the dagger that he had dropped and quickly backed away.

'Mother! Intruder! Intruder in the house!'

Karugdog was just scurrying back into the hole when he saw that Aling Tere was still asleep, and stopped. Tentay, recovering from the initial shock and panic, screamed again.

'Who are you!? Mother! Intruder in the house!'

But Karugdog was again on top of her, stifling her cries with his palm pressed hard against her lips.

'Be quiet!'

Karugdog grabbed the dagger that he had dropped and pinned the woman down with his knee.

'You're dead if you make any sound.'

He grabbed Tentay's hand and pressed it against the sharp, pointed tip of the dagger that was aimed at her breast. Tentay gasped when she felt the knife. 'Shush . . . I will kill you!'

It was then that Aling Tere began to wake up, but she was still too groggy to make out what was happening. Tentay struggled against the man pinning her down, and when Karugdog loosened his grip, she kicked the sleeping Victor who rolled away and almost fell into the hole. Victor shouted in pain, and Aling Tere was jolted awake. She became aware of the commotion going on inside Tentay's room.

Aling Tere jumped up and rushed to see her daughter who was desperately fighting off the man on top of her. Karugdog was caught by surprise and released Tentay. The old woman, not bothering to find out who the man was, started screaming to the neighbours for help. Juan stood up and moved to strangle the old woman and threaten her with the dagger in his hand. Aling Tere, in terror, just simply flopped onto the floor. But her cries had already reached the neighbours, who had been on the lookout for any sign of trouble at their house.

'Make one more sound and you're all dead! Go back to sleep, old woman.' Juan pointed toward the straw mat where Aling Tere was sleeping earlier.

Karugdog was standing at the door, effectively blocking Aling Tere from rushing to her daughter's aid. As he turned back to Tentay, Aling Tere stood on her feet, and Victor began shouting 'Mr Fiend! He's here! He's trying to kill us!'

Karugdog turned his attention to Victor and gave him a kick that was so hard that the kid crashed on the pile of wooden slats. The women screamed. The neighbours were already banging on their door, shouting to be let in. Aling Tere ran to open the door, but she fumbled as she tried to untie the knots. Karugdog, in his panic, flung himself against the shut window and wormed his way out through the slight opening.

But there were already three neighbours outside. One of them, who had heard the sound of a body crashing onto the ground, saw Mr Fiend as he darted toward the gate. The fourth neighbour, who had just arrived, hit Karugdog with a thick bamboo pole on the buttocks, but the fiend got away and disappeared into the thick bushes.

The night fiend was back in town!

After that, Mr Fiend spent a good week nursing his bruised buttocks. One cheek of his buttocks was swollen, and walking was too painful. One would think his injuries would have taught him a lesson. But on the contrary, Karugdog was, more than ever, bent on exacting revenge not only on Tentay's family, but also on the whole village. He vowed to burn down the village on one silent night, and in the midst of all that chaos, he would deal with Tentay one last time. 'I don't give a damn anymore. Innocent or not, they shall die in the fire.'

Felipe arrived that same week.

When Felipe and Delfin came to visit Tentay, nobody dared to tell them about the incident from earlier that week. But after more than a week of nightly visits, Felipe began to notice something peculiar going on around the house. He observed that a strange man always followed him whenever he left the house. Every time he reached the main road, that man would turn to the right and head in the direction of the cemetery. After about two weeks, Felipe told Tentay about these nightly sightings. Tentay and Aling Tere just exchanged knowing glances. Mr Fiend! Felipe, seeing the two women mysteriously staring at each other, became suspicious.

'What's going on? Who's that man?'

Aling Tere quickly regained her composure.

'Oh, I don't know. It could be one of our neighbours living in the back. You know, people leaving the village always pass this way. It's quicker than going through the main square.'

Felipe did not press on. But since then, he was more watchful whenever he would leave the house. He would keep an eye out for any stranger who was tailing him, before heading straight home.

There were nights when he did not notice anything, but on other occasions, he would see the silhouette of a man scurrying away as he looked back. Then, one evening when he decided to spy on the area, he spotted a dark figure milling around in front of the house soon after he had left.

'What are you doing here?' Felipe asked in a commanding voice.

The strange man was caught by surprise. He did not recognize Felipe, and he did not realize that the other man was still in the area. He was overwhelmed by fear and shock.

'Oh, I must be at the wrong address! I was looking for my friend who lives in this area, but I can't seem to recall where his house is.'

'A man? There's no man living in that house.'

'Oh, my. Thanks for letting me know.'

And without further saying a word, Karugdog turned his back and went on his way.

Felipe stood for a while outside the gate. He hesitated to go back inside the house to tell Tentay that there was a strange man lurking outside. He had a bad feeling about this strange man—very likely a person who was once a frequent guest at Tentay's, now surprised by his presence at the scene. He began to wonder whether that stranger snuck in every night, unknown to Tentay. He remembered that when he told the women about the strange man tailing him, Aling Tere had struggled to find an excuse. Felipe began to wonder whether Tentay was being unfaithful, and if Aling Tere knew about it. Felipe was never the jealous type, but this time, he felt anger seeping in and coursing through his body.

Felipe was so preoccupied in his thoughts that he did not realize Karugdog was still there.

'Pardon me, but I don't think I got your name?'

Felipe replied, 'Well, I am an intimate friend of the family that lives here.'

'Is that so? You must be that man from the East, the one engaged to the young woman who lives here?'

Felipe was dumbfounded. How could this man be asking these questions?

'Yes. Indeed, I am.'

'Oh, so you're the man!'

'Why are you so curious, and who told you about me?'

'Oh, nobody. Okay, goodbye.'

Juan Karugdog, in a seemingly mocking manner, just turned around and walked away, leaving Felipe seething with wrath. Felipe looked menacingly at Karugdog from head to heel.

Felipe thought to himself, 'Did Tentay tell him about me? That means Tentay must be very close to this man!'

Felipe resisted the urge to run after Karugdog and decided he would deal with this man another time. He watched as Karugdog disappeared around the corner, then started to walk home. On the road, Felipe kept thinking about the mystery of this strange man, an unwelcome intruder in his sanctuary of hope and trust.

* * *

Felipe did not speak to Delfin or Gudyo about what was troubling him. He just stopped seeing Tentay for several nights, but he went there just the same to find out if Karugdog would return. On the one hand, he wanted to catch Tentay in the act, thinking she might have been seeing another man. But he prayed that was not the case.

But Karugdog did not return. Four nights had passed and still, there was no sign of him at all. Felipe got tired of waiting for Karugdog to show up again. And so, before the week was over, Felipe resumed his nightly visits to Tentay. But then, as soon as he resumed his courtship rituals, they began to experience a strange disturbance in the house—stones coming from nowhere, pelting the roof and the walls of the house. Felipe thought that this was the right time to ask the women who that strange man was, why he was throwing stones at the house, why he was lurking outside at night, and how the stranger knew who he was.

Felipe asked the women and this time, they told him everything that had happened, down to the smallest detail. Aling Tere begged Felipe not to run after Karugdog, and asked him to keep out of harm's way.

Felipe and Juan met again at the house. Karugdog turned up, once again, to ask for forgiveness and to seek an audience with Felipe, with the assurance that he only meant to befriend Felipe. The women thought that this was the most opportune time to introduce Juan to Felipe. Aling Tere stood with Juan to usher in Felipe, who was just coming up to the house. The men were formally introduced to each other, and they sat down to have a man-to-man talk. Nobody suspected that things would go downhill from there.

From the beginning, Felipe could already tell that Juan was an odd man, but he still made the effort to be polite and diplomatic. But it was not a simple matter to deal with a person lacking in mental faculties. After three hours, Felipe got tired of listening to the garbage spewing from Karugdog's mouth.

Tension rose when Karugdog boldly declared, 'Now that we've become good friends, I hope you don't mind if I continue courting Tentay. There's no need for animosity between us if both of us can court Tentay. You have three days a week, and three days also for me to court and woo her. May the best man win.'

Felipe could not decide whether to be amused or enraged by Juan's audacity.

'Have you gone mad? You know that Tentay and I are already engaged to be married, right?'

'Oh, don't be so sure. Tentay could still change her mind about you, and she might eventually fall for me.'

'Whatever. We have nothing more to talk about. It's late and I haven't had dinner.'

'Me, too.'

'Uh, but I'm already tired and sleepy.'

'Don't be so rude.'

Felipe was taken aback. This madman even had the nerve to call him rude! But Felipe just reined in his emotions. He knew that the best way to cope when speaking with an idiot was, 'in through one ear, out the other'.

'Somehow . . . I have this feeling . . . that you want to lord over everyone in this house.'

Felipe did not respond.

'Oh, so you think you're so much better than me?'

Felipe stood up, went to Aling Tere, and asked the old woman to turn Karugdog away, as his patience was already running thin. The two women, who had thought that everything was going well between the two men, jumped up and rushed in to find out what was happening. Mr Friend told the women what happened between him and Felipe. Aling Tere, sensing that something had gone wrong between the two, pleaded for Karugdog to just leave.

'Why only me? Why don't you ask him to leave as well? Is he already your son-in-law that you cannot turn him away?'

Aling Tere was furious.

'Why would it hurt that I asked you to leave? You of all people have no right to be here!'

'No, I am not leaving! I will fight and die, if I must!'

Felipe could not put up with Karugdog any longer and grabbed a thick piece of firewood that he saw in the kitchen. He lunged at Karugdog to beat him up, but the women pushed him back.

Karugdog then pulled out his dagger, and Aling Tere screamed in terror. Just like in a traditional play, the commotion drew in the neighbours who entered the house, and Juan, realizing that his life was in grave danger, cowered in fear. And when the neighbours started punching and kicking and hitting him, he knelt and begged them to stop, on the solemn oath that he would leave and never return. The beatings stopped. Karugdog was asked to surrender his weapon, and when Felipe searched him for his gun, all he found was an empty holster.

Karugdog presented quite a laughable sight as he walked toward the gate like a dog with its tail between its legs. The neighbours who, a while ago, were raging mad, burst out laughing.

Aling Tere made Felipe stay for the night.

'Don't go home anymore. You can live with us here. We need a man in this house. My little boys are hardly men. Don't you take that man's word that he will never return. If you will stay and live here, that man will definitely think twice before showing up here again.'

And from then on, Felipe went home to Tentay. Oh, how sweet it was that his heart's desire had come true! Somehow, Felipe felt strongly indebted to the idiot, Mr Fiend!

Chapter 24

Madonna and Child

It was said that there was no pain more excruciating than that of a mother who was in labour. Meni, who was always gentle and meek, went stark raving mad, deliriously crying out while in labour. Nonetheless, the birthing took place without complications.

It was a boy, the fruit of a tumultuous love affair, and it brought happiness to the young couple. The joy and bliss they felt were something they had never experienced before.

Meni was a curious sight to behold. In the morning, she would get up and forget to comb her hair. With her eyes still shut, she would rise upon hearing her infant's cries. She would sing lullabies to the baby in her arms, planting sweet gentle kisses on his lips, forehead, cheeks, eyelids, hair, palms, and all over, like she was burying her face in satin sheets. She would carry the child to Delfin lying in bed, put it down on Delfin's chest, or tuck it by his side. And Delfin would open his eyes to see the mother and child beside him, and it felt like the most wonderful dream.

'Your son wakes up early, unlike you!' Meni teased Delfin. 'Look at him, already giggling! Cooing back whenever spoken to!'

The two showered the baby with tender kisses.

'There, make your lazy father get up now!'

'Oh, my sweet, sweet boy!' Delfin exclaimed as he pressed his lips on the child's forehead.

'Why do you always do that on the child's forehead?' Meni asked.

'That looks like a good head on his shoulders! I'll certainly have him learn great knowledge!'

'What great knowledge?'

'The knowledge to be able to teach the ignorant, help the weak, and defend the oppressed.'

'To teach, to defend . . . so, you want him to be a teacher, or a lawyer?' asked the mother.

'I don't know what kind of college degree that is. I don't think we have it here in the country just yet. But there seems to be the beginnings of it here now.'

'So, what is it then? Isn't it the same knowledge that you have?'

'Oh, if it were the same, I'd rather he hadn't been born into this world. He wouldn't have to die.'

'What? My child . . . to die?'

Meni quickly picked up her son. 'Every living soul in this world will, but not my boy!' she muttered to the child, who looked up as if he understood every word the mother said. She showered the child with more kisses. And when Delfin moved to kiss the baby, Meni moved the boy away.

'You want to kiss him, even though you wanted him to die!'

Delfin chuckled, and kissed the mother's cheek instead. 'Don't be silly! You're putting words in my mouth. He is also my child.'

'Isn't that the case now?'

'Oh, look at him. He's a mini-me! Little Delfin!'

'Little Delfin! Little Delfin!' Meni said as she tickled the baby's chin and cheeks. 'What knowledge would you have him learn?'

'I don't know what it's called, just yet. I said what I said earlier only because I don't wish him to suffer the same fate that we have. If he were to struggle and suffer, it would be because he defended the lives and rights of the oppressed.'

'What should I teach him, then?' Meni asked.

'Teach him to be pure at heart, and I'll teach him to have a great mind. Together, we'll raise him to be a kind-hearted and honorable man, a whole individual, and perhaps, a hero for humankind.'

While the two were debating on their child's future, Delfin's untiring mother was already up and about, preparing breakfast.

Delfin would go to work late, only after he had completed his morning ritual of postnatal care for the mother, and playing with his infant son, whom he could not seem to leave behind. Whenever he would move away, the child would tug at his shirt, and he would once again swoon over the boy. Against the wishes of her mother-in-law, Meni would take the baby outside to see Delfin off as he went to work.

'There, your father's off to work. Tell him to bring home rice cakes for you! Go, tell him . . . da-da . . . *pu-to.*'

'Oi! What nonsense are you saying to the baby?' the neighbours who saw the mother and child at the gate would often remark.

While Delfin was away, Meni kept herself busy watching over her baby boy. A slight whimper and she would sing three or five lullabies to comfort him. She must have sung all the songs she knew, as she sang each one to silence the baby's cries. She would only find rest when the baby was asleep. Then, she would turn to sewing clothes and diapers for the infant, or mending Delfin's torn clothes. Thankfully, her own clothes did not need any mending, since most were still good as new. The old skirts she had turned into diapers, blankets, and bedsheets. The smooth scarfs and blouses, she had made into little clothes for the baby. She was most excited to complete the garments for the baby's christening, which she fashioned from fine silky white fabric, delicate trinkets, and other accessories. She went against tradition by not taking gifts from godparents. She once swore that 'When I raise my own child, I won't subscribe to this custom of taking money from the godparents, be it for the baptism or confirmation, fiesta, Christmas, or whatever.'

Meni was also busy thinking about whether to serve food or not, after the baptismal ceremony. She could not bear the thought of not throwing a once-in-a-lifetime party for her one and only child. She worried about what her neighbours would say, especially since she and Delfin had often been invited to similar occasions. It would be a shame not to invite friends and neighbours, and Delfin would surely be teased by his colleagues if they heard about the christening. She did not like the idea of keeping it a secret from her own close friends, who would surely be more than glad to send gifts.

But they did not have money to spend on the occasion. Delfin was already scraping the bottom of the barrel, and she did not want to pressure him to borrow money just for the baptism. From his measly salary of forty pesos a month, only half would remain after spending on their daily needs, and this half was hardly enough to pay off the debts incurred by her medical needs. There was no way they could provide a budget even for a moderate feast.

While mulling over these concerns and worries, she paused now and then in her sewing and cutting of fabric, and stared intently at the floor, then at the ceiling. She turned to gaze at her sleeping baby, teared up, and sobbing, bent down to kiss the infant.

'My poor child! How unfortunate you are! You'll grow up knowing only hardship!'

She stopped so as not to rouse the child from sleep.

'Your father was right. It pains me to think you'll suffer the same fate as ours. You might as well die at a young age! But I can't bear to think of your early death!'

She couldn't resist the urge to lift the mosquito net that covered the baby's face. As she bent down to plant a kiss, the tears that welled up in her eyes fell on the child's wide forehead. Oh, that wide, round forehead she took as a sign of great intelligence, born amidst such pain and suffering! Strangely, the child woke up, lay still, scowled, and started to cry.

Meni shuddered upon realizing that the child felt her own pain.

'Such awareness and sensitivity for a child so young! My child, you must endure the same fate that befalls those born in rags! Oh, how I wish you were born in my father's house, surrounded by the luxuries that I cannot ever give you.'

Meni sobbed uncontrollably and hugged her baby tightly. Her mother-in-law came in as the baby began to wail.

'Oh, stop weeping! You're acting like a mad woman!'

* * *

Meni could not deny what had just happened. The old woman must have heard everything she said.

'From the day this child was born, I knew you wouldn't be able to put up with our poverty. I'll have to talk to Delfin. He needs to know how you really feel about our living conditions here. I may not be your mother, but it brings me great anguish to see the two of you weeping like this! I can't help but blame myself and my children for the added burden you have to endure!'

The old woman broke down in tears. Meni was dumbfounded; she did not expect to hear such mournful words from her mother-in-law.

'Mother, why do you say that?'

'I feel so guilty for not being able to contribute, especially now that you're so hard up.'

'But that isn't what saddens me, Mother. It is the fact that my siblings haven't seen my son.'

'Yes, that's another thing. Just because you married a poor man!'

Meni felt as if another wound had been inflicted in her heart. She did not feel anger towards the old woman, since she knew her to be very emotional and delicate. But so was she. She wished she did not have to put up with the old woman's tantrums.

'Mother, please stop bringing up old issues that I've already left behind!'

'But I did hear you weep and say, how you wish that your son were born into your father's house.'

Meni thought to herself, 'Ah, she heard even that!'

'If only you didn't show any sign of regret for choosing this life with us, I'd do everything I could to serve you and your husband. I feel like I am walking on clouds, whenever I see you happy and content. And when there's something you need that your husband can't provide, I'll gladly do anything just give you what you need. And it pains me to see you work around the house! If Delfin's father were still alive, the old man would surely do everything within his power just so you wouldn't have to shed a single tear!'

The old woman surely knew how to create a scene as she reminisced the past days when she lived in relative comfort before the passing of Delfin's parents. Her reminiscing was interrupted when the child, who was suckling at Meni's breasts, began to cry once again.

Meni raised the child and gently rocked him to and fro, as if to console him.

'Look at what you've done. You shouldn't be crying while nursing your baby.'

Meni just said nothing. She held the baby in her arms and continued to nurse him, but the child struggled and kicked, appearing to be throwing a major tantrum.

'What's wrong with the baby? Here, give him to me! Your tantrum is rubbing off on him.'

Meni reluctantly handed the baby over, and within moments, the old woman had calmed the child. Ah, such was the magic possessed by old, wise parents!

'Trust me, my child. I've given birth to many children, that's why I know what is good and bad for you and your infant. You let your tears fall on your child's face, and surely, your child will grow up to be a weakling! Not good for a boy! Tears can poison your breast milk. Sure, there are emotionally distressed mothers who breastfeed their babies, but those are battered wives! But Delfin is a good husband, so you have no reason to let this baby drink up your misery.'

'Mother, I'm not miserable.'

'Ah, just rest for now!'

Meni did not resist anymore. She just flopped onto a chair and sat there, brooding. When she tilted her head to the side, the old woman was alarmed.

'You've a headache now? I told you, that's what's going to happen . . .'

'No, Mother, my head's fine.'

'Really? Don't you deny it. You must have overexerted yourself.'

The old woman went up to Meni to check if she was running a fever.

'See what I mean? You're running a fever!'

Meni felt her neck with the back of her hand, and when she felt warmth, she immediately protested. 'Oh, it's nothing, Mother. I don't feel any different.'

'You don't believe me? So what's that headache? And that fever?'

'I'd be a corpse if I turned cold,' Meni smiled teasingly.

'Oh, don't you crack jokes now. You shouldn't think a slight fever is nothing.'

'Don't worry, I might go and see the doctor later.'

'The doctor, again? Why do you believe all that medical nonsense? Doctors are powerless against death. Stop taking those medicines that are too expensive. Tonight, I'll burn camphor incense for you. Which reminds me, good thing I kept some of the placenta when you gave birth. That would be the best remedy for your fever. Apart from God, it sure saved my life many times when I fell ill after childbirth. I'll take care of everything. Don't you go outside the house at all!'

Meni did not have any clue what the old woman was rambling about, but she began to worry that, perhaps, the old woman was right that she had fallen ill.

* * *

Every day, Delfin went home for lunch. He would shuttle between Sampaloc and Quiapo on foot, since he wanted to save all the money he could for his growing family. He did not mind the dust, grime and sweat from the long walks, as if these were just a gentle breeze. He felt a whole lot better, every time he thought of all the happy moments in his life. He would shrug off the exhaustion as he climbed up to his house, where Meni and their son waited. One gentle pat on his wife's cheek and a kiss on his baby's lips were all that it took to wash away all the aches and pains of his body and soul.

'Oh, my wife and child! What an absolute joy to behold!'

Meni, despite showing early signs of wear and tear from hardship and illness, still made it a point to groom herself and dress neatly. Although she was just recovering from sickness, to Delfin she was as fresh and bright as before.

Delfin was on his way home, just as the argument between Meni and her mother-in-law subsided. After putting the baby to sleep, the old woman got up and went out to finish cooking supper. Meni packed away her sewing materials and prepared to greet Delfin at the door.

Over dinner, Delfin's aunt broke the story of what happened earlier that day. Despite Meni's silent disapproval, the old woman spoke: 'I'm telling Delfin about this not because I want to put you in a bad light, Meni. I just want him to know that you're unhappy living here with us. Perhaps it's best that I take the little children with me to live at a friend's in Uli-Uli. And there, maybe I can earn a living by setting up a small store.'

Delfin stared at his aunt, wondering whether there had been fighting while he was gone.

'Where is that coming from?' Delfin turned to Meni and whispered, 'Have you two been fighting?'

'Absolutely not!' Meni shook her head.

The old woman, upon hearing the hushed exchange between the two, went on. 'No, there's no special reason, except for my desire to unburden the two of you. I can imagine how difficult it is for you to house three more people, including two little children who can hardly be of help around the house.'

'Maybe Mother is already getting tired of taking care of me.'

'Oh, no, it's not that.'

'You don't have to leave. I'll just go back to my father's house.' Meni's tears began to well up once more. Delfin was torn between his aunt and his wife, who both looked glum.

'Hold on. What's going on here? You two were never like this before. Tell me, Auntie, what went wrong between you two?'

'Nothing. Ask her. Really, nothing.'

'So why are you acting that way toward each other then?'

'Okay, the truth. I didn't like what she said to her baby, earlier.'

'What was it?' Delfin was already getting agitated and Meni could feel her heart beating against her chest.

'Earlier, she was in her room sewing clothes while the baby slept. And then, after a while, she was sobbing and mumbling about how unfortunate her child was for having been born in poverty.'

'That's what this is all about?'

'Oh, child! Do you understand what she meant by that? She's tired of living in these conditions! Of course, she wouldn't have to suffer if she were to live in her father's house!'

Delfin understood why his aunt was hurt by Meni's words, and he also wanted to sway the mind and heart of the old woman. The aunt, seeing that Delfin was not going to take her side on the matter, made a surprising revelation.

'You need to know how much suffering your wife can endure. I didn't want to say this because you, Meni, might think that I dislike you. I only want to prove my point that my children and I—we're making things worse for the two of you.'

Meni wondered what secret her mother-in-law was about to reveal.

'Yesterday, someone told me that Meni had sold her finest clothes and scarves to the wife of that American friend of Masay, who was just here, a couple of days ago.'

Meni's face looked as if it were suddenly soaked in white vinegar, while Delfin stood as if a wooden stake had been driven into his heart.

'Allegedly, she sold those fine pieces for four pesos, even though they were worth fifteen pesos or more. That's how she was able to give me a two-peso bill yesterday. The money I spent on our food up to today was from the sale of those clothes. And she also bought fine fabric for the baby's baptismal garment. I was curious where she got the money, given that it was almost the end of the month. But then, I thought maybe you took out a loan from the office. In fact, I just found out about it this morning, at the local store, but my source swore me to confidentiality. Meni, you would never have done anything like that if we weren't so poor. But alas, it was still so embarrassing.'

Delfin couldn't think of anything to say after the old woman's revelation and just sighed repeatedly. Face flushed, he stared at Meni who could not look up from her plate. He rose without finishing the food on his plate and went to the bedroom. He was in deep anguish. He pitied Meni and was filled with shame.

The old woman stood up to clear the table. Seeing that she had complicated the already delicate situation between the couple, she realized the gravity of her revelation. She felt uncomfortable knowing that she created a rift separating the husband and wife. She did not imagine Meni and Delfin would be at odds with each other. She did not think it was ever possible for the two, who had always loved each other dearly, to have a grave misunderstanding. So she resolved to patch things up between the two. She approached Delfin who sought refuge inside the bedroom and then went to Meni who sulked at the table, staring blankly into empty space. The old woman acted like a marriage counselor, trying to determine whether the couple were meant for each other as husband and wife. After a while, she called out to Delfin.

'Come here, my son! The two of you are acting like little children! You may have disrespected the grace at the table, but I won't have you disrespect and disobey me.'

Delfin knew his aunt so well. She would not take it lightly if her motherly love were to be rejected. Besides, he also wanted to speak to Meni and tell her how he felt about her selling her finest clothes. He came out to join the two women at the table.

'All I want is that you don't bear ill feelings about what I'd shared with you as a parent. I told Delfin about your clothes because I knew you'd never tell him, out of embarrassment. There should be no secrets between husband and wife, whether for justifiable reasons or not. Go, talk it out between you two, so I'd know what your decision is about my leaving this house.'

Without waiting for an answer, the old woman stood up and walked away with a smile, as if she had just come out of the church after professing to God about a good deed she had accomplished.

* * *

'Meni! This by far is the most hurtful thing you've done to me. But I've no right to blame you. You, the daughter of the great Don Ramon Miranda, selling off her finest garments! I feel so bad about myself.'

'No, don't! I sold those clothes because I've no use for them anymore, and they were poorly made anyway. It would be a waste to let them rot in the closet.'

Delfin didn't believe what Meni just said. It was simply difficult to ease the pain that he felt.

'I hope you don't think I'd forgotten about the jewellery that you pawned some time ago, which I've yet to retrieve. I shudder to think if your siblings found out, they would accuse me of taking advantage of your material possessions.'

'Why do you need to bring that up now? I pawned it to a friend of mine, not yours. And so what if my siblings found out? We've nothing to be ashamed of. It's not like they didn't know that I'd been ill. And it wasn't as if you gambled away the money! We spent it on my medicines. If anything, they should be ashamed of themselves. They're the ones taking advantage of what's rightfully mine! If only you . . .' Meni didn't finish her sentence as she knew Delfin hated arguing about her inheritance.

'Not that again!'

'I only mentioned it because you had to bring up my siblings!'

'They have every right to be mad at you, for you married a poor man like me . . .'

'So what? I fell in love with a poor man and chose to spend the rest of my days in poverty till the day I die . . .'

'Those are empty words! Earlier, you were weeping about how your child had to live in a shabby hut, instead of a rich man's concrete house!'

'No, I don't regret having to live in this house. I was just worried about the baptismal celebration. Surely, all of our friends will be coming.'

The conversation gradually turned to the subject of the christening. The gloom and despair hanging in the air slowly lifted, and the two began to talk animatedly about the plans for the celebration.

'What are your plans for the baby?' asked the father.

'Why, let's baptize him before he turns two months old!'

'Two months! Let's wait till the fifth month, or until he's big enough and able to walk on his feet! So the godfather wouldn't have to hire a carriage.'

'Silly. By then, he would already be able to talk to the priest.'

'All the better. He could listen to all those Latin phrases coming from the priest's mouth.'

'And that's exactly why Mother hates your sense of humor, for you to even joke like that about your child's baptism. She did express concern that we think nothing of raising a pagan child in the house.'

'A pagan child! Don't pay too much attention to the old woman. She's just filled with superstitions and old beliefs. You can tell her this: Oh, is it a good idea to pour water on the child's head? The baby might catch a cold or get sick. You did say we should not give the baby frequent baths, right?'

'So when would you like to baptize our son, then?' asked the mother.

'Whenever you want . . .'

'Wait, so we will not throw a party?

'A party? In this time of scarcity?'

'Even a modest one. We have to. It would be so embarrassing to disappoint our friends and the godparents.'

'Who are the godparents?'

'I don't want a wealthy person. Poor though the godfather may be, as long as he's wise and intelligent, just like the baby's father. What about you? Do you have someone in mind?'

'Me? Felipe would be the best choice!'

'Felipe, whose thoughts and whereabouts are always a puzzle to me?'

'Yes, him. And if he declines, then it will have to be one of my colleagues at the press.'

'I leave the decision to you,' Meni said. 'But what name are we going to give to him?'

'If you ask me, I prefer a Tagalog name.'

'But there are no Tagalog saints.'

'So what are we, devils?'

The two laughed heartily, their sudden outburst rousing the sleeping infant. The old woman heard the cheerful sounds inside the house, felt delighted and uttered a short prayer of thanks. 'Thank you, Blessed Mother and Child, for reuniting the two.'

Delfin picked up the baby and brought him to Meni to nurse.

'Let's give this child a beautiful name!'

'Yes, a beautiful name, indeed. But not one that comes from the Spanish calendar! We can give him a name like Hero, Honour,

Dignity, Purity, Revolution, Victory, Sun Ray, Great, Free Man, Meteor. You choose!'

'Hey, hey, hey! You're crazy!' The old woman blurted out upon hearing her nephew recite Tagalog names. 'Don't be a smart ass! Do you think you're greater than the creators of the liturgical calendar? Why don't you just take the name of the patron saint of the day the child was born? When was that? Could you check?'

April 14th. The patron saint on this date was San Pedro Telmo, and the martyrs were Tiburcio, Valeriano, and Maximo.

'I don't like the name Pedro,' Meni protested. 'That name is everywhere! And they're usually nicknamed Pendong or Penduko.'

'Then call him Pedring, or Pedrito.'

'Whatever pet name you give, it's still Pedro.'

'What time was the child delivered?' The old woman asked Delfin.

'Wasn't it around daybreak?'

'That's it! We have to use the first name. If you don't like that, then go for Tiburcio, because the sun was already up when the child was born.'

'No, not Tiburcio, either. It has an even uglier nickname, Tibo.'

'Call him Usiong then.'

'No, that's very close to the name, Bosiong-kan!' Delfin quipped.

The two burst into laughter again, and the old woman joined in glee.

'Well, if that's what God has given your child, so be it. What other names do you have there?' The aunt further pressed Delfin.

'Valeriano and Maximo.'

'I don't like any of those, either,' Meni still protested. 'Valeriano . . . Bale for short. Not that my baby has a broken nose!'

'Then we can call him, Anong. What a sweet and lovely name.'

'Oh, no! So very close to Manong!'

'What about this last one? Maximo . . .' Delfin said.

'That would be Simo. Those are all ugly names! They don't quite capture the absolute beauty of our child!'

And Meni planted a kiss on the child's face.

'For the love of God, stop being so picky,' the old woman said. 'Ugly, you say? There are no ugly people in heaven, my dear, only angels and saints! You may pore over the whole calendar and still not find any name you'd like.'

'Why is that? Isn't Delfin's name in the calendar?'

'What are you saying, my dear?' Delfin exclaimed.

'I like the name Delfin! Let's name him Delfin! Beautiful name, don't you think, my dear husband?'

'The father is named Delfin, and the son is also named Delfin,' The old woman muttered. 'That's a very Spanish custom. The father is named Jose, the eldest son is called Pepe, the second son is Peping, and another is called Pepito! And all of them are named Jose! Whatever, you two decide! Go follow the likes of kings and popes: Alfonso the First, Alfonso the Second, Leo the First, Leo the Second, and so on and so forth. Of course, the kings and the popes did that because they had titles and duties to uphold. What do you two have?'

Delfin choked back a snigger, lest he earned the ire of his aunt. He turned to Meni.

'As I said, let's give him a Tagalog name. End of discussion. We are all Tagalog, after all.'

'Yes, you're a native Tagalog,' Meni answered in a teasing manner. 'But me, I am a mestiza! That's why we are very pretty!' Meni punctuated and smiled sweetly.

'Indeed, you're a mestiza, descended from a long line of spoiled brats.'

Meni's face turned grim, and she turned and snubbed Delfin.

The old woman could tell Meni took offence.

'Delfin, you were mean. That joke was insulting.' The old woman said.

Delfin realized he had made a mistake, so he hastened to appease his wife and bring her back to her jolly self.

That was one good thing about Delfin's aunt. She was always impartial and called out Delfin for his wrongdoings, unlike most mothers who would always take the side of their son and turn against their daughter-in-law.

Thanks to the old woman's counsel and Delfin's efforts to woo her back, Meni recovered from the momentary hurt. The old woman returned to the subject of the name for the newborn.

'Think about it. If you don't choose a name from the liturgical calendar, the church might not baptize the baby.'

'Why not?' Delfin argued. 'I'll take him to an Aglipayan or Protestant church, if they refuse.'

The old woman gasped and made the sign of the cross. 'Oh, my Jesus!'

'Oh, no! Not an Aglipayan nor a Protestant church,' Meni also objected. 'For generations, our family's been baptized in the Roman Catholic Church! This child will be no exception!'

'But that's because we only had the Catholic Church in the olden days.'

'That's beside the point. When he's old enough to decide what's best for him, he may choose to convert to the Aglipayan or Protestant faith.'

'All right, whatever church it may be, we still have to decide on the name to give him. Let's decide now. I go for either Sun Ray or Hero.'

'It's none other than Delfin for me.'

'Neither Hero nor Delfin! It should be Tiburcio, if we are to remain virtuous in the eyes of God. In case you didn't know, it's a mortal sin to deviate from the names given in the liturgical calendar. Whose name are we going to call out to when the holy priest gives the sacrament of the anointing of the sick? The rightful patron saint will turn a deaf ear to our cries for intercession when your son is about to pass on to the afterlife. Even his guardian angels will forsake him. So you better think twice before choosing a pagan name.'

Meni and Delfin exchanged knowing looks and thought to themselves, 'Yes, Mother, as you wish, if only to end this argument.'

It was almost two in the afternoon and Delfin had to rush back to work. But before he left the house, the old woman forced the couple to finish their lunch. The husband and wife shared a hearty meal, as if nothing had happened just hours before.

Chapter 25

Felipe, the Godfather

'Oh, look! It's the man of the hour!'

Meni's greeting rang in the ears of Felipe and Tentay as they stood by the doorway.

It was a Sunday afternoon. The day before that, Delfin and Felipe had a preliminary discussion about the upcoming christening just before they left the press. It was agreed that Felipe and Tentay will come over to see Meni and her child, the following day. And so Tentay and Felipe had come to visit. That was Tentay's first visit to Delfin's house, and the first time she was meeting Meni, as well. Since Tentay and Felipe had started living together, Tentay had not gone out. When she learned that Felipe was going to see Meni, she decided to tag along to meet Meni for the first time.

'There you are, our man of the hour! Felipe, you must have been extremely busy ever since you got married. I haven't seen you in quite a while!'

Got married! Tentay felt a suffocating atmosphere enveloping her. She was cold, all the blood drained from her face, and she felt shame coursing through her veins like the venom of a snake. Even now, she couldn't quite come to terms with the notion of being a wife. Perhaps that's the way it was with newlyweds. But Meni's words reminded her that, on the contrary, she and Felipe were not a married couple. She felt she did not deserve to be called a wife, since she was nothing more than a domestic partner. Yes, that label, she felt was rightfully hers. As her Catholic religion would have it, a couple that lived together without the blessing of the holy priest and the Catholic Church could never be recognized as husband and wife. It did not matter that Tentay and Felipe had completely surrendered their love to the Almighty. And it would be immaterial if they were to be married by an Aglipayan church, or a Protestant one, for that matter, as their marriage outside the Catholic church would still be deemed illegitimate and meaningless. But being a common law wife was a matter of necessity for Tentay. She simply had no choice.

But what other options did she have? Tentay still clung to the hope that Felipe would someday agree to have a church wedding, and then they would not have to live in sin. With these thoughts in mind, Tentay regained her composure and accepted the warm greeting from Meni. She deferred to Felipe who comfortably and cheerfully responded to Meni.

'Oh, please don't say that just because I haven't been able to visit lately.'

'Was it Tentay's fault that you haven't seen us for so long?'

Meni gleefully teased Felipe as she gave Tentay a look-over, from head to toe. Tentay smiled. She was smitten by Meni's charming manner and thought to herself: 'Meni is really such a sweet thing!'

'Who, Tentay? No, she didn't restrict me at all! In fact, she's been looking forward to meeting you. The two of you will surely get along well. You may be from a well-off family and Tentay may be the opposite, but you two have very similar attitudes!'

'Me, from a wealthy family? Don't ever mention that again, please!'

'But you come from a wealthy family, too, Felipe,' Delfin remarked. He had been observing the exchange quietly and was now laughing in amusement.

'Please come in, Tentay!'

Meni clasped Tentay's hand as if she was welcoming a very good friend and close confidant.

'Leave the two men as they have a lot of catching up to do. Come, I'd like you to see my baby! Oh, I know you two don't have a child just yet, but in due time . . .'

Meni was all giddy as she dragged Tentay to the bedroom, where the baby lay sleeping. Delfin thought Meni was acting a little crazy as she bragged about her little baby.

'Look at these two. They're becoming fast friends!' Felipe remarked.

'Indeed. They had grown intimate with each other from the stories told to them about the other's life,' Delfin agreed.

The two women inside the bedroom struggled to keep their voices down as they did not want to disturb the sleeping child. But Tentay was so full of excitement and delight that she could barely restrain herself from smothering the baby with kisses.

'Look at him! A spitting image of his father! He looks just like Delfin!'

Meni, upon hearing Tentay's compliments, felt delight as sweet as honey overflow from within her. Tentay uttered the very words she wanted to hear from anyone who saw her baby for the first time. 'He looks just like his father!' But of course, this child was the fruit of her love for Delfin!

'A spitting image of Delfin!' That's precisely why she had wanted to name the baby after the father.

'Yes, he should be named Delfin!' Tentay exclaimed. 'And may he grow up to be wise like his father and happy like his mother!'

But Tentay's kisses roused little Delfin. The child opened his eyes and blinked, neither giggling nor crying. Just then, Delfin's aunt came into the room and smiled in amusement at the scene.

'Careful now. I hope you're not running a fever. The child might fall ill,' warned the aunt.

Tentay was startled for a moment, but went back to playing the child after Meni introduced Delfin's aunt. Little Delfin smiled as he rocked his tiny head.

Meni gasped. 'Look! His dimples show whenever he giggles!'

'He's so adorable!' Tentay gushed.

'Oh, yes. As soon as he came out, we cut a portion of the umbilical cord and pressed it on his cheeks. That's why,' the old woman proudly explained.

'Yes, that's how it should be, according to the elders,' Tentay agreed.

'Right now, he may look reddish and rather dark-skinned, but I tell you, when my grandson grows up, he'll have fair complexion! And as a young man, he'll surely break a lot of young ladies' hearts!'

'You mean, just like his father?' Meni teased the old woman.

'Oh, I'm telling you this not because he's my nephew, that Delfin has always been a true gentleman. He's nothing like his father and grandfather, who really broke their wives' hearts.'

'You mean to say, they were unfaithful? Wouldn't it be likely for Delfin to follow in their footsteps? What was that saying? The apple doesn't fall far from the tree! Sure, he may be a good boy now, but eventually . . .' Meni quipped.

Delfin, who overheard Meni's words, interrupted the women's' banter as he rushed in from the living room.

'Hey! What nonsense are you saying?'

Meni stiffened like a child caught in an act of mischief and crouched behind Tentay, for she knew Delfin would retaliate by tickling her.

'Aha! I'm right, ain't I?'

A round of laughter, teasing, and chasing ensued. When the excitement died down, they sat down to talk about the christening.

'So, Felipe, when do you propose that we hold the baptism?' Meni asked.

Felipe winked at Delfin's aunt. 'But do we really need to proceed with the christening? It will be such a waste to give money to the Church.'

The aunt froze and her eyes widened. Without uttering a word, she glared at Felipe, as if to say, 'Some kind of godfather you are!' But Felipe went on with his admonition.

'With all due respect, Auntie, they will just feed salt to the child, pour water over his head, anoint him with tallow, whisper to his ear, give him blessing, and . . . make him cry. I can do all that right here in the house.'

'What sacrilege!' the aunt exclaimed.

Delfin echoed his friend's sentiments. 'That's exactly what I told Nanay. But she disagreed. And she rejected the names that I suggested: Rays of the Sun, Great, Hero . . .'

The old woman spat on the floor. 'You might as well call him Devil, then!'

'Nanay, Devil is not a Tagalog name,' Delfin countered.

Felipe pressed on. 'Oh, that's easy. The emphasis should be on the last syllable—DeVIL!'

The old woman decided that she had had enough of the two men's irreverence. She turned away and joined the two ladies who were secretly chuckling in amusement.

Delfin and Felipe proceeded to have a serious talk on the subject.

'Delfin, my friend, all kidding aside, if Tentay and I were to have children, we would do away with baptism altogether.'

Delfin pleaded with his friend. 'No, Felipe. Don't be too rash. We can't change the world overnight. Be patient. It is not yet our time. Let's wait it out, until the New Day that we all aspire for happens.'

'Hmm . . . Why don't we call the child Radiance, then?'

'Radiance!'

'Yes! Not Sun Ray, nor Great, nor Hero, nor any other name! That child will be raised in the age of the New Enlightenment, and he'll grow up in an era when governance, way of life, faith and worldview are reborn. He'll have strong allies in rebuilding our society. Yes, Delfin. If he is to be baptized, he'll be named Radiance!'

'I just hope the child will have the same inclinations as ours.'

'Why not? As they say, like father, like son! As early as now, you should teach him our ways so he becomes an upright man.'

'True. I don't think we'll have a problem with this child. Look at his wide forehead, calm expression, and bright eyes—these are all signs of great intelligence, virtue, and compassion for others. And that bright, steady gaze speaks of courage. But going back to the name that you suggested, Radiance, we'll surely get in trouble with my aunt and the mother. Meni doesn't want any name other than Delfin, and

Nanay insists on Tiburcio! Neither is she in favour of a Tagalog name, for they think Tagalog is a language ignored by God. As Nanay said, the church will never baptize the child if he isn't named after any of the saints in the liturgical calendar.'

Felipe scoffed. 'Ah, don't listen to them! We'll not have him baptized by the Roman Catholic Church, or any other church for that matter, if they don't like the name.'

'It would have been a lot simpler if it were our child. But this child belongs to Meni and I, and when it comes to matters of the faith, Meni is still unwilling to break the law of God. Let's just go with the flow, my friend. Let them have their way while the child is still innocent. In our country, for any reform movement to succeed, it will need to ally itself with the religious institution. Where their faith calls people to take action, they will surely stand united and fight with us. We can use some of the religious teachings and principles to further the socialist cause. That boy is still a child of the Catholic Church. You, the godfather, and I, the father, may no longer adhere to the tenets of the faith, but we will still have to coexist in harmony with the Church. Consider that carefully . . . You, Felipe, are as volatile as fire.'

'Yes, indeed. I am like a fire that consumes and reduces all things to ash!'

The two friends burst into laughter. What began as a debate on the necessity of baptism ended with a lofty discourse on ideology and reform. Meanwhile, the two women were deeply engaged in intimate conversation around domesticity, marriage and motherhood.

* * *

Over snacks, they began to talk about other things, particularly about Tentay and Felipe's life as a couple. It was customary for guests to inquire about their hosts' affairs before speaking about their own. And so it was that Tentay and Felipe brought up their agenda when it was almost time for them to take leave, just as Delfin recounted the events that happened between Tentay, Karugdog and Felipe.

'I was telling Meni just how absurd it was that Tentay almost married Karugdog . . .' Delfin laughingly recalled.

'No, I didn't almost marry Karugdog!' Tentay objected, flushed and amused at the same time.

'True! If I hadn't come home, you would have succumbed to the fear of his fake revolver!' counseled Felipe, which made all of them burst into another round of laughter.

'Tell me again, how did it all happen?' Meni asked.

'You mean, Delfin hasn't told you?' Felipe asked.

'All I know is that you came home at the right time, confronted and threatened Karugdog never to return. He is gone, isn't he?'

'Oh, no, he never did leave!' Tentay remarked.

Felipe added, 'Yes, in fact, he went crazier than I thought he already was! I must have kicked the hornet's nest. When Karugdog found out that I was staying in at Tentay's house, he began stalking me night and day. A week had passed when, as I stepped out, I chanced upon a letter on the ground right outside the gate. You wouldn't believe how absurd the letter's content was. The first few lines were written as it were by a madman— Karugdog, no less, who signed the letter with the pen name, "The Fearless". Too bad I didn't bring the letter with me now, Meni! How I'd have loved to show it to you, the twisted handwriting and all! The ravings of a madman, indeed!'

'What did the letter say?' pressed Meni.

'Dear Mr Felipe . . . I write to challenge you to a duel . . . If you're a real man, meet me later at exactly midnight at Paang-Bundok, and there, we shall settle scores! I'll send you to your death and bury you in the pagan cemetery where you belong . . . And how dare you live-in with Tentay? She isn't your wife! You shameless pig! Don't you know I've already slept with her?'

The last part of the letter made Tentay's face turn blood-red in rage.

'That fool! What a liar! Mudslinger!' Tentay exclaimed.

'Oh, don't listen to the words of an idiot,' Delfin replied nonchalantly. 'There's nothing he could say that would tear Felipe's mind and heart away from Tentay.'

Delfin's reassuring words didn't help dispel Tentay's feelings of shame and self-doubt. She became teary-eyed and felt so humiliated that she sunk her head very low to avoid the gaze of the people around her. Felipe broke the solemn mood, seeing Meni rubbing tears off her face.

'Come now, this is no occasion for grief and sorrow.'

'Perhaps, our coffee cups are too hot?' Delfin teased.

'No, it's the onion in our rice cake!' Felipe retorted.

Tentay brightened up a bit and gently smiled.

Felipe added, 'Ah, such proud and stubborn women! No profession of undying love ever satisfies you, and you prefer to wallow in self-pity and misery. It shouldn't matter if I spoke of what happened with Karugdog. I wouldn't remain by your side if I believed all those lies!'

Meni counseled, 'Indeed! Ipeng, please go on and continue reading the letter for us.'

'That was all there was to it,' Delfin said.

'Yes, it was all that and then the signature,' Felipe added.

'What did you do with the letter?' Meni asked.

'What else would I do with it? I didn't tell anyone else right away, when I entered the house. That same night, I went out to scout around for any sign of Karugdog. I searched the whole perimeter of the house, and fearing that he might have broken inside the house, I went back inside. But the door was shut. Very slowly, I opened the door and peered inside.'

Meni gasped. 'Why on earth did you even dare to go out? That man is indeed crazy and dangerous!'

'I didn't want him to think that I was afraid of him, for he might just be too emboldened to try and harm us again. Especially since he once threatened to burn down our whole village . . .'

'So, did Karugdog show up at all?'

'Not at all! I was up until daybreak waiting for him to show up. Then Tentay woke up and called out to me. She gently scolded me, accusing me of sneaking out at night to spy on our female neighbors.'

'That might as well be!' Meni ribbed Felipe. 'So typical of men to be sneaking out in the dead of night to roam around town. Right, Tentay?'

'True. I didn't believe him at first, until he showed me the letter.'

'And what would you have done if you caught that madman?' asked Delfin. 'Would you have shown up at Paang-Bundok?'

'Absolutely not! I would have squared off with him right at the gate! I would have shown him I am not one to mess with!'

Meni reprimanded Felipe. 'Please, never go out again! Who knows if he might sneak up on you when you least expect it? Just stay inside, even as you keep an eye out for any sign of his presence.'

'I'm not afraid of him! Despite the ultimatum he had given me, he never had the courage to actually fight. Once, I saw him right outside Quiapo Church. When he saw me, he appeared to retreat, but it was too late because he knew I had already spotted him. He didn't say a word when our paths crossed. I wanted to ask him about the letter, but he just walked away, pretending he didn't see me. So I walked on, but when I looked around as I reached the Zorrilla Theatre, he was following me. We met up on Calle Cervantes, and he asked me how I was. I wasn't sure what he was up to, but I decided to play along and be civil toward him. When I asked him about the letter, he denied writing it. He apologized profusely, saying that he just went to confession where he was told by a Jesuit priest to repent and change his ways. And then he began rambling about how he could not forget Tentay, his true love whom he dreams about every night. He even told me to tell Tentay to remember him should she become a widow in the future . . .'

The last bit really brought the house down as Delfin, Meni and Tentay burst into boisterous laughter.

'You should have just smacked him in the head,' Tentay remarked.

'In short, your dear friend is waiting for you to die,' Delfin added.

'Indeed. So, I played along and told him I'll tell Tentay that should I die, she should marry him. Then, he laughed gleefully! And since that last encounter, he has left us in peace. And every time we chance upon each other, he asks, "How's Tentay?"'

'Thank goodness no untoward incident befell you,' said Delfin's aunt, who had been listening all along. 'That's why it's best for you, Felipe, to be at your best behaviour, always. There's always a peaceful way to resolve any conflict. And repentance always leads us to the path of righteousness. The Jesuit priests are indeed wise preachers.'

Delfin, Felipe, and Meni exchanged knowing glances, as if to say, 'And here goes our old woman preaching again!' Tentay, who was unfamiliar with the old woman's character, was totally clueless.

* * *

Felipe and Tentay stayed on until after dark. Tentay, who was normally quiet, really opened up and spoke engagedly with Meni.

'I wonder what the two of you have been chatting about,' asked Felipe.

'Tentay was just telling me that ever since you started living with her family, you no longer kiss her mother's hand at Angelus.' Meni said.

The four kindred spirits, once again engaged in joyful banter, only breaking up when the baby woke up and started crying. Tentay was about to say goodbye, but Meni begged her to keep her company as she nursed the baby.

The two women had become so intimately close that each had shared their private lives. But when Tentay asked about Meni's relationship with her father and siblings, Meni fell silent. Tentay, not realizing that she had hit a raw nerve, pressed on.

'So, until now, you haven't returned to your father's house?'

Meni heaved a sigh. 'What father would accept my family and I?'

'Why not?'

'All because I chose to marry Delfin, my father just packed his bags and left the country! He swore never to return until his dying day.'

'But why did you just let him leave? I wouldn't have let my father leave like that, no matter how angry he was. I'd have chased him to the port, prevented him from boarding . . .'

Meni realised, hurtful though her words were, that Tentay was right. Had she not been too blinded by her love for Delfin, and acted more like a loving daughter, she should have exerted all efforts to keep her father from going away. Meni did not quite know how to respond to Tentay's admonitions.

'My dear Meni, we should never forsake our parents, no matter how cruel they are. You've already lost your mother. Your father is all that is left.'

'Oh, my friend! Indeed, I'm an orphan now! I've lost my mother and my father, and my siblings!' Meni paused for a moment, weighing the words in her heart. 'I've lost my father, for I don't know where he is now; if he is still alive, or if he has died in his travels overseas. He's been gone four months, and he's never written to me. No word, even from my siblings. He might as well be dead for all I know, for he had already left his last will and testament before his departure.'

'And you haven't heard any news of his return from your siblings?'

'According to Talia, on the day that he left, he said he'll be gone for only six months. Only much later did we realize he was never coming back. Oh, Tentay! My father wouldn't have left if he weren't so furious with me. We wouldn't be suffering like this if he were around. I would have welcomed you in a much better home than this.' And Meni finally broke into sobs.

Tentay was deeply moved, and went on to console her dear friend. 'But then, you and I wouldn't have met . . .'

'Why so?'

'You might not have married Delfin. And even if you did, Felipe wouldn't have been the godfather of your child. And you'd be living in your big house.'

'Oh, but Felipe also comes from a wealthy family.'

'Yes, but he chose to be a journalist and live with a poor woman like me. Surely, it would be your father's rich friends who'd be chosen to be godparents.'

Meni felt pangs of guilt upon hearing those words. Indeed, Tentay couldn't have been more right! She wouldn't be speaking to Tentay now, had she married a rich man.

'But even as a child, I was never one who only looked at a man's wealth. I wouldn't be with Delfin, the love of my life, if I had such a high regard for wealth and social status.'

'I agree. But what about your father and your siblings?'

'No matter. You came here to meet me, not them.'

'If I may ask, why haven't they come to see you for so long?'

'All because I didn't have their blessings when I chose to marry Delfin. That's why they have cut ties with me and abandoned me. That wouldn't have mattered to me if my own father hadn't disowned and disinherited me. Out of spite, they took away from me, everything that's rightfully mine. For the first two months after I got married, they sent money. But when they learned that Delfin didn't want me to be anywhere inside my father's house, they stopped giving aid and never spoke to us again.'

'Why did Delfin forbid you from visiting your father's house?'

'Oh, that's a very long story, which I will tell you another time. All I can say is that Delfin and Felipe found out that it was through the machinations of my brother-in-law that I lost my inheritance. He persuaded my father to leave me out of his last will and testament.'

'Oh, my!' Tentay was aghast.

'That's why Delfin has forbidden me from ever seeing my family again. And then my family stopped sending me updates on my father's whereabouts.'

'And your father never wrote to you?'

'Never. Not a single word.'

'But you know, parents, when they learn that they have grandchildren, they always have a change of heart . . .'

'Oh, no! Not my father!'

'And your brother, what does he think of your situation now?'

'Siano is an imbecile, less of a man than my sister Talia! Otherwise, he wouldn't have let my brother-in-law manipulate my father like that. When I had a falling out with my sister and her husband, Siano also forbade his wife from seeing me.'

'Don't they know you have already given birth?'

'No.'

'It is indeed quite difficult to sway a heart full of resentment. Why don't we invite them to the baptism?'

'Oh, I don't think they'll come.'

'Then go and send for them.'

'Delfin wouldn't have any of that.'

'Nonetheless, you should at least let them know of the child's baptism.'

And that was when the two women hatched an intricate plan to invite Meni's family to the ceremony, or convince Delfin to drop by her old house on the way from the church, after the ceremony. After everything had been settled, Meni and Tentay called the two men, and the four agreed to have the baptism at the end of the month.

It was seven-thirty in the evening when the guests finally took leave.

Chapter 26

Grief Amidst Gladness

Delfin came to work late, one morning.

On the road, he kept thinking about the unpleasant conversation he had had with his wife at bedtime, last night. He could not decide on how to respond to Meni's request. His heart brimmed with greater love for the woman who had endured so much pain to become his wife, and who bore him a son who was his spitting image. But he was deeply bothered by Meni's desire to invite her family to the baptism. He didn't like Meni's idea to bring the child over to her family's house, with or without him. Meni clearly had hopes that seeing her child would wipe away her family's anger and resentment. But Delfin had already vehemently denied her request. He was afraid that Meni and their child would be scorned and turned away. Worse, her setting foot once again in that house of riches and luxury would just remind her painfully of how much she had given up for their love.

But he also felt guilty for depriving Meni of the chance to be reunited with the family whom she dearly loved. He stopped in his tracks and thought about turning around and not showing up at work. He was anxious about leaving his wife alone in the house after their long argument last night. This morning, when she got up, Meni did not put the child on his chest—something she had always done to rouse him from sleep. She rose from bed and went out to help his aunt prepare breakfast. Then she called him to eat, but without the usual warmth and enthusiasm in her voice. She also did not join him at breakfast, and when she sat down at the table, she barely took a bite before quietly standing up to go outside.

Delfin stood frozen under a tree by the roadside. After a moment's hesitation, he turned and began walking back to the house to tell Meni that he had changed his mind. He could not bear the thought of Meni falling ill again, for that, would also mean the child would get sick. He was going to let Meni see her family, on the condition that she would tell them that she did so without Delfin's knowledge or permission.

But then something held him back.

'No, that cannot be!' Delfin thought to himself. 'That will only make Meni think she has won. There are some things that women desire that once granted, will give them power and dominance over men. If I give in now to her wishes, surely she'll bargain for more in the days to come. She'll think I've no conviction and will always give in to her whims. It will certainly doom our marriage if I followed everything that my wife wanted.'

Delfin's musings continued. 'It's not that I'd want to assert my dominance as the man of the house. I don't wish to treat my wife as a slave, disempowered and disenfranchised, nor do I intend to abuse her and confine her to domesticity, like most men do. But that doesn't mean I'm willing to sacrifice my honour and integrity as a humble man just to give her what she wants. That Madlang-Layon, along with Talia and her brother—their nature is dictated by their lust for money. If they truly cared for Meni, they wouldn't have let Don Ramon disinherit her altogether.

'True, we could contest her father's last will and testament in court. But where will we get the money to pay for the attorney's fees? And if we do get the money that is rightfully Meni's, I don't wish to become one of the *nouveaux riches* and be accused of marrying Meni for her money. And I can't, in conscience, lay my hands on riches that I didn't toil for. No, I won't.

'I can't let Meni have her wish. She needs to understand and accept that we'll never rely on the wealth controlled by Madlang-Layon just to have a comfortable life. I stand firm on my conviction—the comfort and security of my family will only come from the fruits of my own labour. I can't live a privileged life while others are suffering from poverty. No, my conscience will not allow it.'

Delfin stood at the street corner mulling these thoughts over in his mind. He resolved to never again let Meni rejoin her family. Finally, he decided he did not want his colleagues at the press waiting, so he turned and walked on to work. He would take an early leave and go home earlier than expected.

He was on his way back to the house when he chanced upon Talia and Siano's wife on a horse-drawn carriage coming from the direction of Santa Mesa. He saw them from a distance, and he could not quite make up his mind whether to greet or ignore them. As the carriage drew close, he looked up just when Talia turned to gaze at him. Siano's wife pointed at him and cried, 'There's Delfin!' But Talia did not even say a word of greeting toward her brother-in-law, who had stopped in his tracks. She merely craned her neck and slightly opened her mouth, and in disgust uttered, 'Pueh!', as the carriage moved along past Delfin.

'What a gesture of disdain!' Delfin thought to himself. He wondered if Talia had just come from their house. He looked back at the carriage and hastened to his house, his heart beating wildly in his chest. When he got home, Meni was cradling the baby while talking to his aunt.

'Why are you home so early?', asked his aunt.

'I wasn't feeling well. My head was hurting, earlier.'

Meni was curious about Delfin, not knowing whether to pry further or not. After Delfin had changed his clothes, Meni began asking him questions. 'Did you go to the press at all?'

'Yes, I was there.'

'Why didn't you just take a carriage if indeed you weren't feeling well?'

'Why would I pay for a ride? We barely have enough for sustenance.'

Meni, who had not yet forgotten about their disagreement, was stung by Delfin's words. She was not used to Delfin being coarse and harsh. She and the aunt were just talking about their argument the night before, and the aunt was consoling her when Delfin arrived.

The old woman thought Meni, being the youngest sibling, should be respectful toward her older siblings who now stood as her parents in the absence of her mother and father. She reminded Meni that she would be setting a bad example for her child if he were to grew up in a divided family. She promised that she would speak to her nephew about the matter.

'Didn't your "beloved" sister, Talia, drop by to see you earlier?'

'Oh, no, not at all. Why, did you see her earlier?'

'I met her on the road as I was walking back home. You've no idea how she treated me with absolutely no respect!'

Meni was struck dumb.

'Why, what did she do to you?'

'From a distance, I saw her with Siano's wife in a horse-drawn carriage coming from Santa Mesa. I stopped to greet them, but when she passed she spat and snubbed me as they went on their way. I was taken aback by such rudeness. It's hardly to be expected from a well-educated person such as she. I've never felt so humiliated and scorned!'

Meni felt deep shame for her husband. She dispelled the doubt that emerged that her husband would invent such a story. She stood speechless.

'None of that matters now, my dear wife. If you really must see your family again, then I don't wish to prevent you from doing so.'

'And why would I want to do that, after what they have done to you? Did you really think I wouldn't stand by your side after they humiliated you?'

'I don't know, Meni. You're free to do as you wish in matters concerning your family. The incident earlier notwithstanding, I came home early just to let you know that I don't want your family to drive a wedge between us, and that you're free to visit your old house. I couldn't bear the thought of you harbouring deep resentment toward me and you know I can never resent you for anything. Last night, I couldn't sleep . . .'

'And you think I was able to?'

'Oh, you fell asleep. I was talking to you, but you weren't saying anything. I was tugging at your hand, but you were snoring.'

'Really?'

'Yes.'

'Well, I haven't been getting enough sleep because of the baby. But wait, did you really see Talia earlier, and did she really spit on the ground upon seeing you?'

'Indeed.'

'Then I swear to you that I'll never set foot in that house ever again.'

And true to her word, Meni never spoke of seeing her family again. She intended to write Talia to ask why the display of utter disrespect to her husband, but Delfin dissuaded her. And so, Meni cut all ties with Talia.

* * *

In the days that followed, it was as if the couple were on their second honeymoon. The house was filled with happiness. All despair and worry would vanish at the doorstep, as soon as Delfin saw his beloved son. It was as if the baby could ward off the spirit of gloom with a mere wave of his tiny hands, driving away any fear of mortal danger. Not even all the riches of Don Ramon could equal the treasure trove of joy that they cradled in their arms.

As for Meni, she needed to prove her love for her child by pushing through with the baptism. She felt the irresistible urge to show the world how happy she was at being a new mother. She refused to forego the usual pomp and circumstance and did not care at all about the cost it would entail.

'Where would we get the money to pay for all of it? Do you really think we could limit the amount of food we serve once the orchestra you have invited begins playing?'

'Oh, don't worry about it!' Meni said dismissively.

'I can't not worry about it. Do you really think that twenty or thirty pesos will be enough, given our situation?'

'That's a small amount!' Meni smiled. 'I don't suppose you wouldn't do everything you could for your only son?'

'No, it's not that at all. It's just that we're in dire straits right now. Even as we speak, my next paycheck is bound to instantly vanish into thin air, with all the expenses on medicine, the store credit, your physician and many other things. It is wisest to wait a few more months until we can cope with our expenses.'

'Are you suggesting that we postpone this Sunday's baptism?'

'If possible. But if you insist, let's get on with it, without all the expensive rites. We can have the feast at a later time, when we have the means.'

'Why invite people then if there's no celebration?'

'What would you have us do, my dear wife? We simply don't have the money! It would be such a disgrace to put up a feast and be buried deep in debt because of it.'

Meni fell silent as she broke out in a cold sweat. She thought of the shame it would bring if people found out that they had to borrow money for the occasion. But then, she decided it would be more disgraceful if they went on with the baptism as if it were only an ordinary Sunday Mass. 'Such woes befall a woman married to a poor man!' Meni thought to herself.

Delfin, seeing that Meni was utterly quiet and looking disheartened, relented.

'Oh, Meni, you don't know how it rips me apart to see that I've failed to give you everything you deserved. It's terrible to be married to a poor husband, you must be thinking.'

'Why bring that up again? Don't change the subject, please.'

'Look, about your employer, since it's highly unlikely they'll lend you money, perhaps it is best to . . .' Meni paused as she studied the intent expression on her husband's face as he hung on to the words she was about to say. 'Before I go on, please promise me you'll take what I am going to say in good form. I've an idea that will solve our problem.'

'What is it?'

'Swear first that you won't take any offence.'

'No, what is it? I can't promise anything without knowing if what I'm about to hear is bad, or impossible, even.'

'In that case, I won't tell you.'

It took a little coaxing and gentle teasing from Delfin before Meni spoke her mind.

'All right, all right . . . I was thinking . . . maybe we could take my earrings to the pawnshop, and pawn them for twenty-five pesos, perhaps?'

'What!? Why would you even think of doing that?'

'I've no use for them as I never wear them anyway. Didn't you say that it was a sin to waste money on idle things like jewellery? What's the use of having them if I can't exchange them for money that I can spend?'

'No, Meni. It would be okay if you were going to invest the money in a business that can sustain us. But not if you're just going to throw it all away at a lavish party! And if truth be told, I wouldn't have people think that you were forced to sell off your possessions because we were dirt poor. And if your siblings found out, surely they'd point an accusing finger at me. Forgive me, my dear, but I cannot allow it. No money, no baptism!'

Meni waited for Delfin to calm down before she gently pleaded her case.

'Look, Delfin, you're more concerned about my siblings asking about my heirloom, when in fact, I've all the reason to ask *them* about *my* inheritance. What right do they have to question what I do with what is rightfully mine? It's not like they're still giving me something. Besides, the money is going to my child.'

'Your child! You mean your guests!'

'Yes, but it's because of my baby.'

'And where will you get the money if your child gets sick?'

'No worries. We're just pawning it. We can get it back as soon as we've the money.'

The argument between the two again dragged on aimlessly. But in the end, Delfin caved in. The next day, Delfin's aunt brought the earrings to the Monte de Piedad. Although the monthly interest was manageable, the offer was a only meagre twelve pesos. At the old shop in Binondo, the interest was high, but the offer was no more than twenty pesos—not even enough to pay for the reception. Meni insisted on twenty-five to thirty pesos, since the item was already worth one hundred pesos when her mother had bought it.

The old aunt went to one of the shops in the port area in Escolta that was owned by an American who was known to pay a good price for excellent jewellery. The old woman asked around and by noontime, she had arrived at the shop's doorstep. The old woman was ecstatic! She was offered thirty-five pesos! She hurried back home on foot, not wanting to take a single cent to pay for a carriage.

'Had I known, I should have gone straight to that shop. These Americans really know gold and precious stones when they see them, unlike the Spanish and the locals here!' The old woman was brimming with excitement as she spoke to Meni about the shops that she had visited.

Meni said, 'That's not why Monte de Piedad gave a very low appraisal. They offer very little because should the pawned item be forfeited, they'll earn so much more.'

The two women chatted happily, conveniently glossing over the unfair and opportunistic practices of the local pawn shops. They were all praises for the American capitalist, not concerned at all about the exorbitant interests that they would have to cover. But Delfin was nowhere near happy or ecstatic about the whole thing.

He struggled to put on a smile and barely nodded as he listened to the two women. But there was nothing that he could have done about it. It was done. The preparations for the upcoming celebration were now underway.

* * *

On Sunday morning, right after the High Mass, Tentay arrived at the house with her brother, Victor, in tow. Meni and the child were already properly dressed for the baptismal rite. 'Where's the godfather?' asked the aunt.

'Felipe's already there waiting for us in church.'

'Some godfather! Don't tell me he's ashamed of his godson. He should be here accompanying the child as he is being welcomed into the house of God!'

Delfin spoke on behalf of his best friend. 'Felipe and I agreed that he should be there first to take care of the registration.'

The old woman scoffed. 'And he had the gall to send over a rundown carriage for your son!'

'Oh, don't be so picky. Meni and the baby wouldn't fit in a horse-drawn carriage anyway.'

'Well then, he should have rented two carriages. There are many decent rides around that could have been rented.'

'Nanay, it wouldn't make a difference. Rundown or brand new, the child will still make it to his baptism.'

'I would have you know, this doesn't bode well for your child, on his first day of becoming a baptized Christian! If the child is initiated into the Catholic faith under impoverished conditions, he will surely live and die under the same conditions.'

'Oh, you really should let go of these old superstitions.'

'They're all true! Look at me. All my children were taken to church in carriages for their baptism. The eldest was baptized in the cathedral. And there was a marching band in the procession. Even when your uncle was ill, we managed to rent a decent carriage for the baptism of your youngest cousin.'

'Don't make a fuss over it, Nanay. It's a Sunday. Most likely all the new rides have already been booked, so Felipe had to settle for this old carriage.'

'Why can't you just admit what a cheapskate your best friend really is!' The old woman exclaimed with scorn as she spat on the ground and turned to go back inside the house. She came to Meni and whispered. 'Look outside. Felipe had hired a rickety old carriage to take you and the child to church. Really stingy of him!'

Meni who was powdering her cheeks stood up and frowned upon seeing the old carriage waiting outside the house. 'A very old carriage, indeed. My goodness, why couldn't Felipe find a more decent ride?' She thought of calling Livery Stable to hire a fine carriage, but then she decided that would be inappropriate and rude behavior. She quietly accepted the situation, went out, and with eyes half-closed, boarded the carriage.

It was too late to turn back now and change anything. It was hardly the time to throw a tantrum over things that mattered very little.

* * *

And so the child was baptized and named Tiburcio. The church rejected the Tagalog name proposed by the godfather, and they also did not like

Delfin, which the mother wanted. The parish priest said. 'You may call him whatever you want at home, but here, in the house of God, you can't do as you please.'

With sad eyes, Meni looked at the babies lined up for the baptismal rite—six infant girls, not one boy. She heard the chimes of the bells as the priest administered the rite, and she was taunted by the orchestral accompaniment at the baptism of one child. All of it seemed to make her think: 'Poor Tiburcio! How unfortunate you don't have all these to celebrate your initiation!'

It was a good thing that nobody amongst the crowd gathered in front of the altar knew who she was. Otherwise, she would have felt deeply ashamed. She did not regret marrying a poor husband; it was the fact that she was born to a wealthy family that gave her a deep feeling of resentment. But seeing how Tentay, who knew nothing but a life of miserable poverty, was so happy to have witnessed this modest celebration of her child being welcomed into the Catholic fold, Meni's heart began to feel lighter. 'If I were in Tentay's shoes, I'd feel blessed to witness my child's baptismal, even without all the pomp and circumstance surrounding him.'

Her epiphany put her in a joyous mood for the reception that followed, and Meni delightfully celebrated with all the guests who were waiting for their arrival at home.

There were numerous guests, many of whom were neighbours who had offered to help with the chores. The invited ones just started pouring in—colleagues of Delfin's and Felipe's, and several young men and women from Sampaloc and Uli-uli. At the eleventh hour came the musicians—Meni's female friends who played the native mandolin. They came from Santa Cruz, followed by a cartload of old women and young children, who were probably relatives of the musicians.

The party came alive when the musicians with their native mandolins, the guitarist and the bassist started playing. More and more people began to pour in and mingle amongst the guests. That was when Delfin saw that they would soon run out of food and drinks to serve. Meni's friends from Quiapo and Santa Cruz came up out of the blue, and it suddenly appeared to be a party hosted for the affluent society.

Clearly, their house was unfit to receive such noble guests. Meni was surprised how her old friends found out about the reception. She did not tell anyone else, aside from the two women who had brought the musicians to play at the party. The only ones she invited were Dr Gatdula, her physician, and his wife. Even her old teacher, Miss Ines, came with several companions. There were just too many social butterflies to count!

Naturally, these uninvited guests were not part of the equation when they had made the preparations. A small roast pig, six or seven whole fried chickens, and a pound of meat for two viands—these would not be enough for the multitude that had come unexpectedly.

True, there were guests who came bearing gifts, but what good were baby clothes and house decors and dining accessories in feeding these gatecrashers? It would be pointless to blame his wife, or curse at the uninvited guests. It was the local mentality that he really abhorred. He wondered how so many people could be so callous as to ignore the humble status of the hosts.

As the musicians strummed the native mandolins and in the air floated the fast-paced waltz and the two-step tunes, they sat timidly tapping their feet to the rhythm, unsure whether the fragile floor of the house could withstand the pressure. They shook their heads, winked and muttered to each other, while some pointed toward the empty lot in front of the house where they said a dance floor could have been staged.

But Delfin would not have any of that. His house simply was not built for ballroom dancing. They could very well celebrate Tiburcio's baptismal party without all that jumping and flailing and twisting and turning.

As for the child, indeed he was christened Tiburcio by the church. But Delfin and Felipe, dropping the earlier Radiance, introduced him to the guests as Hero. Delfin's aunt no longer protested, for she thought that they had already fulfilled their moral obligation of baptizing him with a Christian name, and that it was enough that they put God's will first before man's whim. She regarded it as an alias, for she only saw the world as divided between the evangelized and the pagans. After all, she was a woman who grew up following the tenets set by the Christian doctrines.

As soon as the baby returned home, she officiated the Catholic rituals of welcoming the newly baptized Christian, then cradled the boy in her arms as the guests came to honour him. She abandoned the kitchen altogether and welcomed everybody to the house, leaving Delfin to supervise the preparations of the meal.

* * *

Delfin was still worried about the food for the guests and expressed his concern to the old man who was preparing the meals. The man stood up from the pan he was stirring, looked at Delfin and smiled.

'In your estimate, how many mouths are we going to feed?'

'By my count, there are five to six tables, ten heads each.'

'So, six platters, ten people. That makes sixty, no?'

'Yes, at the very least. Forty people are crammed upstairs, but as soon as food is served, more people will pour in. We're expecting more neighbours to show up.'

'Don't worry. We won't fall short. I've been through worse situations, you know,' the old man said as he threw a glance at the people gathered upstairs. He was just about to ramble on about his misadventures in similar situations in feasts past, but Delfin cut him short, for he was not interested in hearing about any disaster other than the one that was now happening to him.

'So, what should we do now?'

'What time are we serving lunch?'

'At twelve, which will be very soon.'

'All right, I know what to do. Just relax.'

The old man waved at a woman slicing onions at the table not far away from him and instructed her to bring out the huge platter of the Spanish rice dish covered with banana leaves. He tossed the Spanish rice dish back into the wok and poured copious amounts of coconut milk.

'You see, this rice dish alone will immediately curb their appetite. This is a better starter than soup at a time of scarcity, like now. If you feed them something oily early on, then they will lose interest in more oily food that would come later. The rice dish alone will make them stop craving for more food to eat. They'll gobble this up, sure, because it's delicious. And yes, let them all use forks and spoons. That way, they can eat slowly, and no food will be wasted. We'll prepare really salty dishes. Don't cut up the meat. Let them struggle to carve out a piece of the stringy meat. We'll serve the ham and lechon much later. And before I forget, hide the pickle made of grated, unripe papaya. We don't want to serve them anything that can clean their palate or further whet their appetite.'

The old man's plan actually worked! Delfin felt like he had just seen the miracle of the feeding of the multitude with five loaves of bread and a single fish. All that was needed now was to turn the water in earthen jars into wine. But Delfin held on to his conviction not to subscribe to the tradition of serving wines at feasts. As a radical opponent of the Enlightenment, he refused to serve beer to his guests.

Delfin sighed with relief as the 'noble' guests did not seem to complain about the food or the absence of beer. And when the old man told him that there were still two platters of food untouched, he very nearly kissed the old man's greasy hands out of sheer gratitude!

After the guests had eaten, the celebration began to grind to a halt. Indeed there was music, but nobody was dancing. None of the ladies wanted to sing a number. Meni was coaxed into rendering a song that she knew from her younger days, but nobody echoed her courage. The afternoon was sweltering. Many could not suppress their yawns with their handkerchiefs and fans, and the guests started to feel uneasy. A few thought of leaving, but were too shy to say goodbye to the very hospitable and accommodating hosts that were Delfin, Meni, Felipe and Tentay. The guests who did stand up to take leave were pulled back to their seats by Meni. 'Oh no, don't leave just yet. Stay for just one more number from our orchestra, please.'

And it was through that tugging and pulling that the party came back to life.

But no one foresaw the wicked twist of fate that was about to unfold!

Meni was singing another waltz when a man on horseback stopped abruptly at the gate, startling the crowd at the party. He was carrying an envelope.

Delfin went up to the man whom he recognized as the coachman in the employ of Talia, the same man who used to carry his love letters to Meni when he was still courting her.

'A letter for you from Señora Talia, sir.'

Delfin was nervous as he took the envelope. In it was Talia's card and a folded yellowed paper. On the card was written: 'Meni, read this heartbreaking message!'

Delfin read what was written on the piece of yellowed paper. The letter was in English, posted from Boston, United States of America, and had been sent by Doroteo Miranda, a cousin of Meni's, who was studying there. It said that 'Don Ramon Miranda had been murdered by his companion helper at a hotel in New York, on the night of 9th of June . . .'

The telegraph also described how the victim was attacked in his sleep and sustained three fatal stab wounds in the left of his chest, in the face and in the neck. The crime happened in the evening, but it was not until noon, the next day, that the other guests at the hotel discovered the body.

The remains were now in the custody of the state, to be immediately shipped back to the Philippines. The said culprit took all of the old man's money. The nephew had rushed to New York upon hearing the news, and he was to bring the body back home.

From inside the house, Meni could see Delfin holding the letter and people huddled around him. Fear suddenly crept inside her. She stopped singing and rushed out of the crowded house. She was utterly surprised to see the familiar coachman after so long that she blurted: 'Why are you here?'

She turned to Delfin. 'What is that letter you're holding?'

Meni snatched the letter from Delfin's hand. After reading the opening of the message, she cried out in grief, dropped to the ground and fainted. Delfin held her as everyone around them began to sob in mourning when they learned of Don Ramon's tragic fate. 'God bless his soul,' uttered those who knew the life that Don Ramon had lived, while others still gripped with shock gasped, 'It can't be'.

The news of Don Ramon's untimely death spread like wildfire throughout the neighbourhood. The house nearly crumbled under the weight of more visitors, who came to express their condolences to the bereaved.

Even the baby who was quietly sleeping in his room wailed suddenly, as if he knew of the tragedy and was now grieving with his parents. Meni was already back inside the house when she regained her consciousness. Thank God they had a doctor amongst the guests!

The festive mood in the house was now gone, with the heavy atmosphere of grief and sorrow taking its place. It was as if a phantom had broken into the house and stolen their hearts bursting with joy and delight, and replaced them with ones filled with suffering and pain. Felipe sat still, trying to come to grips with the shocking death of Don Ramon. He never saw eye-to-eye with Don Ramon, his godfather, on many things. They were polar opposites in terms of political leanings, and oftentimes, they fought openly on matters of principle. He also could not wrap his head around Tikong having murdered Don Ramon. He had always thought of Tikong as a loyal servant to his master. He could not quite fathom what his reasons for killing the old man in cold blood could have been. Tikong was known to be kind and obedient to his master and lord. That was why Don Ramon chose him for company on his travels, amongst all the other servants in the house, because he was the one who could be trusted the most. He could not believe that Tikong could do something as grave as this, without a sufficient reason to do so.

Inside the house, when everything had subsided and Doctor Gatdula had pronounced that Meni was safe from any danger, everyone began to say their farewells, singly and in groups. The only ones who remained were the husband and wife, as well as Tentay's little brother.

Chapter 27

Coming Home

Flickering daylight, weeping sky, the scent of wet air, grass fields glistening, streets heavily drenched: all-too familiar Manila grinding and belching as throngs of weary workers who had barely stopped to rest, while the angry screams of factory machines blared on relentlessly— this was the unholy hour of worship when the masses would kneel at the heels of the Gods of Capitalism, leading the procession to the shrine of Desire and Pleasure. This was Manila Bay, where gloomy weather and scenes of hard labour were like two sides of a coin.

But on this particular day, even darker clouds loomed over the Captain Luis port in Binondo, where four men were carefully unloading a black, shiny, well-adorned casket. Siano was at the forefront, followed by Madlang-Layon at the rear end.

The arrival of the remains of Don Ramon came at short notice. They were not expecting the ship *Logan* to arrive until the next day, but without warning, at 12 noon on that day, Yoyong received notice from the port authorities that *Logan* had arrived in the morning. Yoyong hastily informed his brother-in-law and made arrangements for a small boat, men to carry the casket, and the funeral parlour.

Talia was left behind at home, for Yoyong was worried that her faint heart might not be able to bear the sight of her beloved father's casket. She waited as if the angel of death was also coming to claim her, soon enough.

Meni and Delfin, although prepared to see the remains at once, were unaware of what was happening, since they thought that *Logan* would not arrive until the next day.

The broken ties between Meni and her siblings had begun to mend. The sisters once again reached out to one another for solace, although they were yet to visit each other's homes.

Don Filemon was amongst those from The Progress who accompanied Siano. Since Don Ramon left the country, his anger and jealousy had washed away. He felt deep remorse when he received the farewell letter and regretted having wronged his dear friend, all because of an anonymous note filled with lies and deceit from a vile and cowardly enemy. He had profusely apologized more than once to Señora Loleng, whom he had almost killed for no adequate reason at all. Oh, how devastated he had been when he had learnt of Don Ramon's sudden death!

He felt responsible for the death, for he was convinced that Don Ramon would not have gone away to save himself from all the disgrace and shame, if it were not for their misunderstanding. If only he had remained in Manila, he would not have suffered such a terrible fate at the hands of his servant.

Before Don Filemon and Siano left the factory, work was momentarily halted. The workers were ordered to get properly dressed to receive the remains of their master at the pier. The labourers at The Progress, like a singular mass, went into a frenzy to obey the command.

'Whoever fails to show up at the docks will not be paid their wages on Saturday!' Hearing Don Filemon's words drove the workers into panic as they tidied up.

Yoyong went ahead of the rest and boarded the small boat to claim the coffin, and the crowds arrived just in time at the docks as the coffin was being unloaded. It was an uncanny mix of people gathered around the coffin—mourners who had come to pay their respects and strangers intrigued by the news of the old man's death. Their eyes were all fixed upon the black coffin. Some spoke in hushed tones about the circumstances surrounding the old man's death. Many felt seething rage upon learning how the Don was murdered. And everyone thought how unfortunate it was that the culprit got away with all of the old man's money.

Two strange men in the company of Yoyong and Siano piqued the crowd's curiosity. Clearly they were Filipinos, but the two were so unlike each other, judging from their clothes and the way they carried themselves. One was tall and rather fair-skinned, wearing a dark linen suit. The suit was too big and too long, looking as if it did not belong to him; the pants too narrow at the legs and too wide at the hem; the collar as stiff as a startled crane's neck; the tie woven like a disheveled scarf; the wide-brimmed felt hat with a crooked top; and black shoes stumpy and flat like the feet of a sea turtle. The other man wore similar garments, although clearly, he was a mere attendant. The two men talked in English, but their tongues buckled and curled as they spoke in Spanish and Tagalog to Yoyong and Siano. Undoubtedly, these two men had just arrived in the country. They had brought the coffin all the way from America.

'I didn't think it was a good idea to just leave it all to Ruperto to bring home my uncle's remains. After sending a telegram about the mishap that befell my dear uncle, I didn't want my cousins to think I was unsympathetic. I felt it was just proper to take a break from my studies in Boston.'

So this man must be Doroteo Miranda, Don Ramon's nephew, the one who sent Talia the telegram. And who might this Ruperto be? A fellow student in the United States of America? But he seemed more like a servant to Doroteo with the way he fumbled upon every word of instruction as he tended to the coffin. He could not be another nephew of Don Ramon's.

'Oh, that man?' said Doroteo to answer Siano's question.

'He's a poor Filipino working as a bartender in New York City. I just met him there. He left the country when he was young and never saw nor heard from his family again. That lucky kid's been to almost every place in Europe, before coming to America. In New York City, he had no permanent residence until he found work in a bar where he's been stationed for a year now. He offered to help me bring home

Don Ramon. The bar where he worked was near the hotel where the crime took place. He may seem rough around the edges, but he's a good lad. Very fluent in English and a few European languages. His life story is so tragic as well.'

As the student from Boston spoke, the funeral carriage paced along San Fernando Road, followed by a procession of five horse-drawn carts and carriages carrying the friends and relatives, who came as soon as they learnt of Don Ramon's passing. Behind the carriages trailed the throngs of workers from The Progress, walking in a disorderly fashion. The young women, still shaken by the threatening words of Don Filemon at the factory, lifted their skirts and trampled on the thick mud as they dogged the carriage carrying their master's remains. Many did not heed Don Filemon's stern warning and chose to stealthily break away and flee from the procession. No one amongst the watchers seemed to care if the people had already disappeared from their ranks.

The people who saw the funeral march were filled with awe and grief. In silence, they uttered their prayers for the dearly departed: 'May he rest in peace! May the Lord forgive him for his sins!'

* * *

The coffin was brought straight to the old man's house instead of being taken to the cemetery, as was customary. The house had already been fully decked and well-prepared to honour the remains of the great father. In and out, the old man's house was miraculously transformed to look like a great church.

It was nighttime when the body of Don Ramon arrived, and the vigil was going to be held until the afternoon of the next day, when the remains would finally be laid to rest. Everyone who came to visit saw the gruesome appearance of murder: a long, deep slash wound on the man's left cheek, and another down his neck up to his collarbone. Many wondered about the chest wound beneath the corpse's shirt. The flesh had already darkened from the embalming that it was nearly as black as the funeral suit.

Meni came in the evening as soon as she received word from her siblings. On that occasion, the siblings set their differences aside and reunited once again, for it was their moral obligation to pay their respects and honour their dearly departed father, as one family. This was their solemn moment to cast away all past hurts, and for the orphaned children to shed only tears of grief. Those who bore witness could not discern any hint of the old grudges or the long-endured pain of separation between the siblings. Standing there before their father, their bond as Don Ramon's children and as brother and sisters was undeniable.

Even Siano, Yoyong, Delfin, and Felipe cast aside their differences and worked collectively in handling the matters pertaining to the wake, ushering guests who steadily poured in, and in tending to the two sisters who had been driven to hysteria and delirium. Many times, Talia and Meni had thrown themselves onto the coffin to pry open the glass cover, as if wanting to take the place of their father who was lying inside the coffin.

Throughout the vigil, the guests constantly flocked around Doroteo Miranda and Ruperto. After paying their respects to the dead man lying in his coffin, each and every one of them approached the two men, curious to hear the details surrounding the murder of Don Ramon at the hands of his servant, eager to learn the whereabouts of the dastardly culprit, or whether he had been apprehended and sentenced to death. But nobody asked why Tikong had committed the murder, despite the knowledge that Don Ramon had chosen him as his servant companion for his meekness, obedience and humility.

Only Felipe, due to his innate curiosity, had the courage to dig deeper into the crime. The following day, he invited Ruperto to have a private chat in the room of the house where he used to stay.

'My friend, I've been meaning to speak with you since last night. The first time I saw you, you acted like a servant companion to that foreign student who came here with you, which made me rather curious. It's my hunch that you know more than you care to let on about the real circumstances surrounding the murder of my godfather.'

'Are you Don Ramon's godson?' exclaimed Ruperto, staring intently at Felipe's face.

'Yes, I am. It should come as no surprise to you, this desire to know everything about the string of events that led to his gruesome death.

I myself couldn't believe Tikong would be capable of committing such a terrible crime. He and I were roommates, and we actually shared that bedspace right there. I knew him very well, just like I knew Don Ramon quite intimately. What about you? Did you know them?'

'Yes, I know them very well, Don Ramon and Tikong. The bar where I worked in New York City was right beside the hotel where they were staying. But before I go on, my friend, since you mentioned you are the godson, may I know your name, please?'

Felipe immediately sensed uncertainty and hesitation in Ruperto.

'My name is Felipe.'

'Felipe?!'

Ruperto was struck by what he heard and fell silent.

'You seem surprised. Why, have we met before?'

Ruperto could not say a word. His eyes and tongue froze. He wanted to respond, but he could not seem to muster enough courage to do so.

'Why? You don't believe what I just told you?'

'I'm sorry, not at all. It's just that . . . you and I . . . may have . . . mutual acquaintances . . .'

'Where? America, do you mean?'

'No. Here in Manila, in Santa . . .'

Ruperto fell silent again. He looked confused, hesitant and anxious, from where he stood.

A sudden realization hit Felipe in the chest. He began to recall a distant memory.

'Wait, didn't you say your name was Ruperto?'

'Yes.'

'Ruperto . . . that was the name of . . .'

Felipe was utterly dumbfounded and could not move his tongue to speak. He stared at Ruperto from head to toe, as if trying to discern any familiar characteristic or resemblance to the people he knew so intimately.

'Felipe?!'

'Ruperto?!'

The two men stood face-to-face and gestured to give each other a welcome hug, but neither moved an inch closer. A strong feeling of doubt pulled them back.

'How long have you been away from the country?'

'Oh, it must have been seven years now, by my count.'

'Seven years? Didn't you go away with a certain Spanish gentleman?'

'No, a Latin American, from Argentina, who was a ship captain.'

'Don't you have a family? Father, mother, siblings?'

'Yes, I do.'

'And their names . . . ?'

'Alejandro and Teresa, my parents . . .'

Felipe was stunned. The revelation sent a chill running down his spine and gave him cold shivers all over. He was dumbstruck for a moment.

'Do you know my parents?'

'As a matter of fact, yes, I do know them very well. But alas, your father . . .'

'Why, what happened to him?'

'Mang Andoy had passed away . . .'

'That can't be!'

Ruperto was speechless, and he stood there like a melting candle.

Felipe instantly regretted telling him that he was now without a father, but it was too late to take it back. He attempted to shift the conversation to another topic, but Ruperto did not oblige. The thought of his father who had gone on to the afterlife, and his mother and siblings who were left behind, pierced his heart. Seven years had passed that he did not see his parents and siblings! That was the only reason he offered himself as a servant companion to Doroteo Miranda—so that he could finally return home. He had planned to go back home for so long, but he did not have the money to do so, and it did not help that he had stern, unbending masters. His wanderlust also distracted him, taking him to foreign lands that he had longed to see.

Since he left the country, he had never received any news about his family back home. It was only through Tikong, that servant who killed his own master, that he was able to gather some information about his loved ones. But it was only bits and pieces. Tikong, whom he had met in New York City, only told him that Don Ramon had a godson named Felipe, a young man born into a wealthy family,

who, because of his socialist leanings, was disowned by his own father
and cast away by his godfather. That this Felipe fell in love with a
poor woman named Tentay, the daughter of Aling Tere and a certain
Mang Andoy, who had very young brothers. That this Felipe had a best
friend who fell in love with a daughter of Don Ramon's, and that the
old man left out of spite because he did not want his daughter to marry
a poor man. Ruperto realized that this Andoy, Tere, Tentay spoken
of by Felipe, godson to Don Ramon, were undoubtedly his very own
father, mother, and sister.

As luck would have it, he was handpicked to assist in ferrying the
remains of a man who happened to be a fellow Filipino! For Ruperto,
what really mattered, more than the murder of Don Ramon, was
that he was finally on his way home, and he did not have to spend a
single penny to do so. He did not care about the way Tikong killed
Don Ramon, for he thought Tikong could not be blamed, and the
murder was all the old man's own fault.

But this was hardly the right time for the two men to continue
discussing the gory details of Don Ramon's murder. In the light of
this sudden revelation, Ruperto could not wait to hear more about his
mother and siblings.

'Where are they now? Where can I find my mother and my siblings?'

'They're in San Lazaro, here in the town of Santa Cruz.'

'Can you take me there?'

'Yes, but how? Your master might be looking for you.'

'Master? He isn't my master. I'm sick and tired of serving masters!
He was merely a means to an end, a free ticket to my homeland. Thank
goodness I met you here, otherwise it would take forever for me to find
my way back to my family. Oh, Felipe, my friend, if you only knew the
torment I had to endure, separated from my mother and my siblings
for seven, long years!'

'I've had my own fair share of that, I think.'

'I doubt that even comes close to being stranded on the other side
of the world, for seven long years! Away from my mother, my sister and
little brothers!' His eyes glistened with unshed tears. 'I wonder who's
been looking after them . . .'

Felipe could not respond, worried that it might shock Ruperto to learn that Tentay now had a husband, and that husband was him. Ruperto had a hunch that this Felipe before him was the same person referred to by Tikong as the man who had fallen in love with his sister, although he was not entirely sure what became of their love affair. The two stood weighing their own doubts and uncertainties. But Ruperto could not wait any longer to be reunited with his family.

'How do you know my mother and my siblings?'

Felipe was taken aback by the very straightforward enquiry. Overwhelmed, he grappled with the answer, still doubting whether he should tell the truth. It would be pointless to deny the truth, he thought.

But then, he decided it was not the right time, either.

'That's a very long story. I'll take you now to where they're staying, and they can tell you all about me. What matters most is that you see them right away.'

'I'm grateful beyond words!'

'So, should we be on our way, then?'

'Yes, without further delay. I'll just tell Doroteo where I'm going so he wouldn't come looking for me when I'm gone. The burial wouldn't be until this afternoon. That gives me enough time to see my mother and Tentay, then return here right away.'

They went off to tell the foreign student of their plan. Doroteo knew full well why Ruperto had offered to tag along as his aide. As there were just too many servants around, he allowed Ruperto to go and see his family. The two men left, leaving Delfin completely unaware of what had just happened.

Chapter 28

The Seven-Year Chronicle

Ruperto was just eleven years old when he left the country in 1898. He was away for almost seven years and did not return until 1905. He lived onboard sea vessels for many years, traveled around Europe, reached Cuba, and later settled in the United States of America. He came back home a young adult, very American in garb and mannerism. And here he was, standing right before Aling Tere. When he had gone away, Tentay was just a young girl, Lucio was just five years old, and Victor was two. 'Mother!' he cried as he hugged Aling Tere tightly and kissed her hands. His siblings watched in awe, bewildered and confused.

For the mother and son, this was a moment that could last forever, unsurpassed even by eternal life in heaven!

Aling Tere did not seem surprised. She let out a soul-wrenching cry as she looked up and gazed into the eyes of the long-lost son who had called out to her.

'Ruperto! My son!' She had risen to receive Ruperto in her loving arms and wept. Such was the bond between mother and son, unshaken even after long years of painful separation.

Tentay was utterly dumbfounded. Her eyes were intent on her mother being hugged so tightly by this young man who had just come out of nowhere. She heard it all, mother and son calling out to each other, but it all seemed like a dream to her. A miracle, a vision, a mystery. Their words echoed in the deepest recesses of her soul. Her whole body froze and her face became pale. She could not utter even a single word! Although they were all so very young when they got separated, she could still remember Ruperto's face. She had thought that after what seemed like a century, Ruperto must have long been dead. There was no way *he* could be standing here before them. Or was he just a phantom coming to tell them that, indeed, their brother had gone on to the afterlife?

Felipe, seeing his wife in a state of bewilderment, jolted Tentay back to her senses.

'Tentay! Don't you recognize him? That's your brother, Ruperto...'

'Yes ... Ruperto! Pentong! It's you!'

Tentay, roused from her mesmerized state, hugged Ruperto and cried with joy.

Lucio, who had just returned from fetching water outside shouted 'Kakâ Pentong! Kakâ Pentong!' ran, and wrapped his arms around his big brother. Little Amando stood motionless. He was still in his mother's womb when Ruperto had left, and he was clueless as to what was going on. He could not quite decide if he should come close and join in their embrace.

'That's Lucio!' Aling Tere introduced the young boy with his trousers rolled up.

'And this young boy?' Ruperto turned to Amando, who was regarding him with a blank stare.

Tentay blurted, 'Oh, he doesn't know you. Mother was still carrying him in her womb when you left. That's Amando.'

'This is Amando?' Ruperto grabbed the little boy, carried him in his lap, and planted kisses on his forehead and cheeks. Julian, the infant child who was roused from sleep by the noise in the house, bawled and rolled over on the floor.

'And this little one? Whose child is this? Are you married already, Tentay?'

Tentay and Aling Tere looked at each other before turning toward Felipe. Neither could say 'yes, indeed', for they were ashamed that

Tentay was not actually married in church. But Aling Tere thought that was immaterial and decided they could explain the whole matrimonial situation to him at a later time.

'Yes, Tentay has a husband now.'

'Is that baby yours?'

'Oh, no! That's our two-year-old sister.'

Ruperto picked up the screaming child. Tiny Juleng kicked and shrieked as if her fingers and toes were being mutilated. Ruperto barely kissed the baby before he gave her to his mother.

'So, you're married, Tentay? And who's your husband?'

'That man.' Aling Tere pointed to Felipe.

'Oh, him! It's you! Thank you!'

The two men hugged each other like brothers. Then, Ruperto suddenly remembered his other younger brother.

'Wait, where's Victor? He was just two years old when I left.'

'Oh, he's not here. He's in Tondo with your aunt. But Ruperto, your father!'

And the whole house was suddenly filled with screams of grief. Ruperto could no longer hold it in and broke down and sobbed like a child.

'Hush now, don't bring that up anymore. Ruperto and I had already talked about what happened to his father.'

It took some coaxing before Felipe could pacify the grieving mother and children. They all sat in silence, eyes still wet with bitter tears.

'It's late. Are we still heading back for the burial?' Felipe asked his brother-in-law.

'It's up to you. If you think we should . . .'

'You just reunited with your family. I doubt they'd want to see you leave anytime soon.'

Aling Tere and Tentay protested. 'Are you going to the burial? You don't have to!'

'I don't want to, but all my clothes and my things are there. Besides, I don't want my companion to think I've abandoned him now that I'm home.'

'Indeed. I also have to return and join the funeral procession. If you agree, Pentong, let's go back now. I want to introduce you to my best friend. It's only two o'clock, and the procession will start at four. Why don't we stay a bit, and you can tell them the story of where you've been all this time?'

The women and the children eagerly pleaded in unison. 'Yes, please!'

And so began Ruperto's story of the last seven years.

Ruperto's father sold him to the Spanish foreigner as an apprentice, so he could learn to read and write. The foreigner was a seafarer who often visited various islands in the Philippines. Ruperto traveled with the man and was given light duties, for he was just a young boy. The boy served the foreigner for one year, and the two became very close. Mang Andoy traded his boy for thirty pesos: but he only got six pesos, because he had to pay one year's advance lodging for Ruperto to stay aboard the ship. During that one year, whenever the ship docked in Manila, Ruperto would come home to visit his parents. Seeing that Ruperto had learned to read and speak phrases like '*sí* señor', 'no señor', '*mande usted* señor', Mang Andoy thought it would be best to let Pentong stay with the Spanish voyager.

At some point, the Spanish foreigner decided to go back to his home in Mexico. He turned Ruperto over to the Argentinian captain of the *President Sarmiento*, who was a close friend. Just like that, the young boy was abandoned by his former master as the *President* sailed away one day, in November 1898.

The *President* had many marine soldiers from different races, and there were cannons and weapons for warfare.

As the ship left Mariveles, Ruperto was hysterical and wanted to jump off the ship. At first, his shipmates were amused, but before long, they took pity and consoled the young boy. The Argentinian captain promised to teach him the ways of an excellent seafarer, so that one day he could become a high-ranking naval officer.

Seven days later, they docked in Singapore, and from there on to Colombo, where they disembarked and stayed for three days. The natives of Colombo were barely clothed: both men and women wore nose rings and worshipped Buddha. They avoided the cholera outbreak in Bombay and proceeded instead to Aden, passed through the Persian Gulf and sailed on the Red Sea, where the troops onboard conducted military practice. They met with extremely hot weather in the months of June and July and terribly cold temperatures in December. They reached Mocha in Yemen, a land ruled by the Turkish empire, through which no sea vessel could pass. They took a detour through the Suez Canal, where the sanitation authorities ordered them to strip naked and subjected them to quarantine protocols. Then on, they went to Port Said where they loaded coals.

Next stop was Alexandria, and there, the passengers had alighted. They docked for five days before heading on to Pireas in Greece near Athens. Ruperto tagged along with his new master and stayed there for three days. He rode a ferry boat for the first time and saw the sights of ancient Greece.

Back on the *President*, they sailed off to Pola in Austria-Hungary, then to Venice in Italy. After two days, pretty female guests came onboard and there was merrymaking. The Venetian streets were too narrow for any vehicle, so they had to travel on foot. It was Ruperto's first time seeing an Italian opera perform at the Teatro Malibran in Venice.

From Venice, they went to La Maddalena, a coastal town inhabited by Italian military troops, then moved to Naples, where they wandered around for five days. In La Spezia, they stayed for twelve days, as the *President* had to be serviced and cleaned. There, Ruperto had the first photograph of himself taken as a souvenir of his life as a vagabond.

The women and the children gasped at the mention of the photograph, and they were wide-eyed as they listened to his descriptions of the places he had visited. They asked why he never sent any mail, but Ruperto insisted that he did and that it was the captain himself, who had sent a copy of the photograph via post.

'So you never got my mail?'

'No', said Aling Tere and Tentay.

'I wonder where it went? But no matter, let me tell you more about my adventures abroad.'

'Yes, please continue!' They all urged Pentong.

'All right. So after all the work on the ship was done, from La Spezia, we traveled to Toulon in France, to a huge naval port very near Marseilles, where the French Revolution took place. We were afloat on the Gulf of Lion between France and Spain. As we were heading to Barcelona, there was a huge storm that almost toppled us over. We saw waves bigger than cathedrals and mountains. I thought we were done for.'

'Sweet Lord Jesus!' Aling Tere exclaimed. 'Where were you? What did you do?'

'I stayed close to my master and followed him as he ran around on the ship deck.'

'Holy Madonna and Child! Didn't you get dizzy?' Tentay asked in disbelief.

'Oh, I wouldn't!' Lucio boasted confidently. 'In fact, I'd just watch as the waves hit the other vessels.'

'Well, I didn't feel dizzy at all.'

'Oh, stop being silly, children!' Aling Tere was feeling sick in the stomach.

'My master threatened to throw me off the ship if I felt nauseated.'

'Jesus! What a soulless man!' Tentay nearly screamed.

'Aw, he was just trying to scare Pentong,' Felipe countered.

'Oh, if you're caught in a tempest like that, underneath skies black as night, amidst torrents of rain, you won't see anything, Lucio. You'll hear nothing but the sounds of cannons fired from nearby ships calling for help. The French vessels were there to help those that couldn't withstand the storm.'

'The French are kind, indeed,' Aling Tere remarked.

'Why, that's how people should be when others are in peril at sea, Mother,' Lucio seconded.

'How would you know? You've never sailed far out enough into the ocean.' Aling Tere teased.

'I have heard such stories from the seafarers at the pier in Escolta and San Fernando, where I used to work as a porter for sea travelers,' Lucio insisted, and Ruperto confirmed. 'Yes, Mother, what Lucio is saying is true.'

Tentay pressed for more stories. 'So, you were stuck there in France?'

'No, we had to let the storm pass. Which reminds me, one of the crew members was killed in that storm. He was working the rig when a huge wave threw him off the ship. He was swallowed by the sea and was never seen again. Poor soul!'

'So, the next day, we went on our way to Barcelona, the most beautiful and lively place in Spain. There you would find countless factories and places of trade. It was also the breeding ground of anarchists. The people, especially the Catalans, were the fiercest and most rebellious in all of Spain.'

'How could you tell they were anarchists?' Felipe was curious.

'We stayed there for more than a week. My master, who absolutely loved women, wasted no time gallivanting around the city with me in tow. But whenever a particular woman caught his fancy, he would send me off to wander around by myself. And that was when I would see all those riots by the factory workers. One time, there was a huge crowd of several thousand rioters barricaded around a particular factory, throwing rocks and breaking down doors. And there would be people being chased down the streets, thieves stealing bread from a bakery. The local authorities could do nothing to arrest the offenders running wild all over the place. So they brought in the soldiers from the neighbouring towns to break down the barricades and catch the rioters. But the more they fired warning shots, all the more people poured out into the streets to join in the fray. And when it was already impossible to quell the riot and the masses had begun to push and hit back, the soldiers started shooting the people. Five people were killed, and many wounded. Several of my crew mates very nearly joined in the riot when they saw the troops killing civilians. I heard them rant about the labour unions, the *Internationale,* socialism, anarchism, of which I knew nothing at all. Two officers were assaulted, and the riot escalated. Finally, it took the Spanish cavalry to disperse the rioters, who then fled to the town plaza to regroup. There, the labour leaders preached to the masses gathered around, who responded with loud cries and raised fists. I did not get to see how the rally ended, because I soon got hungry and needed to head back to the ship.'

Felipe, who was listening intently to his brother-in-law's story, could not help but comment. 'That's nowhere near how riots and rallies here are carried! When will our local labourers learn to rise as one against oppression?'

Aling Tere had a dissenting opinion. 'It's best that we don't take after them. Or they will have to yield to gunfire!'

'I'm not scared of guns. It wouldn't matter if we, our wives and children, were all to die of starvation. I'd rather we died fighting!' Felipe could not be swayed from his conviction.

'That's exactly how it was in all the lands I visited in Europe!' Ruperto confirmed.

Aling Tere felt uncomfortable at this turn in the conversation. 'Anyway, enough of that! Pentong, so from Barcelona . . . ?'

'Ah, yes. From Barcelona, we crossed Cartagena, sailed along the Mediterranean, and passed through the Strait of Gibraltar. I thought of abandoning the ship and stowing away with a Spanish and Tagalog crew mate, as I was already growing tired of the sea. We were headed for New York City, but strong winds and high waves forced us to seek refuge in Madeira. From there, we sailed all the way to South America. For twenty-five days, we did not see land at all, until we reached the Carribean islands. Then we were in La Guana in Venezuela, Santiago de Cuba, and finally, we stopped in Havana, the capital of Cuba. I was shocked to see so many Filipinos in Cuba working as slaves for Spanish traders, or as staff at trading houses, or as tobacco farmers. I was so fascinated by Cuba that I decided to abandon the *President* and stay behind. And that turned out to be a wise decision because two days after it set sail, the *President Sarmiento* got caught in a storm and sank to the bottom of the sea.'

'Oh, Blessed Virgin Mary! Thank you for saving my boy!' Aling Tere exclaimed.

'Fate was indeed kind to you!' Tentay agreed.

'So I stayed there in Cuba. Another Filipino took me to work as a helper at his Spanish master's house, but after two years of unpaid labour, I grew restless and went away to work at the tobacco farm. I started earning my own keep, and had money to buy my own food and clothes. I was already doing well, but then I got involved in a huge strike at the farms. The workers tried to make demands, but the landowners refused to listen and retaliated by firing those who had joined the strike. Half of the labour force was laid off. The ones who remained were the docile farmhands who remained loyal to their masters. Just to survive, I worked as an assistant at a Cuban watch repair shop where I learned to fix timepieces and bicycles, but left just the same, when the owner died. I decided to try my luck in the United States, where there were a lot of job vacancies. Together with other Cuban nationals, I went to San Francisco via New York City, worked at various breweries until I moved to New York City itself, where I found a job at a bar that paid twenty dollars. That's where I met Don Ramon and Tikong.'

'How did you meet them?' Felipe asked excitedly.

'Well, how could I not meet them? They were billeted at the hotel right next to the bar. Don Ramon would visit the bar every night. Oh, such a ladies' man, he was! Every single time he was with a different American woman. Quite a heavy drinker, too! Tikong and I would often bring him up to his hotel room, totally wasted. He was a violent and aggressive man, when drunk. Tikong and I became very close friends, and he would always complain how the old man treated him so badly, how whether drunk or not, the old man would beat him up all the time. More than once, he begged me to help him find a job for he really wanted to leave the cruel and heartless old man. I tried my best to help him out. Once, he asked whether he could run away to Cuba, but I dissuaded him. Repeatedly, he expressed his desire to abandon Don Ramon, until that horrible crime happened. He had been afraid he might lose his mind and end up murdering his master.'

Ruperto's mood changed and he began to speak in a low tone.

'I'll tell you this, but this should never leave this room. I knew exactly when the murder was committed. Tikong told me exactly how he'd kill the old man.'

'Oh, dear Lord!' Aling Tere gasped in horror. 'So, where did Tikong flee after that night?'

'New Orleans. There are lots of Filipino immigrants there, I tell you. He's hiding there. And should the police close in on him, he said he'd flee to another country.'

Felipe suddenly blurted out what he had been thinking all along. 'I knew it! Tikong wouldn't just snap like that for no reason at all.'

'Earlier that day, before he was killed, Don Ramon was again giving Tikong a heavy beating. The old man would have shot Tikong dead, had he not fled from the old man. Later that afternoon, the old man beat him up again. Tikong could not take it anymore. So, that same evening, as the old man slept in his bed, Tikong slaughtered his cruel master.'

Felipe nodded. 'Cruelty begets cruelty!'

Aling Tere felt a profound fear for her son. 'Ruperto, never tell anyone what you know of the crime. Lest . . .'

'Of course, I wouldn't even dare to think of telling anyone else.'

'All right . . . You should be on your way to the funeral. You're already running late.'

Only then did the two men realize that they should head back to the funeral right away.

Chapter 29

How the Rich are Buried

Many carriages were already parked in front of Don Ramon's house. The funeral car had been waiting outside to carry the old man to his final resting place. It was almost time for the procession to start.

Black cloth draped the banisters that led up to the main house. The scent of large, burning candles filled the rooms inside. Silver and gold candelabras stood like royal guards around the coffin. The black floral carpets on the floor rustled as the guests milled around, as if to remind everyone not to disturb the dead. The coffin lay on a three-foot-high riser decorated in black lace. There were also garlands of silver flowers handcrafted by a famous silversmith from Santa Cruz, a relative of Don Ramon's deceased wife. A small ladder was placed on the side for people to step on the platform from where they could view the remains of Don Ramon.

At the foot of the coffin, on one side of the main room, stood a large shrine filled with candles, flowers and hanging decorations. In the centre of the shrine was a portrait of the crucified Jesus Christ, face turned away as if to refuse the offering that lay at His feet, head hung so low in deep sadness and resentment over the excessive glory given to such a cruel and sinful man.

Upon their arrival, Felipe and Ruperto went up to the terrace to avoid the crowd that had gathered in the living room. Felipe looked around for Delfin, and while he and Ruperto were speaking, the door to the bathroom near the terrace suddenly opened. Felipe was surprised when he recognized the face that peered out through the door. It was his sister, Marcela!

'Marcela! You're here!'

'Felipe!' Marcela, teary-eyed, stepped out, wearing the garments and accessories typically worn by the wealthy. 'Father and I just arrived earlier at noon.'

'Where's Father?'

'He's inside.'

'Is Mother with you?'

'No. She stayed behind at home.'

'Is Father still mad at me?'

'Yes. He told me not to speak to you if ever I see you here.'

Felipe bit his lip as his sister stood in silence. 'Then, please don't tell him I'm here.'

'No, I won't.'

'I'll stay away from him. But what are you doing here?'

Marcela glanced toward the bathroom near the terrace before she replied. 'I wanted to console Talia and Meni, to be with them in this time of grieving.'

'And here you are, looking just as miserable. Where are they?' Felipe went inside the bathroom without hesitation.

Ruperto just stood there completely mesmerized, as if he had just seen an apparition. He could not quite believe that Felipe that had such a beautiful sister! 'How on earth could Felipe choose to be with a poor woman like my sister, Tentay, when he could have any woman as gorgeous and noble as this Marcela!' Ruperto wondered in silence.

Marcela paced around the terrace as Ruperto watched her in awe. She felt uncomfortable with Ruperto staring at her like that. She wondered who might this man be, for clearly he looked like he had come from America.

After a while, Ruperto gathered enough courage to address the young lady before him.

'I'm sorry, Miss Marcela, you are Felipe's sister, right?'

'Yes, I am. And you must be a friend of his?'

'Well, I just met him today, and we're actually more than friends.' Ruperto hesitated to tell her that Felipe was his brother-in-law, for he was unsure how Marcela would take that revelation. He was afraid that Marcela might feel offended if he told her that Felipe was already married to his sister.

'So, how do you know my brother?'

'We're . . . oh, it's nothing, really. We're just friends.'

Marcela gave Ruperto a piercing look from head to toe, a look that Ruperto thought could have turned him into a pillar of salt. 'Liar!' Ruperto could almost hear her thoughts.

'I don't understand why you would lie to me.' Then she turned to leave Ruperto alone.

'Wait, don't go, Miss Marcela!'

Marcela turned around to face Ruperto, who was staring intently into her eyes then down at her breasts, which prompted her to cover herself with a handkerchief.

'What do you want?'

'I owe you the truth about Felipe and I.'

'Ah, no need! I am in no mood to play games with you! I've to go. They're waiting for me inside.' Then Marcela left without hearing what Ruperto had to say.

Ruperto felt a strong emotion that he had never felt before. He was just a young boy when he had left home, and even as a virile young man living in America, he had never felt an attraction like this for any woman. In America, money could buy love, and it was absolutely easy to find love and indulge in the pleasures of the flesh. But this was the first time he was ever truly smitten. And by a lady from his own country.

Ruperto mused to himself. 'But I don't wish to play games at all. I'm serious.' He scratched his ear, pulled his hair, and bit his lip. He blamed himself for pushing away Marcela like that. He thought it unfair that his refusal to reveal the truth about him and Felipe would leave him without his muse. He felt the urge to run after Marcela and beg on his knees for forgiveness.

After a while, Felipe returned, followed by Marcela. He had just seen Talia and Meni, who were hiding inside the bathroom, each slumped on a chair, weeping inconsolably.

The mourners had begun to bring down the casket to the funeral car.

Talia and Meni chose not to join the procession. They did not even care to put on proper clothes and fix themselves up for the guests. They hardly left their father's side during the wake. Meni even neglected to breastfeed her infant son, who had to be cared for by a surrogate nursing mother. Talia was seven months pregnant at that time. Thankfully, Dr Gatdula was around the whole time to keep a check on the condition of the two women.

The sisters watched from a distance as their father's coffin was carried away. Señora Loleng, sobbing hysterically, asked Felipe as they came out from the bathroom. 'Where are the sisters? Oh dear, Don Ramon is gone!'

Marcela, taken aback by the old woman's weeping, asked what she was to Don Ramon's family, but Felipe only turned up his nose and shrugged.

'Talia! Meni! They're taking your father now to his resting place! My goodness!' The old woman cried out to the sisters.

'Father! Father!' The two sisters ran the old woman over as they hastened to catch up with their father, whose remains were now being loaded onto the funeral carriage. Señora Loleng, unaided, struggled to pick herself up as the sisters darted off, screaming and wailing like babies. Felipe, who had caught up with Talia, was spotted by his father, Captain Loloy, who did not say a single word to him. Marcela and Ruperto rushed to restrain the two sisters and took them back inside to calm them down.

The funeral marchers stopped upon hearing the commotion going on inside the house. Don Filemon ran back to the house and upon seeing Señora Loleng sprawled on the floor, rushed to help the old woman back on her feet.

And so, Felipe, Marcela, Ruperto, Don Filemon and Señora Loleng did not get to leave the house anymore, leaving Yoyong to lead the funeral procession.

The townsfolk who saw the procession gasped in admiration. 'A funeral fit for a king! A noble man being laid to rest!' Indeed, that was the truth, for it was the Lord of Riches, the Master of Leisure, the God of Capitalism himself who was being borne away by the cortege.

The people gossiped about what became of the 20,000 pesos stashed away by the old man in a bank vault in New York City, and how the rest of the money and Meni's inheritance were stolen by the murderous culprit.

The eight horses that drew the funeral carriage were all dressed up in embellishments. Atop the carriage was a wooden statue of an angel kneeling down in solemn grief—a symbolic gesture, as it were, of the funeral owner's sincere grief over the passing of this very wealthy man. Before the wooden angel stood the Angel of Death, scythe in hand, standing in fervent prayer. The funeral carriage, and the entourage that followed, was brimming with flowers, garlands and wreaths that had been sent by the funeral parlour, The Gate of the Sun, and the famous florist from Singalong. One would wonder whether these had been sent to console the grieving or to rejoice for the departure of a very wealthy man, for clearly the extravagant arrangements meant good business for the mortuary and the florist.

Behind the funeral carriage was a long line of carriages that seemed to compete with each other in grandeur. High-ranking government officials, Americans and Filipinos, trade leaders, colleagues at The Progress, tobacco farm owners, representatives of the press, Spaniards, Chinese, mestizos (who were great in number); lawyers, doctors, two Jesuit priests, a Capuchin friar and members of the clergy . . . and at the very end of the procession was a huge mass of factory workers at The Progress and tobacco farmers from all over. This mass of workers followed on foot, squirming like a huge snake on the dirt road.

Being a devout Roman Catholic, Don Ramon was brought to the church for his final rites. Surrounded by towering candelabras, he was blessed with holy water and consecrated with frankincense, as members of the clergy recited the sacred prayers for the dead. Don Ramon should have been taken to the church in his native Santa Cruz, but his relatives preferred the bearded and barefooted Capuchin monks, who closely resembled the lowly Jesus of Nazareth. They held on to the firm belief that these monks could better intercede for the eternal repose of the old man, who had unfortunately died without receiving the final sacrament.

The Capuchin Church on Real del Palacio Street in Intramuros looked magnificent that afternoon. Multitudes thronged the churchyard, but only the distinguished gentlemen were able to squeeze in. The workers contented themselves with hearing the melancholy tolling of the bells and the mournful chorus of the Rizal Orchestra, for they could not see past the relics and artifacts that guarded the cultic ritual going on at the altar.

It was nearly five o'clock when the church rites ended, and the funeral march headed to the great cemetery in Paco, where Don Filemon, Delfin, Felipe, Marcela, and Ruperto were already waiting.

* * *

As if the Capuchin rites were not enough, more of the blessing of holy water, prayers, and dirges followed at the burial ground. The mourners stormed the heavens with their prayers for divine intervention, so that the soul of the dearly departed would be saved from the fiery pits of hell. Woe to the poor and the lowly, for unlike the rich, they had no means to appeal for the salvation of their souls at the pearly gates of Heaven!

Then came the long-winded eulogies, first, by the High Commissioner, who spoke about Don Ramon's great deeds as an exemplary citizen and a businessman who worked tirelessly for the nation's progress, and as a political figure who had cooperated with the American government. Next spoke a distinguished member of the trade council, who spouted flowery words on how Don Ramon was a brilliant entrepreneur, and how he invested his inheritance and built his own business empire. But neither of these two gentlemen made even the slightest mention of Don Ramon's opportunistic character, for during the Spanish regime, he was loyal to the Spaniards, but when the Americans came, he became a close collaborator. If truth be told, Don Ramon was never loyal or kind to his own countrymen. At The Progress tobacco factory, he was abusive and ruthless toward his workers, just as he was toward his slaves and servants in his house. He was a womanizer, an alcoholic, an extortionist, an illegal gambler and a game fixer, all rolled into one. But nobody cared for all these vices, for now the evil man was dead.

At last, Don Filemon stood before the crowd to deliver his prepared speech.

'Distinguished gentlemen, my fellow countrymen, my dear friends . . .' He paused as he struggled to speak. He took out his handkerchief to wipe off the tears that streamed down his grey mustache. It was already dark and many amongst the crowd who no longer had the patience to hear more speeches began to leave the assembly. Those who remained couldn't bear to miss his talk about his special friendship with Don Ramon.

'Distinguished gentlemen . . . my fellow countrymen, my dear friends . . .' He muttered once again. 'Please bear with me as I simply couldn't abandon my solemn duty as a friend to speak of our dearly departed. May his soul rest in peace.' His long pauses were punctuated with sobs and cries of grief more dramatic than Señora Loleng's. Don Filemon rambled on and on, and all the listeners could glean from his broken speech were his praises for Don Ramon as a true friend . . . The women began to wail uncontrollably. Julita, the maiden from San Miguel, whom Don Ramon had courted, attended the funeral with her American suitor named Jack, who stood beside her, consoling her as she wept. Julita met Jack soon after Don Ramon had left the country.

It was an entirely different scene with Marcela. She had been dodging Doroteo Miranda, whom she absolutely abhorred. She shielded herself from the man's unwelcome advances by sticking close to her father, but her father kept moving away to mingle with the distinguished gentlemen at the funeral. Ruperto could tell that Doroteo bore malicious intent toward Marcela, so together with Delfin and Felipe, he provided a safe perimeter around Marcela. And when he saw an opportunity, Ruperto took Marcela aside, away from the crowd, so they could speak in private. The two stood in silence for a moment.

'When are you heading back home?' Ruperto asked Marcela.

'Perhaps three days from now.' Marcela replied.

'Can I come with you?'

'I don't know, it's up to you.'

'Do you want me to come with you?'

'You may do as you wish.'

'Will I ever meet happiness once we're there?

Marcela fell silent. She just stared at Ruperto from head to toe.

'I'm concerned that you might not like it there.'

'Oh, I can put up with anything just to be with you. What would you have me do?'

'Befriend my brother. Court him if you will, and you just might discover the way to win my heart.'

'And should I succeed? You would be a lucky woman!'

And that was how the two parted that evening, just as Madlang-Layon was ending his eulogy and thanking everyone for coming to the funeral. Soon, the body of Don Ramon Miranda, newly arrived from the United States of America, was lowered into the hollow ground and covered with earth.

Chapter 30

Darkness and Light

It was not by design that Delfin and Felipe parted from the rest of the mourners. The two walked side by side at a slow pace until they reached a quiet area between the rows of niches. Felipe told Delfin all the stories he had heard from Ruperto—how Tikong murdered Don Ramon, and how Ruperto had lived a vagabond life.

'Despite his hardships, I envy your brother-in-law. He has seen the world. As a young boy, I would have grabbed any opportunity to travel to distant lands. It would matter little if I were a lowly slave. I'd still get the chance to learn new things. It would have been a wonderful life, especially for an orphan like me!'

'Sure, you would have learned many things,' said Felipe, 'but you probably wouldn't have the same principles and beliefs you have now. Living so far away from home truly changes a person's character!'

'Ah, yes, to have seen the glory of Western civilization! One would be filled with idealism and great knowledge. But alas, most of our countrymen who have travelled abroad, return with a fervent desire to recast their native land after the Western countries.'

Felipe nodded. 'Indeed, the West has always been the paragon of civilization and culture. Darwin had been right all along. Survival of the fittest. Civilization is like wine, and the civilized is the drunken one.

The attainment of high culture corrupts the moral fibre of society, and the civilized individual becomes the centre of the universe. Man becomes intoxicated with self-entitlement, expecting the rest of the world to deliver unto his feet all the comforts and pleasures that he believes are rightfully his. That, my friend, is what has become of the civilized world.'

'That's a serious matter, indeed,' Delfin agreed. 'But going back to Tentay's brother, do you think he really learned anything of value in his exploits abroad?'

'I think so, although not much, I'm afraid. I mean, how could you expect him to really learn something if all he did was to serve foreign masters? Fortunately, he lived in Cuba, otherwise he would be forever a slave, or a seafarer, at best. Despite what he had seen in Italy and in Barcelona, it was in Cuba that he faced the inevitable harsh realities of life; where he learnt the value of earning his keep. And when he moved to the States, although he was a mere wage earner, he still got to see what the labour movement was like. I would consider him as one belonging to our own ranks.'

'Very well, then!' Delfin was pleased. 'We better head back now. It's getting dark, and the rest of the mourners may have already left us behind.'

True enough, they were alone in the cemetery. The undertakers had already completed their tasks and had left by the time they returned. All around the cemetery, there was nobody in sight, except for the caretaker who was just about to lock the gates.

'Hold on for a bit, will you? We just buried our father. We won't take long.' Felipe offered him a cigarette, and after the caretaker left, the two sat in the dark as they continued talking about the life and death of Don Ramon.

'Felipe, my father-in-law has now been laid to rest. Let's not dredge up his wrongs. Let the dead rest in peace.'

'And what?' Felipe protested. 'Shall we take after those three old fools who eulogized on all the good and nothing of the bad? We came to this funeral for a reason, Delfin.'

'Yes, I know.'

'Then why shouldn't we memorialize all his evils, his greed, his carnal ways, his oppression of the poor? I have always hated the hypocrisy of our old ways. Upon a rich man's death, his life should be an open book in which all his wrongdoings are exposed, so that no one shall ever follow in his footsteps again.'

'I don't agree with you, Felipe. On the contrary, exposing a man's wickedness would only awaken the evil that lies dormant in others. But I see the benefit in extracting socialist teachings from the life of Don Ramon, for clearly, our country can learn a great deal from the death of a wealthy man.'

'Yes. The death of a man like Don Ramon should mean freedom for the oppressed, not the death of one's source of livelihood.'

'And even with the death of the likes of Don Ramon and your father, Captain Loloy, the cycle of oppression will remain unbroken so long as the agency of inheritance is in place. It's just money and authority changing hands.'

'If only the rich would willingly give up their claim to wealth and power, just like how you and Meni rejected Don Ramon's, and how I refused my father's.'

'And we have been branded as fools because of that! I long to see the day when people would see the light of reason in the choices that we have made!'

'But when will that day come, Delfin? Will it ever happen?'

'I am just as tired of waiting, Felipe. I feel like I'm already in my twilight years after having seen the affairs of our countrymen. But we must be patient and let things run their natural course. Nations and their people, like everything else, evolve over time.'

'But we can take action now, Delfin.' Felipe's eyes glared. 'We certainly can bring about change through revolution!'

'Yes, Felipe, but a revolution cannot take place before evolution. A nation will only rise up in arms if it can no longer stand to be oppressed. A revolution has to gather steam first before it can explode.'

'That is precisely why I say it is high time we should take up arms. The oppressed masses are already desperate.'

'I don't think that now is the right time. Look at them, they are not part of an organized movement just yet. They are not lashing out.

They won't move without a leader or a martyr to rally them to action. The revolutionary movement should come from below, if we are to bring down the pyramid of oppression.'

'Let's not forget the government,' Felipe added. 'We may succeed in bringing down the capitalist order, but it will be for naught if there is no change in our local government. We must also prevent the transfer of wealth and power to the oligarchs in government.'

'Oh, I assure you, Felipe, the rise of the revolutionary system will also bring about the ascension to power of the socialist republic that will look after the common welfare of its constituents.'

'But what good will it do to have an alternative ruling system? We will still be placing the power to rule in the hands of a few. I say we should abolish any form of government altogether and allow a self-governing system to flourish instead.'

Delfin chuckled softly as he shook his head. 'Felipe, Felipe! I don't disagree with what you're proposing. But let me stress once more, we are not yet ready to stage a revolution. The evolution of a nation has three phases: first, the preeminence of the Divine; second, the age of revolutionary heroes; and third, the rise of the egalitarian state. Looking at the state of affairs here, we are somewhere between phase one and phase two.'

'So, what now?' Felipe leaned back, sat on a stout branch of the frangipani tree behind him.

Felipe stood transfixed as he waited for Delfin to speak. 'It's true that our lives are still very much dictated by religious beliefs, but that will soon change. Right now, we're taking our first steps into the age of revolutionary heroes. We've seen the likes of Jose Rizal and Andres Bonifacio stir the revolutionary sentiments of our masses, and we have come to fashion our ideals after these exemplary heroes. They've already changed the course of our history. But I believe that we need more heroes to rouse our poor masses from their deep sleep. Only then can we say that we have progressed well into the second phase. And then we can move on to the third phase, which is when a true social revolution can take place.'

'And then, what comes next, Delfin?'

'Then, my friend, we'll achieve a true egalitarian state. The time will come when we no longer subscribe to the notion of a Supreme Being as the be-all and end-all of things, when we no longer worship individuals but instead regard each and every member of society as our equals. But then . . .' Delfin paused and shook his head once again.

'What are you worried about, Delfin, if what you say is true?'

'It's already late, Felipe. The caretaker has waited long enough for us. We should be on our way.'

'No, we still have time. Go on, what was it you were hesitant about?'

'First and foremost, I believe in what the anarchist Grave said about socialist revolutions. He underscored the importance of disseminating socialist ideas beyond geographic borders. We forget to consider that respect for human rights has to be universal, which means that the same socialist ideals should also be upheld in other countries such as those in Asia, Africa and the Pacific. Twentieth-century Western civilization had already seen the dawn of socialist reformation, thanks to the teachings of the likes of Fourier, Owen, Marx, Kropotkin, and many others.'

Felipe was exhilarated. 'Yes, thanks to the martyrs of anarchism, we now have the instrument with which to oppose the ruling class and dethrone the false kings.'

'You speak of means that can only lead to bloodshed, Felipe. We can't achieve peace and harmony amongst men through violent means.'

'Not if it means cutting loose the oppressed masses.'

'Even so. We're talking about putting lives at stake . . .'

'Lives! What about the lives of those martyred by the ruling class? What about the millions whose blood they've shed?'

'I get where you're coming from. But that doesn't mean that we should be just as cruel.'

'Yes. An eye for an eye, a tooth for a tooth. Only death can put an end to abuse of power.' Felipe was adamant in his argument.

Delfin pleaded his case. 'Be that as it may, what you're saying is highly unlikely to happen in the near future, especially here in our country. And more importantly, what will become of humankind if you get rid of all the kings, leaders and governments in the world?!'

'To your first point I say, why not? To the second, after tilling the land, the harvest will be bountiful, and the riches can be equally distributed amongst our people.'

'And then what do you think will happen after that?'

'That's it. Things will just keep on getting better. It can't get worse thereafter.'

Delfin clasped his hands. 'Cannot get worse thereafter! Think about what you're saying, Ipeng! History tells us otherwise. Man's progress has always been a spiraling movement, a continuous cycle of birth, death and rebirth. Like the seedling sprung from underneath the ground, growing, flourishing, aging, then dying, with its offspring taking its place. And then the same cycle repeats itself all over again. There is no escaping the natural order of things. The same phenomenon can be observed in the rise and fall of the great civilizations of ancient Egypt, Greece and Rome that gave rise to the modern empires of France and Spain. At the height of these empires, nobody ever foresaw their downfall. But, lo and behold, indeed they fell, and they crumbled to dust. Sure, there are remnants of these great empires to this day. And if you look at the insides of what is left of these great empires, all you will see is decay. Look at France. Between the French Revolution that demolished the great monarchy of the Middle Ages and the French Republic that took its predecessor's place, not much has changed. They are still plagued by the same ills. Didn't the revolutionaries promise radical reformation?'

Felipe suddenly stood up and patted his backside that leaned against the trunk of the frangipani. Delfin paused as he waited for a rebuttal, but Felipe was just quiet, as if he was waiting for the rest of the speech.

'It can't be denied that the French Revolution of 1789 gave rise to the Modern Age as we know it. The last two centuries saw great leaps of progress in our way of life. Now, I don't mean to diminish the significance of that revolution, or even our own revolution of 1896, but what kind of socialist state are we aspiring for? I daresay that even if at first we are able to establish a communalist regime, that regime will not last long. There will always be some force, whether internal and external, that will rise to undermine it. We have seen it happen before.

Even the United States of America will wither and die at some point, just like the old Western civilizations that came before it. The time of the great West has passed. Now is the time for the East to rise from the shadows. Japan is already breaking new ground. Who knows, maybe it's time for the Philippines to keep pace with Japan, if only a supremacist presence weren't standing in our way: the United States of America. Then there is China, which will awake from its sleep, at some point. And Australia, where the aborigines are being extinguished just like how the American Indians were wiped out by their colonizers. India will be next, for it has long been under the influence of the British colonial power. If all these countries rise up, then the wheel of fortune will turn. I am no psychic, Felipe, and I don't pretend to know everything myself. But think about it, all it takes for a social revolution to happen is for every country to be prepared to take part in it. You see, it will take ages for Asia to stage a coup at the scale of the French Revolution of 1789!'

Felipe broke his silence. 'Hah! And you think it will ever happen if we don't start it now?'

'Yes, we need to start somewhere. The seeds have been sown, thanks to the revolutionary movement of the Katipunan in 1896. We need to set up our own ways of governing our affairs. Once those are in place, then we can work on establishing a socialist state. I am not a pessimist, Felipe. On the contrary, I am every bit an optimist. The future of our society lies in the hands of heroes in our country. But we can't force the hand of destiny. We need to be patient and allow things to run their course. The wheel of fate will inevitably turn. The old regime will die, and in its place will rise a new regime that will be as bright as day. But until then . . .'

'When will that be!' Felipe exclaimed despairingly.

Just then, the gatekeeper approached them and said in a rather annoyed tone, 'Gentlemen! It's already late!'

The two were startled. They threw a meaningful glance at Don Ramon's tombstone and then they started to walk.

'Yes, it's evening. We shall take our leave now and let the dark of night run its course.'

Chapter 31

The Martyrs of Redemption

After the funeral, the mourners dispersed and went straight home. The only ones who remained at the mansion were Don Filemon, Captain Loloy and Marcela, Doroteo and Ruperto, and Madlang-Layon's spinster sister, Turing.

The house was dark and gloomy. The guests who had gathered inside were quiet and brooding, save for the small group of Don Filemon, Madlang-Layon, Captain Loloy, and Doroteo, who began to chat about America. Doroteo prattled on about his experiences and his studies overseas. Captain Loloy and Don Filemon eagerly lapped up his stories.

It came as a surprise when Delfin entered the house, alone. Felipe was outside as he did not want to be seen by his still very angry father, whom he respected very much. The last time he saw his father was when he and Gudyo had left for Manila. His mother and sister already knew he had been living with Tentay, but not his father. For some time now, he had been vacillating between going back home to Lazaro and staying put in Manila, for he missed his father and sister. He wanted to see his father, but he did not want his father to see him. Because he could not quite make up his mind just yet, he went to the servant's quarters in the basement of the house to have a chat with the coachman.

Delfin greeted the three gentlemen gathered in the living room. As he hesitated to shake hands with the other two guests, Madlang-Layon stood up to make the introductions.

'Oh, you three haven't been introduced?'

'It will be my honour to make their acquaintance,' Delfin politely said.

'This is the Honourable Captain Loloy. And Doroteo Miranda, Don Ramon's nephew, who's a student in America . . .'

Captain Loloy and Doroteo held out their hands, even though Madlang-Layon hadn't mentioned Delfin's name. Doroteo had to ask, 'And you are?'

Madlang-Layon caught himself. 'Oh, yes, where are my manners? This is Delfin, the husband of Meni.'

Doroteo's jaw dropped when he heard the name and felt a chill run down his spine. He quickly dropped Delfin's hand. He was filled with silent rage, and in his mind, he wanted to scream, 'So this is the man who brought about my uncle's downfall!' Captain Loloy held a similar expression on his face. The furrows on his forehead deepened as he sat down and glared at Delfin from head to foot. He thought to himself, 'So this is the man who had taught the ways of the wicked to my son!'

Delfin knew the looks on these two men's faces all too well and thought to himself, 'The disdain and their faces! In due time, the light of Truth will be revealed when the dust has settled!'

Madlang-Layon felt how uncomfortable the atmosphere was and awkwardly invited Delfin to sit with them.

'There's no need, thank you. Where's Meni?'

'Meni? I think she's in one of the rooms with the other women. Go on inside, then.'

'Oh, no. Could you tell her to come out as I have something to tell her, please?'

Meni heard Delfin's voice from inside the room and came to the door to speak with her husband. As Delfin turned his back, the three men whispered to each other. Doroteo and Captain Loloy turned up their noses and very nearly spat on the floor out of contempt for Delfin. Madlang-Layon's wry smile could have been out of disgust, or plain indifference. Captain Loloy could not contain himself and muttered, 'And he had the gall to show his face around here! He must have a gut of steel!'

Meanwhile, Meni and Delfin were talking about going home soon. For Delfin, they had already buried the dead, and that was all the responsibility that they needed to fulfill and nothing more. Meni, on the other hand, was tired from all the crying and wailing she had done with her sister. She was just having a conversation with Talia, Turing and Marcela about her baby whom she had left behind at home, when Delfin came to pick her up. Delfin did not tell Meni anymore about the scene in the living room. He just told Talia that they were leaving and waited outside the door.

'Delfin, come join us here.' Madlang-Layon called out when he saw Delfin standing outside the door alone.

'We won't be long as it's already very late.'

'Wait, you're going home?'

'Yes, we have to, as there's a baby waiting for us at home.'

Delfin watched the three men from where he stood. He began to feel strong emotions welling up inside him. He was sure the three men speaking in hushed voices were talking about him. Between the old man as imperious as the late Don Ramon, the foreign student embezzling his dead uncle's fortunes, and Talia's husband, whose grasping hands were enclosed around Don Ramon's estates, their talk could only have been about his bad character.

Although from where he stood, try as he might, he could hardly decipher a single word from the living room. He spotted Ruperto looking out of the window. At first, he thought Ruperto was admiring the garden. Before long, he realized that Ruperto was eyeing the window to the right, the room where Talia and the other women were gathered, where Marcela now and then looked out to exchange glances and make meaningful gestures at Ruperto.

Delfin thought of going down to tell Felipe of what just happened inside the house. They hatched a plan for Ruperto to act friendly with the men in the living room and act as their eyes and ears. Felipe sent the coachman to bring Ruperto, who was reluctant to leave, at first, for he wanted to have more stolen moments with Marcela. After receiving instructions from Delfin and Felipe, Ruperto went back inside and in a beguiling manner, joined the three men.

'Are you staying here again for the night?' Ruperto asked Doroteo.

'Probably not. I'm expected at my place. My siblings have been waiting to see me since I got back.'

'Well, then, this is where we part. I'll be going home to be with my family.'

'Ah, so you've found your mother?'

'Yes, after asking around.'

'That's good. But don't leave just yet. Come sit with us for a bit.'

Doroteo motioned for Ruperto to take an empty seat not far from the group and join in. Don Filemon, who had rejoined the small fraternity, and Captain Loloy, were befuddled since Doroteo and Ruperto spoke in English. Madlang-Layon whispered something in Doroteo's ear that prompted the foreign student to interrogate Ruperto.

'Is there anyone else in the salon?'

'No. There's no one there.'

Madlang-Layon was curious. 'Didn't you see a man in black who just stepped out of the living room? Did you see where he went?'

'Oh, that man. Delfin, that's his name, no? He went down to the basement.'

Don Filemon butted in. 'Delfin? Yes, I saw him go down the stairs as I was stepping out of Loleng's room.'

The men had been talking about Delfin and his wife, and about Don Ramon's last will and testament. At first they spoke in hushed tones, wary that someone could be eavesdropping from the salon or the bedrooms inside the house, but they livened up when Don Filemon joined in. They were unaware that amongst them was a spy.

Don Filemon and Madlang-Layon were describing to Captain Loloy, Doroteo, and Ruperto, the wrongdoings that Delfin had done against Don Ramon. Madlang-Layon blabbered on about Delfin's malicious character and his socialist beliefs, how Delfin forbade Meni from communicating with them, and how they were not invited to the baptism of Meni's son. Madlang-Layon made Delfin out to be precisely the reason Don Ramon dropped Meni from his last will and testament, to protect his wealth from an unworthy man. At this point, the men all felt pity for Meni, whom they felt deserved much more.

Don Filemon suggested something. 'Shouldn't we be making plans to separate the two, then?'

'Separate them? That would be extremely difficult!' counseled the lawyer.

'Once Meni's separated from Delfin, she can return to this house and you can take care of her.'

Yoyong shook his head as if to reiterate the impossibility of divorce. One would think that he was also worried that if Meni were to come home, she would get her share of her father's wealth, and that would mean Talia's would be diminished.

Captain Loloy was agitated. 'Look at what's happening now. He allowed Meni to come home, and even he stepped inside this house. Why? Because he wanted to see for himself just how much wealth his wife is entitled to.'

'Indeed!' Doroteo and Madlang-Layon both agreed.

Don Filemon urged the lawyer. 'Honorio, hold on to the reins tight! Make sure the last will and testament is fully enforced! Never let that bastard get his hands on the money before Don Ramon's nephew, a Miranda by name, gets his share. '

Yoyong carefully considered Don Filemon's words. He thought the two old men's intentions were malicious, but he also understood the implications on his ambitions and desires. He just kept nodding in silence.

Captain Loloy pressed on. 'I am sure you are quite aware that this Delfin has been a terrible influence on my Felipe! Because of him, I disowned my only son!'

Doroteo was mildly amused. 'Could it be that your son has gone mad?'

But Madlang-Layon spoke in Felipe's defense. 'No, Felipe isn't crazy. He really is just stubborn and hot-tempered. It's just unfortunate that he mingled with the wrong crowd of socialists and anarchists. Compared to Felipe, Delfin is level-headed.'

'True! I don't know where Felipe got those traits! No one in my family ever turned out the way he did. Don Ramon and I both believed that it's better to cast off children like that and not give them any inheritance at all. Meni was just collateral damage, for she would just give in to her husband's whims. Honorio, you had better tighten your grip on Don Ramon's estates.'

'As far as I'm concerned, I'm only sticking to what's clearly stated in the last will and testament. In fact, I'm more worried about Meni, especially now that she has a child . . .'

'That's why you should find a way to separate the couple,' Don Filemon insisted.

'I'll talk to her tonight. I'll instruct her. I know that they've been hard up, barely able to eat three square meals a day. I heard she had even sold off her jewellery. Clearly, Delfin's measly salary of forty pesos a month could barely sustain her, more so because she was sickly. I'll ask her to tell Delfin that she'll be staying here with us. And should Delfin resist, she'll have to tell him she can no longer live in such poor conditions. And should Delfin beat her up, all the better, for then she'll surely stay away from him for good.'

Captain Loloy cautioned Madlang-Layon. 'And what if Delfin doesn't resist? Don Ramon is dead, and he's here now, snooping around.'

The men paused when they heard footfalls approaching the door to Talia's room. Thinking that it was Meni about to come out through the door, Don Filemon and Captain Loloy went to speak with her about their plans, followed by Madlang-Layon, who went straight to Talia, and Doroteo who approached Marcela.

Ruperto was left all alone in the living room. Nobody thought of tagging him along. He realised it was the opportune time to sneak out and report to Delfin and Felipe, who were waiting in the basement. He was already descending the stairs when he realised a few things: 'What if telling them of what I'd heard and seen would just divide them further? And if Captain Loloy were to find out it was I who told them, I'd surely lose my chances with Marcela.' He stopped just a few steps from the landing. 'But I promised I'd tell them everything I heard, and it would be really bad to break that promise to my brother-in-law.'

Ruperto also thought that the two old men were unjustly harsh toward Delfin. He knew too well how cruel and inhuman the wealthy could be. He also felt bad that Madlang-Layon and Don Filemon only cared about Don Ramon's wealth, and how they were filled with contempt over the fact that Delfin, a penniless man, became Meni's husband. 'I myself am also a penniless man. If I were to pursue Marcela, who's to say they wouldn't do the same to me?'

Ruperto decided to do as he had promised. Delfin and Felipe were already impatiently waiting for him. He told them everything that he had heard, and warned them that the two old men were already talking to Meni as they spoke.

Felipe burnt with rage upon hearing Ruperto's report.

'What do you intend to do now, Delfin, against these men who harbour ill intentions against you?' Felipe was shaking with anger. 'I really don't care anymore about my father's wrath. But you, on the other hand! What they're doing now is outrageous! I want to burn this house to the ground and let the flames consume them!'

Ruperto cautioned Felipe. 'No, don't. You're forgetting that your sister, Marcela, and Delfin's wife, Meni, are there with them!'

Delfin sat in absolute silence, thinking about what to do next.

'Let's get up there and face those men, Delfin!'

'Wait, Felipe!' Delfin held Felipe back.

'Your reluctance and timidness will only make things worse, Delfin! If you don't want to get rough with Madlang-Layon and Don Filemon, then let me handle them!'

'No, calm down, my friend. We didn't come here to start a fight, or murder people. Let me and Ruperto go up and deal with them. Stay here for a bit and come up later. I'll speak to Meni in private to see if she would tell me what the two men told her, and I'll ask her if Madlang-Layon and Talia have conspired with them.'

'And then what?' Felipe asked pointedly.

'I'll tell you of my plans over supper, later.'

Delfin and Ruperto went on to go back inside the house. Delfin waited in the kitchen and told Ruperto to secretly send a message to Meni to meet him there.

Ruperto was just entering the house when Captain Loloy, Don Filemon, Yoyong, and Doroteo stepped out of Talia's room. The small fraternity headed for the living room and quietly resumed their talk. Ruperto just pretended to marvel at the grand paintings in the salon. Doroteo called out to him to ask about Delfin.

'No, he hasn't returned,' Ruperto lied through his teeth.

Momentarily, Meni stepped out of the room, followed by Marcela, who looked straight ahead and did not even glance at him. Meni no longer looked bereft, but she had a very grim expression on her face. In the salon, Marcela spoke to Meni. 'I told you to stay a bit longer. You've to stay and join me at supper!'

'Ah, Sela! They really think my husband is an evil man, despite all his humility and patience!' Meni sighed and began to cry.

'Please excuse my intrusion!' Sela, thinking that Ruperto was going to approach her, turned around and smiled. Ruperto went up to Meni and whispered something in her ear.

'Wait here, Sela. I've something to take care of outside.'

And the two lovers were left alone, finally, in the salon.

'What was it that you said to Meni?' Marcela was curious.

'Oh, nothing important. I just gave her Delfin's message before he stepped out.'

'What message? What did Delfin want to tell Meni?'

'Oh, I'm afraid that Delfin won't like it if I told you something that he didn't want others to know.'

'Others? Including me?'

'I was told to tell only Meni and nobody else.'

'Well, if you're not going to tell me . . .'

'If I told you, I'm sure you would think I'm not someone worthy of trust. You might say I'm one who doesn't know how to protect someone's secret.'

'No, I'll never think that of you. Come on, I really want to know what you told Meni.'

'I just told her to meet Delfin, since the two of them had important matters to discuss between them.'

'But didn't you just say Delfin left the house?'

'Yes, he went down to the basement, and then he came back up through the stairs leading to the kitchen.'

Marcela did not ask further, but she threw a furtive glance toward the living room.

'Father might see us here, alone.'

The two then walked up to the window. They now had the entire salon all to themselves, save the servants who were occasionally passing by to run errands around the house.

Ruperto spoke up. 'It's my turn now to ask questions. What did you and Doroteo talk about earlier?'

'Please, I hardly said anything to him.'

'Oh, really?'

'Well, why don't you ask Meni if you don't believe me, Sir?'

'Let's do away with the pleasantries. It's just the two of us here.'

'Oh, no. What if somebody heard us talking like this?'

'So? Why would it matter if I'm being too casual with you? After all . . .'

'After all . . . what?'

'I now hold the key to your heart, and you've the key to mine. Isn't that the case here now?'

'Is that the case?'

'Elang, please tell me straight!'

'Wait! Somebody might enter the salon. Father might see us. I think . . . I should go back inside . . .'

'You're going back inside? Don't leave me here hanging in uncertainty and doubt. Don't taunt me with your ambiguity. My whole life is in your hands now. I know that your father will disapprove, for the two of us are worlds apart. Your father will surely take you away from me if he ever finds out I'm in love with you. He'll only give your hand in marriage to another, more deserving suitor.'

'Another suitor? But I'm not seeing anyone else at all.'

'Really? Cross your heart . . . ?'

'Yes, there's no one else, because Father forbids it.'

'And me?'

'I only have eyes for you.'

'What do I know? I haven't known you for long . . .'

Marcela turned up her nose. 'Why did you let yourself fall in love before getting to know me first?'

'There's no need for that, Sela. Love does not grow over time, nor does it follow rhyme or reason. It just sprouts and blossoms when you least expect it. That's the way love is. Don't you feel it growing inside your heart, an intense feeling of affection for me?'

'Yes, indeed.'

'Isn't that love?'

Marcela just gazed at Ruperto with loving eyes.

'Isn't it?'

What a persistent man, Marcela thought, as she looked at Ruperto staring at her, as if waiting to respond with a sweet kiss.

'My sweet Elang! Tell me, please. Have I already won your elusive heart?'

Marcela just smiled, her dimples showing as if to say 'yes'.

Ruperto was just about to say something, but Turing suddenly burst into the salon, startling the two. Turing gave them a knowing look, for she was sure there was something going on between the two. She shrugged off the thought, for she knew it was not her place to judge the secret lovers.

'Where did Meni go?'

'She went outside,' said Marcela, 'to deal with something important.'

'As soon as she gets back, please tell her that Talia wants to speak to her.' Turing left as quickly as she entered. Shortly, they heard footfalls approaching the salon. Ruperto hastily went to the window, pretending to look out onto the garden outside the house. Marcela, from where she stood near the doorway, could see Don Filemon pacing back toward the group gathered in the living room.

'I must go back inside now.'

'Wait! Don't leave just yet,' Ruperto protested.

'How? I'm afraid . . .'

'Don't go without leaving behind a token of your love.'

'And what would that be?'

'Whatever you would like to give . . .'

'I'll give you something when we reach home. Aren't you traveling back with us?'

'Yes, but I can't wait any longer.'

'What can I give you? How about this handkerchief?'

'Is that all your love is worth?'

'My fan, then?'

'What will I do with that?'

'Then what is it that you want? Hurry! Here comes Meni!'

'Just . . . one . . . ' Ruperto pouted his lips.

'Oh, no, I can't. Here, take this.' Marcela took off her ring and handed it to Ruperto. Ruperto pressed Marcela's finger before the woman quickly turned around. She met Meni by the door as she stepped out of the salon.

'Meni, Talia would like to have a word with you.'

'No, they can all just shut their mouths!' Meni snarled.

The small bell rung in the dining room. Supper was ready to be served. It was already eight in the evening. The men gathered in the living room dispersed promptly at the sound of the bells. Madlang-Layon went to get Talia, who had to be coaxed into coming out for supper. Before long, everyone inside the house had flocked to the dining table. Don Filemon passed by Don Ramon's room to fetch his wife, but Señora Loleng was in no mood to socialize. Siano and his wife, who had stayed in their room since after the funeral, also came out to join the rest at the table.

Madlang-Layon prevailed upon Meni to have supper with them, but Meni just sat without saying a single word. Then came Delfin and Felipe, ascending the stairs to the main house. Delfin had to be swayed to stay and have supper. Finally, everybody was seated around the dining table, except for Felipe, who could not bear to be in the same room with his father. Felipe stayed outside in the salon to wait for whatever was going to happen next.

Captain Loloy sat at the head of the table at one end, while Yoyong sat at the other end. The men were on one side; the women on the other. They were thirteen in all: six women and seven men. What an unlucky number!

Everyone around the table spoke softly, heads bowed low as if in deep prayer. Talia, Meni, and Siano hardly raised their tear-stained faces, for it was rude to let the guests see their miserable state at the dining table. Only Marcela and Ruperto were in a light mood. Seated across from each other, they bowed their hands and only looked up once in a while to catch stolen glances and smile at each other, before anyone else could notice them.

Captain Loloy could not help but notice Meni seated next to him, all quiet and barely touching the food on her plate. He turned toward Delfin and saw the same thing. As he looked away, from the corner of his eye, he noticed his daughter staring at the man sitting across from her. Marcela turned to throw a furtive glance in her father's direction and saw the old man glaring at her. Marcela recoiled like a snake that had just struck with its venom.

After a while, when his daughter no longer dared to behave in a disgraceful manner, Captain Loloy spoke in a loud voice in an attempt to lighten mood in the dining room.

'Meni, please eat some more. Remember, you still have a baby to nurse. And Talia, the same goes to you. You've a baby still growing inside your womb. Your father's gone now, and there's nothing we can do about it. We're all going to meet the same fate, some earlier than others.'

Everyone turned to look at the sisters, especially Meni, and they all noted what Captain Loloy had observed.

Meni, who had been keeping her boiling emotions at bay, suddenly burst.

'No, Captain Loloy. It's not my father I am sad about! It's about my husband and I! It is bad enough that my father forsook and banished me from this house, but to hear you speak of such treachery and malice! I've enough respect for my own honour and dignity not to eat the food served at this table!'

She abruptly stood up and dropped her fork on the plate before her. Her whole body was shaking with anger.

Everyone at the table stared at her, visibly shocked by the look on her face. Yoyong, Talia, Captain Loloy and Don Filemon could not quite believe such an outburst from Meni, whom they had known to be gentle and meek; hearing those blunt words had left them speechless. Delfin shifted uneasily in his chair, but when he saw his wife's face, he just nodded and casually sat back.

Meni continued to speak in a nervous voice.

'Who was it? Who dared speak lies as to why we came here? How dare you say we're here only because my father is dead, that my husband is here to contest my father's last will and testament, that we're here to claim my inheritance? Yoyong, why go behind my back and not tell it straight to our faces? Now is your chance. My husband isn't a coward! Do not treat us in such a shady manner!'

'Meni, mind your words!' Madlang-Layon objected. 'Why single me out?'

'Because this is all your doing!'

'What do you mean this is all me?'

'Oh, please, don't even try to deny it!'

'Delfin, your wife is so out of line here! Why do you just sit there and let Meni speak ill of others in front of our guests?'

Delfin was about to reply, but Meni beat him to it.

'Me? Rude and disrespectful? Toward your cohorts?!'

Captain Loloy, Don Filemon, and Doroteo were wide-eyed.

'Weren't you just talking to them about these things earlier, in the living room? Didn't you all come up to me to convince me to leave Delfin?'

The faces of Yoyong, Doroteo, and the others turned pale.

'They want you to leave me, huh?' Delfin said. 'For what reason, pray tell . . .'

'Yes! It's true!' Talia said, clearly full of contempt toward Delfin. 'Because if it weren't for you, my sister wouldn't be suffering the way she is now. And . . . our father wouldn't have deserted us if he weren't so dejected. This is all your fault! We've to endure all this suffering. And you had the gall to show your face here and speak to us in that tone?'

Things escalated rather quickly when people abruptly rose from the table. Delfin was so overwhelmed by Talia's harsh accusations that he was at a loss for words. Doroteo, Madlang-Layon and Siano whispered to each other. Turing ran to her brother's side and muttered words to calm him down. Only Ruperto remained seated in his chair, unable to look at anyone else around him. Señora Loleng, who had just stepped out of her room, came by and called out to her daughter, Isiang. Felipe, upon hearing Meni's loud voice, moved closer to the door to peek at the scene in the dining room.

When Delfin did not speak a word, Meni turned to face her sister.

'Talia, don't you talk like that to my husband. He has done you no wrong! I love him dearly, that's why I married him. Don't bring Father into this mess. Yes, he left because he was so disappointed in me, but you do know that was because I fell in love with a poor man.'

'Hold it right there!' Talia shouted in a hoarse voice. 'Even you've become so hard-headed, and now you've the temerity to turn your back on those you're deeply indebted to!'

'I'm grateful for everything you've done for me. But that's exactly why I don't understand why you're doing this to us. You were all kind and doting in the past, but now you treat us like dirt after getting your hands on the spoils of our father's last will and testament. You hid from me the fact that it was your husband who presided over Father's estate.'

'But you know that was your father's dying wish,' Madlang-Layon said. 'I merely did as I was told. If you wish to contest the will, the courts are open for you to file a lawsuit.'

'Yes, sue us if you must!' Talia seconded.

Delfin could no longer contain himself. 'Yoyong, Talia, let's settle this amicably. We don't wish to take this to court. Let's not squabble over money that isn't really ours. I don't really care that there was no full disclosure in the administration of your father's estate. You've no reason to be alarmed. There's no need for secret meetings nor a conspiracy to ruin my reputation or destroy our marriage. And you mustn't think I'm interested in my wife's inheritance. That means nothing to me. You of all people should know where I stand on these matters. I am dead serious. I don't want anything to do with your family's money, period. And while I'm still around, you don't ever have to worry about Meni's welfare at all.'

'Not ever at all!' Meni reiterated in a loud voice.

Madlang-Layon spoke to defend his wounded pride. 'Why do you say that? You think we're depriving you of what's rightfully yours? Are we . . . ?'

But Delfin cut Yoyong short. 'We don't have to get into that. I say we're even.'

Delfin walked away from the table and went around to get Meni. Husband and wife spoke to each other inaudibly, and in a moment, they motioned to take their leave.

Talia nearly threw herself in Meni's path. 'You're not going anywhere with him! He can leave, but you're staying here!'

The women ran to restrain Meni as she struggled to break free from her sister. They tugged at her blouse, held back her arms, and pulled at her skirt. But Delfin did not let go of her hand.

'Let her go!' Talia screamed hysterically.

'Please, just let us take our leave,' Delfin said calmly.

'There's no way you can do that!' Talia was defiant. 'I'll call the police if I have to. You're starving my sister to death! You can't even feed her!'

Delfin smiled wryly. 'I can't feed her?'

'Let her choose, then! If she wants to stay here where she'll never grow hungry again . . .'

Talia released Meni, and as soon as she did, she dropped to the floor, dragging Isiang along.

The men just stood there and looked on. Only Siano ran to Talia's aid. Although he had been quiet at the table, he had been intently watching Delfin's every move.

'Just stay here, you crazy woman!' Siano told Meni.

'No, please don't leave me here, Delfin!' She broke down when she saw her husband walking away. Delfin turned around, but Talia stood in his way and pushed him back. Meni, finally breaking loose, threw her arms around husband's waist and broke down.

'Delfin! I want to be by your side, even if it means living in poverty!'

It was an ugly sight to behold—Meni ripped apart by her love for her sister and her devotion to her husband.

'Please, just let me go. My poor baby needs me.'

'Your baby can stay here as well!' Siano insisted.

'No!' Meni protested. 'I want my son to grow from humble beginnings. Only then will he know true happiness in life . . .'

Meni's words pierced Delfin to the core. Meni's conviction was so fervent that he decided he could not leave his wife behind and so he very nearly pushed Talia aside. When Yoyong and Siano saw Talia falling back, they lunged at Delfin. Felipe, seeing that his friend was about to be mauled, rushed to join in the fray.

'Fear not, Delfin! You're not alone!' Felipe shouted. Madlang-Layon cowered when he saw and heard Felipe. But Captain Loloy, who had spotted Felipe from a distance, went behind him and smacked him hard in the head. Felipe, not knowing what hit him, was stunned.

'You meddlesome bastard!' The old man growled.

Felipe turned around to retaliate but froze when he saw it was his father! He was so shocked that his raised arm hung in the air. His angry eyes softened upon recognizing his old man, but quickly, he shifted his attention to the madding crowd around Delfin. His wrath turned to pity at the sight of Delfin, and in his mind, he saw the image of the righteous poor, clearly outnumbered, being trampled to death by the rich. He turned around to face his old man and began to speak in a loud, booming voice.

'You dared to lay a hand on me, Father, when all I want is to help my friend here who is in distress and overpowered! He's merely claiming what is rightfully his. He isn't forcing himself on his wife, and she is more than willing to go with him. But you want to take her away because you think you have power over him? You're all wretched; twisted in the mind! Just because you're rich, you think you can have it all! Why don't you respect Meni's freedom of choice? Why do you trample on Delfin's rights? Why tear this loving couple apart from each other, when they don't want any of your money? Be very scared, for the day will come when you'll all get what you deserve. Someday, all your wealth will mean nothing, and you'll all stand as equal to everyone else!'

Felipe took Delfin and Meni by the hand and led them out, away from the rest, who were all left aghast and appalled by the words that were dripping with contempt.

Only Ruperto had the right mind to follow them, saying 'There's still hope for my homeland, for surely amongst us, there are now heroes of the New Order.'

THE END